Critical Praise for *VanOps: The Lost Power*

"Avanti Centrae's *VanOps: The Lost Power* opens a tantalizing new series that combines historical mystery and cutting-edge science into a masterwork of international intrigue—with the promise of more to follow. Written with a dynamic, cinematic style and full of action and suspense, here's a book that defines page-turner. Don't miss this riveting debut!" ~ James Rollins, the #1 *New York Times* bestselling author of *Crucible*

"Just a good ole' fashioned rip-roaring adventure from start to finish. Enjoy the ride." ~ Steve Berry, *New York Times* bestselling author

"VanOps: The Lost Power takes readers on a fast-paced roller coaster of a ride across the globe in a top-notch thriller with high-stakes and plenty of edge-of-seat action." ~ Robin Burcell, *NYT* bestselling author of *The Last Good Place* and (co-written with Clive Cussler) *The Oracle*

"A high-stakes, daring adventure charged with suspense and mystery!" ~ Ann Charles, *USA TODAY* bestselling author of the Deadwood Mystery Series

"The narrative flows quickly and is unstoppable." ~ Stacey Donovan, *NYT* and national best-selling editor

"The mystery of finding the weapon, the responsibility on the young woman's shoulders, and the constant threat of being chased was a perfect combination that had me sitting on the edge of my seat and holding my breath. This is one of the best action/thrillers I have ever read and I can't wait for the next novel in the series." ~ Reader's Favorite. Five/Five Stars

"Every family has its secrets, only some are deadlier than others." ~ Chanticleer Reviews. Five/Five Stars

"The writing is superb. Easy to read and captivating. There is a mixture of mystery and action that keeps me turning pages. Readers who like Indiana Jones, or the books by James Patterson, Tom Clancy, and Vince Flynn, will enjoy Centrae's first installment in her VanOps series." ~ John Bernstein, Professional Reviewer

ACKNOWLEDGMENTS

Mom taught me to read about the same time I learned to walk and has supported my love of reading and writing ever since. Michelle listened to my obsessive meanderings about titles, character names, plot devices, etc., contributed blue-ribbon ideas, and is the worthy president of my fan club. My first editor, Stacey Donovan, taught me the sin of gerunds and provided encouragement to a new author who needed to hear from an expert that she could succeed. My agent, Donna Eastman from Parkeast Literary, took a chance on my writing and negotiated that elusive first book deal with Black Opal Books. My editor, Faith, helped me fine-tune the plot and provided world-class editing. Black Opal did a lovely job with formatting and distribution. David Ter-Avanesyan, my cover artist, was patient as a saint, eventually creating a work of art. Olivia Bernard, author of *The Balance and The Blade*, helped bring out the most visual elements of the story. My dear friend, Kathy Bridges, has been an unending source of inspiration for my work. I'm grateful for each of their contributions.

I wish I had space to name all my other friends, family, and beta readers who helped polish the book or get the word out. Special shout outs to: Sandy, Betty, Anita, Karyn, Carole, Lori, Susan, Joanne, Dani, Trish, Paul, Claudia, Margaret, John, Mari, Eileen, and Ruth.

Many authors showed incredible kindness and support. Their generosity amazes me, and I'm deeply grateful.

Although they were all a huge help, any errors in the book fall on my shoulders alone.

VANOPS: THE LOST POWER

AVANTI CENTRAE

A Black Opal Books Publication

GENRE: THRILLER/SUSPENSE

VANOPS: THE LOST POWER
Copyright © 2019 by Avanti Centrae
Cover Design by David Ter-Avanesyan/Ter33Design
All cover art copyright © 2019
All Rights Reserved
Hardcover ISBN: 9781644371961

First Publication: NOVEMBER 2019

Published by Black Opal Books **http://www.blackopalbooks.com**

For mom

"I am part of a light, and it is the music. The Light fills my six senses: I see it, hear, feel, smell, touch, and think. Thinking of it means my sixth sense. Particles of Light are written note. A bolt of lightning can be an entire sonata. A thousand balls of lightning is a concert...

~ Nikola Tesla

Ripped from recent headlines:

"The US Air Force has hit Iraqi TV with an experimental electromagnetic pulse device called the 'E-Bomb' in an attempt to knock it off the air and shut down Saddam Hussein's propaganda machine. Iraqi satellite TV, which broadcasts 24 hours a day outside Iraq, went off the air around 4:30 a.m. local time."
~ CBS News, March 25, 2003

"SOME METEORITES CONTAIN SUPERCONDUCTING BITS. FIND ENERGIZES SEARCH FOR EXOTIC MATERIALS THAT CONDUCT ELECTRICITY SANS RESISTANCE."
~ Science News, March 7, 2018

PROLOGUE

Aragon, AD 1057:

Ramiro needed a way to halt the spheres of ball lightning that killed and tormented his troops. They fell like a meteor shower, unstoppable arrows of piercing light.

But first, he had to survive. Ramiro parried a thrust, lunged with satisfaction, pulled his sword free of the man in front of him, and gasped for air. As his opponent collapsed to the ground with unseeing eyes, Ramiro grunted and looked to the crest of a nearby hilltop. Tendrils of gray mist obscured his vision as he searched over and over again for the lightning's source. *Where is that hellish-blue fire coming from?*

Frustration at the lack of a clear view warred with his relief at winning another swordfight. The back of his throat burned, so he gave in to the desire to spit. He was tall, but his opponent had been taller, larger of limb, and stronger than he. Ramiro hadn't been sure of his victory until that final opening had presented itself.

Over the clang of surrounding swordplay, horses' hooves pounded the wet earth behind him. He turned as his six-man honor guard approached.

The group was led by his son, Sancho Ramírez, who reined in his muscled chestnut warhorse. Sancho's chest heaved with exertion under his chain mail. He looked at Ramiro, pointed down to his side, and yelled over the din, "Father, you're injured!"

"I will find the physician later." Focused on the battle, Ramiro had moved away from his guard while fighting. He'd also ignored the wound. A trickle of blood oozed from a gash above his right hip bone. It wasn't deep. He'd warded off his opponent's sword move just a little too late. Infidel or not, this last challenger had been a worthy foe.

Before his son could insist, Ramiro watched another blue ball from hell sail through his ranks, harvesting his men like a scythe. The bizarre display threatened to unnerve him, but he refused to be swayed from his course. He planted his feet, wiped his sword on the dead man's sleeve, and deepened his breathing.

Sancho wasn't as steady. "Father, we must act soon!" His voice broke as he shouted.

Ramiro agreed but had yet to find what they needed. With the return of his guard, who now surrounded him for safety, he could look again. Searching through the dusky haze for a good view of the lightning's source, Ramiro peered around and at the hilltop.

Several long weeks ago, his Iberian lands had been invaded by Moors, a people better at conquest than weeds taking over the spring fields. His holdings, bequeathed to him by his own father, were situated in the foothills on the west side of the Pyrenees and were usually verdant in midsummer. But there was no green to be seen now. Instead, the land looked like the remains of a funeral pyre, black and charred.

To help protect the land and his people, his troops were scattered about, fighting in small, unorganized clusters. Many lay on the ground, dead or bleeding. Since the beginning of this battle, lightning had rained violent yellow from the dark skies above and unusual blue from the hillock beyond. Sounds of his men screaming from the impact of the strikes hung in the air and haunted his mind. It smelled as he imagined hades would, putrid and sharp. A breeze stirred, cooling his face, and the mist parted for an instant.

Sancho also gazed up the hill. "Do you see what I see?"

Through the screen of light vapor, the hilltop appeared. Before this summer, he'd never seen a storm with lightning such as this, and he suspected the reason had just come into view. Protected inside a group of warriors, a Moorish priest stood with both arms raised to the sky. Legs held wide in an arrogant stance, he wore a dark brown, deeply-hooded cloak that obscured his face. As lightning flashed, Ramiro's heart pounded. There were two blood-red objects in the priest's raised hands.

"At last, yes!"

"It's the proof we've wanted to see." Sancho pulled the silver relay horn off his belt. "Give the order!"

Ramiro was proud that his son was ready for action even against the unknown power. But before he committed himself and his remaining troops, Ramiro paused to be certain of his next step, as there was no way back if it failed. This was the fifth battle where he had watched more of his men die from the round blue lightning than from the sword. After the last skirmish had been lost, Sancho had suggested a spy be sent into the camp of the Moors. It was a clever idea.

"Are you sure about what the infiltrator reported back?" Ramiro asked.

Sancho moved his nervous steed closer and bent down next to his father so they could talk. "Yes, Father. He was careful and heard the guards talking one night after a meal. Our man is convinced. The Moors think those ancient obelisks help them create the lightning that kills."

But Ramiro wasn't satisfied. "What about Alexander of Macedonia? Did he use these rods in his conquests?"

"So, the Moors believe. Egyptian priests crafted the obelisks from a fallen star of old, obtained from a distant country. Alexander used the obelisks during his campaigns after he took Egypt."

At first, both assertions appeared to be uneducated, superstitious nonsense, but after watching that priest kill a hundred of his best men, Ramiro believed the spy had spoken the unfortunate truth about Alexander and the power of the obelisks. No wonder the Macedonian had such success.

But could it be Satan's hand at work here? Ramiro's priests were convinced the devil was involved. Ramiro wasn't sure. However, for his people to have any chance of defeating the Moors, he must take the risk, capture the obelisks, and determine for himself if they were evil or merely being used that way.

"And this is the only time we can get them?" Ramiro insisted.

"Yes, Father, I told you, when not in use, the Moors lock them inside a sturdy metal box and guard them well. Only carefully trained priests can touch them." Sancho sounded impatient.

Ramiro wanted to have the obelisks for himself, so that he could learn more about them, and find out from where they had come. He held out hope that, with time and study, he could learn to command the obelisks in a fruitful way. But if they proved unable to be tamed, he must make certain to keep the power safe and out of his enemies' hands.

Reassured that he had no other option but to commit his troops, Ramiro nodded to Sancho. "We shall proceed." A sizzling sound, like fat dripping onto a fire, warned Ramiro. "Look out!"

Another ball of lightning passed inches from his son's head and exploded nearby, between Sancho and a guard. Mud flew high into the air, pelting Ramiro with dirt and small, sharp rocks. He didn't notice the pain, intent on his decision. Beside him, Sancho struggled to keep control of his mount.

"I've been spotted. It's time." Ramiro took a deep breath and bellowed across the field, "Aragon, to me!" the sign his men had been waiting to hear.

Sancho repeated the signal by blowing into his silver horn. Two long, haunting notes cut through the sounds of the melee. Bleeding soldiers, who had been lying on the ground feigning mortal injury, stood, false ghosts rising from the mist. Others appeared from the wood on the far side of the hill. The apparent disarray of Ramiro's troops coalesced into an organized mass, honed and focused like a spear.

As one, they charged up the hill, determined to wrench the mysterious power from the Moors.

CHAPTER 1

Napa Valley, California, June 25, 8:56 a.m., Present Day:

Through the crosshairs of his long-barreled sweetheart, Ivan scanned the wood-casement window of the vineyard's stone-walled residence, and waited for his intended target to walk into view. His movements were slow and meticulous.

Lying in the loft of an old barn, he calculated range, altitude, temperature, barometric pressure, wind speed, and humidity. His skin was irritated by the coarse hay that surrounded him, but he ignored the sensation and focused on his calculations. Click. He made a minor adjustment on his rifle to account for the drop of the round due to air density. And another for windage.

Although misty rivers of fog swirled into gray whirlpools around the winery, the computer-enhanced scope of his Springfield EBR allowed him to visually lock onto the home's large bank of windows. Human movement flickered behind the glass.

He didn't want to pull the trigger. Nevertheless, Ivan waited for the perfect moment, the perfect shot.

CHAPTER 2

8:57 a.m.:

As she headed toward her father's vineyard, Maddy drove as fast as she dared down a familiar tree-lined Napa country lane. Today, she didn't recognize the road. It looked eerie and unnatural. The area was draped in sheets of fog from yesterday's unseasonable rain, and the silver half light gave the trees an ethereal patina.

"Sensei, would you kill someone if you had to?" AJ asked.

Surprised, Maddy frowned. "I'm not a sensei yet, remember?" She paused for a moment before she replied to his query. "Where did that question come from?"

"We were talking about it in the locker room at the dojo after class. We know aikido is about non-violence, but what if you don't have a choice?" His voice dropped to a dramatic whisper. "What if it was kill or be killed?"

Maddy shook her head. The things children thought about. "I would always look for another way."

She glanced over at AJ, glad she'd brought him along today. His ears stuck out and his face was dotted with freckles. She found him adorable.

"Okay. Can martial arts masters light paper on fire with just their hands?"

Maddy halted the car at a stop sign and peered through the swirling patchy-dense fog, trying to get her bearings while she figured out how to answer this question. The mist distorted everything. She turned right.

Without warning, a smothering mass of black rustling feathers flew toward the car. She flinched in her seat and slammed on the car brakes. Her heart pounded. She stopped breathing and scanned the road ahead of her. After a long moment, she realized with chagrin that she had just scared a bunch of ugly, red-faced black turkey vultures into flight by turning onto a new road after a stop sign.

She took a deep breath. It wasn't like her to be so jumpy. She was, after all, shodan, a first-dan black belt. But the sudden movement of wings, obscured through the morning's foggy haze, had pulled her off balance. Maddy gave the car some gas and it inched forward down the road.

Maddy looked over at AJ. "Are you okay?"

AJ laughed. "I'm okay. But that scared you!"

"Did not!" Maddy replied, twisting her ponytail.

"Did too—I saw you jump! And you smashed on the brakes."

Maddy grinned for a moment at the childish banter and AJ's creative language. It could be a happy day, in spite of everything. She loved AJ, she and Vincent had even talked about adopting him. Vincent, her *former* fiancé. Of course, that was before the breakup. Since then, she'd been feeling brittle, and the nightmare last night didn't help. The dream was gut-wrenching. Although the sensation had faded in the dim light of morning, much of it lingered like a bad relationship. That dream was probably why she was on edge and had jumped at the thrashing wings.

She looked at the dash clock—only a few minutes late. Heart still beating faster than normal, she turned down the long shadowy driveway of the once proud vineyard.

CHAPTER 3

9:02 a.m.:

Up in the old barn, Ivan was close to the target, only seventy meters from the glass curtain that separated him from his quarry. Although the misty morning limited his visibility, he felt confident in his ability to execute the task Baron Sokolov had assigned to him.

Ivan recalled much longer-range kills. Two months ago, from a nearby skyscraper, he'd eliminated a traitorous spy during a French soccer match, piercing the man's forehead as directed. His record was just under two thousand meters, one hundred fifty meters shy of the longest recorded sniper kill in history. But he reminded himself to stay vigilant and cautious, traits that had earned him medals as one of Russia's most accurate shooters.

Being watchful was his nature. It was the silver lining of his disorder, congenital analgesia, which made him insensitive to pain. *My gift from Mother*, he thought.

Ivan wondered where on his body he would mark this job. His left arm was covered in sets of hash marks—scars, where he had marked his kills. He started scarring himself in school to impress the other children, and in time it had become a blood ritual after a task to remind himself to be careful, that he too could die. After this morning, it would be time to add another scar. At one hundred and fifty-five confirmed kills, he had scars on both thighs, both arms, and was running out of room for the marks.

Soon he would catch up to the kills his grandmother had recorded during World War II. After Germany had invaded, she had volunteered for the military and had one hundred and seventy-nine confirmed kills to her credit. Impressive. He remembered how she had taught him to shoot when he was young. She had a fondness for killing rabbits and he could still picture their crimson blood sprayed on the bright Siberian snow. However, patience was her favorite lesson and it had served him well.

A puff of wind tugged at a windmill in the distance, and the melancholy creak of metal scratching metal disturbed the morning silence. He held his breath and listened for any sound to indicate he'd been discovered. There was nothing further, only an unnatural, muted quiet.

Focused on his breathing and the window, he continued to wait for a clean shot.

He was tired of killing, but he had to do his job. This last job. Or his son would die.

CHAPTER 4

9:05 a.m.:

Maddy's car hit a pot-hole on the vineyard's long gravel driveway. It annoyed her that Dad hadn't said what was so urgent, and she'd been too distracted with the breakup to call him back.

As she drew closer to the house, she was irritated to see Will was playing fog-fetch with the dog in the front yard. *What is he doing here? Did Dad call all the siblings? Bella, too?* Will waved, walked toward an obnoxious sky-blue convertible that must be a rental, and opened the trunk.

Maddy parked by Will's car, near the house. She wished Dad would get the place painted. It was overdue and made the house look dilapidated in the gloom. Barking, her dad's middle-aged golden retriever ran up to the car.

"A dog! Can I play with the dog?" AJ asked, true excitement in his voice.

"Sure, just don't head too far into the vineyard," Maddy replied. "His name is Squirrel."

AJ bounded from the car and ran off, chasing the dog through the murky, fog-bound yard.

Will closed the trunk of the Mustang, moved around to the side of the car, and watched AJ and the dog playing. Dressed in his usual style, he wore tan cargo shorts, leather sandals, and a dark-blue Ralph Lauren polo shirt. Ever prepared for disaster, he had a small flashlight hanging from the front of his shorts, and she figured he had a knife in his pocket. He was holding two small travel bags and managed to cradle a book in his hand. Without a doubt, a geeky physics book.

Maddy had avoided prolonged contact with Will since their senior year in high school when he had pulled that awful prank. She had turned her back on him then, and her face flushed with the memory. As she opened her car door, she stood and swung her hair out of her face. Then she shut the door and walked over to him. It was so foggy and quiet, she didn't even hear songbirds.

Maddy tried to keep the annoyance out of her voice. "Hello, Will."

After they'd spent time apart, she was always surprised at the strength of their emotional bond. She couldn't believe he was happy to see her—he had no shame! She had felt some connection to her boyfriends, Vincent included—*I hate you right now, Vincent*—and sometimes to her students at the dojo. But the connection was always strongest with Will, her twin, like it or not. He felt content now. She had almost missed his charm.

Will flashed his irksome, boyish, lopsided grin. "Hey, Maddy, it's good to see you! Did you have a safe drive?"

To meet her, he walked around toward the front of the car. She noted his dark curly hair looked ruffled and a little shorter than the last time she'd seen him. His green eyes looked pinched, as if he were worried about something.

Dad sometimes teased that they all had Spanish olives for eyes, but she enjoyed sharing the feature. She just wished she'd been blessed with Will's long eyelashes, instead of having to create them every day with mascara.

Maddy studied Will's face. She noticed that the scar on his chin was almost hidden by a fashionable new beard that he'd grown since she'd seen him last year at Christmas dinner. The scar was always a painful reminder of the childhood accident that killed their mother.

As he put down the bags, he scratched the beard, casually leaned back against the hood of the Mustang, and crossed his long lanky legs.

She knew protocol called for a hug, and considered it. Rejecting the idea, she also ignored his worrywart question about the safe drive. "Did you leave Maria in Brazil?"

Maddy could tell from his eyes that Will didn't understand her cold shoulder, and she didn't care. He had never made amends for that thoughtless stunt back in high school and she wasn't going to let him off the hook.

"No, I brought her with me," he replied.

Remembering her nightmare, Maddy's gut clenched. She tried to ignore it.

"We've both been working too hard."

Instead, she lashed out, her voice rising more than she intended. "Was that wise? Bringing her? Do you even know what Dad wants?"

Will took a deep breath. "Gee, sis, simmer down. I thought I was the worrier of the family." He met her gaze. "Maria was up for a change of scenery so we planned a romantic wine-country vacation. You know, the train, mud baths, that sort of thing? We might even stop by Safari West. Besides, you brought company." He nodded toward AJ. "Who's the little guy?"

"His name is AJ. He's a foster kid from the dojo and it's his birthday." She watched AJ and the dog play a spontaneous game of tag. "Is that all Dad wants with us? A vacation? He sounded concerned on the message he left me. And didn't mention you'd be here, or Bella. Is she coming? He didn't even say why he wanted me to come, which just seems odd. Did you talk with him?"

"Bella is on her way, but no, we didn't talk before I came up. I hope nothing is wrong. We just got here and haven't had a chance to visit much, but he did mention he had some disconcerting news." He paused. "You feel upset. What are you not telling me? What's the big deal?"

On days like today, Maddy hated that the emotional bond between them worked both ways. She didn't feel like telling him anything, especially about the dream. Irritated, she looked around for a way out of the conversation but didn't see one. The sun was hidden, the vineyard foggy and subdued, like it was holding its breath.

She clenched her teeth and took a deep breath of her own. "I had a dream last night."

Now his tone sharpened a notch. "What kind of dream?"

"A bad one. Maria was in it. I woke up early and it's stuck with me since."

"Tell me," he demanded.

"I don't know…there was blood on her face."

She remembered another dream she had when they were six. The night before their mom died. She knew by the look on his face that he was remembering that dream, too.

"Blood on Maria's face—" He frowned, thinking, questioning.

"Yes, it was horrible. Splattered like a Pollock painting. I don't remember much else. But the feeling is still with me." Her mood picked up a little, having gotten it off her chest. "It's probably nothing. I just wish you hadn't brought her."

"Interesting," he said. "You haven't had one of those dreams in a while, have you? A real one?"

"No," she said. "It's been a few years and the last was about a boyfriend cheating on me. The dream ended that relationship."

Will put his hands on his hips. "How is Vincent?"

She grimaced.

Irritated, Maddy turned and headed up the sidewalk toward the house. Will grabbed the bags and his book, and followed her, his feet padding on the concrete.

As they walked, she remembered the lush landscaping that had been here once. It had provided a jumbled, colorful contrast to the acres and acres of straight green vines in the fields. Her father's landscapers, back when he could afford them, had done well in this entry area. She couldn't see it, but she inhaled the light scent of gardenia, and she recognized remnants of some sort of native grass, night-blooming jasmine, pansies, and roses. Vincent had brought her roses only three weeks ago. *Bastard.*

"I see," Will said. "So…maybe this dream was a reaction to whatever is going on there?"

"Maybe—" she said. "I hope so." Then she added, "Let's go see what Dad wants."

CHAPTER 5

9:15 a.m.:

Ivan tugged on the two-stage trigger, testing it. He was used to his Soviet bolt-action SV-98, but in the interest of time and ease of entry into the country, he had purchased a black-market rifle in the States. He was pleased with his choice, and glad it had come with a suppressor. The Enhanced Battle Rifle was decent—he tested it out yesterday in an isolated vineyard he found for the purpose. The rifle was a little heavy, but he liked the trigger-shoe modification the prior owner had done, as it gave the pull a more natural feel.

He drew his attention back to the wood-casement window and twice glimpsed the oblivious inhabitant, dancing his way to death. A minute ago, the sound of car tires on gravel had come to him through the fog, so his partner, on lookout, should be reporting in.

On cue, a voice in his head broke the morning stillness, "Green Prius has parked at the front of the house." The sniper appreciated that he could hear his partner's Russian voice clearly through the high-tech device, as he was old enough to remember missions without such advanced technology.

"Driver?" he subvocalized the question, also in Russian, into the tiny molar microphone that had been custom formed to fit his teeth.

"She's female, young, maybe thirty. Slim, with an olive complexion. Has sexy, long, dark hair in a ponytail, and is tall. Pretty tall for a woman. Rape-bait if you ask me. Dressed in jeans and a snug purple T-shirt," his partner said.

On this job, his partner was here as much to keep an eye on him as to help, Ivan knew. The man's simple mind and cruel nature were evident every time they worked together. The idiot had caused them to run late this morning. This part of the job should have been over an hour ago. Now it was getting complicated.

"That's not what we're here for," Ivan hissed.

"Maybe. If so, you need to take your shot." A few beats later his partner continued, "She was talking to the tall man next to the blue sports car. They look alike. Now they're headed to the front door."

There was a long pause. The sniper adjusted his hold on the rifle, concentrating. He'd read the dossiers on Maddy Marshall and her twin brother, Will Argones. Argones was an engineer, no real threat. But the Marshall woman. A world-class athlete and national ski champion who had been a favorite for Olympic gold, she'd used her lightning-fast reflexes to become a warrior in an unusual martial art. And she was gifted with a keen intelligence. A dangerous combination. In another time and place, he'd have been interested in her as a mate.

He swore. Based on his orders, their arrival meant he had run out of time.

A low whistle pierced his ear.

"Ivan, she's got long legs. You know I like long legs, right? Why don't we stick around and have some fun?"

"You're a pig and the baron was clear in our instructions," the sniper replied, with heat in his tone.

"You're a bore. Oh, she had a kid with her in the car."

"A kid? What kid?" The dossier didn't mention a child! That wasn't part of the deal. *I may go down in flames if the baron makes me shoot a kid. This target is one thing but—*

"How do I know what kid? He looks like he's eight or nine. Red hair, big ears. He's playing with the dog in the vineyard."

Ivan hoped the kid and dog were off in a different direction. At home, Ivan's son might be playing with his own dog. But that thought was dangerous. "Just make sure they don't come this way."

His attention back on the window, Ivan finally got a complete look at one of the other inhabitants: a short, dark-skinned woman. She wore a pale pink blouse above a blue skirt and Ivan prayed she would get out of the way. He didn't like killing women. However, he knew that, whether he liked it or not, the latter part of the baron's plan already called for its share of female bloodshed.

The older man, near a black sofa, came into Ivan's sights for a brief moment. It appeared that he and the younger woman were moving into the room with all the windows. Ivan knew it was time.

Ivan was glad now they'd chosen a fast getaway car. "I must focus— go get the car ready."

The older man came completely into view. He was tall, clean-shaven, tan-skinned, with owlish glasses. His receding black hair was streaked with gray, and he wore slacks and a white button-down shirt. *Yes, finally.*

But the woman was directly behind the target! *Move,* he willed to her. *Please.*

This was the best shot he had. Time had run out! He had no choice but to urge her to move at the last minute.

He took a slow, steady breath and tugged again on the two-stage trigger. Only this time, it wasn't a test.

CHAPTER 6

AJ and Squirrel, done with the chase and on to a game of fetch, ran around the side yard, enjoying the grass and the feel of morning in the dense, wet fog. AJ loved all things nature.

Feeling happy today made him miss his parents. He had vague memories of joyful times when they took him to his grandparents' Ukrainian dairy farm. When the Russians came and killed his grandparents, his parents and he had fled to San Francisco. Then, one day, his mom and dad had been caught in the crossfire of a convenience store holdup while stopping for milk. That's what he'd gathered, no one had told him.

Since his parents' death he'd been in foster care, because all of his family back in Ukraine were dead, too. He didn't like his foster family because they ignored him, but he loved Maddy and did whatever his foster creeps asked so that he could go to the dojo. Maddy treated him the way his mom used to, warm and caring.

Today, he was full of pleasure—hanging out with Maddy, getting to chase a dog outside. More than anything, he wanted a real family again. And a dog, just maybe not one named Squirrel. Someday, he'd get a big dog to protect him and name it Rufus, or Damien.

AJ threw a stick and tried out the new name. "Damien, fetch!"

After several minutes of chasing the stick in the side yard, AJ decided they should play a new game in the rows of vines. "C'mon, Damien," he called as he ran into the shadows, followed by the panting dog.

The morning was blissfully perfect as they ran up and down the rows. Then a loud crack sounded from the direction of the barns, like a tree branch breaking. He called his new canine friend and they headed off to investigate.

CHAPTER 7

9:21 a.m.:

Together, Maddy and Will reached the stout, carved mahogany double doors of her father's home. A muted clap, in the distance, roughly cut through the morning silence. The sound of breaking glass clattered somewhere in the house.

Maddy turned, looking for the source of the noise. Will's eyes darted everywhere, too. A woman shrieked. Maria? As Will pushed open the right-hand door, the screaming died off. Maddy looked at Will, made eye contact, and could feel his fear mirroring her own.

"Let's go!" Maddy yelled.

Oh god—was that a gunshot? Had it been a *real* dream?

She ran through the door and pressed down the long hallway. As she kicked into gear, she felt as if she were flying down the travertine alley. *Oh god, oh god, oh god, oh god.*

Her dad's occasional housekeeper was in a side bedroom off the main hall. The woman was holding a feather duster like an upright sword blade, turning from side to side, wide-eyed, and shaking.

Maddy paused. "Get down! Get under the bed and stay there!"

She sensed, more than saw, Will pass her by. She ran on.

High on adrenaline, she headed into her father's living room, now a step behind Will. She took in the scene—broken glass window with a spider web pattern—her father lying face down on the floor in a crumpled heap. *Oh god.*

Other, odd details. A picture knocked onto the floor, their father and his namesake, Grandpa Max, arm in arm. Papers scattered about like fallen leaves.

She turned, dreading what else she'd see. Her sister-in-law was sprawled on her back, eyes glassy, a dark stain spreading down her neck and onto her pale-pink blouse.

The blood-splattered face horrifically mirrored Maddy's morning dream.

CHAPTER 8

9:22 a.m.:

That horrible, gun-like sound still echoed in Will's ears. Frozen with fear, he stood in the living room doorway. Maria and Dad were sprawled on the floor next to each other.

Will's breath stopped. His stomach clenched and his heart turned to ice. For a moment he remained motionless, then, in a flash, he was on the floor at Maria's side. He still couldn't breathe. She didn't look right. Part of her head was—

He couldn't look. She was gone. Pain washed over him, he closed his eyes tightly, doubled over, and clenched his hands into fists.

A long minute later, a small sound caught his attention. Will managed a shallow breath, which he held while he straightened up and opened his eyes. The murmur came from Dad's direction. Will turned, knees on the hardwood floor. Maddy knelt on the other side of their father, near his broken eyeglasses. There was a ragged hole through the upper left side of his dad's shirt.

Then Dad's chest moved. Barely. Surprised, Will and Maddy both leaned over their dad and searched his face for signs of life.

Maddy's eyes filled with tears and her cry sounded hoarse. "Dad!"

Before Will could utter a word, Dad's eyes slowly rolled open and focused on the two of them. "Love you—so much—torney—go to Sacramento attorney. Go now," he choked out, weakly turned his head, put his right hand on his wound, and coughed up blood.

Will grabbed his father's other hand, feeling as if he'd snagged a fragile branch while sinking into quicksand.

"It's okay, Dad," Will said, the words sounding surreal and inadequate. Their eyes met for an instant before his father's green eyes fluttered shut and his head relaxed back. "Shhh…"

"No—called you here—saw a ghost—think…about Ramiro's legacy—think it was—" Dad's last, shallow breath doused Will's tiny flame of hope.

For the briefest instant, his father's essence exploded throughout the room, and then all of him was gone.

The delicate branch broke, and Will sank into despair. He closed his eyes, pulled his hand away, slammed his fists into the floor against all the grief, and somehow managed to keep the scream inside his own head. Maria was gone. She was his life and love. His father was dead. Will's heart was a coal pit of grief, while his head exploded with white fireworks of pain. Tight with the effort of holding himself together, he trembled.

Long seconds passed.

After a time, Will became aware of Maddy's violent sobbing. Her hand gripped his arm tightly.

Eventually, Will opened his eyes and took a deep breath. He couldn't look at the bodies, so he peered around the living room. Who would do this? And why?

His eyes found the cracked window, and, with a jolt, he realized the shooter could still be out there. Probably was still out there. He reached for his phone to call the police.

And where was AJ?

CHAPTER 9

9:25 a.m.:

AJ liked playing cowboys and Indians. As he moved through the patchy fog toward the broken-branch sound, he imagined that he and Damien, the renamed dog, were Indian braves sneaking up on stupid cowboys who had gotten too close to their tribe. In his head, he made war whoop sounds.

Holding onto Damien's collar, he tiptoed down the tall rows of vines, around the house, and toward an old barn, where the noise had come from. The brave warrior paused at the edge of the vines, about ten feet from the gravel driveway, and lay down on the ground, pulling Damien down beside him into the mist.

He heard a new sound in the distance. A siren.

As he watched from the shadows, two men ran out of the barn and jumped into the front seat of an evil-looking car with tinted windows and a BMW emblem on the hood. One of the men was carrying a long weapon, and AJ watched him throw it on the dash before the man jumped in after it and started the car. The brave Indian role abandoned AJ as he realized two things at once. The breaking branch had been a gunshot, and these men were dangerous.

AJ burrowed into the ground and tried to make no noise. He felt scared, knowing the car would drive right by his hiding place. Afraid to move, he shivered, held his breath, and tightened his grip on the dog's neck, wishing Squirrel wouldn't pant so loudly.

CHAPTER 10

9:30 a.m.:

Maddy rubbed tears from her eyes and stood. Will had just called the police. How long would it take them to arrive? Her head reeled with questions about the murder of her father and Maria. Why on earth would someone want to kill them? Where was the son of a bitch who did it?

"*Merda!* Where is AJ?" Will swore in Portuguese as he stumbled to his feet, too.

It took Maddy only a moment to realize Will was right about AJ being in trouble. Where was he? The threat wasn't over.

"Don't panic yet. Let's go find him," she said.

Maddy could sense Will trying to get ahold of himself. Her sobbing done for the moment, all she felt now, deep in her chest, was the powerful urge to locate the boy. She was razor sharp and focused. As fast as she could, she studied the bodies, the window.

Wanting to see if AJ was in sight, but also wanting to be careful, she hugged the wall and peered around the window casement, looking outside through the shattered glass, too aware that the killer was out there somewhere. At first, there was nothing to see but the barn through the fog. Then she noticed the upper hay window at the top of the barn stood open, a lidless third eye in the face of the barn.

She pointed. "Look! I'll bet that's where the shot came from."

"I'll bet you're right," Will replied in a hushed tone.

Maddy took a final look and ran back down the hall. Will was not quite able to match her long stride. Tires crunched on gravel. She cracked the front door open. A black Seven Series BMW sedan sped around a corner. The passenger's window was down, and blond hair leaked out underneath the man's black cap. She couldn't make out any details about the driver. The car fishtailed away as it careened through the foggy vineyard and down a service lane.

"They got away," Will growled through clenched teeth.

"I know—but I didn't see AJ in the car." She raised her voice and yelled for him, "AJ! AJ! Where are you?"

Will joined the chorus. "AJ. Come on out, buddy!"

As they both moved toward their cars, Maddy turned around in a slow circle to peer in all directions.

After a minute, Squirrel came bounding from behind the house, AJ close on his heels. Tears glistened in the boy's eyes as he ran to her and rushed into her arms. She embraced him, awash in relief. Maddy hugged AJ tightly for a long minute as he cried, her own eyes moist, too. After a minute or two, the rush seeped out of her and a deep chill entered her bones. She shivered when AJ stopped crying and separated from her.

The three of them moved to the front steps and collapsed. AJ huddled next to her and Maddy put her arm around him. For a minute, they all stared in the direction the BMW had gone.

"What happened? Why were those mean men here?" AJ asked.

Maddy considered sugarcoating, but chose the truth. "Our dad—and Will's wife—were killed by those men."

AJ let out a fresh sob and a tear rolled down his freckled cheek.

Will reached for a cigarette. "Don't cry, buddy, it'll be all right."

"Will it?" AJ asked, and Maddy wondered exactly the same thing.

CHAPTER 11

11:00 a.m.:

As he stared out the window of his father's den, Will considered reaching into his pocket for another cigarette. Too bad they were indoors. He wanted a smoke. Filthy habit. But it might make him feel better.

The heaviness in his chest made the day seem dream-like and bizarre. *Dad and Maria aren't dead.* He wasn't being interviewed by a cop, no. The smoke would have to wait, so he scratched at his itchy new beard instead.

A blackbird flew into the window pane with a dull thud and dropped to the ground. It flew off again, but Will, not in the best of moods, figured it for a goner. The murders were spreading evil ripples like a pebble thrown into a pond. Staring at the smudge on the window, Will sat rooted to his chair.

"Where did you meet your wife?"

Will ignored the police sergeant's question.

The den reminded Will of a gentleman's library from days gone by. His dad had enjoyed the masculine feel of high, beamed ceilings, dark shelves full of books, a broad, traditional desk, and multiple narrow, patterned, stained-glass windows.

Another unwelcome stab of pain arose as he thought about Dad on his way to the morgue, never to sit at his desk again. The shadowed space felt too close, and Will could smell the sergeant's haze of stale-coffee breath from across the desk.

Earlier, Maddy had left the den in which the police had set up an interview room. Before their younger sister, Bella, and the police had arrived, she had fumed for a while, pacing and kicking gravel in the driveway. He figured they were all in shock. Just ten minutes ago, while in the bathroom, he almost lost it during a long, bad moment and knew he'd mourn more later, when he was alone. As Maddy had stalked from the room on her long legs, he could tell from the storm in her green eyes that she was angry as a disturbed rattlesnake.

The police had questioned AJ, too. Now it was Will's turn in the den's hot seat. He had tried, with no success, to avoid a conversation with the portly Calistoga police officer named Pete. The cop came with a balding pate, heavy black glasses, Groucho Marx eyebrows, and a thick, drooping mustache. For someone with such a hang-dog comedic appearance, the man had an annoying air of self-importance.

"I said, where did you meet your wife?"

Will cleared his throat. "I met her after I relocated to Brazil. I was living on my sailboat and working as an electrical engineer."

Will didn't mention he'd moved to South America to escape Maddy's anger, his own guilt, and his need to stop living in her shadow. They were close when they were young, but high school was hard. She was a straight-A student. He was a B student. She was a star snow skier. He hadn't done sports. She excelled at everything and he had done okay. Since Maddy was the firstborn, it was typical psychology, but living it had been a rough ride. After high school, she hadn't wanted anything to do with him. It was all so uncomfortable that he'd sought out a new life. But he still felt loyal to Maddy and this walrus of a man didn't need to know those details.

Sergeant Pete fidgeted with a pencil on the desk. "How'd you hook up?"

"Maria and I met at work, she was an engineer, too—we worked together on a project to improve manufacturing quality. I was a tester. She was a respected and successful project manager. We were happy and married a year and a half later."

A kaleidoscope of memories whirled through his mind: lazy mornings on the boat eating bacon and eggs, dancing in the midnight clubs, wine over dinner, walks through the noise-filled market. His head was dizzy with grief.

"Why exactly did you come up to California this week?"

Nervous, Will twirled his flashlight's keychain ring around his finger. "I don't know why Dad asked for a visit, but on the voice mail he indicated it was important. So, we came. Maddy and I arrived first, our younger sister ran late and missed the whole thing." *Wish I'd missed the whole thing, too.*

The sergeant went over the events of the morning, bit by painful bit. Will indicated he hadn't seen the shooter and had only caught a brief glimpse of the BMW sedan.

"Any idea who would want your father or your wife dead?"

"No. The vineyard had been on a downhill slide but wasn't bankrupt, Dad hadn't dated in forever, and I don't know of any shady business partners. And Maria, everybody loves Maria." And then he added under his breath, "loved."

Will remembered yesterday morning's laughter, lovemaking, and kisses before they got out of bed. When his heart constricted further, he looked for something else to think about. His father's mention of Ramiro came to mind, but he decided not to share that tidbit with Sergeant Walrus either.

Sergeant Pete stabbed his pencil at Will. "What about a will, how much will you get from your dad's murder?"

Will tried to keep the defensiveness out of his voice. "I suspect this place is mortgaged to the hilt, so I doubt we'll get anything."

Will didn't like where this line of questioning was going. He expected some sympathy, not to be treated like a suspect. He was still wobbly, cut off at the knees.

"What about life insurance on your wife?"

The question, like the man, was too blunt. and Will's temper began to flare. "I vaguely recall that there's a life insurance policy on my wife through work."

"How much is it worth?"

Ridiculous as it was, Will could sense the man narrowing in, like a hunting dog that had just found a scent.

"Six or seven hundred thousand, I don't recall exactly."

The sergeant's eyes lit up. "Really? And you don't recall the exact amount?"

Will could almost see the cop's nose twitch with the aroma of motive. "No. No, I don't."

"And why's that?"

Will's ire was up now. "Well, I don't even know my own policy. Maybe a million. Something like ten times my annual salary. I'm just sad she's gone."

"I'll bet you are. All seven-hundred-thousand tears." The sergeant smirked. "How much does it cost to hire a hit man in Brazil?"

Will stood and leaned toward the desk, knocking the chair down behind him. The dread in his chest had been replaced by the heat of anger. His face felt hot and his hands were clenched into fists. Using every ounce of self-control he possessed, he grated, "Are we done here?"

The sergeant stood, too, and stared Will down. "Yes, just don't leave the country." The final insult was delivered with authority and dismissal.

Will did his best not to slam the door on the way out, but it still thundered in his ears. *Christ Almighty! On top of it all, I'm a suspect.*

CHAPTER 12

12:30 p.m.:

Police questioning over, Maddy tripped and swore as she stepped out the front doorway and onto the porch with Will. In a foul temper after dealing with the interviews, she wanted the truth about what had happened here and was not at all sure when she was going to get it.

The sergeant with the wild eyebrows and bushy mustache had seemed a complete idiot, asking her the same questions two, and sometimes three, times, so she had no faith he was going to be of any help in tracking down the killers. Especially since Will told her he'd been treated like a suspect, which was absurd. She and Will had been released at last and were heading for his blue Mustang.

As the heavy front door shut behind them, Will said something she didn't quite hear. The rage she felt at the murders, mixed with the angry stew she'd felt toward him since high school, began to boil over. She didn't want to talk to him, but their dad was dead! Ugh, she was going to have to deal with him. He smelled of tobacco and part of her questioned when he had taken up smoking. It was a disgusting habit and threw her right over the edge.

Maddy turned toward him to express her annoyance. "You stink! When did you start smoking?" He kept walking so she grabbed his arm to get him to stop, a little harder than she intended. "Hey, I asked you a question."

Will turned and looked at her with long-lashed eyes that held deep pools of sorrow. Her anger evaporated, like mist in the sun, and she reproached herself. She sniffled, once, twice, and then her reserve failed, and she broke into tears, sobbing. Will pulled her close and held her.

After a minute, she pushed him away. "I'm sorry. It's just you were such an ass in high school, and I'm still mad at you."

He looked down. "I'm sorry for all that, Maddy."

She tried a grin. "Let's just drop it. We have bigger problems right now."

He pulled out a piece of paper and waved it gamely. "I found the attorney's address while you were working with Bella to get AJ back to the city."

"Great, I want some answers. Since we can't make any funeral arrangements until after the autopsy, let's go find out what Dad was talking about." She got in the passenger seat. "His tone was urgent and we can start notifying people of his death on the road."

"Sounds good. Who do you think those guys were in that black Beemer?" Will asked.

"No clue. And whoever they were, why would they want to kill Dad and Maria?"

Will engaged his seat belt. "You've got me. And I don't trust the police to figure it out."

"Me neither."

Will fired up the Mustang and started down the driveway. She noticed the vineyard roll by. The fog had cleared and the sun shone brightly out of a robin's-egg blue sky. Somehow, it had become a beautiful Napa Valley day. Life went on. A sad line from an old Johnny Cougar song rewound through her head.

"That was nice of Bella to take the dog. And get AJ back home."

Maddy thought back to her younger sister's frightened arrival and agreed. "It was. Maybe I shouldn't have brought AJ. He got lucky. I hope he'll be okay."

"You can take him to the roller coasters some other time. I'm sure he'll be fine."

The boy did seem resilient. Maddy was reminded of a scene from the dojo the day before: AJ was still trying to figure out how to perfect his backward roll. Some moves just didn't come as naturally to him, and she'd been assisting the sensei. She showed him how to tuck his head to the side and how to bring his hand up to help distribute the weight across his shoulders. Each time she gave him a slight nod to let him know it was his turn. When he finally figured it out, he'd given her a huge smile and hug.

Was that just yesterday? Today AJ didn't want to leave her, and she had to bribe him with a promise of an ice-cream cone, before he agreed to get in the car with Bella.

So much had changed in a day. She felt as she imagined World War I soldiers in the trenches might have, shell-shocked and dazed.

Will pulled out of side streets and onto Silverado Trail, a local route that paralleled the main drag through Napa Valley. She sat back in disbelief. Only yesterday, hell, even this morning, she had cried in the shower, sad from the breakup with Vincent. Helping out at the dojo, her aikido training, and part-time gig developing computer apps were all that she had to worry about. She fought against another sobbing attack, thinking about Vincent, Dad, and Maria. A lone tear rolled down her cheek.

After about ten minutes, Will turned on to Highway 128, a shortcut through the coastal range to the Central Valley and Sacramento. Although filled with stunning scenery of woodland oaks, golden rolling hills, and even a picturesque creek along her side of the road, it had more than its share of hairpin turns.

Maddy felt nauseous at the thought of all those curves. "I might get carsick if we take this route. Are you sure you want to go this way instead of taking the freeway?"

"Well, it's shorter, and we'll miss traffic on the interstate."

"True. How about I drive then?"

"Okay, let me find a spot to pull over." Just having passed the Lake Hennessey Recreation Area, they were already in one of the curvy sections of road. "I remember a turnout up past the lake."

Maddy rolled down the window to get some air and tried to focus on the thoroughfare ahead, which was probably why she saw the black car before Will did. It was parked where the road from the left met up with the highway.

She pointed at the black BMW. "Will—look there! Don't stop!"

Will turned his head to the left then looked back at her with a terrified glance. He swore under his breath and gently accelerated past the BMW. The driver and blond passenger were looking down at something. Perhaps a map.

Maddy turned in her seat and mentally crossed her fingers. "Hope they didn't notice us."

"Me, too!"

She reached for her cell phone to dial the police. She glanced at the screen. "No reception!"

Swearing, she shoved the phone into the glove compartment, closing the plastic door with enough force that it bounced open. She slammed it shut again.

Tires squealed behind them. Maddy looked back in time to see a large cloud of dust bloom from behind the BMW. "Punch it!"

Will threw the car's transmission into "Sport" mode, downshifted, and accelerated through the next corner. Maddy was thrown back in her seat and watched the pursuit using the side mirror instead of craning her head back around. The German sedan seemed to sail around the corners, gaining on them, Maddy held her breath through a series of small S turns.

Coming out of the last curve, a short straightaway ran in front of them, leading to a decrepit one-lane bridge. Will sped toward the crossing. From the opposite direction, a late-model white Ford truck barreled down the road, also headed for the narrow passage. Will slammed the horn and the truck skidded to a stop on the far side of the bridge. The driver stuck his head out his side window, and Maddy read a questioning look in his eyes.

His confusion didn't last long. Shots rang out from the BMW and one of them hit the windshield of the truck. Will fishtailed onto the bridge, glancing off one side. They passed the Ford, the driver slumped over the wheel. Blood was plastered on the back window. Poor guy. Maddy touched her heart in shock as they raced by.

Maddy looked ahead and couldn't see around the next corner, which hung to the left. She jumped as a bullet pinged off the back of the Mustang.

Will downshifted again and braked into the turn. "Hang on!"

The car went into a skid until Will hit the gas. Their tires screeched, and she smelled burned rubber. For an instant, the BMW came into sight, but then her right-side mirror exploded.

Her heart lurched in her chest. *We're going to die!* Her shaking hands grabbed the dashboard as she realized she was truly terrified for the first time in her life.

They accelerated down a straight stretch of road toward a U-turn that she recalled from prior trips, the BMW gaining on them in the straightaway. Will took the turn to the left way too fast and braked to avoid the railed drop-off that yawned beyond the road's gravel edge. Tires squealed as their car slid into a full spin.

Maddy's pulse hammered in her ears and her stomach did a Tilt-a-Whirl lurch. Pebbles flew.

Will jammed the accelerator and corrected the car. It rocketed forward.

Abruptly, a female deer jumped onto the road and Will jerked the car to avoid it. They brushed past the doe and a heartbeat later, brakes screamed.

Maddy whipped her head around. The black sedan narrowly missed another deer but skidded out of control and hit the guardrail. The railing was no match for the fast-moving feat of German engineering—the car sliced through it and bowled down the canyon. It rolled twice before it burst into flames.

"Will, stop the car. They've gone over the edge." Relief rang clear in her own voice.

Before he pulled over, Will continued on another fifty yards, until the road widened into a turnout. Without speaking, they got out of the car, walked back down the road, and looked into the abyss beyond the violated guardrail. Several hundred feet below, the car at the bottom of the canyon was a crumpled, dirty, smoking mess. Flames flared from the engine. Somehow, the vehicle had landed right-side up in the creek. The horn blared.

The noise stopped, and she could make out the sound of a roaring fire over the rushing of the creek.

The passenger's half-submerged car door opened, and a blond man stepped into the thigh-deep water. Not just any blond man, the shooter from the vineyard. At this distance, it looked as if flames were coming from his hair and shirt. Perhaps his entire right side was on fire. She couldn't be sure. The shooter threw himself into the water, executing a perfect shallow dive.

Maddy turned and looked at Will.

His eyes were wide and scared. "We need to go."

Her heart pounded again, loud in her ears.

CHAPTER 13

1:15 p.m.:

As Will put his hands back on the wheel of the Mustang, he noticed they were shaking and fought to control them. *Fear or adrenaline?* he wondered. He gripped the wheel hard with one hand and shifted into "Drive" with the other.

Once they were back on the road, Will turned to Maddy. "Holy Mother of God! I've never had to drive like that."

"Wow. Just wow." Maddy's tone was quiet and shocked. Then she found her voice. "I've never been so terrified in my entire life."

"Me neither," Will said. "I can't believe that guy survived the crash."

"Crazy."

"I guess they're after us, too."

"Yeah."

"Do you have cell reception yet?"

"Let me look." She grabbed the phone from the glove compartment and glanced at it. "No, not yet. We're still in the boonies."

Will piloted the car through the curves at a normal speed. "So, who wants us dead? Maria, Dad, and now you and me?"

"I have no flipping idea. Maybe Dad had some kind of sketchy business deal go awry?"

"Unlikely," Will disagreed and checked off points on his fingers. "Dad's land company was pretty tame. All he did was run the vineyard. He hadn't dated anybody in decades, pretty much since Mom died. Maria and I have no known enemies—you don't either, right?"

"Right. Unless I ticked off some kid's parents at the dojo while teaching them to roll," she replied facetiously.

Will chose to ignore the sarcasm. "Sounds questionable. So much for the usual suspects. That leaves Dad's odd mention of our old ancestor, Ramiro."

Maddy looked out the window. "Speaking of which, does the attorney know we're coming?"

"Uh, no. I didn't think to call. I was a little…distracted."

She looked down again at her cell phone. "We must be getting close to Winters. I have reception now. I'll call nine-one-one and then the attorney."

The hills had given way to the orchards of the Central Valley. Will lit a cigarette and decided it was definitely fear, perhaps terror, and not adrenaline that had made his hands shake.

As Maddy made her calls, Will scratched at his beard. At least the fear had chased off the sadness for a minute. Now that his breath had returned to normal, the lead weight of grief weighed him down again. *What will I do without Maria? I loved her so much.*

Once Maddy was done wrangling an urgent appointment with the attorney, he turned on some classical music to fill the silence. The battle to keep his hands steady on the wheel was won for the moment, but he often looked in the rearview mirror and wondered what he would do if that blond guy got his hands on another car.

CHAPTER 14

Midtown Sacramento, 1:45 p.m.:

After they had parked in the neighborhood parking garage near the attorney's address, Maddy scanned the area for a possible attacker. At this point, she was feeling jumpy and raw, but nobody leaped out of the bushes. They had argued over where to park, just like old times. She had voted for a closer spot on the street, but since Will was driving, he vetoed her vote and went for the parking garage, using the "It will be cooler" logic.

As they stepped out of the shaded garage and onto the tree-lined street, she agreed to herself that he had a point. The car dashboard had read 103 degrees, a typical scorching Sacramento summer day. "There's a reason I live in the Bay Area. It's bloody hot here."

"It is." Will looked up and down the street. "I can't believe I'm asking this, but are you hungry?"

"I lost my appetite in Napa but will keep you company when we're done here."

Will checked the address on his piece of paper against a 1920s-style bungalow that was painted a modest light green with tan trim. "Okay. This is it."

She appreciated that, although nearly one hundred years old, the house was well kept. It even had an inviting porch swing, which, to her taste, may have pushed the envelope a bit between cozy and professional. But she didn't mind. However, she did mind the Coors beer can on the sidewalk. It didn't belong. She picked it up, emptied out the remaining contents in the landscaped ivy, and carried it with her up the broad set of stairs.

Inside, a too-sunny, too-young, too-nervous-looking receptionist with short dyed-blonde hair and long nails looked up from her typing. "Can I help you?"

"Yes, Madeline and William Argones here. We have an appointment with Ms. Bridgewater," Maddy said.

The receptionist looked pointedly at the beer can in Maddy's hand. Maddy, in turn, looked down at the gold fingernails, noticing a tiny red star embedded in each. Maddy wondered how the woman typed.

Maddy felt too tired to be petty. "Do you have a trash can? I found this on your sidewalk."

"Of course. Here you go." The sweet young thing reached under her desk and offered a waste basket.

Maddy promptly took advantage.

The receptionist pointed toward a fashionable set of chairs at the other end of the room. "If you'll have a seat, Ms. Bridgewater will be right with you."

Several minutes later they were ushered into an office. It looked like it had been a dining room at one time, as it had a swinging door, probably to the kitchen, at the opposite end of the room from where they had entered. The office was painted a warm, light-green color. Maybe she should consider repainting her apartment with the shade, as it nicely set off the polished oak floors and the wood double-hung windows. The glass offered a view of the front porch, the swing, and the empty Midtown street. A tasteful antique desk, chairs, and a side table comprised the furnishings.

The attorney, a partner in the Bridgewater, Simon, and Stratford firm, was female, and in her early fifties by the laugh lines around her eyes and the salt and pepper in her hair. She held herself with a competent, businesslike demeanor that was reflected in her tailored suit. Either she had managed to avoid glasses or was wearing contacts in her dark-brown eyes.

The attorney wasted no time in offering sympathy as she shook their hands in both of hers. "Please sit down. I'm so incredibly sorry for your loss."

Will sat across the desk from the attorney. "Thank you." His long legs didn't fit between the desk and the chair so he scooted the seat back.

"We appreciate your condolences," Maddy added, pulling her own chair back for her legs before taking the seat next to Will. "Weren't you friends with Dad?"

"I do-uh, did—consider your father a good friend. We met years ago at a wine tasting and had gotten to know each other well over the years, as he ran all his business through our firm. I will miss him."

"Well, we're sorry for your loss as well."

The attorney's eyes looked red. Perhaps there had been something more to the relationship.

"Thank you. So why are you here? It's a little unusual to discuss his affairs so soon. In most circumstances, we would wait for a death certificate."

Will made a small motion with his hand to get their attention. They turned to him. "I know Maddy didn't go into details with you on the phone." He paused and looked away.

The attorney prompted, "Do you want to share those details now?"

He took a deep breath. "Yes, it's why we're here. Dad was shot this morning, brutally murdered, along with my wife. They were both taken out with one bullet, intentionally or unintentionally, we don't know. We heard the shot and ran into the living room. My wife was gone, but Dad got out a few words. He told us to come here." Will's voice cracked but didn't break.

The attorney's expression became flat and closed.

"He mentioned 'Ramiro.'"

Bridgewater's eyes narrowed for the briefest instant. "The first king of what eventually became Spain. And your ancestor. Interesting." She paused.

Maddy imagined the attorney was making her mind up about something.

"I'll need to confirm the death," the attorney said.

"Please do," Will said.

Will looked at Maddy, and she got the sense he was asking permission to add additional elements to press the point. She nodded.

He went on, "Also, on the way here, we were followed by the murderers. Shot at."

The attorney's eyebrows rose. "You're all right?"

"Well, we're as fine as we can be," Will said. The fear in his eyes, though, leaked through. "The shooter's vehicle crashed, and we hope the police have apprehended them. We've had an extremely long day already and want to know why Dad pointed us here."

"Okay. I'll get on it. Please step back outside for a moment. Help yourself to coffee."

Maddy and Will walked into the young receptionist's domain. Was the girl even out of high school? She wore ear buds and ignored the twins as she continued to type. Will looked out the window, then picked up a magazine and began to skim it. Maddy checked her phone to distract herself.

There was a text from Bella indicating that AJ was back at home safe and sound. The message even had a picture of him waving, with a somber smile on his freckled face, which produced a small return smile from Maddy as she texted a thanks. There was a breaking-news article from her *New York Times* newsfeed about a Russian attack on someplace in China. She skipped it. Her buddy Aaron, the sensei who owned the dojo, had texted that classes had gone well today. Her computer coworker had left her a text asking when she was going to be done with wireframing the new shopping app they were creating. And nothing from Vincent. Of course. All normal correspondence. But after the day's events, normal correspondence seemed unreal.

The door opened and Ms. Bridgewater called them into her office. Outside the windows, the hot summer street held no movement. The porch swing was still as death. They sat down and the attorney handed them each an eight-inch-by-fourteen-inch yellow manila envelope. Maddy's felt heavy.

The attorney interlaced her fingers. "Your father made arrangements for you, and your sister Bella, to have these. If he'd died a nonviolent death, you'd get them after the funeral, but he had the foresight to indicate that, should he die in violent or unusual circumstances, you were to receive them right away."

That farsightedness surprised Maddy. She opened her packet and noticed Will opening his, too. Hers contained a letter-sized envelope addressed to her in her father's handwriting. Something swished when she moved the envelope. She'd open it later, after seeing what else was inside.

The packet's contents then got odd. She found ten gold coins. Upon closer inspection, each was a one-ounce gold American Eagle.

"What the hell?" Will muttered.

Maddy glanced over to see him opening a small black velvet bag. When he spilled the contents into his palm, her breath caught. He held a handful of small diamonds. They sparkled in the sunlight streaming from the window, like a tiny galaxy of glittering stars against the night-black setting of the bag.

Inside Maddy's envelope was not only a similar bag but also a wad of several thousand dollars in cash. Large denominations. That concluded her quick inventory. *And I thought Dad was broke*. She shook her head at her father's strangeness then looked up to press the attorney for additional information.

"So, about Ramiro—" Her question was cut short as swift movement outside caught her eye. Through the window, a charred version of the blond-haired shooter pounded up the street.

CHAPTER 15

2:10 p.m.:

William ignored the rock of grief in his stomach and looked with dismay at the packet of wealth in his hands. He had figured on a paltry inheritance when his father died. What was it with all this cash, the diamonds? Why leave them liquid assets?

The implied stealth made him feel uncomfortable, and he was certain this was undoubtedly the harbinger of a dangerous scenario. An engineer by training and a skeptic by nature, getting shot at in the morning and being handed diamonds in the afternoon was just not his cup of tea.

"Will!" Maddy hissed in a loud whisper, frantically pointing outside to the attorney's front porch.

Why did she care about the porch swing?

Maddy stood and poked him in the shoulder. At her insistent, not-so-subtle prodding, he looked out the window. The shooter from the vineyard was running up the stairs, a gun held in his right hand. Burned clothes and half a scorched face drifted by the window. The front door slammed open and a man's loud, thickly accented voice boomed in the lobby. Had the guy hijacked a car?

Fear flooded through Will all over again, and he sprang from his chair. *And how did the man know we'd be here?*

"*Merda!*" he swore. He had moved so fast that the chair was knocked over behind him. Not the best way to stay unnoticed.

Will reached for the inner-office door lock and turned the bolt, thankful for modern renovations in the old house.

Maddy threw the fallen chair under the door handle and grabbed both manila envelopes. The attorney's face held a wide-eyed, slack-jawed look. Shock.

"Let's go!" Will whispered as he ushered them both toward the swinging door at the back of the office.

Maddy moved fast, but Will had to grab the attorney by the elbow and manhandle her out of her chair and toward the door. Right before he made it through the doorway to the kitchen, an ominous thump came from within the foyer. Will hoped the good-looking receptionist hadn't been the target, but he felt a lump in his throat as he guessed she had.

Together, Will, Maddy, and the attorney raced through the small kitchen toward a back door, Maddy in the lead. Brewing coffee gurgled as they sped through. Maddy led them outside, into a long, narrow, fenced yard.

Will looked at the attorney. "Which way?"

"The back alley," she said, pointing to the fence.

They sprinted across the yard and through a small wooden gate. On the other side, a narrow, unpaved alley ran in both directions.

The attorney headed to the left. "There's a mall just down the street. I'll run in there and call the police."

"Thanks! We'll get out of here," Will said over his shoulder.

They ran down the backstreet to the right, in the direction of the parking garage.

Halfway down the alley, a Rottweiler jumped into a chain-link fence and Will instinctively jumped to the left at the sudden, angry assault.

"Get down!" Maddy yelled as she ran by.

Will looked behind him. Clear. But, as they turned the corner at the end of the alley, the shooter rushed through the gate, into the alley, and took a practiced two-handed pistol-shooting stance.

Pop! Pop, pop!

A telephone pole near Will's head splintered with a loud crack. They raced for the Mustang.

Will ducked. "Faster!"

They hit the parking garage at a dead run and jumped into the car. The keys were in the ignition before Maddy had even shut her door. Will had never moved so fast in his entire life. But was it fast enough?

CHAPTER 16

2:17 p.m.:

Maddy sought to catch her breath as Will gunned the car engine. Tires squealed as they careened out of the Midtown parking garage and drove away from the attorney's office. She prayed the shooter wouldn't follow them.

"Where to?" Will panted.

His dark curly hair was damp with sweat.

Sensing Will's fear, Maddy was somehow gratified that he was as freaked out as she was. Then she criticized herself for being so shallow. "Away from here. Take a freeway."

The street they were on led to a freeway on-ramp. Will took it and headed south on Highway 99. A short minute later, he had the option to turn off toward either Lake Tahoe or San Francisco. He took Highway 50 east, toward Lake Tahoe. Maddy watched behind them for signs of pursuit but saw nothing unusual. Will checked his mirrors as well.

"I don't see anybody. Do you think we're being followed?" Will asked.

"You may have lost them by heading east, but I'll keep an eye out, too."

"How do you think that bastard found us?"

Scared and pissed off, Maddy turned again and studied the traffic behind them. "I have absolutely no idea. And why does he want us dead?"

"Really good question."

"His voice sounded Russian when he spoke at the attorney's office," Maddy offered.

"It did?"

"Yes, I recognized it from some of the kids at the dojo. AJ's family spoke Russian, and I have one other student who is also fluent."

"Hmm, I wonder—no, that's being paranoid."

Maddy tried to keep her tone level, but she was still on edge. "What?"

"You mentioned to the cops on the phone that we were heading to the attorney's office when you called in the car accident, right?"

"Yes."

Will checked his side mirror. "Well. Maybe the guy has connections."

"You mean connections inside the police force? Perhaps. Does sound a bit farfetched. He or his friends could have tapped our phone conversation, too, I guess."

"True. Of course, he did kill Dad and Maria this morning. That would have sounded implausible yesterday."

"You're right. Either way, we're kind of screwed. I don't feel safe making any more phone calls. At least we seem to have lost him, for now."

Will yanked the wheel and pulled the car over to the freeway shoulder. He grabbed his cell phone, and handed it to Maddy. "We need to destroy them."

"Why, so they can't be traced with the GPS?"

"Exactly."

"You're in too many Facebook techy science groups." Maddy didn't want to take his cell phone, but turned it over in her hands. "Wish they still made removable batteries."

"Me, too. Put them under the tires."

Maddy pulled out her own phone and got out of the car, trying to think of another way to deal with the problem. She failed to come up with any other option, so as the highway traffic rushed by, she placed each phone behind a wheel, feeling as if she were cutting off a limb.

Will rolled down her window. "Ready?"

"Sure. Go backward."

Black tires rumbled over the small devices. The loud crunch of the breaking electronics made her wince. She sighed and closed her eyes. How much worse could the day get?

Will pulled the Mustang forward and she confirmed both phones were pancake flat. Small pieces of gorilla glass and silver metal caught the sun and flashed. Leaving the piles of litter pained her, but she got back in the car and Will sped off.

They sat in silence for a minute or two as the car continued down the freeway. Will lit a cigarette and rolled down the window. Maddy tried not to gag on the smoke and rolled her window down, too.

Will broke the silence. "Do you think he killed the attorney's assistant back there?"

"I don't know. I hope not."

"Yeah, me too, but I definitely heard a thud as we were leaving."

"God, that would be awful, even if she did look like a child playing dress-up."

"She did not. She was good-looking."

"Are you serious?"

The silence in the car was thicker this time and lasted a little longer.

Bothered by the directionless driving, Maddy finally asked, "What do you think about heading to our old house in Lake Tahoe?"

"Dad sold that place over a decade ago."

"Exactly—it's not in any of our names any longer and the new owners are never there, except weekends during winter. They're snow bunnies."

"Do they even still own the house?"

"I think so. I have a friend who would have told me if they'd sold."

Will tapped his fingers on the wheel, a sign, Maddy knew, that he was feeling nervous. "I don't know if it's such a good idea. It's not exactly legal," he said.

"But they won't think to look for us there. Better than a hotel or going back to my loft. We'd be sitting ducks. And we're already moving in that direction."

"True, but we would have to break in. We could get caught."

"There was a broken latch on the bathroom window. Maybe they never fixed it. I'd rather take my chances there than have that thug find us again. Wouldn't you?"

"All right. You win." Will paused. "Think the lion statue will still be in the front yard?"

"I hope so. It would make it feel like home."

They had spent much time as children playing with, and around, that four-foot bronze statue of a guardian lion.

Maddy took one more look behind them, then pulled out the manila envelope and shook her father's letter. "Feels like there's something inside it."

"Besides a note, you mean?"

Maddy rolled her eyes and opened the letter-sized envelope. "Yes." She spilled the contents into her other palm.

She gasped. It was her mom's favorite necklace.

"What is it?"

Maddy picked the necklace up by the chain and held it so Will could see. She fought back fresh tears.

"I thought she'd been buried with that!" Will said.

"Guess not." Maddy studied the necklace. A carved silver lion's head hung from a delicate silver chain. An expensive looking piece, it was a little over dime-sized, but thicker, the head in slight profile. "The king of the jungle. Mom, the Leo, sure loved her lions."

Will bit his lip. "She did."

"Guess astrology was a thing then."

"Nice that Dad saved it for you."

She put the necklace around her neck and fastened the clasp. It was a nice length. Not too long. Not too short. "Yeah. Want me to read the letter?"

"Sure, maybe it'll explain some things."

"I hope so." She smoothed the seams out of the pages and began to read:

"'Dearest Maddy,

"'If you're reading this, I'm gone, hopefully, at a ripe old age and passed in my sleep. I've written similar letters to Will and Bella, wanting to say something unique to each of you, besides the standard "I love you," although that is as true today as it's ever been.

"'You were such a beautiful child. Your mother and I adored you. You were a bright, curious girl with a keen mind. Do you remember learning to read? You curled up on your mother's or my lap for hours and we read you one story after another. You've always been such a gifted athlete as well, learning to ride your bike before all the other kids in the neighborhood, running circles around them on the playground and no one could beat you on the slopes when you skied competitively in high school. I still think it was a shame you missed the games that year. You'd have made a great Olympian!

"'Watching you grow up and become a lovely young woman has been one of the keenest joys of my life. I'm proud of how well you did in college, graduating at the top of your class, proud of the computer work you do to make cell phone apps easy for old farts like me, and proud that you made black belt at the dojo. Your mom would be proud too. I was saving her favorite necklace as a special wedding day gift, but if you're reading this, please feel free to wear it now.'"

She paused for a moment, tears welling in her eyes. To maintain control, she looked out the window and held her breath. The seemingly endless suburbs of Sacramento had given way to the oak-studded foothills of the Sierra Nevada. The view reminded her of the morning's car chase through the similar landscape of the Napa hills, prompting her to check behind the car for company. But they still seemed to be without a tail.

"You okay?" Will asked.

"Not really, it's just all so weird."

"I know."

She took a deep breath and flipped through the pages of the letter. "Okay, skipping other sappy parts. Here's where he talks about Ramiro.

"'What follows is shared only at the passing of a generation. I learned this family secret when your grandfather passed away a few years after your mom and grandmother died. The secret is not to be discussed outside the family, or with your future children, unless you have explicit permission from the current king. These are Ramiro's wishes and they are wishes we honor.

"'As you know, Ramiro I founded this family over a thousand years ago and went on to create a dynasty that has contributed to, not only the current Spanish ruling class, but also to the royal families of nearly all the other current European monarchies. We have rich blood in our veins.

"'Many attribute his power to whatever is inside the Aragon *Châsse*, a small box that he supposedly hid before he passed away. The *châsse* is said to contain an arcane object of immense power—if you can find it by following the clues he left behind. Family legend indicates only Ferdinand and Isabella have found it to date, and we all know their legacy through Columbus.

"'Me? I couldn't find the Aragon *Châsse* but didn't have time to look. You kids were young and more important to me. Your grandfather did have time, but in retrospect, I think decades of fruitless searching made him angry and bitter before he died. Perhaps, with your smarts and the help of your siblings, you'll have better luck.

"'Your first clue will be found in an old book, or codex, held by your great-uncle, the current king of Spain, at the family castle. Once he hears of my death, he'll be expecting your call.

"'Although there is just one codex, all your cousins receive similar letters as inheritance. The cash and diamonds are universal currency to aid you in your quest. It's all I could save up. I wish it were more.

"'Remember to quiet your mind and "listen" as you go. Family rumor says that will help. And good luck! Know that I'll love you forever.

"'Yours always,

"'Dad.'"

She put the letter in her lap, feeling curious, perplexed, and immensely sad. "Is he out of his mind?"

"Seriously. Careening around the world on a random hunt for some old, arcane object? What the hell?"

Tears slid down Maddy's face. "Crazy. It must be important though, to mention it when he was…dying. He must have neglected the vineyard to save up money for us."

"Yeah." Will's face looked sad too.

They rode in silence for a minute.

Maddy fiddled with the letter. "He mentioned 'quieting your mind.' Think that's why he taught us to meditate while we were growing up? At least meditation is what I think of it as now."

"It seems to fit. Have you practiced much?"

"I've tried using it with aikido, but have a hard time shutting up my mind. What about you?"

"Nah, hasn't been my thing."

Maddy took a final look over her shoulder. "Let's talk about this more later. It's all too much. I'm going to take a nap. Wake me when we get to Tahoe City so we can get some Thai food on the way to the house."

"Sure, sis, will do."

Countless concerns passed through Maddy's mind, but she was so exhausted from the day that she nodded off within a mile.

CHAPTER 17

Tahoe City, California, 6:30 p.m.:

As he neared their old lake house, his sister asleep, Will reviewed the afternoon's revelations.

The Aragon *Châsse*? How had none of the grown-ups slipped up and told them about this? Or did it have to do with the furtive looks he had caught them sharing at family reunions when he and Maddy were young? Could it be connected to his father's murder? Or was it mere coincidence? He was skeptical of legends, especially those that involved stories of great wealth or power. It was no wonder his dad hadn't pursued it.

When Will pulled into the driveway, he was glad to see their childhood home. It was a classic Tahoe log-style house with a blue metal roof and rock fireplace, out of the way on a large lot that backed up to the national forest. He was gratified to see the sitting lion statue still gracing the front yard. *Home.*

The knot that had been in his stomach since the morning relaxed a notch as he floated for a moment in a pool of happy memories. That statue had been his mom's idea, and he remembered chasing her around and around it, laughing with glee. Always good for a mom-ism, she'd told them to "Go outside and blow the stink off." Later, she'd joined them. It was one of the rare memories he had of his mom and he treasured it.

There were also some less-than-happy memories from this house, too. Dad's letter reminded him of all that Maddy had accomplished in high school, and all that he had failed. It was hell to live in her shadow.

His momentary reverie finished, he put the car in "Park" and poked his sister. "Wake up, Maddy, we're here."

Maddy yawned and stretched her back. Her green eyes still held sleep. "You didn't wake me up, but I smell Thai food. Thanks for stopping. Let's go see if that window latch is still broken."

"At least you were right, they're not home. Hope they haven't installed an alarm."

They walked around to the back of the house and peered at the latch of the bedroom window with dismay. After pushing on the window a few times, they concluded that the new owners had truly repaired the latch, so they went around the house and checked all the other windows. They were all locked but, as they stood looking over the back of the house, Maddy pointed out that the house was not alarmed.

"Let's just break a window," she suggested in a too-loud voice.

Sound travelled in the forest. Will lowered his own voice and looked around. "You're nuts! That's breaking and entering."

"Only if we get caught. This place is seriously isolated. I'll buy them a new window, or we can replace it, and they'll never even know we were here."

"This doesn't sound like a solid plan."

"You'd rather the Russian sniper find us? You have a better idea?"

Will sighed. "No."

Maddy broke a small bedroom window with a stone from the yard, used the same rock to remove the glass shards that were left in the frame, then crawled in, and let him in the front door. At least the neighborhood was quiet tonight. The house was secluded, the nearest neighbor a five-minute walk down the road. Still, he moved the car into the garage and drew the curtains for privacy.

After a quick review of the changes the new owners had made to the house, Will uncorked the bottle of German Riesling that he had bought from the liquor store next to the restaurant, opened the food containers, and turned on the TV to watch the news. "I doubt the murders will have made the news up here."

"Probably not," Maddy agreed.

Instead, the breaking news was about Russia. The announcer's headline was, "New Russian e-bomb knocks out Chinese town's electronics."

They exchanged a glance about the mention of Russia, and Maddy's chopsticks paused for a moment.

After a commercial, the news footage showed a quick, brilliant flash over a Chinese TV station in Yanbian, a town near the Russian Far East. The video was grainy, captured by a cell phone, but it was followed by interviews with several experts who postulated that this was the deployment of Russia's first electromagnetic "e-bomb." The Chinese TV station and the surrounding areas were reportedly still off-line, so the expert's theory made sense.

The announcer indicated that this type of weapon was a warhead that, when exploded, emitted a high-energy, high-powered microwave pulse that fused electrical equipment within range, rendering it useless. *Dangerous technology*, Will thought.

To punctuate the newscaster's point, they interspersed the cell phone video footage with images of destroyed cameras and TVs from the Chinese broadcasting station. Melted circuits made the TVs look like dripping Salvador Dali paintings. Will shivered.

Putting the sound on "Mute," Will turned to Maddy. "I'd heard that we, the United States that is, used an early version of an e-bomb to knock out an Iraqi TV station back in the Gulf War to stop Saddam's propaganda machine."

"If those melted electronics are any indication, it's an effective weapon. That TV oozed like blood from a wound. Let's see what else they have to say."

Will turned the sound back on in time to hear the introduction of an expert on emerging weapons technology. He was with Decisive Weaponry Corp., in Herndon, Virginia.

The expert said, "Although much of the work on this type of weapon is classified, we believe that the US military has actively pursued these types of high-powered microwave 'HPM' weapons since the 1940s, when scientists first observed the powerful electromagnetic shock wave that accompanied atmospheric nuclear detonations."

Nukes. Will and Maddy shared a glance.

"Current efforts are based on using high-temperature superconductors to create intense magnetic fields." Summing up the interview, the expert continued, "A well-made e-bomb could unleash as much electrical power *in a flash* as the Hoover Dam generates in twenty-four hours. The power blast could knock a city off the grid by burning out batteries, frying semi-conductors, melting wiring, and exploding transformers."

Will's mind raced with the implications. The Western world's weaponry was highly sophisticated, with intricate electronic circuits, software, and computer chips. Not to mention the economies of nations that relied on electronics for banking, telecommunications, and shipping. Or, his own personal reliance on the power grid, the internet, phones, stoves, refrigerators, and cars. What didn't utilize electronics these days? Will stared around the house and shivered again, feeling cold all over.

The announcer wrapped up the segment with the theoretical good news that the Russians were said to need a reliable source of high-temperature superconductive material for the weapon to pose a viable threat.

Will again muted the television and turned to Maddy. "Two Russian incidents in one day. Coincidence?"

She hadn't touched her food. "Maybe. Maybe not. But where's the e-bomb connection?"

"I have no idea, but Russia would probably kill ten of us to enable a weapon like that." Finished with dinner, Will twirled his flashlight's keychain ring around his finger, sending the flashlight round and round. The rhythmic movement comforted him somehow.

"My god, can you imagine the world without electronics? No internet?"

Will shuddered. "I can but would rather not. I'm already having phone withdrawal. It would completely screw our ability to defend ourselves from an attack. Think about all the electronics embedded in our modern weapons."

"And I couldn't stream *Walking Dead*, which might be ironic. Did you see that melted TV? Can you say Dali? But seriously, are you seeing some kind of World War Three scenario?"

"A weapon like that, in this day and age, would be the mother of all weapons. Sure, I could see another world war if someone attacked the United States and didn't fully succeed in wiping us out. We'd attack right back and things would escalate from there."

"Great. Just great. The entire world killing each other. That's even better than the murders this morning and our near-death lunch experience. I've lost my appetite and am going to bed." She threw her dishes into the trash and strode to her old room.

Will knew he tended to see the world through a half-empty glass but this did indeed seem dire. Mechanically, he drank more wine as he mulled over the information. With Russia's aggressive behavior in Ukraine, he wasn't surprised by this latest attack on China, but it was disconcerting, to say the least. The Dali-esque image of the melted TV haunted him.

After Maddy's light went out, Will smoked on the deck, worried about Russians, and fighting grief. Maria was gone, his father dead. He couldn't even bury them. His heart ached with the loss. It felt almost too much to bear, like he was scuba diving without air. As his father had taught him, he tried focusing on his breathing and listening to the wind in the trees, but he couldn't slow the train of his thoughts. His heart ached and he nearly wanted to die, just to stop the pain.

Later, as he slept, he dreamt he was dropping down through a void, falling forever through black emptiness.

CHAPTER 18

June 26, 8:27 a.m.:

Maddy woke with a groan as she left the nightmare behind and reached for Vincent. In her dream, spiders were crawling out of the heater ducts and swarming all over her, biting her neck and shoulders. She was unable to move, had been trapped. At least *that* wasn't a real dream. Wait. Not only was Vincent missing from her bed, but there was also a Russian sniper intent on killing them. She groaned again.

The right side of her neck was stiff, so stiff that it pained her to move it. She lay in the strange bed, in the familiar room, for a long minute, massaging her right shoulder and the back of her neck.

The truth was, she felt hurt on a number of levels. Besides the discomfort in her neck, there was a weight in her chest and a heaviness throughout her whole body. It was how she had felt in the aftermath of her first failed aikido belt test: basically, beat up. Facing the day seemed too daunting. What if the killer found them? What was this Aragon *Châsse* that Dad thought so important? What would happen if the Russians made more e-bombs? *And what the hell is Vincent doing this morning?*

Anger, frustration, and tears threatened, but she fought them off, not wanting to feel any of it, afraid the feelings would consume her. Instead she pounded her fists on the bed once and forced herself into the shower to see if she could at least get her neck to loosen up.

After dressing in the same clothes she had worn yesterday, she went out to the kitchen and was amused that Will had gotten over his reluctance at imposing upon the owners. The smell of coffee wafted through the air and, from the packaging on the counter and the crumbs on his plate, he had eaten a frozen waffle. He sat at a round table in the breakfast nook nursing his coffee and looking out the window, a pack of cigarettes on the table. Thankfully, it smelled like he'd smoked outside.

"How'd you sleep?" Maddy asked.

"Not very well. You?"

"Me neither." Earlier in the shower, she'd had some ideas about their situation. "Do you think we should call Bella and let her know we were shot at in Sacramento?"

"Bella, our dear sister, is married to Marty, studly fireman and poster child for the NRA. And no, as we discussed yesterday, I think we need to stay off the grid. Want some coffee?"

"Yes, to coffee. But how practical is going dark? How are we going to know what's going on, or—" She almost couldn't say it. "—or make funeral arrangements?"

"I know. I want to notify Maria's family. I wish I could bring Dad and Maria back, but I can't. Mostly I want to keep us safe and figure out who is behind this nightmare. Don't you?"

Maddy sat down across the table from Will. "Of course, I do. But I'm already tired of running."

"It's not your style. You're a fighter. However, in this situation, are you prepared to use aikido against guns?"

She rubbed at her neck. "Not really."

"Okay, so my suggestion is that we get a *Chronicle* at the grocery store, or a Napa paper if they still carry one up here. Maybe the paper will give us a report about the murder. Dad hooked us up with plenty of cash, so we're good to hang low for a day or two."

"The paper is a good idea but I want to warn Bella. Let's discuss it all further." She twirled her hair around her fingers. "Perhaps over some real food?"

"Sure, that waffle was lame. Where do you want to go?"

"How about the Fire Sign Café? We can shop at the thrift store in Tahoe City and get some new clothes after we get that newspaper."

"All right, let's go."

An hour later, they were seated in the crowded café next to an old stone fireplace, trying to make small talk while waiting for their order. Will looked dapper as always in a light-green hoodie, and she had found a long-sleeve T-shirt and a North Face fleece for the mountain chill that would come in the evening. She loved sitting on the café's outdoor patio, but the wait to sit out there would have taken forever.

Their polished wood table stood under a window that was crowned by a black-and-white checkered valence, and it held a single yellow flower in a juice glass for decoration. Sun shining through the lake side of the café, the charming knotty pine walls, and the happy patrons provided an elegant juxtaposition to her edgy mood. As *the* breakfast destination on the west shore, the café was a little crowded for her taste, but she'd always enjoyed the delicious food. She hoped she could eat. Maybe it would make her neck feel better.

Will sipped his steaming coffee. "So how are your aikido skills coming along? Seems they might come in handy if we get attacked at close range."

"I'm no Steven Seagal, if that's what you're hoping."

"Bummer." He gave her a disappointed smile. "How close are you?"

"He's seventh dan and I'm trying to pass the test for second dan." She left unsaid that she'd failed the test twice already.

"What can the seventh dan types do that you can't? I don't remember any of those kinds of details from my abbreviated participation back in our summer-school program."

"They're much better at many things, but particularly working with and directing energy. Some of the masters hardly touch their opponents. They just take the energy of the opponent and use it against them."

"That's for real? Not woo-woo stuff? I have a hard time believing it."

"I've seen a few exhibitions. Once, I saw a skinny master pin a huge weightlifter with a single finger."

"No way!"

"True deal. A one-finger pin."

"So, what do you think it's like to direct energy?"

In frustration, she clenched her fists together under the table. This was the big reason why she hadn't passed her test. "I don't know. My sensei talks about it."

"Sounds weird."

"Remember when we were kids and you would sometimes feel what I was feeling?"

It had never been predictable, but every once in a while, they'd felt an emotion the other was experiencing. She'd always thought it a twin thing.

"Yeah," he answered.

"Maybe it's similar. He has me doing visualizations during meditation to try and move my own energy around. I have a long way to go with that and still have some fear to work through, too, which will help unblock the energy."

Will took another sip of coffee. "Fear, huh?"

"Yeah. My sensei recommends that I don't become a teacher myself until I get better at feeling and directing energy."

"You're a black belt though, can't you teach now?"

"Technically, I could teach once I get to *nidan*, my next level, but my sensei would consider it arrogant to teach too soon. Fourth dan is more common. I'm excited to get there but want to do it the right way."

"I see. What's he say the energy feels like?"

She sat back, thinking. "He says when he meditates and the power starts to move, it feels like a river of sunshine—or something to that effect. Apparently, hard to put words to it."

Will got a faraway look in his eyes, as if he were remembering something. It was either too good a memory, or one now too sad, as he changed the subject. "Want to check the paper and see what we can find?"

Guessing the memory was about Maria and energy they had shared, she didn't push it. "Sure."

They both grabbed a couple of sections, and she skimmed the contents for anything related to yesterday's events.

After several minutes of searching, she put her part of the paper down. "See anything?"

"Not yet." Will scanned the Metro section. "Wait. Here we go." He broke into his lopsided grin. "Aha! You were right about him being Russian."

She leaned over the table to try to get a look at the paper. "Oh yeah?"

"Yes, this article says that a Russian citizen was found dead in a car at the bottom of a Napa Valley canyon. They indicate his companion is still at large."

She reached for the news. "Let me see."

He handed the paper to her and she scanned the short article but learned nothing new.

All of a sudden, a bulky shadow fell over the paper and her heart jumped in her chest. It wasn't the waitress.

Maddy looked up and recognized Teddy Thorenson, AKA Bear, a strong, short, stout friend from high school who once had an embarrassing one-way crush on her. They had all gone to the same high school, and he'd enrolled in summer aikido as well.

His wide smile shone through a fashionably scruffy beard, and she noticed he was wearing dark-blue jeans, black boots, a tight T-shirt over a strong set of shoulders, and a bandana over his military-style blond hair. His light-blue eyes sparkled with amusement that he had made her jump.

It was too bad that he just wasn't her type, as he was more rugged and handsome now than he was in high school. He'd grown up and filled out. Exclusively, she liked tall men, and he was still a good several inches shorter than she. Pity.

Bear looked down at them both and said, in his trademark Southern drawl, "Madeline Argones and Sir Skeptalot. Y'all mind if I pull up a chair?"

CHAPTER 19

10:25 a.m.:

D'Angelo sat in his car outside the Fire Sign Café, pulled off his navy ball cap, and subvocalized into his throat mike on a secure line. "The process has been set in motion."

Tasha, his assistant back in Washington, DC, at VanOps headquarters, responded in the affirmative. "Yes, Director."

"I'm en route now, heading to the Reno airport."

"Thank you, sir, safe travels."

He smiled. Maybe he'd take a turn at the slots before his flight left.

The mission was off to a good start. One of his IT staffers had hacked into the rental car company database and used that data to track the blue Mustang Will Argones had rented at the airport. D'Angelo had predicted they'd flee to Lake Tahoe: animals always sought their den when hunted. But he hadn't known how long it would take. They had headed straight to Tahoe, so last night, he'd unleashed Master Sergeant "Bear" Thorenson. And Thorenson just completed the initial rendezvous as planned.

Perhaps Lady Luck would smile on him at the airport. Cha ching.

At any rate, the timeline had just accelerated, and that was a good thing indeed.

CHAPTER 20

10:26 a.m.:

Will and Maddy, in unison, answered in the affirmative that, "Of course," Bear could pull up a chair to join them for breakfast.

Will didn't appreciate the high school "Sir Skeptalot" reference to his cynical personality and felt uneasy at the overt masculine energy emanating from Bear—it was like a strong smell. He hadn't remembered Bear's shoulders being quite so...hefty. Although he was a running back on the high school football team, Bear had a definite presence to him now, but Will wasn't sure he could trust him. In his experience, most men with that many muscles didn't have much in the way of brains.

And why was he here? There'd been a lot of coincidences lately and this one, on top of yesterday's grief, made Will feel uneasy.

Bear sat down and the waitress brought another menu. Ignoring the menu, he ordered a full breakfast of four scrambled eggs, toast, and bacon. And iced sweet tea.

Will looked at Bear, figuring him for military but didn't want to assume. Military guys didn't sport beards. Perhaps he had become a pro football player? "What are you doing with yourself these days, Bear. Do you still live around here?"

"I'm visitin' my mom and stepdad. Was just here having coffee with a friend. I'm in between tours, trying to decide if I'll re-enlist."

"Re-enlist in the service?" Maddy asked.

The waitress brought their food.

"Yeah. Joined the marines after high school. Piloted a 'copter in Afghanistan to gather intel. Crashed once. Eventually led a unit with a great bunch of guys and a few gals."

Will drank some of his coffee, ill at ease with all things military. "That's intense, I'll bet."

"Is."

Will remembered that Bear had never been exactly loquacious and, even though he'd grown muscles, they didn't extend to his vocal cords.

Bear looked at both the twins. "You guys headed off to college if I remember right. What are y'all doin' now?"

Maddy looked at Will, and he sensed her urging him to divulge their adventure to Bear. But Will wasn't ready to do that, so they chatted idly throughout the meal, sharing how he ended up in São Paulo after college for a good engineering job, the details of his sailboat, a brief mention of Maria.

Maddy shared her desire to start her own dojo someday and talked about her job developing mobile apps for cell phones. She also shared that she'd taken on their mother's maiden name, Marshall. A disrespectful move, but Will said nothing about it.

After they were done eating, Bear excused himself to use the restroom. Both twins watched him walk away.

Maddy turned to Will. "He has a limp now, see it?"

"Yes, a small one. Maybe from that 'copter crash."

Maddy leaned over the small checkered table, looked intently at him with her green eyes, and lowered her voice. "Will, we need to tell him."

"Tell him what?"

"Don't be coy. That we're being chased by a crazy Russian who wants to kill us! And it may have something to do with the Aragon *Châsse* and the royal part of our family."

"Why tell him? How do you know we can trust him?"

"We've known him for years," she insisted.

Will kept one eye out for Bear's return. "But we haven't seen him for over ten years, and now he's in the marines."

"I don't know, but it seems to me as if we need a friend right now. And a friend in the military sounds even better."

"But we're not supposed to tell anyone, remember Dad's letter?"

Bear came out of the bathroom.

Maddy's eyes shifted to Bear, too, and her tone was soft but urgent. "Of course, I do, but we're getting shot at! Let's just leave the letter part out."

"Okay. Tell him but leave out the letter."

"Fine." Maddy pretended to smile at him for Bear's benefit.

Will gave her a fake grin in return.

She tugged once on her hair, her irritation plain.

Bear sat back down at the table and, over a refill of coffee, Maddy filled him in on the blatant murders, the wine-country car chase, and the likely demise of the receptionist at the attorney's office.

Concerned, Bear's eyes narrowed to slits. After several other clarifying questions, he asked, "And, Ms. Marshall, this all happened yesterday?"

"Yes," Maddy answered.

"Do you have any idea what the killers want?"

"No," Will put in before Maddy's resolve could falter. He and Maddy had to get their story straight.

Bear looked from one twin to the other, wheels turning. But he let that line of questioning drop. "Where did y'all spend last night?"

Maddy shuffled the newspaper into an organized pile. "At our old house, why?"

"Doesn't somebody else own that now?"

"They do. We were desperate."

"Then I suggest y'all regroup at my place."

Will shook his head. "We wouldn't want to put you or your family in danger."

"C'mon, Argones. We have weapons at the house. Even a guard dog."

Although still cautious, Will liked the idea of adding some firepower to their group. He could also sense Maddy's relief, so when she looked at him to see if he was game, Will acquiesced, not wanting a repeat of yesterday's fatal encounters.

But as they left the café with Bear, Will's gut was tight with the sense that they had somehow misplaced their trust.

CHAPTER 21

Kings Beach, California, 5:15 p.m.:

Maddy and Will left the Fire Sign Café and drove back to their old house, followed by Bear in his almost antique, dingy-white Ford pickup truck. With a Safeway grocery pit stop, they restocked the box of waffles, then they cleaned up the kitchen, made arrangements to have the broken window fixed, removed all other traces that they'd been there, and left. Maddy's guilt at breaking and entering subsided as the house regained its clean appearance.

Afterward, they drove to Bear's parents' house, which was about five minutes from the market in downtown Kings Beach, up a side road and situated so the redwood deck had a gorgeous, wide-open view of the distant lake. The day was clear, so the few snowy mountain caps around the lake stood out like points on a white crown.

The snow reminded Maddy that she and Vincent had come up skiing a few times last winter, since it had been a good snow year. She half missed him and half wanted to kill him for leaving her for another woman.

Although it was hotter than various shades of hell in the valley yesterday, the summer mountain air was warm and fresh. Bear's parents had done a great job designing their house: green metal roof and cedar siding on the exterior, knotty pine vaulted ceiling on the interior. The rock fireplace showcased an old pair of snowshoes and there was an ancient set of wooden skis on the opposite wall. Classic. It felt like home, all sugar cookies and Christmas presents.

Bear showed them his den, a granny cottage behind the main house. It was small, but cozy.

While getting settled, Maddy was so relieved to have Bear's help that she caught herself humming. And her neck started to feel better, too.

After the tour and unpacking, she, Will, and Bear chatted on the broad deck in the late afternoon sun. Mountain Chickadees talked to each other as they flitted between the Jeffrey pines and tall white fir trees. Colonel, Bear's mom's German shepherd, lay on the deck next to Bear's chair. Will jokingly referred to the place as their "safe house."

They had just opened some beer when Bear's mom, Phyllis, arrived home and came up on the deck, bearing a bag of groceries in each hand. She looked much older than Maddy remembered, but it had been over a decade. Phyllis's blonde hair had turned half gray and the laugh lines around her light-blue eyes bore testament to a life well lived.

Bear relieved his mom of the grocery bags and set them on the table. "Hi, Mama, do you remember Will and Maddy from high school? The Argones twins?"

"Of course, I do, child," she replied in a Southern accent twice as thick as Bear's.

She gave both twins a warm hug.

Maddy recalled that Phyllis had grown up in North Carolina and had met Bear's dad when he was stationed at Fort Bragg. Although kids had made fun of Bear's drawl in school, Maddy had always rather liked it.

Phyllis inspected the twins. "You both look a little tired. Working too much?"

"Something like that," Will said.

Phyllis looked at their beer glasses. "I see y'all found some beverages. Are you hungry?"

"We had a late breakfast," Maddy replied.

"Well, they had a sale on salmon at the store and I'll barbecue it in a little while. I have plenty." She looked from one twin to the other. "Has Master Sergeant Teddy Thorenson told you all about his medal yet?"

"Mama, that's classified information."

"These are your friends, Theodore. And it was just supposed to stay out of the press. Anyway—" She turned to the twins, her hands on her hips, "—Teddy and two friends helped stop a terrorist in a market in Afghanistan!" Phyllis paused.

Maddy suspected the pause was for effect, so made the appropriate comment. "What happened?"

"He and two buddies were at a market and saw a man, a terrorist, pull an AK-Forty-Seven out of his cloak. They rushed over and subdued him. The gunman got off a few rounds, tragically killing several women and children before the boys got to him. Teddy was bruised, and one of his friends was shot in the shoulder."

Will looked captivated, in spite of himself, and she was impressed as well. It was hard to think about how she'd react in a situation like that. Yesterday had been bad enough.

Maddy turned to Bear, curious. "What was that like for you?"

Bear shrugged his massive shoulders. "I don't know…I just acted. He was shootin' innocent folks and had to be stopped."

"Were you scared?"

"I didn't have time to be scared then. After we got his gun and I saw my buddy John was hurt, I felt a little sick for him."

Phyllis smiled brightly. "His stepfather, Tad, and I are so proud of him. It's too bad Tad isn't in town tonight, I'm sure he'd love to have a drink with the lot of you."

Bear seemed uncomfortable with all the praise, so Maddy wasn't surprised when he threw the ball for the dog to chase and changed the subject. "Mama, do you mind if the twins spend the night tonight?"

A quick look of surprise passed over her features before years of Southern hospitality kicked in. "Of course not, dear. We can put Maddy up in the guest room downstairs and Will can have your old room upstairs. You kids have a nice visit."

"I figured you'd say that. They're already settled."

Phyllis picked up the bags of groceries and headed into the house. "Good."

Two hours later, after what was the best salmon Maddy had eaten in a long time, Phyllis cleaned up while the three of them enjoyed the last of the dinner wine. As the summer twilight deepened into dusk, Colonel chewed on a bone. Citronella candles kept the mosquitoes at bay and added a citrus aroma to the pleasant forest air.

A Steller's jay cawed in the trees. Maddy wondered if Will and Bear had a little too much to drink, especially when they all began to argue about their next steps.

"Where will y'all go from here?" Bear asked.

Although certain it was the right next step, Maddy wasn't sure how to broach the topic of Spain without mentioning the codex. "I think we should go to Spain and tell our great-uncle in person about Dad's death. It might get us out of the killer's sights."

"Do you think that will throw off evil-killer Russian sniper man?" Will asked in a mocking tone.

"How's he going to know what we're doing?" Maddy countered.

"I don't know. How'd he know we'd be at the attorney's office?"

Bear reached down and scratched Colonel under the chin. "That's probably easier than knowin' you're halfway around the world, at what, a Spanish castle? Have you ever been?"

"No." Maddy sipped her wine. "Does seem a perfect chance to see the world. And Dad hooked us up with some resources. I wonder if he knew…"

Will lit a cigarette. "Knew what?"

Frustrated that she couldn't tell Bear the whole story, Maddy curled her toes under the table and tapped them. Watching her tongue was not her normal form of communication, but she did usually play by the rules.

She said carefully, "Knew we'd be attacked by the Russian jackass."

"How would he know that?"

Maddy bit back her exasperation. "I don't know, but why'd he give us the, um, resources?"

"He was probably just covering his bases."

Bear poured more wine. "Could be."

Phyllis opened the back door. "Teddy, will you come here for a minute and say hi to Tad? He's on the phone."

Bear rose and went into the house.

Will turned to Maddy. "So you think we need to go traipsing across the world? And for what? We know who the killer is."

Maddy narrowed her eyes, irritated. "We don't know the motive and what if he had an accomplice?"

Will smiled with triumph. "He did have an accomplice—that guy who died in the car wreck."

"I'm talking about somebody in Russia."

That dashed Will's smile for just an instant.

He recovered. "Oh, on the grassy knoll." Will's eyes sparkled as he enjoyed his own joke.

"Conspiracy theory smartass. Besides, if we don't figure out what's going on here, we'll still be in danger. You'll note that we're both going through electronics withdrawal already." It was true, she kept reaching for her phone and was annoyed it was gone. It was like a phantom limb.

Will puffed on his cigarette. "Okay, that's a fair point. But what about the fact that I'm not allowed to leave the country?"

"That's another reason to go. I'm thinking that if you want to clear your name, we need to figure out why these Russians killed Dad and Maria."

"Perhaps. But what about the funerals?"

"They'll have to wait until we get back. I've heard of other families who have to wait for the service until everyone can gather, and I think it's more important that we stay alive. We'd be, as our Southern hosts might say, 'easy pickins' at a funeral."

"I don't like it. But let's say we are able to put our lives on hold, we get over to Spain, and we find a clue in the proverbial dark and stormy castle. Then what?"

"You're in rare form. Then we follow the clue. If this was truly put in motion by Ramiro a thousand years ago, how hard could it be?"

Will put out his smoke. "Hard enough that whatever is at the end of the rainbow has only been found once, Ms. Eternal Optimist."

Angry, Maddy waved her empty hand. "This is the age of the internet—if we can ever find a way to use it again safely."

Bear walked out of the house and rejoined them at the table. "What did y'all decide?"

Maddy stroked her necklace. "We haven't agreed to go yet."

"C'mon, Marshall. I was thinking I'd come watch your back if you want." Bear's smile was wicked. "I'm good with a gun."

Will motioned down the hill with his head. "You wouldn't rather be hanging out at the beach?"

"I've always wanted to see Spain. Seems like a good excuse. I have some time off work yet."

Maddy was surprised. She hadn't seen Bear's offer coming and exchanged a glance with Will. He took a quick drink to hide his own shock, but she sensed that he felt comforted somehow. She, on the other hand, worried that Bear's motives might relate to his high school infatuation. There were no weird vibes today, but still...why else would he want to tag along? Sense of adventure, perhaps?

"Could be dangerous," Maddy said. "We do have an angry Russian killer stalking us."

"I've probably faced worse." There was no tone of condescension in his voice, just the tenor of rock-solid confidence that made Maddy wonder, with sympathy, what he had faced along the way.

Before she could stop him, Will reached his hand out to Bear. "All righty, I'll go if you go."

Bear shook the proffered hand. "It's a deal then, let's get some sleep. We'll have a busy day tomorrow."

As they broke apart for bed, Maddy realized she'd won the argument, but she couldn't help but worry at the implications of bringing Bear along for the ride.

The next afternoon, Bear felt like a kid on the first day of school as he and the twins packed for the trip to Spain inside his parents' guest cottage. The room was plain except for a framed print of Judas Iscariot kissing Jesus on the cheek and a cross over the door. Luggage and clothes were spread all over the bed.

"Marshall, how'd the chat with your sister go?" Bear asked.

Maddy glanced up from the suitcase. Her deep green eyes looked troubled, like a storm-ravaged sea. "That reminds me, thanks for taking us to the store so I could get clothes and a pre-paid cell to call her. Bella wasn't happy to hear that we'd been shot at, but she agreed to hold the funeral until we get back. It'll take time to wrap up the autopsy anyway."

Maddy shot a glance at Will, which seemed to telegraph some disagreement, but Bear couldn't tell what it was this time. Since he'd found them yesterday morning, he'd noticed more tension between the twins than even their edgy situation called for, and he wondered what the hell was going on.

As Maddy put a large, sealed package into a backpack she'd borrowed from him, Bear could see a chamois cloth, but not much else. *What's worth keeping waterproof?*

She continued, "Bella said she'd be careful, and no, she doesn't want to leave her husband and kids to join us. Before I tossed the phone, I also called the family castle and they're expecting us tomorrow after the red-eye lands in Madrid."

"Good thing, since we're ready to go," Will said.

"And our fake passports?" Bear asked.

Maddy folded a shirt. "Those passport photos we took worked. My ultra-geeky computer friend found some sketchy character to work up Canadian papers for us."

"Practicing your accent, eh?"

Maddy smiled. "Eh. They shipped the passports by courier and they arrived a few minutes ago while you were out back."

"What if Spanish immigration can tell they're fake? I'm not even supposed to leave the country," Will grumbled.

"All the more reason to use false papers," Maddy replied.

"Bear, you're not flying under your own name either?"

"Nope. Don't want to leave a trail."

Will nodded. "Okay. What about that Go-Pro? Find it?"

"I did. Have it packed with the rest of my goods." He'd also wanted to bring a weapon, but knew he couldn't fly with one, so had researched where to buy 3D printed firearms in Europe.

"That'll help us blend in as tourists," Will said.

"Hope so. What else have you packed, Argones?"

"Got my favorite flashlight, the one Maria gave me." Will's face turned glum. "She had 'My handsome Boy Scout' engraved on it to tease me. See?"

Will showed Bear the side of the flashlight.

Bear didn't know what to say in the face of such grief. "I see it. I'm sorry."

"Maybe the distraction of a trip will be good. I just hope I don't get fired."

Bear watched Maddy continue to fold and pack. She had gracefully organized her toiletries and the bed was almost void of clothing. They were going to travel together. He couldn't believe his good fortune.

Bear turned to Will. "What's your job exactly?"

"I find engineering defects early in the product's life cycle. The sooner we find them, the cheaper they are to fix. If a defect makes it to the assembly line, it's costly. I've actually been promoted twice in three years."

Bear was glad to see pride steal some of the grief out of Will's expression. "Cool."

Maddy shut her suitcase. "I'm ready."

Will looked at her, eyes haunted. "What if the Russians are at the airport?"

Maddy crossed her arms over her chest. "I guess we'll find out."

CHAPTER 22

Spain, June 28, 1:30 p.m.:

As they drove across the scenic Iberian countryside in a rental car, Will wished Maria was at his side, enjoying the sights and laughing with him. He clenched his teeth and fought back a surge of anger at her senseless death. He hoped this trip would help him deliver justice to her killer.

Last night, they had purchased flights into Madrid from Reno, paying cash and using their new false passports, which Will hoped would not only put the Russians off their trail but would also confuse the cops. He didn't want a worldwide manhunt for him if the Napa police and that idiot who suspected him of murder, "Sergeant Walrus," figured he was gone.

Still not convinced their decision to depart the country was wise, Will worried at the airport that they'd be intercepted by someone—either the Russians or the police. His concerns proved unfounded, however, and their overnight flight was uneventful, thanks to multiple adult beverages and a long restless nap.

Throughout the travel preparations, Will continued to assert to Maddy that they keep their father's letter secret from everyone but Bella, and Maddy agreed, although how it was going to remain a secret in Spain, Will wasn't sure.

They arrived at the guard station below the family castle in early afternoon. The stronghold had been visible for miles as they cut across the Spanish plain, a hilltop fortress from another age. The day was mostly cloudy and the sun occasionally lit on a fairy-tale stone tower, or crenellated rampart. During the latter part of the drive, while Maddy was oohing and ahhing about the beauty of it all, Will mused that the castle looked more menacing than welcoming. Of course, that could have been his mood. The guard looked at their papers and passed them through.

After rolling through the immense arched and tiled front gate, then underneath the metal portcullis, their second cousin Prince Carlos, the heir apparent, met them in the broad stone courtyard as they stepped out of their rental car.

Will had never met any of his Spanish family and was struck by his cousin's resemblance to his father and grandfather. Prince Carlos, like them, had the same receding hairline, tall frame, olive skin, and green eyes. However, his entire left leg moved stiffly. Will tried not to stare at the pant leg while he recalled a tale from his father that the prince was born a conjoined twin. The twins had shared a leg and the doctors had chosen to give the elder twin the leg when they separated them. Prince Carlos had lived his entire life with the implications of that decision.

There was also a story about the twin brother's death, but Will didn't recall the details. In the moment, he was just glad that he and Maddy were neither conjoined, nor dead.

Will wondered at his cousin's age and guessed mid-sixties, because although he stood tall, his face was heavily lined and his movements were slow.

Prince Carlos's flat eyes radiated the fury of a cold arctic wind, belying his welcoming words, "*Buenos tardes.* Come in, *por favor.*"

"*Gracias,*" Will thanked him in Spanish as he, Maddy, and Bear stepped to the side of the car. "Do you mind if we speak English?"

He nodded to Bear and Maddy to indicate they weren't fluent in Spanish.

"Of course," Prince Carlos replied with just the trace of an accent. "Thank you for calling us yesterday from California to let us know of your visit. I trust your trip was satisfactory?"

With this kind of welcome, Will already wanted to leave. "Yes, we appreciate your hospitality and hope not to inconvenience you for long. Is it possible to see your father?"

Prince Carlos frowned. "The king has much business today and will arrive later this afternoon. He may or may not agree to a dinner audience with you. You must know that your presence puts him in grave danger."

Maddy reached behind her neck and pulled up her dark ponytail to rest in front of her right shoulder. "Why is that?"

"Your father was murdered, was he not?"

Maddy made a small grimace, nodding once in reluctant agreement. "He was."

"You told me of this on the telephone and we have confirmed your story. Based on this sniper attack, the man, or men, responsible, could be after more than one family member. Have they attacked you?"

Will didn't want to look at Maddy. They hadn't rehearsed this. "No, they haven't bothered us."

Will could almost feel Maddy flush with the lie. She was not one to stretch the truth. Nor was he, but special times called for special measures.

Prince Carlos looked from Will, back to Maddy, and then lingered on Will a moment. Will suspected the prince knew he was lying, but Will held his ground and stared back. He hadn't come all this way to be turned back at the gate.

Will added, "Our father indicated at his passing, that it was—" He didn't want to divulge too much. "—or is, customary for the king to grant an audience when an elder passes. We would appreciate the courtesy that has been granted to other family members."

Prince Carlos continued to stare. "Well, we shall see." After a last look, he turned on his heel and motioned for an aide to take their luggage. Over his shoulder he said, "Make yourselves comfortable in your rooms and meet me back here in an hour. I will see that you have a tour of the grounds."

Feeling troubled by the interaction, Will glanced at Maddy and Bear. He wondered if they also didn't trust Prince Carlos. Bear shrugged off help with his bags and Maddy, with a wary expression in her green eyes, watched the prince leave. Will wasn't sure if her similar assessment of their cousin was a good omen, or a bad one.

CHAPTER 23

Argones Castle, Spain, 2:30 p.m.:

Back in the courtyard an hour later, Maddy, Will, and Bear slumped on stone benches around the fountain, surrounded by yellow, red, and purple roses. Maddy sat next to Bear while Will puffed on a cancer stick a few feet away. *Jet lag and grief are catching up to us all.*

Nevertheless, Maddy wanted to remain on guard. Prince Carlos had *not* seemed friendly. They were a long way from home.

Home. Maddy caught Will's eye. "What do you think AJ is up to right now?"

"Hard to say, why do you ask?"

She looked around the courtyard and shrugged. "Kids love castles."

Will smiled a tired smile. "They sure do."

Bear clipped the GoPro on his shoulder harness to record the tour. "Who's AJ?"

"He's a sweet little muffin of a foster kid from the dojo. I was going to take him to Great America the day Dad and Maria were shot. He was with us. It was his birthday."

The conversation lagged. Maddy closed her eyes for a minute and recalled the chat she'd had with AJ on the way to the vineyard that day…

"Are you a princess?" AJ had asked.

Maddy laughed. "No, not really."

Her biological clock was ticking, but the last thing she felt like was a princess.

"But the kids at the dojo say you are," AJ insisted. "It's my birthday and I want to go to a castle!"

AJ's parents had died not long after they moved to the Bay Area from Ukraine, and he'd been living with foster parents since. Those foster parents were busy and appreciated that she did the occasional extracurricular activity with AJ, so she had wanted to take him to Great America to help him celebrate.

"My great-great-great-great-umpteen-great-grandfather was Ramiro I, the first king of Aragon, which eventually became Spain, but my immediate family isn't royal, so I'm not a princess."

"What about the current king of Spain, you're related to him aren't you? Let's fly to his castle today!"

She figured AJ was too smart for his own good. "The king? He's my great-uncle. I've never even met him, his castle is an ocean away, and we're going to my dad's house on a vineyard. We have to go there before we go ride the roller coasters."

AJ made a momentary pouty face. He knew they couldn't go to Spain, but kids loved castles.

Taking a deep breath, Maddy found it odd that she was now in the courtyard of the castle. Maybe when this adventure was history, she'd revisit the idea of adopting AJ, even without Vincent. She sure did miss his freckled face.

She opened her eyes and looked at Will. "Wish we could call, just to check in. This not having our own phones thing is downright inconvenient."

"Yes, but safe," Will said.

Maddy sighed. "I guess." But she felt vulnerable without it.

Letting the conversation lull again, she glanced up at her room's open window. Although the room was handsomely appointed, with an antique four-poster bed and gorgeous side table that looked a thousand years old, there had not been a good place to hide their father's letter, the passports, and their cash and assets. After a too-short nap, she'd resorted to stuffing their resources between the mattress and box spring, but she wasn't happy about it and vowed to keep them close, in her backpack, next time.

Her worry was interrupted by Prince Carlos's brusque arrival into the square. As he walked toward them, looking like her father, another piece of her heart broke off and she fought back tears. She'd cry again later, not now.

Will had reminded her of Prince Carlos's false leg, and she noticed that he walked slowly, not quite a shuffle, but definitely like an older man. If the prince were this old, likely in his sixties, how old was the king? A little math produced a guess that he would be in his eighties. So, Prince Carlos was close to acquiring his crown.

What would it have been like for her grandfather Max to grow up here and know, as the youngest of four boys, that he would never be king? And what was it like for Prince Carlos to be ever the heir? So close and yet so far...

Prince Carlos was trailed by a small entourage that included a gangly young man and a middle-aged woman, who looked like a female version of her own father, Francisco. When Prince Carlos got close enough to speak, he introduced the groups to one another by waving. "This is Antoine, my eldest grandson, and his mother Catherine. I have business to attend, so they will take you on a tour of the castle grounds. Father has agreed to meet you for dinner at seven this evening in the dining hall. Antoine can show you where it is before you complete your tour."

As she sized up these new cousins, Maddy stifled a yawn and doubted she could stay awake until seven. Her father's first cousin, Catherine, moved in odd jerky motions, looking up at the sky for a moment and then glancing at them without seeming to see them, then squatting down to peer at something only she could see on a paving stone. Was Catherine mentally well? Dangerous?

Antoine, on the other hand, was the charming picture of Americanized youth. He was in his late teens and wore a blue-and-white New York Yankees baseball cap backward on his head. His broad smile, at least, seemed genuine.

"Hi!" he said, in accent-less English as he reached out his hand to shake hers.

She couldn't stop her return smile. "Hello."

She was always a sucker for charming men, even if they were related. Antoine also shook Bear's hand with vigor and then went a little more gently on Will, perhaps realizing that Will had more brains than brawn. The family resemblance was clear as the two men shook hands—they were both about six foot two, sported tan skin and fashionable beards, and they shared broad white smiles.

Prince Carlos lurched off. "*Adiós*, enjoy your afternoon."

Maddy breathed a sigh of relief, not liking the shadows moving in his eyes.

Antoine started walking and waved his arm, inviting them to follow. The group moved through the courtyard, outside the arched main gate, and stopped a hundred feet from the wall to take in the panoramic view of the valley below. Maddy looked back. Catherine hadn't tagged along.

The unusual woman continued to sit on her heels, staring at something on the ground.

Antoine noticed the direction of Maddy's gaze. "Don't mind my crazy *madre*. She's been like that since my father died years ago."

Maddy didn't know how to reply, so nodded and gazed around, astounded by the view.

Once he had the three Americans' full attention, Antoine turned in a half circle with his arms out, calling them to his story. "The castle was built during the tenth century by an Arab family, when its position on the frontier between Muslim and Christian territories gave the location strategic importance. It was built above the river as a recreational residence, originally known as the Palace of Delight. Aragonese forces, led by our ancestor Ramiro I's son, Sancho Ramírez, conquered the castle and surrounding lands from the Muslims in 1089. Not such a delight for the Muslims, I'm afraid, and it was renamed Aragones Castle at that time. Somewhere along the way, the second *a* was dropped from the family surname and it became Argones Castle."

Maddy found herself drawn into the story, imagining men in pitched battle, fighting for control of the ramparts.

Will motioned to several large piles of rock that lay outside the nearby walls. "What's up with the piles of stone?"

"In the original construction, extra ramparts were made in the open field surrounding the castle, but as you can see, they've been reduced to rubble."

Will nodded.

"In 1143 the castle passed into Templar hands," Antoine continued. "They added additional walls, towers, stables, a hall for dining, and dormitories. You may even see some Egyptian artifacts around the castle. No one is sure if those artifacts are from the Arabs, Templars, or passed down from Ramiro."

Maddy noticed Bear's eyes roaming the walls. He might also be imagining medieval combat, hearing the clash of sword on shield.

"Eventually, around 1309, the Templars were, shall we say, 'disbanded,' and the castle was retaken by another ancestor. Additional evolution in walls and defenses continued until the nineteenth century, as the fort still held defensive garrisons until that time."

Antoine led them back through the gate and they followed the walls around to a tower. Maddy noticed Catherine was no longer in the courtyard.

Antoine gestured. "The outermost walls of the castle and their seven towers were erected in the thirteenth or fourteenth century."

As they walked along the wall, Will pointed at a cross. It was oddly shaped, with a pointed bottom and flanged ends, and carved into the side of the chapel. "What's that symbol? It looks like a thorned cross."

Earlier, Maddy had seen the mark on an interior hallway corner but hadn't remarked on it.

"That's the royal sign, the *signum regis* of Ramiro. You've not seen this in America?"

"No, not that I recall," Will answered.

"It's in our family crest."

Maddy had likewise never seen either the royal sign or family crest before today. She wondered if America had been a fresh start for her grandfather, so much so that he even left the family crest behind.

They walked along until they stood in front of a tower so high that it made Maddy's neck ache again when she craned back to see the top. She cringed.

"This oldest construction of the Argones Castle is now called Troubled Tower, although some say it was called Minstrel Tower back in the day. Looking at it from the outside, you can't tell that there are actually five internal floors—the whole thing looks like an enormous prism, broken by narrow, I think you call them, 'embrasures.'"

The term sounded familiar but Maddy couldn't place it. "Maybe not, what's an *embrasure*?"

"Slots for cannons or places where an archer stands. These look more like arrow slits," Bear said, around his chewing gum.

Maddy had forgotten his fondness for the stuff. He'd popped some in his mouth on the plane ride and was still working on the same piece. It baffled her. She could chew gum for about twenty minutes and then had to spit it out.

Antoine was agreeable and energetic. "Sure, okay, an arrow slit. Let's go up and inside through the murder hole." He pointed to an upper door that was accessible only by means of a portable ladder, which he lined up. "They used to drop hot oil and rocks down on besiegers from the access hole."

Will shuddered. "Not pretty, but effective. No wonder they called it the murder hole. Hey, I'm going to stay down here and have a smoke."

Will's long-lashed eyes looked a little pinched. He hated heights and had even drunk himself to sleep on the airplane ride from the States. His fear seemed silly but she wasn't all that fond of enclosed spaces, so who was she to judge? She glanced at the small door above and hoped it opened into a larger space. Why not risk it? The view must be fantastic from up there.

Antoine shimmied up the wooden ladder, lithe as a monkey. Maddy and Bear followed.

Once up the ladder, the space did open up.

Antoine commented, "This tower was built as a defensive structure, with a quadrangular base and five levels, which date all the way back to the end of the ninth century AD. In its lower part, the tower has the remains of the old heavy walls. When we get higher, you'll see the walls are lined with planks, simple plaster, and some sort of lime concrete. That lining was thinner to allow the architects to reach greater heights."

Antoine was in full tour-guide mode now. Maddy wondered how many times he'd given his spiel.

On the first level, Maddy noticed horseshoe-shaped arches dividing two separated naves. Looking around, she appreciated the sense of balance and the compound's interesting blend of Eastern and Western architecture. This section was in the Eastern style. She could see the remains of colorful Muslim brickwork in the brick façades. The art was all well and good but how many attackers had been murdered through that entry hole?

Wanting to explore further, Maddy found the ladder to the second floor, climbed up, and stepped off the rungs. The ladder area opened into a narrow hallway with an arrow slot ahead. She headed toward the light and, from behind, someone grabbed her shoulder. Startled, Maddy let loose a martial arts battle cry.

CHAPTER 24

7:30 p.m.:

Later, seated toward the end of a long table in the castle's formal dining room, Will looked across the table, from Maddy to Catherine and back. They were seated next to each other, two seats to the left, heads lowered in conversation. Catherine's hands jerked as she talked.

He fought back the knot of grief in his throat. Maria's hands had moved gracefully. He missed her, still feeling as if the air had been knocked from his lungs. Maria was always the wind in his sails, and now that she was gone, he felt slack and empty and useless.

Which reminded him of the embarrassing events of several hours earlier. From his station below the Troubled Tower, Maddy's high-pitched scream had enticed him four rungs up the ladder before he looked down, became dizzy, fought back bile in his throat, and had to lower himself to the ground, swearing at what a wimp he was the entire time.

It was a long few minutes before Maddy, Bear, Antoine, and Catherine had climbed down the ladder. Laughing, the group recreated for him the post-scream aikido moves that Maddy had put on Catherine when she had reached out to warn Maddy away from a broken floorboard. It turned out that Catherine had been in the tower before they arrived.

Although Will had studied aikido with Maddy and Bear for a summer when they were seventeen, all he remembered was rolling. Front shoulder roll. Back shoulder roll. Repeat. The wrist grab and throw that Maddy had executed on Catherine didn't ring a bell. Even knowing Maddy was training to become an aikido instructor, he'd still been surprised by her quick action.

Now, it seemed, the altercation had somehow bonded the two ladies. As they sat in the dining hall, they were involved in a thick-as-thieves conversation, almost as if they shared a secret. He marveled at Maddy's ability to make quick friends, even with someone who was a little *loca*. It always took Will awhile, as he liked to joke to himself, to make sure new people weren't going to eat him. But once he knew he could trust them, he was loyal to the bone.

The dining hall was in the center of the castle, so there was only a single set of two long, narrow windows that looked down onto an interior courtyard and fountain. With windows open to the warm summer night, Will could hear the fountain gurgle below. Tapestries hung on the stone walls, and at the end of the long room stood two matching stone Egyptian statues. Each statue was sculpted with tall conical headdresses, short square beards, and decorated kilts. In addition, the sculptor had added crossed arms and hands that held on to short rods or scepters.

Five ornate crystal chandeliers were spaced out over the table at two-meter increments. The table was so long it could have seated a small army. Perhaps it had at some point. His active imagination could see Knights of the Round Table types sitting side by side, then he saw one of them poisoned for treason, choking, and—he cut off that imaginary train of thought and hoped tonight's dinner would be safe enough.

The king, white-haired and over eighty, but clear-eyed and jocular, was at the head of the table wearing a garment that looked like a priest's cassock. Will figured it to be a royal robe, as it had the family coat of arms, including the cross-like *signum regis* he'd seen earlier in the day, embroidered over the heart.

Prince Carlos was at the king's right hand, Will at his left. Bear sat next to Will and Antoine next to Prince Carlos, with Maddy and then Catherine at the end of the group on the other side of the table.

They made small talk through a delicious meal of quail, green beans, roasted squash, fresh bread, wild rice, and berry pie.

The king seemed in good humor, joking as he ate. At one point, he turned to Bear. "And how are you called? Bear? Is this true?"

"Yes, sir."

The king's English was heavily accented. "Please. We meet as friends and family tonight. I would like to hear how you got this name, 'Bear.' Was it from your birth?"

Bear laughed. "No, it is what we call a nickname, or a name for fun. It was given to me by friends in high school."

Seeing Bear was going to be taciturn, Will prodded Maddy. "Why don't you tell the story?"

Maddy looked at Bear for permission. He sighed, chewed an ice cube, and nodded his nearly shaved head in agreement.

Maddy patted her mouth with her napkin. "Let's see if I remember the details. When he was born in North Carolina, his first name was Theodore, which became abbreviated to Teddy in grammar school. Many children in America have small toy bears called 'teddy bears,' and from the time he moved to Lake Tahoe in high school he was often teased with his childhood nickname: 'Teddy Bear.'"

The king nodded. "Go on, please."

"When he was fourteen, he went camping with his family. During the trip, his younger brother wandered out of camp and was attacked by a bear. Teddy yelled and jumped on the back of the bear with only a stick! The bear scratched Teddy's shoulder and threw him to the ground, but the noise brought the rest of the family and they scared off the bear. Teddy here saved his younger brother's life and was lucky to live. After word got around, he became known simply as Bear."

The king looked at Bear. "An impressive feat for one so young. And with the shortness of your hair, it appears you have joined your country's military. You are a warrior in your heart, yes?"

Bear's face flushed. "Yes, sir, I am."

Dinner continued, with the king drawing each of them out in turn.

Once the dessert was finished, the king spoke, "Now there is a private matter I must discuss with the twins. Leave us now, Prince Carlos and Antoine. Catherine, you as well."

"But, Father—" Prince Carlos broke in, speaking in Spanish.

"No contradictions. Your time will come and soon enough. Tonight is their time," the king replied, also in Spanish.

Prince Carlos's eyes narrowed. He nodded in acquiescence, yanked Catherine up and out of her chair by the elbow, then followed Antoine out the door. Will decided that he definitely didn't trust Prince Carlos.

Bear got up and started to follow, but to Will's surprise, the king said, "Bear, you can stay."

Before he could stop himself, Will said, "But I thought—"

The king must have understood Will's objection, because rather than ask for clarification, he turned to Maddy. "There is precedence for having a loyal friend here. We'll call him a bodyguard. Would you like Bear to stay?"

Frozen in place, Bear's eyes darted about in confusion.

"Yes, please," Maddy said in a rush.

The king, Maddy, and Bear turned their gazes to Will. Knowing the king was okay with sharing the family legend with Bear relaxed Will's concern and seemed to match the one exception in their father's letter. Will didn't trust Bear yet, but did appreciate his strengths. There was a time for brawn.

"Yes, thank you," Will said.

The king motioned for Bear to retake his seat. Bear's brow furrowed, but he sat down again next to Will without asking what was going on.

"Madeline, please sit here now." The king gestured to the seat that Prince Carlos had vacated. Maddy moved next to the king and sat at his right hand.

Before they could talk, maids cleared the pie plates and brought coffee. Will fought off a yawn, welcoming the brew. Jet lag was a brutal mistress.

The king added sugar to his coffee and stirred. "I am deeply saddened to hear that my nephew, your father, was so suddenly taken from us."

He looked at Maddy and Will in turn, and Will could sense the keen intelligence, perhaps even wisdom, that radiated from the man. Although Will had grown up knowing they were related to the King of Spain, seeing him, actually dining with him, was a humbling experience.

Taking a drink of coffee, the king added, "But every rain is followed by sun, yes?"

Will wasn't so sure yet. He still felt hollow inside.

The king looked at Will. "I'm sorry also, that you, my great-nephew, lost your wife. You are young yet. I hope you will find love again."

Will's throat choked and he couldn't say anything. Instead, he nodded and sipped his coffee.

"I have heard you are an engineer and skilled with languages. Your grandfather was a scientist, too, you know, may his soul rest in peace."

Will colored, a little embarrassed at the praise from this man who had seen so much in his life. "Thank you. Yes, I work as a test engineer in Brazil and do speak several languages."

The king turned his keen gaze on Maddy. "And you, young lady. You look like your Grandmother Emma on her wedding day. I understand you used your martial arts training today and are a computer genius as well."

"I'm so sorry about Catherine—she startled me, and I just reacted on instinct."

"No need to apologize, niece, I am proud of you. But I think you did not travel all this way to hear the ramblings of an old man. What did your father tell you about coming here?"

Will cleared his voice and spoke with an effort to mask his disbelief. "With his last words, he sent us to his attorney, who gave us letters from him that told of a family legend."

The king turned to Bear. "Turn off that camera on your shoulder."

Bear complied and turned off the GoPro. "Sorry."

The king turned to Will. "Go on."

Will couldn't stop skepticism from creeping into his tone. "He said, when a member of the family dies, the heirs can go on a quest to find an artifact hidden by Ramiro One, something that has power. Something inside the Aragon *Châsse*."

"And that the theoretical quest starts here, with an old book you have," Maddy added.

Bear's jaw dropped open.

The king locked eyes with each of them in turn. "You want to know if your father was *loco*, was crazy." It was a statement, not a question.

Maddy nodded.

The king looked at Will, who also nodded. "Crazy, or maybe joking," Will said. "Dad was a prankster. Perhaps he just wanted us to come meet you. See some of the world."

The king took a deep breath and measured it out. "Your father told the truth." He turned to Will and said with clear conviction, "He was not crazy, nor was he making a joke." In a softer tone, he added, "This is a club of sorts, a club you enter when your parent dies only. And now you are part of the club."

Will felt deflated for a moment, he'd been so sure this whole thing was ridiculous. Irritated, he scratched at his beard. Then he had an idea. "If there is something to be found, the Russians might be seeking it, too. The man who killed father and Maria—Maddy overhead him speak. He spoke Russian."

The king's eyes lit up. "Your generation is so bright." His smile waned. "I planned to warn you about this."

"About what?" Will asked.

"My intelligence forces intercepted a recent communication from a scientist at the Russian Ministry of State Security, or MGB." The king paused, looking at each of them in turn, eyes heavy with the mantle of responsibility. "I believe somehow they have learned our secret. They are also after the lost power."

Will swallowed hard.

The room was silent for a moment.

"Can you give us any resources, or tell us anything else?" Bear asked.

"I'm sorry, no. I wanted you to be aware of their interest, but it seems you already are."

Maddy bit her lip. "Any idea how they would know about the Aragon *Châsse?*"

"I do not know. I would not want to believe any of our family would tell them. All who learn are sworn to secrecy as you are now." The king paused and sipped at his coffee. Then he looked at Bear. "You as well."

Bear nodded.

The king put his cup down. "But power can twist a mind. Family legend tells us there is much power to be found. But so hard to find. I did not have time to find it, nor find it did my brothers. My youngest brother, your grandfather Maximillian, was the last to try and the angriest to fail.

VANOPS: THE LOST POWER 79

Only Ferdinand and Isabella have found it in a thousand years, and history tells us of their later accomplishments."

Columbus had sailed the ocean blue but Will was still skeptical. "How do we know they hid it again?"

"That is…how do you say?…part of the deal. If you find it, you must hide it again before your own death."

The king looked around and nodded to himself as if acknowledging the empty room. He reached into the folds of his tunic and opened his large hands to reveal a slight bundle wrapped in black cloth. With care, he opened the cloth, revealing an old book. Light from the overhead chandelier lit the book's cover with blue and green fire.

Maddy gasped.

The gold cover of the enameled book was outlined with dozens of cobalt-blue and emerald-green gems. Another line of sapphires and white pearls formed a bordered frame for a single haloed figure in the center.

"Wow," Maddy said. "Are those emeralds?"

Even Bear's tone held excitement. "Is that a saint in the middle?"

Will was left speechless, shocked by the solid reality of the quest's instigating artifact.

Maddy's olive eyes were wide with wonder. "May I touch it?"

The king ignored Bear's question and slid the codex toward her on its cloth. "Yes."

Maddy opened the old tome. It creaked a bit with age, as the cover swung back. The handful of pages looked even more ancient than the cover.

Bear reached out. Reverence shone in his eyes as he touched a corner of a page. "Vellum."

Will recalled how well Bear had always performed in history classes. It had been a passion for him and his interest was on full display now.

The color of the first page was faded, but an image was clear. There was an artistically rendered mini-painting of a blond, handsome rider leading an army, one hand raised, holding a short scepter the color of blood, his wavy locks half hidden by a lion's head. One eye appeared dark as the night and one blue as the sky. Although clean-shaven, his neck was slightly twisted, so that he appeared to be gazing upward at an angle. Will glanced at Bear who wore a puzzled, questioning look for a moment. Then he leaned back and sat up straight with recognition shining in his eyes. All eyes turned to Bear.

"'Fess up, Bear. What do you see?" Maddy asked.

"The man is Alexander the Third of Macedon, also known as Alexander the Great."

"How do you know that's him?" Will asked.

"Well, the rider is blond and has an army. Alexander was the greatest military leader the world has ever known, so I've studied up on him. The lion's head and his curly hair are dead giveaways, as is his different colored eyes. Also, Alexander had a bit of a twisted neck, which the artist captured."

The king nodded and spoke to Maddy and Will. "Your bodyguard is astute. Many in the family agree with his assessment."

Will considered. "So, what does he have to do with all this?"

"Hard to say without more information," Bear said.

Maddy turned the page and exposed a hand-drawn, muted-colored sketch. "Maybe the rest of the book will tell us more."

A person wearing a tall, rounded ceremonial headdress held up two slight ruby-red obelisks in a *V* formation to the sun. The person and the sun were bordered by three columns of tiny hieroglyphs on one side of the page and two vertical rectangles, also inscribed with hieroglyphs, on the other.

Will had no idea what this drawing represented, and although Bear had hit the bullseye on the first page, he scratched his head as he looked at this sketch. Maddy stared, too, and Will wondered, *Is that person an Egyptian priest? Are those red obelisks the same thing that Alexander was holding on the prior page? None of this makes any sense.*

The king remained silent as Maddy turned the page again.

She gasped.

Where there should have been a third page, the vellum was torn next to the binding. In such a beautiful book, the tear was like a jagged scar on a pretty girl's face. Will winced.

"What happened here?" Bear asked.

"That is a good question, young Bear," the king replied. "Thirty years ago, when my father died and I became king, my uncle showed my brothers and me this book. At that time there was a drawing here, a hand-drawn view of the sky, perhaps a constellation, in similar colors as the other two drawings. However, by the time the book fell into my hands for safekeeping several weeks later, the drawing was torn out."

Bear's face was flushed and his voice tight. "Who would do such a thing?"

"I know not. It saddens me as well." The king paused. "Of course, I asked all my brothers, aunts and uncles, anyone who would have seen the codex and the sky drawing. They all assured me they would do no such thing." The king shook his head slowly from side to side. "The good news is I do not believe it leads to the artifact."

"Why is that?" Maddy asked, stiffening.

That's odd. Why is she holding her breath?

The old man's eyes twinkled. "There is plenty of rumor in the family about this quest for the *châsse*, some of which I suspect are additional verbal clues left by Ferdinand, or perhaps Isabella." He nodded to the final page, "Why don't we see if William can translate this first clue and then we will enjoy our coffee and, how do you say, gossip?"

Maddy turned the book to face Will. In faded hand, the start of the quest was outlined in Old Spanish. Will translated: "'Find the center of the world that looms over an abyss, a bottomless pit. Listen and you can hear the souls of the dead.'"

CHAPTER 25

Spain, June 29, 9:10 a.m.:

*H*ear the souls of the dead' echoed in Maddy's head as she drove the rental car down the twisty mountain road, away from the baroque family castle. Dinner with the king had been revealing, both before and after they looked at the codex. Her head was still spinning with the idea that they were in a deadly race with the Russians to find an ancient artifact that may have been used by Alexander the Great. What dangerous power was hidden inside the *châsse?* What would happen if the Russians found it first?

This morning, they had said their farewells in a large, central, rectangular courtyard that boasted a number of porticoes and two pools, one on each of the rectangle's short sides. Although she'd enjoyed her time with the surprising Catherine, she was not sorry to see the castle fade in her rearview mirror. *Too bad AJ couldn't have seen it. Kids love castles.*

Bear had called shotgun and sat next to her with his usual stick of chewing gum in his mouth, looking out the window. Will was in the back seat, smoking, sitting sideways to make room for his long legs. Her backpack with all their essentials was on the middle of the front seat.

Maddy thought back on the visit. "I think I know why the Russians want to kill us."

"Yeah, why?" Will asked.

"Less competition for the *châsse*."

"Could be." Will muttered something under his breath.

"What?"

Will slapped his thigh. "I just want to go home. What chance do we have against trained killers?"

Maddy gripped the steering wheel tight with both hands. Their odds weren't good, but she couldn't let Will slip into despair. And there was no better choice. "Our best chance is to keep moving. To outsmart them."

"I don't like it."

Maddy changed the subject. "Prince Carlos looked like he wanted to kill us, too. Didn't he just seem like a slithering, angry snake to you guys?"

"He was creepy. I remember hearing that his Siamese twin brother died when they were both boys. That could make a guy angry."

"Your disgusting smokes could make me angry. Why do you have to smoke in the car?"

Will blew smoke toward her.

Maddy exaggerated a cough. "Catherine told me about that death once she came out of her shell. It was called a swimming accident at the time."

"An accident, huh?" Bear asked.

"Yeah. They were twelve. It was in the river down there by that hundred-foot waterfall we saw on the way up." She glanced to the rushing rapids in the canyon below.

To her right, on the other side of the road, was a tall, vertical cliff face. The drive through the canyon reminded her of Northern California rafting adventures with Vincent. They'd been planning a Class IV trip down the North Fork of the American River in late July. She bit her lower lip at the twinge of unwelcome emotion.

"Was it *really* an accident?" Will speculated.

After meeting Prince Carlos, Maddy wondered the same thing, and Catherine's tone when discussing it had been…odd. The prince seemed callous, and Maddy had had a bad feeling when they left.

"Who knows?" Bear responded. "What do y'all think about the clue?"

Maddy was somehow glad that Bear now had the full story. "I've thought about it so much I have it memorized: 'Find the center of the world that looms over an abyss, a bottomless pit. Listen and you can hear the souls of the dead.' I'm looking forward to having internet access to do some research. In the meantime, the destination sounds grim but I have no idea where it actually is, do you?"

"After sleeping on it, I think it means the Well of Souls, under the Dome of the Rock."

"The Dome in Jerusalem? Why there?"

"The Well is a cave underneath the Dome. The name comes from a medieval Islamic legend that the spirits of the dead can be heard as they wait for Judgment Day."

"Why would Ramiro lead us there?" Will asked. "It's nowhere near here."

"The why is a little harder, but I'm thinking that in his day, Jerusalem would have been a pilgrimage site, right?"

"Sure, if you say so." Will's tone sounded doubtful.

Bear blew a small bubble. "Well, as we were leavin' dinner, didn't the king mention that Ramiro came to power around 1035, when he was about twenty-eight, and died in 1063?"

"Yes, I remember thinking it odd he also ruled for twenty-eight years."

"Okay, so the Dome of the Rock is situated in the center of the Temple Mount, the site where the Jewish First and Second Temples stood. Then, for hundreds of years, Jerusalem was primarily Christian. Thousands of pilgrims came by the cartload to experience the places where Jesus walked."

"Can you get to the point?" Maddy asked with a smile.

"Hold your pants. After the Muslim Siege in 637, the Dome of the Rock was constructed between 689 and 691, if I'm rememberin' right."

"How do you know all this crap?" Will asked.

"How do you know all that engineering crap?" Bear riposted.

Maddy felt intrigued that Bear became talkative when discussing history. "Touché. Bear, please go on."

Bear smiled. "Okay, so the crusaders didn't capture Jerusalem until 1099!"

"Thirty-six years after Ramiro passed on."

"Right. During his time, there was likely some Muslim pushback about Christians visiting the town, which is what historians think led to the Crusades. But if you consider Ramiro, during his life and for hundreds of years before, Jerusalem would have been a popular tourist-type destination. As a side note, the Knights Templar believed the Dome was the site of the Temple of Solomon."

Maddy considered this information. "Could Ramiro have belonged to the Knights Templar?"

"The timing's not right. The Templars weren't officially endorsed by the Roman Catholic Church until around 1129."

Will jumped in, "Sixty-six years after Ramiro died."

"You're good at math."

"Thanks, just not history," Will said.

"Leave that to me."

"Deal."

Bear continued, "Anyway, Jerusalem is full of history, religious history to boot, so if Ramiro were a religious man, and who wasn't back then, it would have been a logical place to hide somethin'."

"After dessert, the king did hint that the clue pointed to the Middle East," Maddy added, impressed that Bear knew so much history.

Will blew smoke out his window. "Either that or he was trying to misdirect us."

Maddy hadn't considered this possibility. "Why would he do that?"

"What if we find this weapon, this power? Might we take the kingship from him?" Will asked.

Maddy steered the car around another curve, grateful she was behind the wheel and not carsick. "In this day and age?"

"The Russians want it. He might be worried. Or Prince Carlos might be," Will said, to bolster his argument.

"I could see Prince Carlos going for some misdirection," Bear said.

Maddy considered this but it didn't add up. "But Prince Carlos doesn't know about this quest."

"Maddy the Innocent. How could you live in that house, have relatives pop in every time somebody dies, and not know something was up? There're probably even listening holes bored into that dining room wall," Will said.

"Good point," Maddy conceded.

"Listening holes! I like how you think, Argones. We should assume Prince Carlos knows. But back to where we're headed. The king did mention that all the sites might not necessarily be as old as Ramiro. And don't forget his passing comment about strange lights in Isabella's rooms," Bear said.

Maddy added, "And he mentioned a rumor that the source of the power could come from the relic of a saint. That old codex cover had a saint on it, and he'd heard that Vladimir the Great's finger bone might be in the *châsse*."

"And do you think a saint's bones have some kind of supernatural power?" Will's tone was sarcastic. "I'll bet the king tried to mislead us, and there's no new age or even old age saintly power that we're going to find at the end of the rainbow."

Maddy piloted the car around yet another curve. At least they had made it down the hill and the road had leveled off.

"Mr. Skeptic, why are you okay with coming along then?" Bear asked.

"Going on the quest might lead us to the Russian killer," Will said.

His answer surprised Maddy.

"You said you wanted to go home. Are you sure you want to find them?" Bear asked with quiet insight.

"I do. If I can't turn back time, I'd like justice for Dad and Maria, or at least revenge."

Maddy could see Will's wry smile in the mirror.

She considered Bear's point and wondered if the three of them would be able to subdue the killer if they did find him. Will wasn't exactly the Incredible Hulk and she didn't exactly have a lot of real-world fighting experience. What if the sniper brought a team?

They came around a blind corner, and the waterfall appeared in the distance. She found the narrow road up ahead blocked by several small Spanish-model cars. Some kind of accident?

"Look out!" Bear yelled.

As she braked to avoid the cars, shots rang out, hitting her windshield and the hood. Bear and Will both ducked. Maddy swerved and her mind raced.

She ruled out stopping the car.

She ruled out ramming the group of cars in front of them.

She ruled out turning around.

That left a swim in the river.

She just hoped they could get out of the car—she hated feeling trapped. And all their goodies were in her backpack.

Instead of braking, she gunned the accelerator. The car thrust forward and flew over a small levee. Maddy hit the auto-window "Down" button as they vaulted through the air and plunged into the water with a hard jolt.

CHAPTER 26

9:45 a.m.:

Within seconds, the car sank into the river. Bear was glad it was summer and that he knew how to swim as he slid out of the passenger window into the cold, rushing torrent. He spit out his gum. Maddy sure was a quick thinker, but who were the bastards shooting at them?

Opening his eyes underwater, Bear looked around. Maddy grabbed her pack and squeezed out her window. Will was right behind her through his window.

Bullets traced through the blue water. They swam downstream to avoid them.

Once Bear finally came up for air, the river pushed him into a narrow gorge, below the enemy. The river smelled of water weeds and summer days, and the current separated him from the twins. Bear tried to yell at them but got a mouthful of water for his trouble and could hear only rushing water.

And now they had to deal with the river, which, judging by the lack of visible stones, was deeper than his familiar rocky rivers back home. But to be on the safe side, Bear kept his feet up and pointed downstream to avoid any submerged rocks, or hidden logs and branch snags, all potential death traps.

Bear was a solid swimmer, but the swift moving river was difficult. After a bend, the river left the gorge, widened, and filled with rocks. His feet bounced onto a hidden stone, then off and around to the right. It was hard to maneuver with his boots on and try as he might, he couldn't make any progress against the current.

Touching bottom for a fleeting moment, he tried to stand. The lethal current threw his ribs into a jagged boulder, which forced him to scramble back into the "feet downstream" position. Grasping at rocks also proved futile.

The river narrowed again and the water roiled, taking him down into a trough and then up onto the crest of a wave. As he topped another upsurge, he got a glimpse of sky, indicating a drop-off. He grimaced. It was probably that huge waterfall he'd seen right before the shots were fired.

He used all his strength to swim toward shore, twisting onto his stomach and pulling hard against the current. When he realized he wouldn't make it, he slapped his palm against the water in anger, causing a tall splash, and turned his feet back toward the looming falls.

He came up to the top of another wave with a sickening pitch. When his head popped above the water, he could see Maddy and Will were also headed for the waterfall. The sound of it filled his ears, roaring what could very well be their death song. His stomach gripped with fear.

It could kill Maddy.

He had to admit, if only to himself, that he did still have feelings for her. With desperation born of last chances, he pulled toward the shore with all his might, drawing an arm-over-arm backstroke away from the drop-off. He swore, but the current held him. And then he was hurtling over the falls like a cannonball.

For a long minute as he fell over the waterfall's edge, Bear felt weightless, like he had during his parachute training. Time slowed as he got a peek through the water in his eyes and saw the river far below. Ignoring the scream in his head, he tried to keep his feet heading down as he fell.

And fell.

And fell.

Then, with a bone-crunching splash, he hit, boots first. The jolt quaked his feet, spine, and head before he submerged, churning in an underwater tornado.

Not knowing which way was up, he tumbled, his arms and legs askew. His lungs burned, and he started to get dizzy as he struggled in vain to move against the massive, washing-machine surge. He realized this was a hole at the bottom of the waterfall and recalled the advice to ball up if caught. It was his nature to struggle, but since that didn't get him anywhere, he gave in, clutched his knees, rolled a few more times, and was finally spit out into calmer water.

Relief flooded him. He opened his eyes and turned until he could see the blue sky. With powerful strokes, he kicked up, broke the surface, and gulped the sweet, precious air.

Right away, he looked for Maddy and spied her, wearing her backpack, not far from him in the pool. She smiled at him, their eyes locked and his heart felt warm liberation from his concern for her safety.

Another deep breath, then he broke his eyes away. Will gasped for air behind him. Will's head went down and didn't come right up. Had he gotten caught in the same hole? Maybe took on some water?

Bear dove toward him.

Will struggled, just under the surface. Swimming up behind him, Bear put both his hands under Will's armpits and pushed him up to the air. Will gasped and then went into a coughing fit while Bear held his head out of the water, kicking furiously.

After a long bout of coughing, Will spit out the last of the water. "Bear. Oh my god! I got caught in a whirlpool!"

"It caught me, too."

Will looked at Bear with wide eyes. "You just saved my life!"

Bear had been too caught up in the action to think about it. "I guess I did. Just glad you're okay. Can you swim now?"

Will tried a few strokes and spoke back over his shoulder, "Yes, sir!"

Will headed toward a small beach on the left bank of the river. Bear and Maddy followed suit. They dragged themselves from the river and collapsed on the beach.

Bear threw a stone in the water while catching his breath. "I sure hope those shooters don't come down here looking for our dead bodies."

"Yeah, we need to get out of here fast," Maddy agreed.

CHAPTER 27

Jerusalem, Israel, June 30, 1:35 p.m.:

Inside a taxi, as they twisted and turned through the streets of Old Jerusalem, Maddy caught glimpses of the shimmering Dome of the Rock around corners and between buildings, a golden egg floating in a sea of sandstone.

Maddy wondered again who had ambushed them at the river. The king? The Russians? Her best guess was that Prince Carlos, their cousin, had felt threatened by their hunt for the ancient artifact and ordered them killed.

She was not only glad they escaped but also relieved she managed to grab the backpack with the diamonds and cash in it when they were forced to swim for their lives.

After they had caught their breath, made sure Will was fine, dried off, and checked that the contents of the backpack were safe, they hiked to the nearest town and boarded a bus to southern France. Once over the border, they confirmed that they didn't need a visa to visit Israel even with their fake passports. They then took a train to Marseilles and flew to Jerusalem without further incident.

As they traveled, Maddy experienced a practical sense of anxiety when they were in public. Since leaving Lake Tahoe, she found herself watching the crowds for burned, blond-haired men and listening for Russian accents. After the attack yesterday, her antennae were also tuned for a Spanish threat.

The sun shining off the cupola in the distance reminded her of the mosque's strict visiting hours and that the clock was ticking.

She said to Will and Bear, "So remember, we just have an hour this afternoon."

"Yes, we know," Will replied, while Bear watched the world go by.

"And if we can't find anything today, it'll be a long weekend."

"Heard you the first time."

The taxi pulled to a stop.

Will's demeanor toward Bear had relaxed. Bear's heroics yesterday must have finally earned Will's trust.

"Let's go then."

The instant they departed the taxi, Maddy regretted leaving the cool sanctuary of the cab. The heat was an oppressive force, more intense than the Sacramento heat by what seemed an evil factor of two. Perhaps it was made worse by the head scarf she was wearing to try and fit in with the women in the crowd.

She tried to focus on something besides the heat as they joined the throng and headed for the entry to the Dome, which was through a wooden walkway next to the entrance of the Western Wall called Mughrabi Gate. As usual, she was the tallest woman in the crowd, but today she appreciated the ability to scan for threats.

Israeli security forces checked their bags for weapons, religious artifacts, and anything with Hebrew letters, all which were forbidden in an attempt to keep the peace between Jews and Muslims. They had prepared for the checkpoint and were allowed through.

Bear looked up. "Pretty impressive building, eh?"

"It is," Will replied. "How old did you say it was?"

"Old. It was built around 691. The dome was replated with gold donated from a Jordanian king in 1994."

"Real gold, huh? Pricey. What about all that fancy tile?" Will asked.

"That was added around six hundred years ago. It took seven years to do all the tile work."

"It puts my office tile bathroom in Brazil to shame. Do we have any idea what we're looking to find here?"

"Based on the clue to listen for the souls of the dead, I suspect we look inside."

"Sure, but for what?" Will repeated.

Maddy broke in. "Hopefully, we'll know it when we see it, or hear it—how about we divide and conquer?"

Bear turned to look at her with a twinkle in his eyes. "What do you suggest, Ms. Marshall?"

"How about I look for whatever it is from the ground to head-high? Bear, you can overlap me a little bit from waist-high to above head-high and Will, as the tallest, you get the top section to the ceiling."

"Sounds good, let's head on inside." Bear started walking.

Maddy and Will followed suit.

The first thing she noticed as they walked into the mosque was that the cool interior dampened the furnace of the day down to something bearable. It was still warm, but she no longer felt like a lamb on a roasting spit. She took a deep breath and looked around.

It looked like another world. The sense of open space and stained-glass windows reminded her of cathedrals she had visited, but there was a background noise of tour guides and people talking that had never been present in those churches. Also, the complex symbols, colorful tiles, and rich carpets all distinguished this house of worship as Eastern rather than Western.

There were also inscriptions. Probably Quranic.

Every square inch seemed to have some sort of colorful lavish pattern highlighting its surface.

In the taxi, Bear had mentioned a mosque takeover attempt that had occurred about a month ago, and as she took a closer look, evidence of an uprising was plain. He touched her arm and pointed out the dark smudges on the carpet.

Was that blood? There were chips in several walls. A hole in the stained glass.

She sighed at the desecration. Such a long-standing feud. It lent a disturbing feel to the space that made the hair on the back of her neck rise.

The three of them nodded to each other and split up to draw less attention while they searched.

She walked around the back of the mosque first, behind the circle of pillars. There was gold inside the building, too, up in the dome, and at the top of the pillars, but nothing looked out of place, or like a clue.

Next, she climbed a set of stairs and peered over the railing to get a good look at the Foundation Stone. It was the rock that Jews believed to be the place on which Abraham had almost sacrificed Isaac, the rock that Muslims believed was the spot from which the Islamic prophet, Muhammad, had ascended into Heaven. And, she'd learned, because it was the site of the original temple, many Evangelical Christians believed that the destruction of the Dome would usher in the End of Days.

Okay, Ramiro, why here, at the intersection of three of the world's major religions, and what the hell am I looking for? The grim humor of the spiritual juxtaposition made her smile.

Eyes wide open, she continued to look around for any sort of suggestion that they were on the right track. If the clue did lead here, a good number of her ancestors had been here and left empty-handed.

Before she could get too frustrated though, she reminded herself that Isabella, or Ferdinand, had found something, somewhere, and that lifted her spirits. If the clue didn't lead here, Maddy would keep looking until she found where it did lead.

A bell tolled and she decided that they needed to head downstairs into the Well of Souls. Time was running out for the day.

She looked around, spied Bear, and walked over to him while looking for Will. Will stood twenty feet away, staring down at the Foundation Stone. *Why is he looking down, instead of up?*

As she and Bear started toward him, Will turned and walked over to join them. "Time to head downstairs?"

"I think so," Maddy replied. "That bell meant that there's only fifteen minutes left in this visiting period. They'll be rounding us up and out soon."

She didn't want to go downstairs into what looked like a cramped low-ceilinged room, but she followed Bear down into the cave-like space. No sounds of dead souls greeted her, not even the ghost of her father's voice.

The Foundation Stone above, and the area hewn out of rock below, made the space feel crowded. She felt a bubble of anxiety growing in her belly and watched the stairwell as an escape route. The ceiling was way too low for comfort. In spots, she guessed, Will would have to bend his knees to keep from hitting his head.

"There must be fifty people down here," she whispered to Bear.

"At least," Bear whispered back.

Scanning the crowd, she was glad she'd worn a head scarf. She realized she might not have even been able to get in without one, as every woman in sight wore some sort of scarf, hijab, or full burka.

In the crowded cave, the three of them again broke apart to scan the walls and floor for any sort of clue. The contrast from upstairs to downstairs was extreme—every inch upstairs was covered in some sort of colorful decoration. Down here was just hand-hewn rock, although she did see a shrine in a corner. There wasn't much to look at, but she scanned anyway.

After about ten minutes of staring at blank rock walls, guides spoke above and the throng started to head back upstairs. At least there was a little more breathing room as the crowd thinned.

The three of them drew back together near the side of the stairs.

Will scratched his beard. "I give up, what about you guys?"

Maddy wondered why he didn't just shave his beard off, if it bugged him so much.

"This is so frustrating," she said.

Bear scanned the room. "I think we've looked at every square inch."

Maddy released an exasperated breath, realizing her shoelace had come untied. "Except under these stairs."

She squatted down, retied her shoe, and surveyed the space. There was a slight, black stain on the lower part of the wall, behind the stairwell. *Is that a stain? Or is it a symbol?*

She looked up and around. They were now the last ones in the cave. A sound like a firecracker popped in the distance.

They looked at each other. Will raised an eyebrow and Bear swore under his breath. Another crack echoed through the mosque, and then trampling feet thundered above their heads.

Bear peeked up the stairs.

"That sounds like gunshots," Will whispered.

Part of her realized they might be in trouble but the other part of her continued to look back at the dark smudge. *Focus.* It took shape in her mind.

Bear pointed upstairs. "Get down! It's probably another mosque takeover. Hurry!"

Excited, Maddy ignored him and motioned for Will and Bear to come over. "It looks like a symbol."

Will used his key-ring flashlight to illuminate the spot and, in the dim light, Maddy recognized it as Ramiro's *signum regis* from the castle.

Bear inhaled sharply.

For a moment, she froze. Tentative, she reached out and touched it. As she explored it with her fingers, it seemed to give a little, so she pressed. It gave farther and then something clicked as it released.

Underneath the stairs, where there had, a moment before, been a wall, a low door swung inward. Before she could stop him, Bear ducked down and walked right through it.

CHAPTER 28

2:30 p.m.:

Bear, wait!" Will exclaimed. But it was a futile request. Bear was already disappearing inside a low door. *Where does it lead? Is it safe?*

Above the Rock, through the stairwell that led to the mosque above, loud male voices and more gunfire were getting louder. Closer.

Maddy gave Will a look that he knew meant, "Hurry up!"

She grabbed his sleeve and followed Bear.

Will ducked down and allowed Maddy to lead him into a hand-carved tunnel that began at the low opening. As he passed through the doorway, he moved the beam of his flashlight around. There was nothing but dust and a metal lever on the wall by the door.

Maddy looked at the lever, too. "Quick, shut the door!"

"Not a good idea for us to be up there," Bear whispered.

Will felt like a condemned man about to head to the gallows and could feel Maddy did as well, although her feeling was probably more related to the low ceilings. But he wanted to avoid any more shooting, so he gave in and pulled the lever. The door shut with a solid click.

Shining his small flashlight beam down the meter-wide tunnel, Will followed the light, Bear and Maddy walked behind him. Shadows danced on the stone walls. The ceiling was just tall enough that Will didn't have to duck, for which he was grateful, as his thighs hurt from bending his knees in that cavern above.

They were silent as they followed the dusty passage through its meandering path underneath the Old City, until they came upon a tunnel opening to their right.

Will's flashlight beam lit up the opening. "Are we safe now? Enough to talk? What do you think of this tunnel? Do you think we solved the clue?"

Bear replied in his laconic drawl, "Yeah, we're a little ways away. This is clearly a side tunnel." Bear pointed. "See how it's narrow, compared to this main tunnel?"

"Maybe it's for supplies or ventilation," Maddy said.

"So, we keep on?" Will asked.

"I think so," Bear replied.

The three of them headed farther into the passageway.

Nervous, Will tapped his fingers along the wall as they passed, but after Bear had saved his life at the river, he knew he could trust him.

Maddy touched her necklace. "And I think we solved the clue. Remember, it read: 'Find the center of the world that looms over an abyss, a bottomless pit. Listen and you can hear the souls of the dead.' That was Ramiro's sign at the entrance to this tunnel."

Will couldn't argue with her logic. As they moved along, he lost track of the number of rounded corners they turned, and he also couldn't tell how much deeper they were going underground, although they'd been moving at a slight but steady decline almost since they started.

After what could have been ten minutes, or half an hour, a wooden door appeared at the end of the passage. They stopped and stared at it for a minute.

"Do we knock or just go in?" Bear asked.

"Do you think it's not dangerous?" Will asked.

"Safer than going back," Maddy replied. "It's polite to knock."

Bear rapped on the door three times. "Yes, ma'am."

Will put his ear to the door and was knocked off balance when it swung inward. He fell through the door, and nearly into, a small-statured, gray-haired woman wearing a white smock, white pants, and tiny white shoes. Her skin was pale, her gray hair long and caught up in a bun at the nape of her neck. Her soft brown eyes registered a wide-eyed look of deep surprise behind her silver-rimmed glasses.

Heart racing in astonishment, Will jumped backward and hit Bear's chest with a thud.

As the old woman backed away from the door, she started to speak in a language that Will didn't recognize.

At their blank looks, she tried two other languages before dropping into accented English. "Oh my goodness, come in, come in. It's been decades since anyone has made it through *that* door, simply decades. Are you with the Argones? You must be, they're the only ones who would see—come in. Please." As she gestured for them to come inside, she continued to prattle, "I'm amazed that door still works, I should get Samuel to grease the hinges. And if I hadn't happened by on my way to the library—"

Darting behind them, she shut the door and then moved in front of them again. Will noticed the old king's sign carved into the top panel on this side of the dark wooden door.

They were in a broad stone chamber, lit from...could it be?...oil lamps that hung on the walls. Numerous other doors lined the walls in both directions.

Will could feel Maddy's confusion and excitement, mirroring his own emotions. Bear's head was swiveling everywhere with what Will was sure was curiosity.

"Follow me, follow me."

Before he could ask any questions, she shuffled away, so they fell into line behind her.

Her hands gestured all around, "This is the grand entryway. You can see all the other doors from passages all over the city. Yours was the first, of course, but so long. It's been so long."

Will had no idea what she was talking about.

"Let's see if we can find Samuel for a proper welcome," the woman in white continued.

She sidestepped through a doorway at the end of the entryway and into a dim wood-paneled room, large enough for two old desks, two bookshelves, and multiple antique chairs. Will wondered how the furniture had made its way down here. A man thin as a skeleton, also attired in white garb, sat at one of the desks. His hair, what was left of it, was white and cut so short that he appeared to be bald. His eyes were wide set above a thin-lipped mouth and he had a longish nose, which reminded Will of a lizard.

The lighting was more of the oil lamps he'd seen on the way here. The woman motioned for the three of them to take chairs as she stood near the man.

"What are your names?" But before they could respond, the woman said, fingers fluttering, "I'm Edith and this is Samuel. We're gatekeepers of a sort, the Guardians of the Jerusalem Testing Society, a thousand-plus-year-old institute established by your ancestor, Ramiro. He is your ancestor, is he not? You two have the look." She glanced at Will and Maddy then at Bear. "Looks like a bodyguard, but those days are past. A friend or suitor, perhaps?"

Bear blushed. Interesting. Will figured Bear's feelings to have been a thing long past.

Maddy jumped in, pointing at Will. "Yes, William there and I are descendants of Ramiro. We're here on a quest that he established. Can you help us?"

Edith smiled and touched the older man on the shoulder. "Ah yes, help. If you can call it that."

The man, Samuel, also wore glasses, but there was cautious amusement in his eyes. He put his hand on the woman's forearm in a gesture of intimacy and spoke in a deep baritone. His voice also bore traces of an accent. "Let's slow down and welcome you first. Would you like a beverage and may I ask your names?"

Since Will had already been announced, Maddy and Bear introduced themselves and said they would like something to drink.

"It's a pleasure to meet descendants of Ramiro. Such a lovely surprise at the end of our tenure here. We are getting old, you see, and our eldest will be taking over with his wife soon. We've had guests from many other famous families, but yours is the most famous of all." Samuel shared a guarded glance with Edith. "How are you related to our last Argones guest, Maximillian?"

Will sat up straight. "He was our grandfather but passed away when we were young. Can you explain more about the institute, please?"

"Of course," Samuel continued in his slow, melodic voice. "You must have many questions. Your ancestor, Ramiro One, had something that he wanted protected, something that he wanted only the worthiest of his descendants to have."

Worthy? This doesn't sound good already.

"He established this institute to oversee a series of tests to determine whether his progeny would prove able to handle the power inherent in what he wanted hidden."

Tests? Dear god.

"Later, after newlyweds Isabella and Ferdinand passed through here, flush with success, they spread word of the institute to other European families who decided similar testing was appropriate for their own goals. Those other families have helped maintain the funding required to keep this place running."

What other families?

"But we're not at liberty to discuss those other families with you and if you stay, you must not discuss your situation with other students, nor they with you. This place is a doorway of sorts. For your family, you must pass through here if you wish to find the Aragon *Châsse*." Samuel paused.

"We've heard of the Aragon *Châsse*. What do you know of it?" Will asked.

"Young man, I think the better question is what's inside the *châsse*. Do you know exactly what a *châsse* is?"

Will had a rough idea from their conversation with the king and was about to say so when Bear said, "It's typically a medieval casket with sloping roofs like a small house."

Will pressed his lips together.

"That's right!" Samuel raised his thin eyebrows in a surprised, good-job type gesture. "What else do you know about the little boxes?"

An embarrassed flush crept up Bear's face, so Will jumped to Bear's defense, saying, "He has studied history."

Bear looked up and to the left as he thought. "It was a shape commonly used in medieval metalwork for reliquaries and other containers. To our modern eye, it looks like a small house, although a tomb was the intent. Part of it is hinged and it may have a lock. The word is French and from the Latin *capsa* for 'box.'"

"Impressive," the old man rumbled. "Usually we have to explain those things. So anyway, yes, it's a box and even *we* don't know what is inside it."

Maddy had been watching the exchange. "We want, maybe need, to find the *châsse*. So how do we pass these tests?"

She was always good about getting directly to the point.

Edith's head nodded like a bird. "Ah yes, the tests. If you choose to stay, you will face more than one test. For instance, one test is a duel. The tests are designed to see if you are fearless, can handle pain, and have sound judgment. And they are also designed to protect you, as what is inside the *châsse* holds immense power. The power could harm someone fearful, perhaps...how do you say?...*backfire*." Her voice took on a more serious tone, "There are...risks. Several students have regrettably died over the years, and I'm sorry to say your grandfather, Maximillian, failed."

"Students died?" Will echoed, feeling hollow. He didn't like to fail at anything, but in his view, death was the ultimate failure. And the word had brought him back to his grief.

"Yes, I'm afraid so. These tests were established over a thousand years ago under explicit instructions from Ramiro. Life was different then. He had rather...how shall we say?...elaborate ideas and thought that it would be better to have one of his progeny die than for power to fall into the wrong hands."

Will exchanged a glance with Maddy. How did she look so calm?

Edith added, "You may leave now, but once you begin testing, you must see it through. Also, you must promise supreme secrecy about this location as we have long-standing agreements about who may attend here. If you fail to abide by the secrecy, we will know, and I'm sorry that I must add, you would regret it."

Will didn't like the threat.

"What kind of duel?" Maddy asked, again seeing to the heart of the matter.

"The kind where only one person survives," Samuel said, with a solemn tone.

Maddy swallowed hard, and Will felt his gut clench in fear.

Edith's hands fluttered. "And your friend is not eligible for any of the testing. He is not family."

Will and Maddy turned to look at Bear, who shrugged.

"If you wish, he will be allowed to stay under the legacy bodyguard clause," Edith continued.

Will chose not to ask for details about whatever the clause meant. He could imagine well enough, and Bear did fit that mental construct.

Edith darted about the room, unable to stand still. "Before the duel, the guidelines allow you five days to rest from your journey and train. Then there is a short series of tests to ensure you have no phobias and are of strong heart. If you pass those tests, you progress to the duel. Afterward, assuming you make it through that and a surprise, you receive a tiny brand, about the size of Samuel's thumb, which you must suffer in silence. Any sign of pain, such as a grimace, a moan, or a shout, and the brand will be covered with a larger, circular brand, and you will not be able to continue on your quest."

Will shivered. *A brand? Like a horse? This just keeps getting better.*

Then Edith delivered the final insult, "No tobacco or alcohol is allowed here in this underground town, which is older even than Ramiro."

Will was not even mildly amused that his hand twitched toward his cigarette pack. A volcano of fury was building in his belly.

Edith nodded briskly. "We have shared all the rules and will ask you to step outside now for up to twenty minutes. Please discuss and decide."

As they stood, Samuel boomed, "Think well. There is no shame in turning back now and much danger if you choose to go on."

CHAPTER 29

3:20 p.m.:

As soon as the door to the office of the Guardians of the Jerusalem Testing Society shut behind them, Maddy started to speak, but Will exploded, "What the hell? There's no way I'm sticking around in this underground dungeon to fight somebody—and to the death!"

Maddy thought he sounded almost hysterical and figured it was going without smokes that had him tweaked around an imaginary axle.

"Calm down. Let's make a rational decision about this."

"Calm? Sure, kill or be killed? That's calming. Oh, yeah! This doesn't sound good to me, sis. I say we leave now. Right now!"

Maddy could feel the heat of his anger, or maybe she was also starting to get ticked off because he didn't see why they had to stay. Her tone showed her annoyance. "I think you're just pissed you can't have a smoke."

Will's fists clenched. "Do you *want* to die?"

"We need to stay."

"They said people have *died* down here. Did you hear that?"

Maddy noticed Bear sitting this argument out by looking at the symbols on the other doors. It was up to her and Will to decide what to do.

"No, of course I don't want to die, but have you considered that we might, if we go back out there? Will, there are people trying to kill us!"

"And so are these people!"

"Not exactly."

In the dim light, Will looked even taller than normal. "How do you know?" He raised his voice.

She raised her voice, too. "I do know that out there, people are trying to kill us. That Dad and Maria are already dead. And you forget I've been training for years."

"Have you ever had to kill someone?"

"No, and I don't want to. Killing someone contradicts all of my aikido training. Perhaps there's some way out of that, but we won't know unless we stick around to find out."

"Well, I don't want to stick around. I know there's no way I want to get branded. Pain isn't my thing. Let's leave."

"And then what? Let the Russians find the *châsse* and do god knows what with it? Go home with our tail between our legs? Or stay on the run, scared of our own shadows, not knowing why Dad and Maria were killed? I thought you wanted justice!"

At these last words, Will deflated.

"I do," he spoke the words as if they were forced out of him by the torture he so vocally wanted to avoid.

Maddy didn't want to stick around either but knew she was right, so she pressed the point. "It worries me that the Russians want the *châsse*. And I want the truth. There's no other way, Will. If one of us succeeds in passing, we at least have a shot at figuring out who wants us dead and what they want so badly. Or else we'll always be looking over our shoulders."

Will took his cigarette pack out of his shirt pocket, threw it on the ground, and stomped on it. "You're killing me, Maddy. I already want a smoke."

Then, tantrum complete, the side of his mouth twitched in the briefest of smiles.

The energy between them shifted. Maddy let out a breath she hadn't realized she was holding and her shoulders relaxed, too. "Good choice, Will. Let's go see what's next."

She squared her posture, walked back to the door, and knocked, already hoping like hell she could find a way out of that duel.

CHAPTER 30

July 1, 6:20 a.m.:

Will awoke with a start, covered in sweat.

He listened to his own labored breathing inside the broader silence. Opening his eyes to the pitch-blackness that enveloped the room he shared with Bear in the ancient underground complex, he tried to calm his breath.

It was another of his falling dreams. He'd had them since his mom died in the car crash when they were four, two years before his grandfather disappeared and died. What a horrible time that was for them, and for his father.

The car crash—he was in the back seat.

His breathing was still rapid and shallow, and he didn't want to remember the car flying through the air.

"Argones," Bear whispered.

Part of him heard Bear but he couldn't answer. Also, he didn't want to remember how unsafe he'd felt, alone in that car with two dead bodies. By wrenching his mind away from that scene, he resisted feeling the terror. He didn't want to delve any deeper.

Couldn't.

His arm had healed, his chin had scarred, but he still blamed himself. They hadn't wanted to take him. But oh, how he had begged to go to that birthday party.

"Will, are you awake?" Bear's southern voice sounded more insistent this time.

Somehow, Will managed to pull himself into the present. "Ugh. Hi. Sorry, did I wake you up?"

"No worries, I heard you moving around and you kinda moaned. Are you okay?"

He wasn't, but men didn't talk about this kind of stuff. "Uh, yeah, I'm fine."

There was silence. Will knew that Bear wasn't buying it, but he understood and didn't press the point.

"What time is it? You want to go get some breakfast?" Bear asked.

"Sure."

As he dressed, Will wasn't sure how many of his memories were his own and how many were from the retelling of the story. He had been so young when it happened.

Still, since his dad's last words had been to send them on this quest, Will held out hope that following the trail would somehow help solve the murders and go a little way toward redeeming himself.

He just wasn't looking forward to the process.

CHAPTER 31

7:00 a.m.:

In the morning, after Maddy woke and realized that her dad was still dead, Vincent wasn't in bed with her, and that she was in some godforsaken cave getting ready to die in some godforsaken fight, she figured a little conversation with Hana, her new roommate, was in order.

She'd never been a morning person, but perhaps a chat about the blond German guy she'd seen at the other end of the dining table last night would improve her mood.

As they got dressed, Maddy asked, "I'm from California, what about you?"

Hana was a good six inches shorter than Maddy, with bobbed blonde hair, bangs, sunny-blue eyes, perfect teeth, prominent cheekbones, full lips, and had a great figure.

Maddy felt like Popeye's tall Olive Oyl next to a curvaceous Playboy Bunny. Especially when she dressed in the same blue jeans she'd worn yesterday, and Hana put on a gorgeous athletic suit that must have cost several hundred dollars.

Hana replied with a Danish accent, "I'm from Denmark. We cannot share last names, ya?"

"I suppose you're right. How long have you been here?"

"Just two days now."

Maddy dug her hairbrush out of her backpack and began to brush her hair. It was a relaxing ritual. "What can you tell me that you've learned?"

Hana shook her head and closed her eyes for a moment. "The training…it is hard. And it is okay to share about the distress tests. But more than this I cannot say."

"So, what kind of distress tests?"

"There are three that we've learned of from other students," Hana paused. "The Guardians don't speak of them. I have not done them yet, you understand, but I have heard."

Maddy hoped small cramped places weren't on the menu. "Go on."

"The first test is to climb a sky-high ladder and walk across a rope bridge, over a cavern filled with spiders and snakes, and to a platform on the other side."

"Doesn't sound so bad."

"It gets worse. The second test you jump into a hole blindfolded and land sometime later in water."

Maddy figured Will to fail that one, even if he made it past the first one, which she doubted, given the height of the ladder. "Screening out people with fear of heights and water in the same test."

"Yes, clever. Lastly, you have to walk through a dark tunnel that gets progressively smaller until you have to crawl on your belly to reach the other side."

Rats! Maddy knew that test would be in there somewhere. She repressed an involuntary shudder. All that weight bearing down on her, trapping her inside—*Stop! Think about something else. Deal with that when it comes.*

"They've been rather, uh, thorough."

"Indeed. Myself, I worry about the spiders. One bit me when I was a child and the doctor said they might have to take my hand off. You?"

Maddy finished brushing her hair. "Small spaces are not my thing."

Hana nodded in sympathy. Dressed, she sat on the bed.

Maddy sat on the twin bed across from Hana. "Know anything else about it?"

"No, this is all."

Maddy tried to push her, but Hana remained quiet, so Maddy changed the subject. "Who was the tall blond man at the dinner table last night? The one sitting with the green-eyed blonde woman and the stocky chap? Sounded like he had a sexy German accent."

This question evoked a sparkling laugh from Hana. "Ah, you have your eye on Juergen. He is handsome, isn't he?"

Maddy nodded as she recalled the broad shoulders, chiseled features, and thick blond hair pulled back into a short ponytail.

Hana smiled. "But what about the man you came with? He is not with you and your brother?"

Maddy wasn't sure how to answer. "He's a family friend."

Hana raised one eyebrow and laughed her sparkling laugh again. "He looks at you in another way."

"He's so short!" Maddy burst out.

"You are tall, yes. Nice long legs you have. Juergen is tall, too. Perhaps you will...how do you say?...hit it off. Perhaps not. I noticed your family friend. He's not so short and seems to have a tall spirit."

Maddy had never thought of Bear that way. "Tell me more about Juergen."

"You will have to discover him for yourself," Hana said.

Maddy wasn't at all sure she was ready to discover anyone new. A little flirting might be fun, but her heart still ached from the breakup with Vincent. And she knew she was still a basket case in the wake of her father's and Maria's deaths. "Really, you don't know where he's from, his interests, nothing?"

"I know nothing more than that he is German."

Twice defeated, Maddy decided breakfast was in order before she began training for the duel that could end her life.

CHAPTER 32

2:00 p.m.:

After breakfast, Will's gut nagged him about their situation. He wondered what the Jerusalem Testing Society was all about and already missed his nicotine. After surviving this morning's nightmare, he wanted a smoke.

According to Juergen, Dieter, and Elena—the Germans he sat next to at breakfast—to leave this place alive, they had to "run the gauntlet," or go through a series of tests such as heights, snakes, etc. That fear testing was five days out, followed by the duel.

As soon as he heard "heights," a sinking feeling began in his stomach. Heights had never been his thing.

But, in the meantime, there was the practice hall. It was a large open space, larger than the dining hall, and Will considered, not for the first time, how this underground town had been built. It had taken a lot of work to create these vast, open spaces out of rock. Perhaps the ancient inhabitants had used caves as starting points and used the complex as a place to escape when invaders threatened.

That was Bear's theory.

Will was just impressed by the resulting underground facility.

Here in the practice hall, there were several mats, sectioned off for practicing with weapons, and walls full of those weapons to choose from. He and Bear stood at the side of the room, checking it all out.

"Looks like they have all the medieval weapons," Bear said.

"Help me out here. I'm not a weapons kinda guy. What are they?"

"Okay. Those poles are quarterstaffs and there are some knives on that wall."

"I'm not an idiot."

"You asked."

Will pointed to the middle of the wall. "You're an ass. What's that thing that looks like a long hammer?"

"Horseman's pick, sometimes called a war hammer."

"How about that long pole with the spiky head?"

"Mornin' star," Bear drawled.

"Poetic."

"Right. You'll also notice there are no guns here."

"Hmm, you're right. I hadn't noticed."

"So, what are you goin' to use?" Bear asked.

Will was surprised by the question. "Me?"

"Yes, you. You need a weapon."

"Screw that. I'm an engineer, not a warrior."

"But you're here now and on this quest. You might need to defend yourself. And what if the surprise they mentioned turns ugly?"

"I'm not going to have time to get good at any weapon. The only thing I ever used in aikido was a wooden knife blade."

"Are you drawn to the sword, that mornin' star, or anything else besides knives?" Bear insisted.

"Not really."

Bear sighed. "Okay, then. I'll show you how to throw 'em."

"Let's hope I don't hit you in the eye with one." Will was only half joking.

Bear ignored him and moved off toward the wall of knives with his nearly imperceptible limp. Once at the wall, he looked over a few, handled a couple, and put them back.

Will was curious in spite of himself. "What are you looking for?"

"Balance."

Bear finally chose three.

He brought them over to Will and they stood in front of the targets about ten meters back. Bear handed one of the knives to Will. "Hold it like a hammer."

Will reached out and took it. It felt cold. Heavy. He caressed the blade with his other thumb. Sharp, too. He'd probably cut himself. "A hammer? On the handle? Don't you hold the blade?"

Bear shook his head. "That's an advanced hold. While you're learning, let's have you hold it like you would a hammer. Like this." He wrapped his hand around the handle, blade up, and even made hammer-pounding motions.

Will understood and shifted his grip. "Now what?"

"Now you throw. Watch me."

With exaggerated slowness, Bear stood with his right foot behind his torso, left foot forward, both arms outstretched parallel to the ground. He brought his right arm up toward his head and then down in a sort of chopping motion. He let go when his hands were even and Will noticed Bear's right leg had also come forward as he threw.

Will was impressed that the knife hit near the center of the target.

"Keep your wrist straight. See?" Bear threw again. "Very important. Try a few from the same distance until you get the hang of it."

Five minutes later, Will concluded that he was pretty pathetic. Bear had to show him three times how to hold the knife properly and five times reminded him to keep his wrist straight.

Finally, Bear pronounced, "You won't kill yourself."

Relieved, Will practiced being pathetic on his own time.

After about fifteen minutes, Hana, who Maddy had introduced him to at breakfast, walked over and started practicing next to him.

When she hit the center of the target three times in a row, he asked, "You're pretty good. Any pointers for a knife novice?" He grinned.

She grinned back. "Practice and keep your wrist straight."

He liked her voice, lilting and with an accent—maybe Danish?

"My wrist already feels like a lead weight."

Hana walked over, stood behind him, and mirrored his stance while almost touching his back with her chest. "That's because you're bending it. Let me show you, here."

She had him slow down his throw while she kept his wrist from moving. Will smelled her perfume, noticed the warmth of her hand, and was filled with a strange mixture of excitement and guilt. *God, I am not feeling attracted to her, am I? Maria isn't even buried yet.*

Her closeness distracted him and his throw was off.

She stepped back. "Okay, you throw again."

He did, concentrating on keeping his wrist straight as he shifted his weight into the throw.

"Better," she said and went back to practicing at her target.

After another ten minutes, he looked at her. "My shoulder is killing me. Want to take a break?" It would be a nice distraction to get to know her a little.

"Ya, sure."

The light in her blue eyes said she'd like to get to know him, too.

He craved a cigarette, but this would have to do.

As they walked off, he worried that, with his luck, she was somehow connected to the Russians who were hot on their trail.

CHAPTER 33

3:05 p.m.:

In the practice room, Maddy watched Will and Bear, then Will and Hana, out of the corner of her eye. It looked as if there was some casual flirting going on between Will and Hana, and Maddy had sensed Will's sudden spike of interest when Hana showed him how to throw from an up-close-and-personal vantage point.

Maddy would have to keep an eye on the two of them. A little diversion would do him good, but too much would set his grieving process back years.

After Will and Hana walked out of the practice room together, Maddy turned her full attention to Joy, her current training partner—a middle-aged dark-skinned woman of average height and build who wore a colorful floral print shirt and tight leggings below hair streaked with a swath of white. She and Maddy were standing on a large mat in a corner of the room.

Joy smiled. "Stop going so easy on me."

"Come on then, but I don't want to hurt you. Have you sparred much?"

"Honestly, I haven't sparred with anyone since my baby brother and I used to roll around in the courtyard."

Maddy had suspected as much. She showed Joy a few aikido moves and then begged off to get a drink of water near the edge of the mat.

Joy walked over to where Juergen and his friends were practicing with a bow and started up a conversation that Maddy couldn't hear. Maddy had learned that Juergen's stocky male friend's name was Dieter and Elena was the name of his reddish-blonde female companion.

Bear walked over to Maddy and joked so only she could hear. "Would you like some real competition?"

"Sure, let's see what you've learned since high school."

Without pause, he reached out to grab her shoulder. Acting on instinct, she grabbed his arm with both hands in a *morote-dori* move, which she followed up with a pivot, twist, and throw. He landed with a grunt flat on his back.

She laughed. "You might want to work on your rolls. Even AJ is better at rolling than you are."

"Give a fella a break, it's been a while."

"Okay, grab one of your staffs. Do you remember it's called a 'jo'? And let's see how rusty you are."

"Sure, I remember that much. Me with a *jo* and you without?"

After throwing him, she felt like a winning prizefighter. "Sure."

"Doesn't seem fair."

"We'll see."

He walked over to the wall where he had placed his quarterstaff and walked back onto the mat, twirling it above his head like a baton. She easily stayed out of the way and waited for him to make a move that would put him off balance.

After a few more twirls, he grabbed the staff in more of a lancing pose and thrust it at her legs. It came at her in what seemed like slow motion, and she simply stepped aside.

He followed up with a more aggressive thrust to her midriff, so she took advantage of his center of gravity moving forward. By grabbing his staff and pulling him toward her and upward in a single flowing movement called *ki nagare*, she caused him to lose his balance, and he again landed on his back.

She thought he might get mad. Instead, he laughed and popped a bubble with his gum. "You've gotten pretty good!"

"Thank you. I enjoy helping out at the dojo and my skills get better along the way."

He rolled backward and came up in a crouch. "Again?"

She nodded and he rushed her.

They sparred for about a half hour, until they were both breathing hard. After she threw him for the fifth time, he looked up at her from the floor and wiped sweat from his forehead. "What do you think about switching to swords?"

"Sure, but let's use real blades."

"Not practice ones?"

"I'm going to be in a duel for my life in a few days. Practice days are gone."

"If you say so."

On the wall, she discovered a slightly curved, samurai-type short katana blade, found its weight pleasing, and wrapped her fingers around its hilt. He went for a straight sword, also single bladed. Swords weren't taught until upper levels at the dojo, so she and Bear were more evenly matched.

The blades were sharp, and she bumped her concentration up a notch as they practiced. She focused on the basics, first gripping and cutting, then balance, center, and extension. He came at her from over his head, sidearm, and tried to take her out at the knees. With each thrust or slash, she attempted to use his forward motion against him, parried, or took an evasive step.

Practicing with Bear was not like working out at the dojo. He was a street fighter who didn't play by the usual aikido rules.

The swords clanged against one another and the others in the practice chamber gathered around to watch.

Maddy's muscles began to ache. As she parried an overhead blow, their weapons caught together in an upright cross. She was about to suggest they take a break when her grip slipped, and Bear's blade swooshed down, slicing the outside of her left wrist. Dropping her sword, she slapped her right hand across the wound. "Time out."

Bear threw down his weapon and rushed to her. "Let me see."

"I don't think it's that bad." She peeled back her hand. A thin band of bright red blood seeped from a two-inch long cut. "It was my fault."

He looked her straight in the eye. "I'm so very sorry."

"Don't be. I lost my grip. If it was the duel, I'd be dead by now."

"Let's use bamboo swords for a day or so."

"Fine," she agreed. "I'm going to go find a bandage."

Afterward, she came back to the practice room and worked off the frustration at her screw up until she could barely lift her arms.

At the end of the day, the Guardians told them to each choose a weapon to keep with them for the rest of their time there. Bear kept his staff. Will took two throwing knives and two sheaths. Maddy kept the sword. If she made it through the fear tests, would she even be allowed to use a weapon during the upcoming duel? And would she make another mistake? A fatal one?

CHAPTER 34

July 5, 5:15 p.m.:

Back in the practice room four days later, Will stood alone, practicing with his knives. It was the last hour of the last practice day.

Although he was still dealing with nicotine withdrawal, he was getting better at throwing the knives. He had realized it involved the basic principles of mechanics that he worked with day in and day out as an engineer. The objective was for the point of the knife to stick into the target with a sufficient amount of force. To be successful, accuracy, distance, the number of rotations, and the placement of his body all needed to be taken into account.

After wishing in vain for an app to work the calculations, he had reached back into his collegiate memory bank and played with some calculus. He chided himself for being such a geek, but the understanding had definitely improved his aim. At least he was usually hitting the target, and once he even came close to a bull's-eye. In that moment, he felt like the kid at the carnival who won the large stuffed dog.

All was not rosy, however. His arm and shoulder were so sore he grimaced every time he threw, and his whole body was out of shape. Worse, a full-blown civil war raged inside his head. Against his better judgment, he'd slept with Hana the night before.

He pictured the scene. Hana had played chess with him after dinner in the common room. It had been good to laugh away the fear and grief. As the others had drifted away to bed, they had lingered over the chess board. Then she had asked if he wanted to sneak into the kitchen to grab a late-night snack.

They took an oil lamp down the hall and into the silent galley, conspirators whispering like children. A leftover blueberry pie beckoned and she had fed him a piece with her fingers. When she leaned in and kissed him, he had resisted at first, but within ten seconds his body seemed to take over and before he knew it, they were entwined.

It had been crazy, wrong, passionate, and irresistible. He was light-headed all over again remembering how she had felt. His knife flew wide and he moved off the mat to get a drink.

Now, in the light of day, he knew their liaison for a rebound thing, a simple attraction, and that he'd done it to forget Maria. It had backfired because he'd fantasized about Maria half the time. He was an ignoble, fornicating bastard. God, at least he hadn't called out Maria's name.

His body felt lighter for the release but he knew that he wasn't prepared for anything resembling a relationship. That was quite clear. And, although he had told Hana he just lost his wife, and she had indicated she just wanted to have some fun, he wasn't sure she was telling the truth.

So, he endured a complex set of guilty, post-pleasure feelings, threw another knife, and grunted with the effort.

After he'd been at it for a while, Maddy walked over and stood behind him, leaning against the wall. She watched him for a moment with her long legs crossed and her arms folded on her chest. Even in high school, she'd always been able to tell when he'd been with a girl. He'd asked her about it a few times, and she'd always said it was just obvious. He could feel the frosty chill of her silent disproval, but since he deserved it, he said nothing.

She was looking good with her sword and aikido moves. No one could consistently take her, not even Bear, although he got lucky once in a while. Will couldn't believe it, but she'd started practicing with two swords at once and wore them now in crossed scabbards on her back.

She broke the silence. "You're looking pretty decent with those knives."

"Thanks, do you think I'll survive the duel?"

She walked toward him. "No."

"Wow, that's kind. What do you really think?"

"I think you should leave now and meet up with me when I'm done here. Take Bear to keep you safe out there."

He was tempted. "Maybe I should. I'll fail the heights test anyway. But why do you get to stay?"

"I have years of experience with aikido. You took it for what…a month?…in high school. And now can hit somewhere on the target most of the times you throw."

He grimaced. "You don't pull any punches, do you?"

"I have been known to be blunt, now and again."

"Okay, but I'm the guy. You're the girl. What do you know about this duel?"

She raised an eyebrow and lowered her voice. "You're the guy? Seriously?"

"Call me a sexist pig, but I worry about you. Have you learned anything useful about the duel?"

"There's a rumor we fight convicts. We're armed and they're not."

Will smiled, relieved. "That's good! You'll have an advantage."

"Who are you and what have you done with my brother?"

"What do you mean?" She might be kidding but he wasn't sure.

"You think fighting an unarmed man to the death is fair?"

He realized she wasn't joking. "Fair? I just want you out alive!"

"Don't worry about that."

"How can I not? You're my sin twister!"

Maddy laughed at his word play. "I'd worry about you, too. But you don't need to. He, or she, is probably not even a convict. Where would they get convicts? I'm sure this is nothing close to legal."

"Legal *smeagle*. They are clearly well funded, and they probably have long-standing agreements with the city jailors. With all the religious tension around here, it probably doesn't take much to exchange a few bucks to get somebody released."

"You're a little cynical about the local justice system."

"I guess I am. But do you doubt my logic?" Will asked.

She took one of her swords out of its scabbard and started twirling it, like a baton. "No."

"So, you're going to be fighting some sort of criminal, perhaps a terrorist, who will want to kill you so he doesn't die?"

Maddy's eyes held a cold expression. "Yes, it looks that way."

"Convicts are often hardened by violence. Doesn't this whole thing bother you?" Will asked.

She sounded heated. "Of course, it bothers me, Will, but what choice do I have? Send you in there to die, back out and let the Russians find the *châsse*, or kill a terrorist. I don't like any of the choices, but of the three, I'll take the latter."

"I just wish there were another way."

"I do, too, and I'm still trying to think of some way out of it. In aikido we're taught to use every other means at our disposal instead of killing. And who knows, maybe I won't pass the fear test."

Will knew he would fail. "There's no way I'll clear the heights part."

"Ah, c'mon, you'll be fine. I heard there is a tunnel, and I'm pretty lousy at small cramped spaces, as you might remember from high school."

Will turned his shoulder to her, as if blocking a blow. "I remember." He wanted to shift the conversation from *that* land mine. "Have you learned how to deal with fear in your aikido training?"

"I wish, but no. There are a few basic methods, according to my teacher: Work out until you can deal with it, ignore it, or sit with it until it passes."

"What's worked for you?"

She put the sword back in its scabbard. "I've been practicing situational avoidance for some time. You? Any ideas on dealing with your fear of heights?"

"Unfortunately, no. I usually drink myself silly when I fly and avoid other high situations, like ladders and tall buildings."

"Looks like time for avoidance is going to run out for both of us tomorrow."

It was true, and he had nothing to add. The conversation lulled. She might not bring up that he'd slept with Hana.

She crossed her arms. "So, why'd you sleep with her?"

Nope. She brought it up. "God, Maddy! Is it any of your business?"

"You're my twin, yes, you're my business."

He threw one last knife. "I don't know!"

Although it landed square in the target's center, he felt no satisfaction. He bolted from the practice room.

He'd failed Maria and knew he'd fail the stress test tomorrow.

CHAPTER 35

July 6, 9:00 a.m.:

On the sixth day, a little bruised and sore from all the practice, Maddy, along with several of the other students, lined up for what Hana had called the "distress" testing. Feeling nervous, she picked at the scab on her left wrist. Will was behind her in line, sweating already. Well, she was sweating, too.

Small tight spaces had been her nemesis during her entire adult life, and already her heart was pounding at what type of test this was going to be. One by one, the students in front of her went through the door at the end of the hallway. There was usually a ten to fifteen-minute wait in between each student.

When Maddy's turn came, Edith led her down a hallway and through a dark brown wooden door, where Samuel stood in a mean, narrow room that contained only two other, similar doors for decoration. Edith left.

Samuel patted her on the shoulder. A paternal gesture. "Are you ready?"

Butterflies were having a party in her stomach. She didn't trust her voice so just nodded once.

His eyes looked kind and his deep voice was soft. "I've noticed you using aikido skills. Are you familiar with your founder's quote about fear?"

She shook her head from left to right and managed to whisper, "No."

"I appreciate his philosophy regarding how to turn an opponent's offensive energy into a peaceful resolution, so I've studied him a bit. One has much time down here. At any rate, I believe he once remarked something along the lines that, in order to be effective, one must be willing to receive ninety-nine percent of an opponent's attack and stare death in the face. Fear of death, Maddy. I think you'll find death at the root of most fears. Once you can stare death in the eyes and laugh, you'll free up huge amounts of energy."

Stare death in the eyes. Lovely. She found her voice, "That sounds like something he'd say. Any tips on how to accomplish that?"

"The only other advice I can share is our motto: Going in is the only way out." He opened the door, put his hand on her back, and ushered her through. "Good luck, young lady."

After the door shut behind her, she stood and stared down the hallway with his advice echoing in her ears. She had felt on solid ground for a second while talking with Samuel. But in this long hallway leading to nowhere, she knew only fear, smelling it in the air, on her body, in the hallway, even tasting it on her tongue.

Involuntarily, she took a deep breath and realized she'd been holding it. She took a few more deep breaths, like before an aikido belt test. *There's nothing here to be scared of, you silly goose. It's a hallway.* She took one halting step and then another. *Breathe.*

Thirty seconds later, the hallway ended in a carbon copy of the other wooden entry door. She opened it six inches and peered through. There was a ladder, maybe one hundred feet high, also made of wood. Looking up, the ladder led to a diminutive, sky-high platform that connected to a rickety rope bridge. In the dim light, she couldn't see what was on the other end of the rope bridge.

To her right, at eye level, there was a glass barrier and below, a well-lit cavern filled with large spiders and venomous snakes. The spiders looked like giant banana tarantulas and the snakes were either coiled or slithering around on the floor. Did the snakes eat the spiders and, if so, how often did they need to replenish the spiders?

Looking around, she surmised that they had designed these tests so that the way out was to continue. Samuel's voice resonated again: *Going in is the only way out.* Heights, snakes, and spiders were not an issue for her, but she knew Will would have a hard time with the heights. And Bear wasn't allowed to test. This was up to her.

She took a last look into the pit and started climbing. The wooden ladder felt sturdy under her hands and feet. The rungs were smooth. She was grateful for the lack of splinters. It took her a while to climb to the top. Indeed, it was a tall ladder. Once there, the platform was larger than it had looked from below, maybe six-feet square.

She didn't linger but started across the rope bridge. It had slippery wooden slats across the bottom and ropes on either side to hold on to at hand level. Even though she wasn't necessarily afraid of heights, it was a long way down, so she kept reminding herself to keep her eye on the prize—the platform on the other side of the chasm, which she could see from up here.

As she moved along the bridge, she slipped once on the wooden slats, then twice. But she held on to the rope and made it across.

On the far side of what she now called "Spider Chasm," she sat, caught her breath, and enjoyed her first success. She recalled from rumors that the next test was a drop into a pool of water far below.

She wanted to build on her momentum and didn't delay. Instead, she followed the platform for about fifteen feet and through an arched doorway. On this side of the arch, the platform became a pirate's plank, complete with a dark, deadly sea below.

As she stared down, she guessed that the water below was about the same distance down as she had climbed up the ladder. Far. But not Acapulco-diver far. *And no sharks*, she smiled to herself. She could do this.

But Will? Will would hate this one, too. Would he even make it this far? Doubtful. She was afraid, but it was a normal sort of fear, wondering how far below she'd land and on what. *Going in is the only way out.* Knees quaking a little, she reminded herself that the waterfall in Spain they had plunged over was probably twice as high. That helped and she jumped.

After a heartbeat, she landed in a large pool of water, feet first. She had done it! The water was cool but not cold. After her exertions so far, it felt refreshing. She floated for a moment, glad to be done with that test.

A small light beaconed and she swam over to it. As she neared, she could see that it was an oil lamp, with a towel and change of clothes laid out for her, along with a glass of water and a snack of dates and almonds. Her belly grumbled, so she took advantage of the food and drink and looked around.

There it was—another door. Three tests. The third and final door.

In her stomach, the butterflies started dancing again. She stood and went through the door. In this room, cut into the stone wall, there was only a narrow dark tunnel and another oil lamp flickering on the wall.

This tunnel. This was what she was afraid of.

She peered into it. There was no light. It was four feet high, but had heard it narrowed. Argh, she'd have to crawl or slither on her belly. Pulling the lamp off the wall, she knelt down and thrust it into the tunnel but couldn't see the end. The tunnel narrowed. She could get trapped in there, not be able to turn around. The earth could crush her.

Her heart slammed in her chest, her breathing got shallow, and her face felt flushed. She tried to quiet her mind like her father had taught them when they were young. It didn't work on her mind or her body.

Panicked, she knelt at the opening, rigid and frozen with fear.

CHAPTER 36

9:50 a.m.:

When it was his turn to test, Will walked up to the ladder and stood there, dumbstruck. Samuel, the male guardian, had told him the only way out was in, but Will wasn't so sure. Couldn't he just turn around and walk back out?

The firelight from the torches made eerie shadows on the spider and snake pit. Looking into the pit with his forehead pressed to the glass and his breath uneven, he felt inadequate. He wanted a smoke. This wasn't going to go well.

Earlier in the week, the three of them had talked about how everybody handled their fears in their own way. Bear had a dogged, small steps desensitization-type approach, and Maddy had a just-do-it-if-you-can't-avoid-it approach. Will decided he was just going to do it. Hell, in a few hundred years, would it matter? He'd be long dead.

The wooden rung of the ladder felt slippery in his palm. While he climbed, he focused on his hands and kept reminding himself that he'd die someday anyway. If this didn't kill him. Halfway up, he started to hyperventilate. Pausing, he wrapped one arm around the rung and held on tight with his other hand.

Then he made the mistake of looking down into the pit.

Will began to shake. He looked across the chasm and, with an almost fatal attraction, again looked down. The view made him lightheaded, nauseous, and he vomited. The splat of his breakfast hitting the ground sounded loud in his ears. *I can't do this.*

Frustration and embarrassment overwhelmed him, nearly to the point of tears. As fear warred with determination, his hand reached out and grabbed the next rung, but his knees were shaking so much that he figured he would die if he continued.

He just couldn't do it. It was so high and he would die. *I'm not safe.* He would fall in the pit and either hit his head or get bitten by one of the creepy crawlies. Surely Maddy would make it through.

Feeling sick, disappointed, and despondent, he crawled back down the ladder.

CHAPTER 37

10:05 a.m.:

D eep in the heart of the Jerusalem Testing Society, Maddy knelt at the mouth of the tunnel and stared into it with the lamp from the wall. How was she going to make it through to the other side? To find the *châsse* and the truth about why her father was murdered, she had to find a way. After another deep breath, she stood and put the wall lamp back in its sconce.

She was having an emotional reaction. Or overreaction. *Why am I so afraid of small spaces? This is completely irrational.* When had this fear started?

Just outside the blasted tunnel, she sat down, brought her knees to her chest, and again stared into the darkness. *Going in is the only way out.* Was Samuel talking literally or metaphorically? Some of the other students had talked about going into their fears to eliminate them and maybe that's what he meant. It hadn't sounded like a good idea at the time the students had mentioned it, but she was desperate. Also, if memory served, her aikido sensei had mentioned the same process once.

It was worth a try. Closing her eyes, she turned off her thoughts and began to let herself feel. She focused on the tendrils of fear in her face, her hands. Her face was a bonfire. Her eyes flew open. *I can't do this.* There had to be another way. As she looked into the depths of the tunnel, she couldn't will herself to enter it.

With no better choice, she took a few deep breaths, looked around, reminded herself that she was safe sitting here, and closed her eyes again. With her mind, she reached out to sense the fire in her face. It was anger. *Go in to it, go on in.* Grrrrrrrrr. Her hands and arms tensed. Tight. Tight. The heat subsided and a tide receded from her face.

There, what was that sensation in her stomach? Heavy. Cold. Her heart, too.

Someone…*who was it?*…was holding her down and pushing her into a closet. Although it was a memory, she could smell the cologne. Old Spice. She tried to shrink in on herself. Inside the closet, it seemed the house was falling down on top of her.

Out!

She wanted to get out.

But couldn't. The door—it was locked. She pushed on the door. Whimpered. Feeling ensnared, caught like a wolf in a trap, she began to cry.

She breathed into the feeling, the stuck feeling. Really felt it. No resistance. She let herself sob. Sank into being trapped.

Sometime later, the feeling shifted—*I am free.* \

The weight left her chest in a rush.

Relaxed and surprised, she opened her eyes, stunned. It had worked!

Wow—that memory must have been from when she was young, perhaps five years old. Dazed, looking into the darkness, she sensed pieces falling into place. Pieces of her psyche that she'd forgotten about, or buried. No wonder she was afraid of small spaces. As a child, she'd been locked in a closet, multiple times. She'd carried that baggage around far too long.

But she was an adult now. An adult who could break out of a cursed closet if she needed to. *I am free.*

The tunnel called to her, challenged her to test her newfound sense of balance. She took a deep breath and crawled into the tunnel on her hands and knees. Like a mantra, she repeated *I'm free, I'm free.* The floor was smooth, as were the walls. No light entered the tunnel but it also didn't get any smaller, for which she thanked all the gods and goddesses she could think of. That must have been a rumor.

After crawling for two long minutes, she noticed a bit of light bouncing off a wall ahead. As she crawled farther, she could see that the tunnel curved to the left. She quickened her pace.

The end of the tunnel was fitted with a door that held a tiny round window. The exit gave to her gentle push and she was out, into the light and into Edith's arms, laughing and wiping a few more tears from her cheeks.

CHAPTER 38

7:00 p.m.:

Will sat at the dinner table and looked around to see who was missing and who had passed at the Jerusalem Testing Society. Although he had failed, the Guardians had told him that since Maddy had passed, as her twin, he had another hour to decide if he was going to stay through her duel.

Or, he could take the safe route and wait for her in Jerusalem. Based on their body language, it seemed they were encouraging him to leave, for his own safety.

He wanted to be there for Maddy, help if he could. But was it safe here if he stayed? Was it any safer above?

Some people were missing from the long table. The faces that remained wore expressions of relief and pleasure. He had heard two other guys, like him, had failed on the heights and weren't there. Joy was gone, too.

Tonight's fish was delicate and delicious, served in a light cream sauce. The prohibition against alcohol had been lifted for the evening, and Will enjoyed the wine served with the fish, a decent chardonnay.

"Joy failed at the bridge," Juergen said with his German accent. "It was touch and go for me on that bridge, too. Can't say I blame her."

Maddy's eyes were glued to him. "You slipped and hung by one arm over the pit?"

"Ya, I did slip. The one-arm part may have happened for a moment. It's all a bit of a blur."

"It's amazing that you were able to pull yourself hand over hand to the far side!"

"I didn't want to land in that viper pit!"

Although Juergen was trying to make light of it, his face was pale and his eyes were pinched. He looked stressed.

Bear looked uncomfortable at the way Maddy oozed over Juergen. Not much Will could do about that heartbreak, though.

Will took another drink of wine, looked over, and caught Hana looking at him. She winked, startling him. He grinned back, happy that she had passed. Maybe she'd be willing to hook up with him again if he stuck around—

That same intense mix of guilty pleasure stirred as memories of making love with Maria warred with more recent visions of Hana. His heart beat faster and his vision blurred for a moment. Pleasure. But too much guilt. No, he couldn't do it.

Will focused with an effort and recalled his walk of shame from the ladder back into the room with Samuel. While ushering Will out, the guardian had reminded him that because they were twins, if Maddy passed, he could stay if he chose. Although, Samuel warned Will that the dangers for him were not necessarily over. The caution in Samuel's eyes was clear: If Will didn't leave after dinner tonight, he was committed for the duration of Maddy's time here.

Juergen cracked a self-deprecating joke and Hana laughed. With the firelight reflected in her long blonde hair and her blue eyes lit with amusement, she looked like an angel. So different from Maria, yet so lovely. Much had happened since Maria's death. It already seemed like a long time ago. The king's words about finding love again came back to him and the sadness in his heart swelled anew. He was in no way ready for love. Even if Hana was willing, what had happened once could not happen again. He sighed.

The end of dinner came and the group moved to a side room to play some cards. Should he stay? Maddy might need his help. He'd gotten pretty decent with his knives. Will gave up on the idea of leaving the underground complex and followed Hana, watching her hips as she walked.

CHAPTER 39

July 7, 8:30 a.m.:

The next morning, the seventh day of their time at the Jerusalem Testing Society, Edith popped her head into the dining room and grabbed Maddy, Bear, and Will. Time had run out and today was the day of the duel.

Maddy didn't feel ready and never would if "ready" meant killing someone. She had never had to use her aikido skills in a dangerous setting and wasn't ready to now, even though she'd implied she was when fighting about it with Will. She felt like a bamboo practice staff broken in two parts, knowing she needed to pass the test so they could find the *châsse*, but also knowing that killing was anathema in her heart and in her aikido practice.

She felt almost dizzy, as if she were floating. When Edith grabbed her elbow, Maddy's stomach went cold. *Stare death in the face*, she remembered Samuel saying.

"Come this way. Come with me," Edith fluttered.

"Weapon or no weapon?" Maddy asked.

"Sorry, no weapon."

Maddy handed her swords to Will and followed Edith on a surreal walk into a round room shaped like a small amphitheater. There was a circular box of sand in the center. A decorated, domed ceiling was held aloft by thick stone columns, the same sandstone material used in the rest of the underground compound. Extra oil lamps lit the space, so that the lighting was nearly as bright as what Maddy recalled to be the light of day.

After leading Maddy to the center of the sand, Edith motioned for Bear and Will to sit on wooden benches near Samuel. They were the only occupants in the amphitheater, which lent the space a vacant, hollow feeling.

Since she was closer to the domed ceiling now, Maddy squinted to see the multitude of blue-and-white tiles that lined the dome. The effect was gorgeous. Was it the last thing of beauty she'd ever see? Or, for that matter, just the *last* thing she'd view?

Samuel rang a bell. A young man entered from a black wooden door on the other side of the room and walked calmly over to stand in front of Maddy. She searched his narrowed brown eyes for a long moment, seeking something...kindness? Compassion? Mercy? Instead, there was icy hatred, and her hope of getting out of this with them both alive dwindled away with the smoke of the oil lamps.

She studied the rest of him, now as an opponent. He wore a black T-shirt and blue jeans with standard workman boots. His clothes signaled nothing, but his muscled arms and chest captured her attention and told her the guy was strong. Probably aggressive. Her hackles rose.

In a voice that filled the empty space in the amphitheater, Samuel announced, "This is a fight to the death. By the laws of this land, this man is a convicted terrorist."

The man spit in the sand. Maddy questioned if he was a criminal. In Jerusalem, it didn't take much to get on the wrong side of the law.

"He has chosen this fight over twenty more years in prison. Today, death or freedom is his fate. Fight well and fight with honor."

That was the end of the speech. Years of training took hold. She took a deep breath, relaxed her body, took a neutral stance, and watched Black T-shirt Man for his first move. Her body and mind became laser-focused. *Okay, Mr. Death, I see your face and I spit in your eye.*

The bell tolled again and, as Maddy had guessed he would, the man wasted no time in attacking her. She used her aikido skills to turn and let him flow by, like a bull chasing the red cape. He stopped himself, turned, grew red in the face, and rushed her, arms outstretched to grab her. As she'd practiced a thousand times, she grabbed both his forearms and pushed him down as he sped toward her. His momentum forced him into a flip. He landed on his back with a hard *thunk* on the sand.

He tried kicking out at her, but she backed away. He cursed, jacked into a crouch, and came at her again from down low, pulling a knife from his boot as he moved in.

Surprised at his use of a weapon, she was too slow to move, and it cost her. The knife caught her right upper thigh. It sliced deep before she twirled out of the way.

The pain was sudden and intense.

Instinctively, she clapped her palm to the cut, and it came away bright with her blood. Adrenaline filled her. The pain in her leg said, *This is no show*.

He faltered, dark eyes locked on her bloody hand. Then he steeled himself and sprinted forward. As he came at her again, she ignored the pain in her thigh, turned to the side, grabbed his blade arm, and twisted his wrist in a knife-disarming move she'd also practiced time and time again. He cried out in pain and dropped the weapon.

She pulled his arm behind his back, twisted more, and he fell to his knees, back arched, helpless in the sand.

Keeping one hand on his wrist in the hold, she leaned over and picked up the knife. Maddy weighed it in her hand to kill him, to end this, and move on. However, it felt wrong, heavy, like she'd grabbed a venomous snake. The blade had her blood on it and grains of sand. She wiped it on her thigh, below the cut, to clean the metal. The lamplight caught the edge for a moment, sparkling off the steel.

With resolve, she tightened her grip on the handle and on him. A small whimper escaped his throat. He was as human as she was, probably scared, too.

She had to kill him, or she and Will would be hunted forever. And the Russians would find the *châsse*, and get all that power. Was one life a fair trade to maintain world peace?

She moved the edge of the knife to the side of his throat and a fine stripe of blood blossomed against the silver blade, red ink ready to cross out the thin line of a life.

His pulse beat in time with hers. She could smell his fear. He was so alive. Time slowed.

Doubt filled her. Was he *really* a terrorist? She pictured the look in his eyes when he saw her blood. Her gut ached with the wrongness of the situation and anger overtook her.

"No!" Maddy yelled.

She yanked the knife from his throat and threw it into the black wooden door, where the blade stuck, hilt vibrating like the tail of a rattlesnake. The loud *thwang* reverberated throughout the hushed silence, a single chord of a stringed instrument plucked in a hushed concert hall.

Released, the man collapsed face-first, into the sand.

Maddy put both hands on her hips and faced Samuel. "I won't kill this man. Fail me if you must."

CHAPTER 40

July 8, 9:15 a.m.:

The next day, in the common dining room of the Testing Society, Bear sat across from Maddy and admired her. How she had managed to bring perfume with her on this trip he had no idea. She smelled divine and looked good, too, sitting there after breakfast, sipping her tea, watching the conversation next to them. Her long, black hair was tied back in her signature ponytail, her twin swords peeked out over her shoulders in a sexy, female-warrior look, and her gorgeous emerald eyes…they looked tranquil, the most relaxed he'd seen since they'd started this adventure back at the Fire Sign Café. She was probably glad the testing and duel were behind her, and maybe she'd grown a bit in the process.

Bear, however, was still on guard and kept part of his attention on the door.

He thought back to yesterday. The Guardians had shuffled them all out of the amphitheater after her dramatic refusal to kill her opponent, and they all worried that she hadn't passed. In the light of failure, he'd considered going home.

Then he wondered how an aborted mission would affect his prospects with VanOps, a clandestine group operating under the CIA's Department of Extreme Threats (DET). The director of the group had arranged for him to come on this mission. He wished he could tell Maddy about VanOps, but he was sworn to secrecy that evening at Jake's, his favorite lakeside restaurant. Home for him wasn't a good option.

While Edith shot up Maddy's wound with a local and dressed it with fifteen stitches, Will had argued with Maddy about what a stupid test it was. Eventually, Samuel had come in smiling and, together with Edith, told them Maddy had passed, that this was a test of compassion as much as martial arts skill. Bear's shoulders had almost dropped to the floor with relief, although he was still a bit angry at the ruse and could tell Maddy felt the same way. Nobody liked being played.

He brought his attention back to the table and wished like hell they had sweet tea here. This Mediterranean mint tea wasn't bad, but it wasn't great either. He scanned the room for threats. Nothing. Yet the hair on the back of his neck tingled like it had in the fight zone when something was about to go down. Why? Someone said something Maddy found funny. She laughed and then turned to look at him with a smile.

Bear smiled, too. "I'm proud of you for making it through the testin' and that duel. I'm especially proud you didn't kill that guy. Seemed like a trumped-up and just-plain-wrong situation to me, so I'm glad you read it right."

"Thanks, Bear. That was kind of a jacked-up exam, testing compassion that way. What if I had made a different choice?"

"Good question. I wonder if they tell you or just fail you."

"Probably fail you with blood on your hands. I'm still a little pissed off about it."

"Understandable. I would be, too. How are the stitches?"

"Starting to itch."

She went back to her tea, and he drank off some of his own while looking around the room. His gaze fell on Will, who was sitting in the corner with Hana. They made a good-looking couple. Will's dark curly hair and tan skin contrasted with Hana's pale skin and blonde hair.

Mulling over the entire week, he wasn't surprised that Will hadn't passed, but Bear had hoped to be wrong. His time in the marines had taught him to take fast stock of a man, and Will was an intellectual, not a man used to his body or his feelings. He figured Will could pick up the knife with some practice, but it wouldn't be easy. Will had improved a bit this week but still had a long way to go.

Maddy was ostensibly listening again to the conversation next to them, but Bear knew she was watching Juergen. What she saw in him, Bear had no idea. Sure, the guy was tall and handsome, but afraid of a little snake? Or heights?

He scoffed to himself, recalling marine training exercises jumping out of airplanes.

And Juergen hadn't handled the embarrassment of his story well. Bear could sense the German was on edge, watching Will and Hana giggling in the corner. Will spun his flashlight around his finger as they talked. At least Juergen didn't seem interested in Maddy. He seemed interested in the blonde, Hana, as did Will. Bear suspected Hana was a rebound honey to hide Will's pain of losing Maria. The engineer wasn't processing his grief, another problem with being an intellectual.

Out of the corner of his eye, Bear spied five figures wearing black clothes and matching midnight balaclavas. They rushed through the doorway in a tight wedge formation, wielding knives, swords, and staffs. All hell broke loose—the vanguard figure wounded a student, blood spiked into the air, and the other four began attacking the remaining students.

Bear swore. This was no test, or perhaps the ultimate test. Probably that evil "surprise" the Guardians had mentioned when they first met.

Moving fast, he upended the table so that Maddy was behind him, protected by the wood. "Get down!"

He grabbed his staff. She unsheathed her swords. Stubborn woman.

Then one of the figures was upon him, swinging a staff of his own. Wood met wood with a force that made Bear's hands ache. He had a brief moment to be grateful for the week's practice before he lost himself in the focus of the fight.

They whirled and danced. The attacker thrust his staff up toward Bear's chin. Bear tilted his head back and swung his *jo* like a baseball bat. It cracked into the attacker's pole, knocking it from its trajectory. Bear followed up with a one-handed blow which landed on his foe's left shoulder.

The assailant grunted and thrust his own staff, which landed in Bear's ribs, provoking a groan of pain. The attacker tried to follow up with a swing to the head, but Bear pulled some aikido out of his memory and twisted away and toward the man.

As Bear fell forward, he was able to do a vital point strike to the enemy's temple. Bear's heart sank as the staff struck home and the black-swathed figure collapsed to the ground, lifeless. Bear knew it was self-defense but never liked to kill.

With his man down, he looked around to see how he could help. Will threw a knife from behind his table, taking an attacker in the shoulder. Hana had smartly taken cover behind the same table. She darted out and threw her knife into the chest of the man that Will had slowed. That finished him. One other assailant was lying on the floor in a pool of blood on the other side of the room. There were two left.

Maddy jumped over their table and fought the last two intruders alone. Her ponytail flew as she wielded her swords, warding off the attack.

Bear snarled and jumped to her aid. One man had a sword and the other, the one closest to Bear, had a knife. Wielding his staff like a lance, Bear lunged toward the knife-bearing opponent and caught him in the chest. The man had been focused on Maddy, so Bear caught him by surprise, but that advantage only lasted a second.

Fury blazing in his dark eyes, the man attacked with a quick viciousness that made Bear call up every ounce of training he'd ever had. The antagonist darted in and out of Bear's range with the speed of a hummingbird—landing a surface cut on Bear's arm before he could get the staff around.

But once Bear realized his opponent's style, he shifted gears, pursued a more defensive approach, and waited for an opening. Time and again Bear countered the aggressive stabbing with his quarterstaff. Each time, the man's knife whizzed through the air with speed that left tracers across Bear's sight.

After half a minute of hard parrying that made his arms ache and left numerous blade scars on his staff, Bear saw his chance. The man's eyes flitted toward another of Will's knife throws. The missile flew by the assailant's head and distracted him for just long enough that Bear was able to jab the quarterstaff at his neck. The strike landed solidly against the side of the tango's vertebrae and he crumpled to the floor, either paralyzed or dead.

Bear turned to see if Maddy needed additional support. She avoided a thrust from the last attacker by turning her body sideways at the last instant. Frustrated, the man came at her again, swinging for her head. Maddy blocked his sword and moved aside.

As Bear waited for a way to help, a strange mixture of worry and pride filled his chest. She danced away three more times. Then the intruder swung at her midsection. Maddy tried to parry his swing, but he was too strong and both swords got knocked out of her hands. She had no weapon!

The attacker, sensing an advantage, rushed in with an overhead chop. As the sword came down, Maddy gripped the attacker's arm and the dull side of his blade. They paused in that position for a second, then she reached up, grabbed him by the nape of his neck, and flung him forward. She pounced on him and pinned him to the floor.

Bear rushed over and briskly struck the man's temple. The assailant's eyes closed in slow motion, like a curtain going down at the end of a theater production.

Maddy's eyes were wide and her voice high. "Did you kill him? You didn't kill him, did you?"

The fallen man's chest moved.

"No, the bastard lives," Bear growled, annoyed at her intimation that he'd done something wrong when he was just trying to keep her safe.

Maddy heaved a sigh of relief but her eyes remained wide. "Good."

"Your aikido honor code is gonna get you in trouble someday. Death happens."

Pissed at whoever set up the ambush, cross at his aching rib, angry at the bodies littered around the dining room, and furious that he *had* been forced to kill today, Bear turned and stalked away through the mess of overturned chairs, tables, and blood.

CHAPTER 41

4:25 p.m.:

A knock sounded on the door of Maddy's sandstone room. She was packing her meager possessions and waiting to be called for the final rite of passage at the Testing Society. Still appalled at the fiasco in the dining room, which had claimed the lives of several black-clad attackers, she almost didn't answer the summons.

She was distracted, too. The moment when her opponent had caused her to drop her swords played itself over and over again in her mind's eye, causing her stomach to flip flop. *I'm not fit to teach aikido. I barely got out of that alive.* The knock came again.

Anticipating that it was Edith, Maddy finally said, "Come in."

It was indeed Edith, who wore her usual white garb. "How are you, my dear? How are you? Come, come, it's time for your final rite of passage."

Maddy's tone was cold. "I'm not sure I'm up for much more excitement today, Edith. How was all that necessary?"

"Yes, yes, it was quite essential," Edith twittered.

"Really? An attack without warning? Bear may have cracked a rib. Other students are wounded, and attackers are dead."

This final rite also meant their departure from Jerusalem, and she'd probably never see Juergen again. Not that he'd expressed any interest, but she had enjoyed their brief interaction and was sorry to say goodbye. She clenched her teeth.

"Follow me. I'll explain."

Maddy hesitated then painfully gimped down the hall after Edith and into a small side room. The deep ache in her thigh burned with every step. "I hope so. Will or I could have been killed."

A smell of charcoal and something that might have been burned flesh, hung in the air. Near two low-backed chairs, there was a small brazier glowing with red hot coals, and several branding irons were stacked nearby. She noticed one of the irons had a small *signum regis* at the tip. Longingly, she looked at the door and fought back tears. *Please, not this, after everything else.*

Edith motioned to the chairs. "Sit down, sit down. Please."

Maddy sat.

"As we communicated before you chose to stay, our founder had some strong opinions about what this society should test and how. Hundreds of years later, Isabella and Ferdinand agreed with Ramiro's opinions. The power you seek is dangerous, and our job is to protect the world from those who would use it as a destructive force."

Maddy considered this statement, but said nothing.

Edith looked at Maddy with intensity. "The goal has always been to allow only the best students to walk out the door as graduates. Best in this case means that you must be able to control your fear, have compassion, know right from wrong, be able to handle yourself in a life-or-death fight, and be able to handle pain."

"I see."

"Without these qualities, you would either fail farther along in your quest or be a menace to the world by having access to immense power without the necessary empathy to wield it well. All who enter know the risks."

Maddy understood, but part of her felt irate. "I still feel sick that those men died today. Everything we learn in aikido is about nonviolence, blending with the attack, turning others' power and aggression against themselves to find a peaceful resolution."

"And what does your school teach you if you're in a life-or-death struggle with someone? When killing is the only option for your survival and the greater good? There are people and situations in the world that would kill you."

"We have a variety of techniques at our disposal that remove the need to kill an enemy. Actually, aikido is about eliminating even the concept that there is an enemy."

"You did this today, right? You killed no one?"

"I guess." Maddy's tone was surly as she remembered the attacker Bear had knocked out.

"Yet, you still feel angry, guilty? What are you feeling?"

Maddy took a deep breath. Good question. "I'm angry at you, at this school, at Ramiro for setting up that lethal test. And I feel guilty, too. I contributed to the fight."

Edith's eyes held kindness. "I understand. Yet, there may come a day when aikido alone can't help you. What good is aikido against a gun at twenty paces?"

Maddy had no answer.

"Ramiro's world was violent, as is the world we live in today. Also, keep in mind that these men were convicted extremists. They jumped at the chance to be released from prison for one last chance to kill infidels, no matter the cost."

"Are you sure?"

"Yes. And, finally, consider that sometimes the only way to a peaceful end is through death, as some won't stop, or can't be stopped, in any other way. So, in a way, they commit suicide."

"Well, that doesn't align with our philosophy, but it's one way to look at it."

Edith's smile was as enigmatic as Mona Lisa's. "Perception is all, dear child, perception is all. I suggest you try to find a way to look at it that feels better, as you can change your thoughts and perspectives far easier than you can change the past, or someone else's actions."

"You have a point."

Although she hadn't fought as well as she wished, she had disarmed her final opponent without killing him. She couldn't force her beliefs on others. Also, she, Bear, and Will had been warned, and Will had been given the chance to leave after failing the distress test. Besides, how commanding was this power that Ramiro had set up a lethal test to protect it, or to protect the world from it?

Maddy thought back through her family's history. "So only Isabella and Ferdinand have found this power?"

"That's right."

"You said my grandfather, Max, was the last of our line to come here. Why didn't he pass the tests?"

"Is he dead, child?"

"Yes, why?"

"We don't discuss results of the living. But since he's passed on, I can tell you he failed because he killed his opponent in the duel."

"I see." Maddy waved her hand. "Do you even know what this power is that we're after? That others are trying to kill us to obtain?"

"It is not for me to know the details of your quest, but I do suspect it will allow you to access the Field of Power, that which you know as *ki* from your aikido studies, that which surrounds us, is within us, the infinite pulse, the unnameable. Perhaps you can access this field in a unique and powerful way."

Several things about this statement gave Maddy pause. For one, the Field of Power concept resonated with her, it was how she thought of *ki*, but she'd never heard anyone else talk about it that way. Secondly, if it were true you could access the Field of Power in some new way, perhaps the testing was necessary to keep the Power from the wrong hands.

It was essentially the power of the universe. Used as a weapon by those with evil intent, it could spell disaster.

Maddy was embarrassed to admit that she wasn't adept at feeling the power yet, but since her lack of skill was keeping her from moving up the dan ranks and someday becoming a teacher. If this old woman could help, Maddy would swallow her pride and ask. "This Power, do you have any hints about how to access it, practice with it?"

Edith's eyes got a faraway look before she gave Maddy a long, penetrating stare. "This is for the one who comes after us to teach, but you ask, you ask." Edith paused as if making up her mind. "You know the basics of meditation?"

"Yes."

"Did you know your own country's military teaches mindfulness?"

"No."

"Useful for warriors. But never mind, I digress. I sense you struggle with quieting your mind?"

Pressing her lips together, Maddy felt chagrined. How could this woman see through her? "Yes."

"This is the first step. When you meditate, listen. Listen with your whole being. Listen to the trees, the wind, the sounds in the room. Listen to something outside of yourself, as it is difficult to listen and think at the same time. Try it now."

"Now?"

"Yes, you don't need to be sitting with crossed legs, this is just a mental state we're talking about. And to be a warrior, you must have a quiet mind while you fight. You did this well today, but you must practice. Close your eyes for a moment."

Maddy closed her eyes.

"Now listen. Listen to your breathing, or to the fire popping, or to the sound of my voice."

Maddy turned on her ears.

The sounds in the room began to come alive. Edith's voice became more melodious and the crackling of the fire became more intense.

"That's it," Edith encouraged.

How does she know how I'm doing?

"No, whenever you have a thought, just let it pass, and listen."

Maddy stopped trying to figure it out and did as Edith instructed.

"Good," Edith said. Then, a minute later, she continued, "Now, now you may reach out toward the Power. It is there, it is always there, but your mind must be quiet to feel it. See if you can feel it slightly below and behind your navel. It will pulse, like a heartbeat. Feel the Power."

Maddy focused on the spot just below and behind her navel. She'd tried this before, but her mind had always been zooming along at freeway speeds.

Edith's voice was a song. A poem in light. "Listen and feel the Power."

The spot glowed in her mind's eye. A moment later, she felt something. *Was that it?* A small pulse, *thump, thump.*

"That's right," Edith crooned.

Maddy no longer wondered how Edith knew what she was experiencing. She didn't care anymore, she was feeling the Power! Her *ki*, her fire within. She was ecstatic.

Maddy opened her eyes and flew into Edith's arms. "Thank you! Thank you! I've wanted to feel that for so long."

After a good hug, Edith pushed her away and held her at arm's length. "Child, there is much more, yes, much more for you to feel than that tiny flame. We have only ignited the spark of your fire within. The Power of the universe awaits you."

"But you've given me a way to get there."

"Yes, but practice you must. Remember, listen and feel the Power."

Maddy grinned from ear to ear. "I will. Thank you."

Edith motioned to the set of branding irons. "Shall we finish this so that you and your friends can be on your way? There is another who will help you access your power."

Maddy smiled. "Well, at least it's a small brand."

"It is, it is. And I must tell you that you cannot cry out, or you will not pass this final test. If you fail, I will have to cover Ramiro's seal with another, larger brand."

"Why's that?"

"So that you will fool no one, on the off chance you find where you're destined to go, even without the next clue."

Maddy nodded, realizing that this brand served as a ticket to her next stop, her next teacher. "Where does the brand go?"

"On your left shoulder, on top of the blade. Please dear, please remove your shirt."

Maddy took off her shirt and sought the calm of listening that she had just discovered. With her mind quiet, she was aware of all the small details in the room, Edith's breathing, the pop of the fire, the warmth of the room. Resolving to bear the pain in silence, she allowed her thoughts to pass and continued to focus on sounds.

The small fire popped and hissed. After several minutes, soft footsteps padded toward her. "Move your arm, dear, out from your side."

Maddy's flesh was seared with the brand. Aware of the sensation, the burning filled her awareness, she was consumed by it. Heat spread from her shoulder throughout her body. She clenched her teeth, her hands, and her stomach muscles, fighting the urge to flinch. She could *not* cry out.

The moment stretched.

But soon she was able to return awareness to other sounds.

It took a long minute for the pain to move from an intense burning to a duller ache.

Through it all, Maddy remained silent.

At last, Edith touched her arm. "You've passed, dear, you've passed. It's so exciting to have one of Ramiro's own to congratulate."

Edith gave Maddy a brief hug that avoided her branded left shoulder. Afterward, she dressed Maddy's wound with a sweet-smelling ointment.

"Please meet Samuel and me tonight around seven thirty back in the office, so that we can send you on your way."

As she left the room, Maddy was determined to find her next teacher, discover the answers they sought, and if Will was right, keep the Power of the Aragon *Châsse* from the hands of the Russians.

CHAPTER 42

7:35 p.m.:

Back in the room they had visited when they first arrived at the Jerusalem Testing Society, Will stood next to Bear and Maddy to receive a final farewell from the Guardians.

Will drummed his fingers against his thigh. Sweat trickled down his brow into his left eye.

Samuel looked at the three of them in turn. "Bear, you are truly brave. A fearless warrior and an excellent bodyguard. You have represented yourself well here."

Bear nodded his thanks. His blue eyes held a thoughtful expression.

"William. Although you have more to learn about dealing with your fears and your grief, be encouraged. Your skills with the knife have come along, and you handled yourself well in the surprise test of the five attackers. You are loyal and courageous."

Will relaxed and felt his chest warm with the praise.

Samuel went on in his deep voice, "As Maddy's twin, you may yet have a larger role to play in the quest. When dealing with your fears, remember the only way out is in." Samuel then turned to look at Maddy. "Ah, Maddy. As you can see, not many make it to where you sit now. You have the royal sign of your ancestor gracing your shoulder and the pride of knowing your own strength, alongside the humbleness of your compassion. You've done well and deserve to see how the next step of your journey will unfold."

Maddy's olive-colored eyes burned with pleasure at the compliment.

With thin fingers, Samuel reached into a drawer and pulled out a gold-worked metal cylinder, about thirty centimeters long and just three wide, which he handed to Maddy. She examined it from top to bottom, tugged off an end cap, and removed a piece of paper.

Will found the cylinder fascinating. He'd never seen anything like it.

"Find the center of the Pagan Empire," Maddy read aloud.

Will figured that, since this clue was in the hands of the Guardians, they would write the words in the appropriate language. But he'd never heard of a Pagan Empire. He, Maddy, and Bear exchanged a puzzled glance.

"It is…yes, it is most appropriate for you to discuss what the clue means after you depart the school. Tradition indicates that you may each take a weapon with you if you like," Edith said.

Will's hands itched to touch the cylinder, so he reached his hand out to Maddy, who handed it to him.

Part of him was aware of Maddy and Bear discussing swords, knives, and staffs, but most of his attention was fixed on the outside of the cylinder. There appeared to be intricate bas-relief images of tiny lines floating in the air above some small trees.

Lines, or are they tiny obelisks, like what we saw in that codex back at the castle? Are they floating? Floating…what types of things might float?

Ever the engineer, he started to consider the lifting Meissner effect of superconductors, when he was interrupted by Maddy. "Will, give it back. It's time to go."

Will let go of the cylinder with reluctance. She pulled it from his hands and replaced it with one of the throwing knives he liked. He made one last mental snapshot of the cylinder as he let it go. Maddy gave the cylinder back to Samuel.

The loss of the cylinder brought Will back to the present. While he contemplated their next steps, he had two ideas. "May I have a piece of paper and do you mind if we take a photograph of this cylinder?"

Samuel and Edith exchanged a glance. "Yes, you may," Samuel replied, while he handed Will a piece of paper and a pen.

"Will, what are you doing?" Maddy asked.

"I'll tell you later. Bear, can you get a pic of that cylinder with your GoPro?" Will wrote on the paper, folded it, put it in his pocket, and passed the pen back to Samuel.

Bear pulled the GoPro off of his shoulder and made quick work of a few snapshots.

When Bear was finished, Will said, "Thank you."

Hugs and handshakes were spread around. Maddy and Bear both picked up quarterstaffs, and Will put his "souvenir" throwing knife in the arm scabbard underneath his sleeve.

They walked out of the office, back into the chamber of doors.

Samuel put his arm on Will's back. "You all have more to learn on this path and will find a wise teacher to complete your education. Go safely—remember to *listen*."

Will wondered what *listening* was. Probably just meditating. The door closed behind them. He sent a guilty farewell to Hana, glad he hadn't slept with her again.

"I'm just glad it's over," Maddy said.

Will looked at Maddy. "Me, too. But now that we're headed back to the real world, think we'll run into the Russians or Prince Carlos on our way to the Pagan Empire?"

CHAPTER 43

8:15 p.m.:

After saying goodbye to the Guardians in the office at the Testing Society, it didn't take Maddy, Will, and Bear long to go back through the chamber of doors and out through the dark wooden portal with the old king's sign.

The passageway back to the Dome seemed much as she had remembered it, a narrow, winding tunnel lit by the dancing beam of Will's flashlight. The difference was that it felt shorter. That was usually the way of things—to Maddy, it always seemed to take less time when she was leaving because she'd traveled that way once before.

When they arrived at the small side passageway that they had discovered a long week ago, Maddy had Will hold up. "Wait here a sec, Will. Can I borrow your flashlight?" When he handed it to her, she took it and lit up the side tunnel. "What's going to happen if we try going out through the mosque at this hour?"

Will checked his watch.

Is that a Rolex? Good grief, is he doing that well with his career? He always did like the finer things in life.

"That's a good point, Maddy. The temple closed for Western visitors hours ago. We'd get arrested, or shot."

Bear motioned with his staff and the muscles in his chest moved under his shirt in the shadow of the flashlight. "Are you thinking of trying this tunnel?"

She was starting to appreciate how Bear seemed to understand her, sometimes even more than her own twin brother. "I think it'd be safer, yes."

Just then, the sound of lightly running feet from the passageway behind them became obvious. Before Maddy had a chance to think that it might be someone dangerous, Hana's pale face burst into their circle of light from beyond the shadows. "Hey, wait for me!"

Will pushed around Maddy and Bear. "Hana!" He gave her a hug.

Maddy groaned to herself. Hana's company on their quest was the last thing they needed. She'd be nothing but a distraction.

"I was hoping I could come with you, just for dinner, before we part ways," Hana said.

"Sure, why not?" Will looked at Bear and Maddy for confirmation, his wide, lopsided smile illustrating his pleasure at seeing Hana.

If it was just for dinner...

Maddy shrugged and Bear nodded in acquiescence.

"We were just talking about heading up this side tunnel," Will told Hana. "I'm guessing it will come out in the square in front of the Temple Mount."

"Good idea," Hana said.

Will pulled a piece of paper from his pocket. "One more thing. Hana, you probably remember that I told you that we had some people— Russians, we suspect—trying to kill us." Hana nodded and Will continued, looking at each member of the group. "In case we run into them, I wrote a false clue about our next destination."

Maddy's eyebrow rose at Will's resourcefulness, amused that he was showing off for Hana. The false clue idea was clever.

In the beam of his flashlight, Will revealed what he had written: *Find the center of the Spanish Empire.* "I figure that will throw them off if they find us again."

Bear slapped him on the back. "Good work, Will. Great to have a quick-thinking engineer around. I like that being-prepared streak of yours."

Hana took the news of Russian killers in stride and asked no questions. Maybe she was too brave for her own good. But, after all, she had passed her own family's version of the tests. Maddy was curious about how Hana's gauntlet may have been different and wished there was more freedom to discuss it.

"I agree. Excellent idea. Now, shall we get out of this warren? I'd like to see some sky," Maddy said.

Hearing murmurs of agreement, Maddy headed up the tunnel, flashlight beam leading the way.

Where the other passage had been wide enough for two or three to walk abreast, this tunnel was a single-file affair and the top of it not much taller than she was. Maddy wished she hadn't gone first, as there were lots of spider webs. After getting two pesky, sticky webs in her face, she started to use her quarterstaff as a sweep.

She missed her swords but figured twin swords on her shoulders, or any sword for that matter, would mark her as trouble. The quarterstaffs would hopefully pass as hikers' walking sticks and would have to do. This one was coming in handy for the time being.

The narrow path led upward in a gentle slope. She had never learned how all the food made it down to the Testing Society and suspected side tunnels like this were used to deliver supplies.

After walking for just another minute, she came face-to-face with an old-fashioned, heavy but plain, standard-sized door. It had a weighted, auto-close mechanism that looked as if it locked securely from the inside. Good, she didn't need to worry about exposing the Society to unnecessary intruders.

Maddy opened the door an inch and peered out. They were outside the main plaza, in a side court. The Dome of the Rock was in front of her, beyond a green-fenced fountain and a set of arches. It was a gold-tipped island surrounded by a sea of space. The sky looked dusky and the plaza seemed to hold only religious ghosts.

She turned to the others. "Right again, Will. The plaza is out there. I'm guessing we're near a side door of that other mosque, I think it was called 'al-Aqsa.'"

"Yeah, I remember that," Will whispered. "Where's the gate that we entered from in the Western Wall?"

"The Mughrabi Gate must be around to the left. So, what's our plan?" Maddy asked.

"I say we waltz out of here like we own the place." Bear leaned on his staff, grinning like a rascal. "Then head into the Old City for some dinner."

"I'm getting hungry, too." Will nodded and Hana's head bounced along in unison. "But be careful."

Maddy saw nothing wrong with the plan. "All righty. Here we go."

She turned off the flashlight and opened the door wide. As she walked through it, she imagined that she was the president stepping out of Air Force One. That image made her feel more like she had a right to be here and less like she was skulking around.

Once out in the air, she took a deep breath, appreciating the fresh coolness of the evening. The Dome shone in the half light above her, gorgeous in its dominion over the plaza.

She skirted the flank of the mosque, walking along its side toward the Dome. She kept an eye out for trouble.

After about a hundred paces, she turned a corner. Their goal was a single-arched gate across the stone-lined plaza. Bear, Will, and Hana caught up with her, and she turned left, heading for the dark mouth of the portal, walking along the tall stone arches of the structure.

Soon, the group left the protective mosque wall and headed into the open court. Few people were about.

When they were about halfway to the gate, Maddy felt Will and Hana hang back. She turned. They stood next to each other, looking up. Will pointed at something. Maddy glanced that direction. The sky was beginning to darken and a thin crescent moon had risen, hanging over the Dome's right-hand edge.

A crack broke the night's silence. Stone chips from the plaza floor bit into her leg. Bear had already grabbed her elbow and was yelling "Run!" by the time she realized shots were being fired.

Maddy ran for her life! Her thigh and shoulder burned anew as she sprinted toward safety.

As they rushed toward the gate, Bear ran between the shooter and her, protecting her. Brief flashes came from a set of arches on the other side of the trees, in the direction of the Dome. *Thunk!* She could hear bullets thudding into the old stone wall behind her.

The darkness of the gate beckoned, and she and Bear rushed through. Missing Will and Hana, she immediately turned. Her heart sank. Hana was lying on the ground, Will's hand to her neck, checking her pulse. "Will!"

As she peered back through the trees for the source of the violence, Maddy saw a single weapon spitting fire. A man, clad in black, was barely visible. He strode toward them.

"Will! He's coming!" Maddy yelled.

Will dropped the false clue and dashed for the gate. Sirens sounded, not far away.

"She's dead! Hana's dead!" Will panted, blood on his cheek, as he thrust himself through the gate like a sprinter crossing the finish line.

Bear pulled Will farther into the shadows and shut the faded-green wooden door, unsuccessfully attempting to lock it. "Nothing you can do for her now. C'mon!"

In front of them was the covered Mughrabi Gate Bridge. With its peaked roof and wood supports, it reminded Maddy of gold-mining era covered bridges from California. Charming though it was, she knew they'd be sitting ducks in there unless they moved.

They ran for it.

The timber ramp was deserted. Their footfalls sounded loud in the twilight. Maddy skidded a sharp ninety degrees to the left, nearly ran into an old man wearing a suit and a black *kippah* on his head, sprinted down the straightaway, turned a small corner that led more steeply downhill, and glimpsed the opening. Her thigh ached.

Before their feet left the wooden planks, Bear halted and put his arm out to stop them. "Listen. I don't think we're being followed."

They listened. No footsteps, no gunshots.

"Maybe he was happy getting the fake clue. I can't believe they killed Hana." Will's voice broke and his chest heaved.

"Maybe the police have scared him off." Maddy's breath came in gasps, too.

Poor Will, another loss.

With tenderness, she reached out and wiped the blood off his cheek.

Bear was not breathing hard. "How'd they find us? Could Carlos have known we'd be here?"

Maddy walked briskly through the opening and headed right, into the heart of the Old City. "No clue. Still, let's get out of here."

"Agreed," Bear said. "If we're still being followed, let's hope the town is enough of a jungle to throw 'em off."

CHAPTER 44

Jerusalem, Old City, Armenian Quarter, July 8, 9:30 p.m.:

Inside a noisy internet café deep in the heart of Jerusalem's Armenian Quarter, Will leaned over a sink and fought back the bile in his throat. They were on the run again. Worse, he was sick about losing Hana.

He had been standing next to her, looking at the crescent moon, when the bullet whizzed through the air and struck her in the forehead. The mental image was gruesome. Will wished he could have done something, anything, to stop it.

In the restroom, with pain roiling inside his gut, he felt sucker punched. After wiping the rest of the blood off his cheek, he almost started to cry, overwhelmed with grief all over again. Something held the tears back, and he splashed cool water over his face to clear his head and emotions.

Eventually, he threaded his way around men smoking water pipes to the small table where Bear and Maddy sat. They had wraps and Armenian coffee in demitasse cups. Except Bear, who had ordered his usual iced tea.

The smoke from the water pipes reeked and burned Will's eyes. A single tear stole out of his left tear duct. Wiping it away, he made an impulsive decision to quit smoking. After all, he'd made it for a week without a smoke and didn't miss it as much as he feared he would.

In the back of the café, the mood at the table was somber. Will sat down, sipped at his coffee, and just stared at his beef and pepper wrap. He wasn't hungry. *Hana was a hell of a fine woman.*

Maddy reached over and grabbed his hand. "I'm so sorry, Will. And I know words just don't cut it. I'll miss her, too."

A tapping sounded overhead. Softly at first, but it picked up steam until it sounded like a rapid, staccato drumbeat.

A rainstorm.

The sound on the café's tin roof made it hard to hear the conversation. At least they wouldn't be overheard.

Will held back a moan. "Thanks, Maddy. I can't believe we had to leave her just lying there."

"We had no choice." Maddy paused and looked at Will, her green eyes alight with compassion. "She wouldn't have wanted you to die, too."

Will's throat closed up for a second.

"How on earth do you think they knew where we were?" Maddy asked.

"I have no idea how they tracked us down again," Will replied.

Bear took a bite of his sandwich. "And who's we? Carlos or the Russians?"

Maddy grimaced. "I hoped we had lost them both. My god, we were underground for a week."

Will looked around furtively. "If they tracked us here, we're screwed. We need to move as soon as we can."

Bear showed them the front page of an *International Herald* newspaper. "I think the situation is even worse than we knew. Get a load of this."

The headline read, "Russia Denies Using E-bomb on Chinese Town." Bear went on, "I read this article while you were in the bathroom. This weapon poses a serious threat. Whatever it was that was used on that town, it knocked out all the electronics: TVs, radio towers, computers, all of it."

"Will and I heard about that the night we stayed in our old Tahoe house. I can still see the image of the melted TV. It was quite disturbing."

"Yes, these weapons are extremely dangerous. From a military perspective, they could wipe out missile targeting systems, airplane and helicopter controls, comms and nav systems, and even sensor systems."

"That's what I was afraid of," Will said.

"What about work arounds?" Maddy asked.

Bear took a sip of tea. "Our troops might still have manual weapons that would work, but without intel and a way to communicate, we'd end up shooting each other."

Maddy pointed at the paper. "So, do you think it was Russia?"

Bear set the paper aside. "There are some analysts who are thinkin' that it might have been a terrorist group like ISIS, but I bet it was actually Russia."

"Commie bastards," Will muttered.

Bear ignored him. "The UN has denounced the use of the e-bomb, and pundits are sayin' the saving grace is that a good source of superconductor fuel has yet to be found."

"Superconductor." The pieces of an idea clicked into place, and Will spoke excitedly, his grief forgotten for the moment. "That's it! That gold cylinder. Bear, let's see those pictures."

Bear pulled up the images of the cylinder on his GoPro.

"It shows obelisks floating above trees. See?" Will pointed. "Floating! Do you know what floats in nature? Not much. But superconductors do!"

Maddy and Bear exchanged a blank look.

Will felt like an alien. He leaned forward. *How do they not see this?* But they weren't engineers with a physics fascination like he was. "Obelisks! There were obelisks on both pages the king showed us. Remember?"

"Yes, but so what?" Maddy asked.

"That Egyptian priest-type person was holding two ruby-red obelisks up to the sun in a *V*. And on the cylinder, it looked like the same obelisks, floating. What if that's what we're hunting inside the *châsse*? What if those obelisks are made of a superconductive material?"

Maddy's narrowed eyes held caution. "Interesting idea, Will, but what exactly is a superconductor? I've heard the term but don't get it."

"Okay." Will tried to slow down. "Let's start with the basics. Superconductivity is the ability of certain materials to conduct electrical current with nearly zero resistance."

"Why is that a big deal?" Maddy asked.

"Well, ordinary conductors have resistance, which restricts the flow of electricity and wastes some of the energy as heat."

"Like copper?" Bear asked.

"Yeah. Copper. Not a great conductor compared to a superconductor, though. Theoretically, an electrical current flowing through a loop of superconducting wire can persist forever with no power source."

Maddy nodded, a thoughtful look in her eyes. "Indefinitely? Wow. That's neat. More powerful computers could be built."

"Yes, exascale and quantum computing, and there are tons of other potential applications."

Maddy drank from her small coffee cup. "Why isn't there more of it?"

"Superconductivity was first observed in 1911, but the problem has been that cold temperatures are typically required."

"How cold?" Bear asked.

"When first discovered, it was below minus two hundred four degrees Celsius, near absolute zero." He could mention the temperature in Kelvin, but since they were more used to Fahrenheit, he did a quick calculation and continued, "Or minus four hundred degrees Fahrenheit.

But scientists keep finding ways to raise the temperature. Last I heard, the record was around minus ninety-four degrees Fahrenheit."

"Still, that's cold," Bear said.

"Yes. Anyway, one of the other unique things about superconductive materials is the Meissner effect."

"What's that?" Maddy asked.

"This guy Meissner realized that some superconductive materials also expel magnetic forces at certain temperatures. So, you can get quantum levitation as a result."

"Levitation? Y'all aren't pulling our legs here?" Bear asked.

He looked around and all the nearby tables were empty. Good. "Yes, no joke, it's a proven scientific phenomenon. Which brings us back to the obelisks—I think they're made of a superconductive material!"

"Will, you sure you're not reaching here?" Maddy asked.

"Think about it, Maddy. It fits. Why else would the Russians want us dead? We've been told we're after are an amazing source of power. Maybe the material in the obelisks themselves is enough to power another e-bomb?"

Maddy swallowed and paled. She must have felt nervous. Maybe she was getting it.

He continued, "You see? It makes sense. Superconductive items can defy gravity! Scientists are just now starting to understand all the things superconductivity can enable. Today, most MRI systems use a superconducting magnet. And that high-speed train in Japan uses superconductors. It was clocked at almost six hundred two kilometers per hour."

They both tilted their heads at him.

Maddy's left eyebrow rose.

How'd I forget? Miles per hour, not kilometers. "That's three hundred miles per hour."

Maddy and Bear both nodded. Bear's eyes widened.

"Applications are being revolutionized all over the place. Superconductors are extremely powerful."

"Do you think knowing they're that dangerous could be why Ramiro hid the obelisks?" Maddy asked.

"Absolutely. I'm sure he didn't want them to fall into the wrong hands. Who knows what else they can do?"

"I still wonder how the Russians knew they existed."

"Maybe our cousin, Prince Carlos, told them in exchange for assassinating his father someday."

"Eww." Maddy frowned as she nodded. "I wouldn't put it past him."

"I know. I have no idea how they found out, but do you have a better explanation?"

"No." Maddy fell silent as she considered.

Bear spoke. "Hey, y'all remember that it was Alexander the Great on the first page of the codex? Maybe wielding one of the obelisks?"

"Sure, but why are you thinking about that now?" Will spun his small flashlight around his finger on its keychain, still excited.

"What if the obelisks themselves are some kind of weapon? What if it's their superconductive properties that make them dangerous?"

"We do keep hearing they have power." Will shrugged. "Science is still unraveling the mysteries of superconductivity. It's possible."

"Okay, consider this. Perhaps when he was in Egypt, Alexander discovered the obelisks, and they helped him win all those battles. He was a brilliant strategist, but maybe he also had an advantage. An unusual weapon, like the obelisks."

Will nodded.

"He ruled from Asia to Persia, much of the known world at the time. Any object of power that might have helped him is surely somethin' to be reckoned with."

Will tapped his leg. "I can see that. Then Ramiro obtained the obelisks thirteen hundred years later and decided he needed to protect them."

"Or protect the world from them," Maddy added.

Bear looked down at the newspaper and then back at Will. "But perhaps the obelisks as a weapon are a stretch. Let's think about what we do know."

"Okay," Will agreed.

"From recent news, we can assume the Russians are after a source of superconductive material. We can also assume they want us dead."

"Unfortunately, yes," Maddy said.

"So, if we also assume for the moment that you're correct about the obelisks having superconductive properties, and it's obvious our government would *not* want Russia to enable that e-bomb—that means our mission to find the *châsse* is critical to stopping a potential war between the US and Russia."

"Yes, I believe so. We're in the middle of a dangerous game." Odd that this conclusion made Will start to feel a little better. "If we can stop the Russians, perhaps all the deaths, Dad, Maria, Hana, won't have been in vain."

"Good lord. This is up to us to stop?" Maddy shook her head and finished her wrap. "I feel woefully unprepared."

"Me, too," Will said.

"But I guess we better figure out where the center of the Pagan Empire is. And fast. Bear, do you have any ideas?"

"Let's double-check with the internet, but I've been thinkin'."

"About pagans?" Maddy asked.

"Yeah. And empires. I suspect either Vilnius in Lithuania or Bagan in Myanmar. Because Vilnius was known as the Jerusalem of the North, I'm guessin' we need to head there. It also seems to be more centrally located to where Ramiro might have traveled. Bagan is pretty far to the south."

With just his eyes, Will glanced around. "I hope we can't be traced at these public computers."

Maddy touched the necklace at her throat. "They wouldn't know what to key in on, so unless they're watching all searches in Jerusalem tonight, I think we're okay. I can also use a special browser."

Maddy got up and walked over to a machine that sat in a row of computers along the wall. Will ate his wrap and took a look at the e-bomb article while Bear watched the door.

After about ten minutes, Maddy came back over and sat down. "Mr. History here is right. When I search for the Pagan Empire, I get both Burma/Myanmar and Lithuania but for different reasons."

"Okay, why?" Will asked.

"According to Wikipedia, Burma was home to the Pagan Kingdom, which was an empire in Asia from around 850 to 1300, and was responsible for the spread of a form of Buddhism. The name comes from the name of a town, Pagan, which became Bagan."

Will scowled. "I don't buy it."

"Let me finish. The Lithuania connection has more to do with what we think of as non-Christian pagans. Lithuania wasn't fully Christianized until 1387. Before that, it was known as a center for pagan worship. After the setbacks of the Crusades in the Holy Land, the popes had a Northern Crusade against Lithuania and other European pagan nations. Apparently, the Baltic tribes were the last people in Europe to convert to Christianity." She turned to Bear. "Nice work."

Bear blushed a little at Maddy's praise and chewed on an ice cube. "So, at the time of Ramiro, Lithuania was a hotbed of paganism."

"Yes, but I'm not seeing much that would make it the center of an empire, per se."

Will finished his wrap and wiped his mouth. "But what did Ramiro have to do with Buddhism in Burma? That's pretty far off his beaten path."

Maddy crossed her arms in front of her chest. "I agree, but the clue read, 'Find the center of the Pagan Empire,' not go to the last holdout of pagans."

"I need more of this lame iced tea but think we should head north, to Vilnius." Bear got up and went over to the counter.

"What do you think, Will?"

"I think he's right. From the perspective of a thousand years ago, Lithuania looks a lot closer than Myanmar."

Maddy held her ground. "Just because it is closer, doesn't mean it's where we should go."

Will pressed, "What about the symmetry of Vilnius being the Jerusalem of the North? Bear mentioned that earlier."

Maddy mimicked Will. "I don't buy it."

"What would Ramiro know about Buddhism?"

"Maybe he's religiously agnostic. Jerusalem is central to Judaism, Christianity, and the Muslim faith."

Will stroked his beard. "Sorry, Maddy, but I think Bear is right. You're reaching. He was Christian."

Outside the café, the rain stopped as suddenly as it had begun.

Maddy grimaced and lowered her voice. "Looks like I'm outvoted. I sure hope you guys are right. It will be a long way out of our way if you're wrong."

CHAPTER 45

The Mediterranean Sea, July 9, 8:25 p.m.:

On the ferry, following a dreadful meal with the twins, Bear excused himself with a sweet tea "to go," grabbed a sweatshirt against the coming chill, and went on a self-guided tour of the ship to make sure they hadn't been followed on board.

Bear reviewed the last twenty-four hours, considering if someone could have tailed their movements. After spending the night at a youth hostel in Old Jerusalem, he and the twins had taken a bus from Jerusalem to Tel Aviv and then purchased ferry tickets to Athens at a dockside kiosk.

To throw off their pursuers, they were heading to Greece by boat and then would take a train through Europe to Vilnius. Their ferry, *Zeus's Pride*, had departed with the afternoon tide. Now the shadows of night were beginning to cling to dark corners of the ship. He hadn't seen anyone following them, figured they were in the clear, but wanted to check out the ferry to be sure.

There was not much to see. The vessel was intended to ferry tourists from Europe to the Holy Land and, as such, was nowhere near a luxury cruise liner. Not that he'd ever been on a cruise, but he'd heard tales. There was no swimming pool, no movie theater, no delicious all-you-can-eat buffet. But what he cared about and, best of all, there was no burned Russian or minion of Prince Carlos.

Most of their fellow travelers carried backpacks and were planning to sleep the night under the stars on lounge chairs. Bear passed the rows of their budget beds and soon found himself at the front of the ship, where he paused to watch the sunset.

The sea gave off that exceptional, intoxicating scent that was unique to salty bodies of water. Bear loved the smell. Although moved by the aromatic textures as he watched the clouds slow dance through the colors of the rainbow, a battle raged inside him.

Am I doing the right thing?

On one hand, he always wanted to work as an undercover agent. The cat-and-mouse game of international espionage got his blood moving. It was his lifelong ambition.

Fighting with the marines over the last decade had held an appeal for a time. He had enjoyed piloting helicopters, gathering tactical intelligence, and it was an awesome feeling to lead a unit. At least until everything went to hell on that mountaintop. That was the side of war that his dead father had known and wanted him to experience: the guns-blazing, bloody, kick-ass side of war.

But since he was young, he had yearned for the covert, stealthy side of war. From studying history, he knew where conflicts were often won. Off the battlefield not on it, in the shadows and streets, through the hearts and minds of lone wolves like him. And in many ways, covert ops were often more dangerous than just being shot at. With no parachute, you had to use your body and your mind as a spy.

Perhaps he should have gone to a military college to become a commissioned officer, but he'd been eager to get out from under his stepfather's thumb. Bear had thought intelligence in the marines would scratch his itch, but he found the experience too focused and tactical. It was not at all strategic or what he'd imagined. He yearned to play a bigger game and one where he'd have more respect from his peers.

That was why he'd signed up with VanOps.

On the other hand, it wasn't his nature to keep secrets from his friends, especially a friend that he wanted to be more than a friend. Maddy.

He knew his feelings for Maddy were a pipe dream. She'd never shown any interest in him, even in high school when he couldn't hide his feelings and he was such a pup he never even got up the nerve to ask her out. She never once flirted with him and, ever since he'd known her, had only dated tall guys, like Juergen.

Yet, his heart sang when they were together. Fool for love that he was, he'd have come along willingly, even if his possible new boss, D'Angelo, hadn't suggested it.

D'Angelo was a director at VanOps, the most secret CIA group in Washington, the blackest of the black. It was an outgrowth of the old CIA Stargate psychic spying program and now had a broader mission—to keep an eye out for any sort of advanced or obscure technology that threatened the security of the United States.

That's why VanOps was under the Department of Extreme Threats. Bear had heard that the definition of "advanced or obscure technology" was pretty loose, and might include any number of things he found fascinating but that the world didn't understand, such as ancient obelisks with esoteric powers. The forward-thinking part had given rise to the name, VanOps, as in vanguard operations.

But how had VanOps known about the Argones family obelisks? Maybe they didn't know, at least when they sent him on the mission, that he and the twins might be the key to stopping the Russian e-bomb threat. Why else would they send an untrained rookie, unless it was a dead-end, milk-and-cookies jaunt?

The only explanation that made sense was that this quest was the VanOps version of what Maddy had just been through. Even though he had some experience in intelligence gathering, was considered a war hero, his dad had been a general, and he had his old master gunnery sergeant's recommendation, getting into VanOps was no shoo-in.

After his latest tour had finished, it was his superior's recommendation that landed him on that arched bridge in DC's Rock Creek Park a few weeks ago for what wasn't even called an interview. The director shared some background about VanOps, asked questions about Bear's service record and his interests. Provided whitewashed innuendos about saving the world. The guy was hard to read and told him to take some time off back home in California, and that they might have a casual way to see if he was a good fit in a couple of weeks.

After two long weeks at his parent's house and just when Bear was going to shave his new beard and re-enlist, he got a phone call from Director D'Angelo and a request to meet at Jake's on the Lake for dinner. That led to a short conversation on the back deck, with the director asking him if he wanted to test drive an undercover role in what was most probably a wild-goose chase with some old friends.

Curious and excited to try his hand at the job, Bear agreed. A new credit card exchanged hands. He ended up minutes later under strict orders to stay quiet, keep Will and Maddy safe, go along with wherever their quest might lead, and to call a memorized number once they were home. The number could also be used in case of a true emergency, but Bear gathered that would be frowned upon.

He'd be told in the morning where to "accidentally" run into the twins. Against the backdrop of a dramatic Lake Tahoe thunderstorm, he was told that he was to, under absolutely no circumstances, share that his finding them was anything other than coincidence. He was to act the friend. So, act he did. But now things were getting more complicated.

He'd not put all the pieces together yet, but he figured Will was onto something with the superconductive aspects of the ancient obelisks. Why else were the Russians on their tail? The complications could also be an opportunity, as he guessed that VanOps might give him a bonus if he could keep the obelisks out of harm's way and talk Maddy and Will into giving them to the government for safekeeping after all was said and done. Family artifact or not, if Will was right, who wanted to have Soviets after you forever? It would be a good way to join the VanOps team.

Somebody touched his shoulder. "Maddy!"

"Hi, Bear, sorry, didn't mean to startle you."

"No worries, was just lost in my thoughts and watching the sunset."

Maddy moved to the railing. "Mind if I join you?"

The last rays of the sun lit her emerald eyes with a golden glow that took Bear's breath away. She used just a tad bit of makeup around her eyes to make them stand out. Bear found them stunning.

He took a swig of his sweet tea. "Not at all, it's a lovely night. Get settled in your cabin?"

"Yes, then I got restless. Will found a book in the trade-in library and has his nose buried in it."

Bear gestured west. "He's missing out on this sunset."

"Pretty, isn't it?"

"It is. I like the sea."

For some reason, Bear felt nervous. He and Maddy weren't alone that often and she stood close to him. A band of sweat broke out on his forehead, and he had to consciously deepen his breathing.

"Me too."

They leaned on the rail together in companionable silence for a time, smelling the fresh salt air, watching the sun sink below the horizon. The colors tonight were incredible. Pink bubbles. Orange lines. Purple swirls.

Bear gestured to Maddy's thigh wound. "How's the leg feelin'?"

"Better today. I think resting a day or two will help." She paused and turned toward him. Her hand found its way to his forearm and, at her touch, tiny, invisible fireworks of pleasure shot off all over his body. "Bear, do you think we're safe out here?"

For a moment, as he looked into her eyes, he had a hard time concentrating. Every fiber of his being wanted to confide in her.

Or kiss her.

Was there any way he could tell her the backstory and stay true to his mission? He swore. No.

"I think we lost them all in Israel. I scouted the ship and didn't see them. You can sleep well tonight."

She gave him a grateful smile. "Thanks for keeping an eye out. I appreciate it."

"No problem."

"Are you sure you want to stick around with us, Bear? This has to be more than you bargained for."

"I'm a marine, Maddy. I've been shot at before."

Her eyes held his for a moment, the demand in them clear. "That wasn't personal. These guys are stalking us for a reason. Why did you want to come along?"

With the sun almost below the horizon, a sudden chill from the breeze gave him goosebumps. Did she suspect? Either his feelings for her or his other, ulterior motive?

To gain a second to think, he put his tea down, took his sweatshirt from his shoulders, and put it on over his head.

"Maddy, I—"

"Hey, what are you guys doing up here?" Will strode out of the shadows. "There's a poker game happening down below. Want to join me?"

Bear heaved an internal sigh of relief.

Maddy gave Bear a last look with a raised eyebrow that let him know she'd ask him again later. They left the sun's multicolored masterpiece and followed Will downstairs.

Spared for the time being, Bear hoped he wouldn't need to keep up the ruse for much longer. Surely, they would find the obelisks in Lithuania and be home in no time. He'd talk the twins into putting the obelisks into the protective hands of the government. Maddy would be so grateful he'd kept her safe that she'd ignore his sins of omission, kiss him passionately, and then he'd get the official job offer from VanOps.

What the hell, a guy can dream.

CHAPTER 46

Vilnius, Lithuania, July 12, 10:25 a.m.:

Maddy looked out the brick-lined, open window of Upper Castle, at the top of Gediminas Hill. The entire city of Vilnius was spread out below her, a picturesque red-roofed medieval town littered with modern concrete buildings.

"You guys are nuts," she said.

Her leg broadcast a dull ache from making the climb, which would have irritated her once, but she'd noticed since Jerusalem that she didn't get irritated quite so easily. Maybe it was the time she'd been putting into her practice. Traveling three days to get here had given her ample opportunity. *Listen and feel the Power.* She even tried directing some of the Power to her leg and it seemed to be healing better. If nothing else, it felt good, and it seemed she was truly on track to become a teacher someday. If they ever found the *châsse*.

Maddy pointed. "Look at that skyline. This town is huge. There's no way this is the 'Center of the Pagan Empire.'"

Will stood a half step behind her, looking out. "Probably some nice pagan bars down there."

Bear explored antique swords behind them.

"William!" Maddy gave him her best "mother-warning" voice to dissuade him from the bar idea.

He smiled the grin of the intentionally ornery. "And good restaurants. After travelling for days, I'm ready for some fine dining. And an adult beverage."

"I could push you off this tower, you know. You're not helping."

He gestured with his head. "Okay, well, how can I help? I can see the river, Old Town. That's the Lower Castle down there. A couple of cathedrals and the Gate of Dawn is over there."

Maddy waved her hand in the general direction of the sprawling city. "I'm guessing the next pointer to the *châsse* is another *signum regis*."

"I'm guessing you're right."

"Okay, but where is it? This is a city of over five hundred thousand people."

Will shrugged. "I don't know. I'm still worried about what Dad's attorney told me when I called this morning while waiting for our bus to depart the train station."

"I'm still not sure that contact was such a great idea. You mentioned you called her, but I'd like details."

"I wanted to pick her brain to see if Dad had told her anything about Ramiro or why he called us together that day. But remember her receptionist—the one that was shot?"

"Yes, hard to forget those fingernails." Maddy's tone was sarcastic.

"Be nice. She's dead."

Maddy didn't feel contrite. "Sorry."

"Anyway, she had traveled to Russia on her last vacation."

That was a surprise. "What?"

"Yes, she lied to the attorney, said she was going to Cancun. Instead, went to Moscow. After the shooting and the dead Russian in that crashed BMW, the FBI did some research and asked the attorney if she knew why the receptionist had made the trip. Of course, she didn't know."

"Another Russian connection," Maddy said.

Will spun his flashlight around his fingers. "Yep. But why would she go to Russia?"

"Good question. Any theories?"

"No, not yet. But I'm wondering if her murder was to shut her up. Tie up a loose end."

Maddy looked out at the red-roofed skyline. "I can see that. Without the travel to Russia, I figure she'd just gotten in the way of our sniper friend...hmm, this means that maybe he didn't even know we were there."

Will reached for a cigarette then let his hand drop. "That's a possibility we need to consider as well."

Maddy was thrilled he'd quit smoking. "The shooter may have thought he hit the jackpot when he saw us leaving out the back door."

"Too bad he missed us."

They grinned at each other.

Maddy turned to Bear, who was inspecting a set of armor on the other side of the old, brick-lined tower. He looked good today in cargo shorts, a blue T-shirt that highlighted his physique, and a matching blue bandanna.

"Hey, Bear."

He walked over and joined them at the window. "Nice view."

"Overwhelming view," Maddy replied.

"I heard y'all talking about the Russian gal. Maybe she put a tracker in all that stuff from your dad."

"A GPS tracker?" Will asked.

"Yeah. We're alone up here. Can I see the packet?"

Maddy pulled the backpack off Will's shoulders and dug around until she found the packet. She handed it to Bear, who rifled through the gold, diamonds, and letters from her father.

"Nothin' obvious, but they're making them pretty small these days. While we're in town, I'll see if I can find an electronic sweeper."

"So, that would be great, but it doesn't help us figure out our next move." Maddy's heart sank further as she looked out the window again. She could see cinnamon-roofed hotels, white-stone government buildings, even a McDonald's. The skyline seemed to go on forever. "It's such a big town."

Will nodded in the direction of the town below. "More like a city. Impressive, in a needle-in-a-haystack-kinda way."

"I'm feeling like our three days to get here was a big waste of time."

"Why's that?" Bear asked.

"This place is not only huge, but also checking out the guidebooks, it seems it was mostly built after Ramiro's time. The first written record of the town was about one hundred years after Ramiro died. According to one book I was looking at this morning, there are one thousand four hundred eighty-seven buildings in Old Town alone."

Bear took some lip balm from his pocket and swiped at his lips. "I do recall the king mentioning after dessert that not all sites were necessarily from Ramiro's time."

"You think Isabella or Ferdinand may have redone a clue?" Will asked.

"It's possible. Much may have changed in the four hundred or so years between their two reigns. The original clue from Ramiro may have, in their time, been in danger of disappearing." Bear redeposited the balm in his shorts' pocket.

"Lame. That means there's a whole lot more to search," Will said.

"Yes, and the search is not without some additional historical challenges. There were five famous fires that destroyed much of the Old Town between 1700 and 1750. It's possible the clue may have perished in one of those fires."

"Oh, boy," Maddy said.

"It gets worse. During the next century, Napoleon and his Grande Armée trundled through here. Also, more recently, both the Germans and the Russians were not kind."

"World War Two?" Maddy asked.

"Yep. Out in the forest, archeologists recently uncovered a hundred-foot tunnel used by a small handful of Jews, called the "Burning Brigade," to escape Nazi death pits. This Brigade was forced to unearth and burn bodies to cover up the killing of an estimated *hundred thousand* people."

Heart pained, Maddy looked away.

"The men dug the tunnel with spoons found on their dead friends and relatives. Only twelve of eighty prisoners survived the escape." Bear paused, anger radiating from his eyes as he gazed into the past. He took a deep breath and stretched his shoulders. "But I digress—the point is, we face the challenge of time."

"That's depressing. You're not encouraging me." Maddy grimaced and put her hands on her hips. "But I appreciate your honesty."

Bear shrugged. "Just setting the stage. I think we owe it to ourselves to look, and I think we can focus on buildings that were built before 1500 when Isabella and Ferdinand had access to them. That will narrow our search significantly."

"It will still take days. Old Town covers one-point-four square miles." Her mind's eye flew to the temples in the south, where her gut still felt they should be. "My sense is we should be in Bagan. And yesterday. With the Russians on our trail, we're running out of time."

Bear waved his hand toward the window. "We do need to hurry, but we're here. We have to try."

"I suppose." She was tempted to leave the two of them there to spin their wheels in Old Town forever but knew it would be safer to stick together. "Shall we follow the same methodology that worked at the Well of Souls, with me looking low for clues, you looking in the middle, and Will looking high?"

"Yes, let's do it."

She turned to Will. "Does that work for you, Will?"

He looked away from the panoramic view and met her eyes. "I guess so."

She gave her ponytail a last, irritated tug. "Fine. Let's go find the needle in the proverbial haystack."

CHAPTER 47

San Francisco, California, July 12, 3:45 p.m.:

The outburst of laughter poured over AJ like a wave. He was with his foster family at Golden Gate Park, where there was a large comedy festival going on. There were over forty comedians who were going to be on stage throughout the day. His foster parents had brought a blanket, six lawn chairs, a cooler, and his three other foster siblings, none of whom he wanted to play with.

For a while, he sat in one of the lawn chairs next to his foster mom and tried to pay attention to the comedian, but they were on a stage that was far away, and he didn't understand what everyone was laughing about.

After a time, he wandered away from the lawn chairs to watch a group of older boys and girls kick around a soccer ball on a grassy area near a long bed of rosebushes. It looked like a fun game, but since they were all teens, he didn't ask to play.

His foster mom waved at him from her lawn chair. "Don't go far, AJ."

He waved back.

Three girls about his own age were playing with hula hoops. One of them smiled at him. "Wanna try?"

Feeling stupid and happy at the same time, AJ agreed and put the plastic loop around his waist. He tried to swing his hips like the girls but the hoop slid to his ankles. He picked it up and tried it again, with the same result. The girls laughed and he laughed along. On the third try, he got the hang of it and was able to swing it around and around in a mesmerizing rhythm. All the girls clapped in time as he swirled it around his hips. Finished and flush with success, he stepped out of the hoop, thanked the girl, and handed it back to her. The three girls went back to their game.

Walking away, a beautiful yellow and black-winged butterfly drew him away from the loud crowd, along a sidewalk, and a little way into the bushes.

He was so focused on the butterfly that it came as a complete shock when a strange hand closed over his mouth and a male voice, in Russian, quietly told him not to scream.

CHAPTER 48

Vilnius, Lithuania, July 13, 8:40 p.m.:

Will tapped his fingers on his leg as he tried to look at the menu. Frustration at the two long, fruitless days they had spent searching for any sort of clue distracted him. Bloody memories of Maria and Hana's deaths haunted him. Guilt taunted him.

He was also disturbed that while they hunted, hysteria over the international e-bomb crisis continued to build around them.

First, the three of them had gone to Old Town and wandered around, checking out the blend of architectural styles while looking for the *signum regis* or any other sign from their ancestors.

They followed the meandering streets to the palaces of feudal lords and landlords, to churches, shops, and craftsmen's workrooms. Narrow, curved streets and intimate courtyards made them feel as if they were going in circles, as the medieval town had been developed in a radial layout.

Every time they passed the university, in unnerving displays of passion, student protestors carrying "E-bombs are E-vil!" and "Books not Bombs" placards chanted and waved the slogans at them. As he walked past the protestors, he remembered the Dali-esque image of the melted TV from the Chinese broadcasting station and shuddered. Their group's lack of progress, and that he might be responsible for stopping what the protesters were up in arms about, made his heart pound in his chest in time with the chanting.

The nuclear mushroom-cloud scenario of WWIII, where Russia attacked America, who attacked back, kept playing in his head like a bad B movie. The flick had an even more disturbing intermission: the still frame of Maria lying on the hardwood floor in a pool of blood.

As Will, Maddy, and Bear sat in a stylish leather booth for dinner, discouraged and hungry, Will kept one eye peeled for intruders, as was his habit. They were in a trendy, overpriced restaurant on Pilies Street, the lighting dim, the music upbeat. He might be paranoid, but he preferred safe to sorry, so sat with his back to the wall and his face to the door. Bear sat next to him, following the same modus operandi.

After ordering his dinner, Will handed the menu to the waiter. The waiter walked away. "I think I saw someone following us today."

Maddy started to look over her shoulder at the door and stopped herself by grabbing onto her dark ponytail instead. "Why didn't you say something earlier?"

"I wasn't sure and I didn't want to worry anyone unnecessarily," Will replied.

Bear took a drink of water and looked surreptitiously at the door. "The hair on the back of my neck rose for a minute there when we were by the bell tower. When did you think someone was watching?"

Will lowered his voice. "No, it wasn't there by the cathedral. It was when we were walking by the fountain."

"Which fountain?" Bear asked.

"The one in the square on our way to the former Jewish ghetto area."

"What'd he look like?"

"He was white, middle-aged, with wavy brown hai,r and wore sunglasses. The navy windbreaker looked a little out of place."

"Sounds suspicious. I wish the electronic sweeper I bought had shown us how they were following us. Nothin' showed up in your stuff."

Maddy gave Bear a small smile. "Thanks for trying."

"I'd been meaning to mention this earlier but—" Bear glanced around to see if anyone was listening. "What do you think about gettin' some weapons?"

Maddy's eyes shone with concern. "What are you thinking, Bear?"

"We're exposed here. Our hiking staffs and Will's butter knife aren't going to do much if they catch up to us. Aikido is awesome for close combat but not so much when someone's tryin' to shoot at you."

Frowning, Maddy nodded slowly. "True. At least at a distance."

Will pantomimed a gun with his hand and pointed it at Bear. "How hard would it be to get them?"

Bear chewed on an ice cube from his sweet tea. "In every town, there's a way to get guns. We might even be able to get some 3-D printed ones. I was looking into those before we left stateside."

"What advantage would those have?" Will asked.

"If they're plastic and not metal, we might be able to get them through an airport scanner."

"Sounds risky. Plus, isn't the technology still not quite there?"

"Real ones would be better," Bear agreed.

"What about shipping an extra set of firearms to Bagan if things don't pan out here?" Will motioned them to silence as the waiter brought their food.

"That might work," Bear said. "We'll have to research shipping."

The waiter deposited their plates and left.

Will noticed Maddy still wore a frown. He said, "I say we do it. What do you think, Maddy?"

Her tone was serious. "I think it does sound risky, as I'm guessing we'd have to find a rough neighborhood?"

Bear nodded. "Right."

"And Will and I aren't exactly crack shots, so this would be for you, right Bear?"

"Yes, ma'am."

A stubborn look entered Maddy's eyes. "I think it's a recipe for disaster."

Will wiped his mouth. "C'mon, Maddy. If we'd had weapons back in Jerusalem, Hana might still be alive."

"This path won't bring her back, Will."

Will's food didn't taste very good. "I know that."

They ate in uncomfortable silence. Bear looked from Maddy to Will and back again. No one spoke.

Bear finished up and put his fork down. "Maddy, do you have a death wish?"

"Of course not."

"Then we need to arm ourselves."

Maddy grimaced and sighed. "So, the aikido part of me hates the idea, but I don't want to die, either. We can cash in a couple of those diamonds that Dad gave us. What neighborhood do you have in mind?"

Bear sat up straight. "The guidebook said to avoid South Vilnius suburbs, including Naujininkai and Kirtimai, so let's head to one of them tomorrow around lunch."

Will preferred to dodge bad neighborhoods. Would it be worth the chance, or just takes things from bad to worse?

CHAPTER 49

San Francisco, California, July 13, 9:22 p.m.:

AJ woke in an unfamiliar place, in a hard bed with a rough blanket and a pillow that smelled of mildew. He had a headache, his stomach hurt, and his mouth was dry and tasted like vomit.

Recalling the last thing he remembered, which was biting a man's hand at the park, he realized that this was not his home, and not his foster home, so he kept his breathing even to see what he could learn from his surroundings, or his captor, while they thought he was asleep.

When he dared to crack open one eye, he saw aged brick walls and a scarred wood floor. The ceiling had open ductwork and long narrow windows with blankets hung as curtains. He guessed it was some sort of old loft or warehouse. Opening his eye made him feel a little dizzy, so he closed it again and rested for a minute.

Where am I and why? He wanted to go home.

AJ turned his head slightly to avoid being noticed. He opened his eye again. A blond-haired man, with half his face horribly reddened, sat at an old table.

Memory came fully back. He remembered trying to bite that man's hand at the comedy festival before he smelled something sweetish and everything went black. The bandage on the man's hand gave AJ a small sense of satisfaction, but more than that, he felt like a tiny ant about to be squished.

He also remembered that this man had shot Maddy's father and her brother's wife at the vineyard. That day was horrible! He still had nightmares about lying in the grass and watching that man throw his rifle into the long black car.

Across the table from the burned blond man was another man. Dark, to the blond man's light. He had tanned or olive skin and long jet-black hair that he wore gathered at the back of his neck. Also, the darker man was tall and had broad shoulders. Oddly, where most people's eyes were the same color, this man had one eye so dark that it looked almost black, and the other eye, where it should have been a color, was white, ringed in a thin circle of black. The white eye reminded AJ of a target. His stomach clenched at the sight, and he wondered if the eye was real, or glass, like a marble.

The blond man was short for a grown-up and a little thin. He was playing with a knife the size of his hand, turning it end-over-end with his fingers. The two men were drinking a clear liquid out of tiny glasses that they poured from a tall bottle. AJ squinted a bit to look more closely at the red marks on the blond man's face.

They looked like burn marks, like what AJ had on his right hand from touching the stove when he was little, before the skin healed into a scar. AJ wondered how the man had burned his face—the wound looked fresh, angry, and painful.

This was a bad, bad situation. He closed his eye again and fought tears. What would Maddy do? He thought long and hard for a few moments and then figured that she'd try to listen, learn, and find a way to escape. Crying would definitely not help, it would only give away that he was awake, and he wouldn't learn a thing.

AJ cracked his eye open and tried to listen. The men were arguing in Russian. Russian, one of the languages of AJ's birthplace in Ukraine before he and his family had come to America. The men were close enough that he could hear what they were saying.

The darker man waved his hand. "You gave him too much of the drug, Ivan. Are you an idiot?"

"No, you didn't tell me how much to give him. I put some on the handkerchief and had him inhale."

The dark man's tone was angry. "I hope for your sake he's not dead. I checked his pulse a time ago and it was running wild."

The burned Russian, Ivan, sounded defensive. He twirled the knife hilt in his right hand. "He's not dead, he's breathing."

AJ realized they were talking about him. A drug! That's why his mouth tasted awful.

"He'd better not be, or you'll be in trouble. The baron will cut your balls off."

Ivan took a drink from one of the tiny glasses. "Fine, let them find another sniper."

"You'll need to find another son if it works out that way."

"It won't. The kid is just sleeping it off."

The dark-haired man looked at his watch. "It's been over twenty-four hours."

"Pyotr. Have some more vodka. If he's not awake in the morning, we'll call in a doctor."

Pyotr crossed his arms on the table. "I call the shots here. If he's not awake by midnight, we call."

Ivan made a disgusted face. "Fine." Then he put his left arm flat on the table, took his knife, and deliberately cut his left arm. A thin line of red appeared.

Pyotr sat back in his chair. "What the hell are you doing?"

Ivan repeated the cut in the same place. Blood oozed. "Marking my last kills."

"You're a crazy bastard."

"I have my reasons."

Pyotr shook his head from side to side. "Sure, you do." He paused and looked in AJ's direction.

AJ shut his open eye. Then, ever so slightly, peeked again.

Pyotr pointed at Ivan's hand. "Looks like your little freckle-faced pet bit you."

Ivan laughed. "He did, but if somebody tried to kidnap me, I'd bite them, too."

Pyotr still sounded angry. "Are you defending him?"

"Yes, I think he's got some spunk. I like that."

"Madonna, help me. You're too nice to him already. Gave him a blanket. Bought him some kid food for when he wakes up. Ice cream. Unbelievable. What if we get orders to kill him?"

AJ shuddered, fear spiking through him like a fever. His eye was riveted to the blood on Ivan's arm. He was cold and hugged the blanket closer to him for warmth and comfort.

Ivan cut himself again next to the first spot. "Right now, we have orders to keep him alive."

"*Da*, this is true," Pyotr said.

"So, I gave him a blanket and some food to keep him alive. Following orders. I'm just a sniper, not trained to work with dark arts like you are."

Pyotr's smile held ice and his white eye gleamed. "My skills scare you, eh?"

"Who wouldn't be? I heard you began training when you were younger than him." Ivan nodded in AJ's direction.

"Not your business. Let it be to make sure you and your pretty face stay safe, eh?"

"I will. I just hope it's all worth it in the end."

Pyotr raised his eyebrow above the odd white eye. "You don't want to see Mother Russia take down America, our great enemy?"

Ivan deepened the second cut. "Sure, I do, but how practical is this plan to take out three of their early warning radar systems with e-bombs? Don't they have redundancy with satellites?"

"*Da*, the satellites are already handled. You are not in the need to know on that."

"How will it work then?"

"If we can find enough superconductive material to fuel the three bombs, we have men in place who can deliver them close enough to take out their upgraded early warning systems."

"Then what happens?"

"Then we deploy nukes into the atmosphere over the country."

"The atmosphere?"

"Yes. Nukes in the sky disable electronics—weapons, phones, power grid, all of it—and within days, New York to Los Angeles will be vulnerable to attack!" Pyotr smiled broadly.

"Americans without their cell phones? They'll be doomed."

Pyotr drank. "They've been so distracted with ISIS and the terrorist threats that they've ignored us."

"They will regret it. Where are the three early warning systems located?"

"What do you care? Your job is babysitting!"

"Back off. I'm curious. This is a major victory waiting to happen. I'm sure I could look the locations up online, so just tell me." Ivan poured more of the drink into their glasses and then poured some liquid from the bottle onto his wounds.

"You're right that the idiots have this information on the internet. There's one system in Northern California, one in Greenland, and one in England. All air force locations."

Ivan shook his head.

Pyotr pantomimed cat claws. "Their other early warning systems are not upgraded, easy for a cyber-squad to take out, so if we take out those three, America will only have three blind mice to protect all its electronics from our war cats."

AJ was glued to the bed with horror. America under Russian rule was a terrifying thought. His parents had left Ukraine to escape Russian influence. His arms trembled.

Pyotr drank off the contents of his tiny glass in one swallow and slammed it on the table with a thud. "I'm going out to find a woman. Your baby over there better be awake when I get back. We have a trip to make."

AJ resolved to make Maddy proud and do what he could to stay alive and stop this plot. He understood that these men were attempting to take over his new home, as they had his old country.

He didn't like it. Didn't like it one bit.

CHAPTER 50

Vilnius, Lithuania, July 14, 10:15 a.m.:

The day they planned to find firearms dawned bright and clear, but by the time Maddy, Bear, and Will set off toward the more notorious sections of Vilnius, thick gray clouds were blowing in and stacking up in the east. Sweat from the humidity and the tension dripped down her lower back.

From their hotel, they took a bus out toward the southern suburbs. It was a quiet ride and Maddy had a moment to feel irritated about the day's objective as she watched the town go by. How was this going to get them any closer to the next clue?

The bus transported them from one world to another in a matter of fifteen minutes, with a train track as the delineation point between cultures. It was uncanny how one side of the train tracks held clean, middle-class streets and the other side had trash in the gutters and tired houses with security bars on the windows.

When the bus deposited them on a gritty commercial street lined with bars, litter, and barely dressed women lounging in doorways, she guessed they were in the right neighborhood. Her sense of apprehension grew.

Yesterday, buying guns had seemed a poor idea. Today, in the grim light of day, it seemed even worse.

Maddy looked up one side of the street and down the other. "Bear, do you know where we're headed?"

With his quarterstaff, he pointed toward a petrol station, walked that way, and the twins followed a few steps behind him. "I have a rough idea, yes."

Maddy turned to Will. "I had another bad dream last night."

"I never like to hear those words come out of your mouth," Will replied.

"I know, especially after the last one, eh?"

They walked by a group of several loud dirty-faced, beer-can-carrying men, one of whom overtly eyed her up and down. Maddy glared at him and was tempted to give him the finger.

Will turned and watched the lewd men walk on. "But my morbid sense of curiosity won't allow me to ignore it completely, so do tell."

"The good news is it wasn't about today's foolish mission."

"That's good. What was it about then?"

"Oddly enough, it was about AJ," Maddy replied.

Bear turned left down a side street and they followed.

Will scratched his beard. "Really? I haven't thought about him in a while."

"Me neither, we've been caught up in other things."

"That's true. Was he in distress? God forbid, dead?"

"It was more like trouble. I had an image of him riding a butterfly, like a magic carpet, and then he got yanked off it."

Bear took a right. They trailed him. Maddy felt like a duckling following its mother.

"Sounds rather generic," Will said.

"It was, but the troubling part is that our blond Russian man was the one who plucked him off the butterfly."

"Oh."

"I wish we could call and check in," Maddy said.

"That would be nice. Hey, what about buying one of those prepaid cell phones here but not using it until we're somewhere else, maybe en route to our next destination, and making it a super-fast call? Think that would be safe?"

Maddy liked the idea and patted Will on the back. "Should be. Even if they trace it back here, we'll be gone."

Will tapped his arm scabbard. "Okay, let's buy a couple. I also want to buy a few more knives."

Before she had a chance to respond, Bear motioned them to slow down. He stopped a young man in his early twenties and attempted a conversation in halting Russian.

He said something that sounded like "arujee," which she guessed was gun or weapon, and she'd heard *pozhaluista* enough times to know it meant "please."

She wasn't sure politeness was valued by hoodlums and in this case, it didn't matter, as Bear struck out. The young man shook vigorously in the universal sign of no, and walked on.

Dark clouds blew in and covered the sun. A cool wind danced down the street. Maddy took a sweater from her backpack and put it on. Bear kept walking, deeper into the neighborhood, deeper into darkness.

Maddy's sense of foreboding grew with every step.

CHAPTER 51

10:40 a.m.:

Bear tried to act like he knew what he was doing, but he had never purchased illegal firearms before. He was modeling his behavior on bad movies, pulp fiction, and raw instinct. With Maddy and Will along for the ride, he hoped it would be enough and he wouldn't get them all into hot water. Or killed.

The first man he'd spoken to had pretended to not understand him. Bear knew his Russian was lousy, but from his time in Afghanistan he was sure of how to pronounce a few words and *guns* was one of them. *Buy* was another. He'd seen the glint of recognition in the man's eyes, but for whatever reason, that one had decided to pass on making a few extra dollars.

As had his second target.

Bear was nothing though, if not stubborn, and by the time the rain started to sprinkle from the sky, making the Vilnius neighborhood smell decent instead of rancid, the third guy he asked accepted the equivalent of twenty dollars before he led them several blocks deeper into the warren of dirty houses.

A short walk later and they turned into a long, narrow, dead-end alley. Bear didn't like the looks of it and said so, in his halting mix of Russian and English.

His guide had wavy sand-colored hair, dark blue bloodshot eyes, a long angular face, a scrawny goatee and mustache, and a long, narrow nose that had either been broken or was naturally graced with a bump. Too slim for a boxer, maybe he'd just seen the wrong end of a fight or two. The guy wore a tan-colored hoodie, jeans, and black sneakers and reminded Bear of the druggie kids he had known in high school. When he replied to Bear that the necessary house was at the end of the alley and that this was the only route to weapons he knew of, his right eye twitched.

Bear didn't trust the guy as far as he could throw him but figured he could throw him if worse came to worse. So, they followed the tan hoodie down the alley and into a small gray house with a tin roof tucked in between several similar shacks. His guide knocked four times in quick succession. The door opened to reveal a robust, middle-aged, dark-haired woman who, Bear guessed, weighed in at over three hundred pounds. She held a cigarette in her hand.

"Vy gavareeteh pa ru-sky?"

Bear recognized the "do you speak Russian" phrase. *"Net. Vy gavareeteh pa anglisky?"* No, he replied, you speak English?

She laughed. *"Da,* you do speak some Russian. I speak some English. You come in, we talk."

Next, she ushered him and the twins inside and shut the door. The guide stayed outside in the light rain.

They stood in a modest kitchen that had room for a rugged farmhouse table with four fifties-style metal chairs, an old gas stove, a dirty white cracked kitchen sink with a faucet dripping rusty water, a type of refrigerator that Bear had never seen before, and cluttered Formica countertops. It smelled of cigarette smoke, burnt coffee, and old sneakers. Bear tried to not wrinkle his nose. *How hard is it to make coffee?*

She took a drag of her smoke. "You sit. You have tea, yes?"

They agreed to tea, although Bear decided to not drink much. It could be drugged. At least she hadn't offered the burnt coffee.

The kitchen seemed too small for the woman, or the woman too large for the kitchen. She struggled around the chairs but managed to get out four cups, saucers, and tea. The water on the stove was already hot.

Eventually, she fell into her chair and knocked the ash off her cigarette. The chair groaned. "You American. In this neighborhood. Not up to good things. What you want?"

"We have some bad men chasing us. Not our fault. We want protection."

Her eyes told him she didn't follow, so Bear added, "Protection…guns." He made the universal sign for a gun with his thumb and finger.

She got that and laughed again, a hearty smoker's laugh. "Ah, bang bang. Americans, you always want guns." Pausing, she looked them over. They were dressed as summer college backpackers. "Guns expensive."

Bear was prepared for this and had asked Maddy to give him two of her smaller diamonds. He took one out of his pocket, polished it with his shirt, and put it on the table. "We want six pistols, two each, with ammo and a backpack." Just in case she didn't get it, he put out five fingers and a thumb.

Quickly, she reached out to pick up the diamond and held it to the hanging bulb that acted as kitchen table light. Her eyebrows went up. She put it back on the table, pushed the chair out, walked over to a drawer, and returned with a jeweler's loupe.

Again, she raised it to the light. "Is real but is small." She pushed it back to him. "I show you what you get for small diamond."

She walked out of the kitchen, trailing smoke.

Maddy took a sip of her tea. "I have a bad feeling about this."

Bear motioned to her tea, shook his head, and moved his forefinger across his throat. "Don't drink too much of that."

Realization of the danger dawned in her eyes and she put it down. "Good point."

Their hostess walked back in, carrying several old Springfield Taurus pistols that Bear hadn't realized were still in circulation. She handed one to Bear, who took a quick look at it and handed it back. His heart pounded.

He hoped this bluff would pan out. "Too old. Probably not work. Sig Sauer or Glock."

The woman looked at him and tilted her head. "I have four Glock. But cost two diamond."

Bear wished for some good ole-fashioned sweet tea to help with his nerves. "Let me see."

Turning, she left and returned, faster this time. She handed him a black Glock. At least it looked newer. "I bring you one. You like, you give me diamonds. I give you three more, with ammo and backpack."

Bear picked it up. A G25. He'd heard about these. Introduced in the mid-nineties in Germany. It felt good in his hand. Solid. He unclipped the magazine. Empty. He popped it back in and then gave her back the jewel. "Here is the one diamond. You bring three more like this, with a spare magazine each, along with a backpack to carry and I give you other diamond."

She grinned. "Deal."

For some reason, her smile reminded Bear of a wolf playing with a rabbit.

Within minutes, they had completed the trade. Two diamonds for a backpack, four guns, empty magazines, and five boxes of ammunition. Bear started to load up one of the weapons.

The woman shook her head and hissed. "No! You load outside."

Bear considered ignoring her, but the look in her eye and the petite gun that unexpectedly appeared in her hand cemented his decision to go along with her request.

All the unloaded weapons ended up in the backpack. Bear toted it like a grocery bag as they walked out the door. A silent sigh of relief escaped his lips as they walked into the empty alley. Their guide had disappeared.

Bear hadn't liked that woman, but he had pulled it off! He gave Will a thumbs-up, which Will reciprocated.

They were two houses back down the alley when movement caught his eye. Four masked men jumped from the low-roofed houses and landed in the middle of the backstreet, blocking their way to the alley exit. *Bad odds!*

CHAPTER 52

10:55 a.m.:

As Maddy, Will, and Bear walked back down the Vilnius alley after completing the arms deal, two things happened at once.

Bear yelled, "Look out!"

Simultaneously, Maddy noticed four masked thugs, thirty feet away, brandishing weapons. Headed their way.

One man carried a small bat, another, a knife. Two appeared unarmed. But one of those was already making a menacing beeline toward her.

Most of their valuables were in the hotel safe. These men either wanted the weapons, blood, or both. Her pulse raced—either the Russians had brought in reinforcements or they'd been betrayed by their "guide."

The thug with the bully stick rushed Will, moving fast. Will gracefully sidestepped the guy. *That worked, cool.* Will reached for a knife and threw it at his attacker, who was five feet away and turning back fast. The blade whistled by the brute's head and landed in a heap of garbage at the end of the alley. Will swore.

In front of her, two men circled Bear, one with a knife and one without. Bear tossed the backpack behind him and whirled his staff like a baton, causing the muscles in his broad shoulders to flex with the effort. The thief's knife glistened in the light rain.

Movement caught her eye. The baton-wielding mugger swung around and came at Will again. Will was able to use his attacker's momentum to grab the thug's wrist and twist, but the man was stronger than Will and broke his grip, then punched him in the stomach. Will doubled over in pain. The brute wasted no time thumping Will on the head.

Like a tall, collapsing building, Will passed out and crumpled to the wet street.

It was clear to Maddy that she'd had a bad feeling about this outing for a reason. Now she felt angry but engaged, lit like a torch. Her unarmed attacker and the brute that had just dropped Will headed toward her. The original attacker got to her first, but came in too fast, and she tripped him. On his stomach, he skidded on the wet street and hit his head on a wall. That left her open to the thug with the bat, who swiped her right arm as he moved toward her. A grunt from Bear distracted her, allowing the attacker to get his arms around her from behind.

With her arms pinned against her body and her back up against his chest, she struggled in his grip. He stank—a potent mixture of body odor and alcohol.

Maddy thrashed and writhed, but she was restrained too closely. Her martial arts moves didn't work. Perhaps he was trained as well. And he was strong! Part of her wondered if this group had anything to do with the people that Will thought were following them, or if the Russians sent them. As she tried to get free, she could hear Bear and an assailant trading punches. Something clattered down the street. *That knife? Bear's staff?* She worried for him, knowing it was two against one.

Resorting to schoolyard moves, she scraped her boot along the front of her attacker's shin. A rewarding grunt of pain followed. His grip on her arms loosened, and she sensed a movement like he had slumped toward her a bit, which prompted her to elbow up at him. He was short and she connected with his face. An eye, a nose? She didn't know, but he yelped and backed off. Maddy turned and kicked him in the solar plexus. That dropped him. A final vital point strike to the temple rendered him unconscious and she said a silent thanks to her sensei for teaching the controversial *atemi*, or striking moves. At least she didn't have to kill the man.

She turned to see Bear in action. Although he had lost his staff, he looked like he knew what he was doing. There was one motionless man on the ground nearby. Bear connected a sound punch into the neck of another. The punch looked bone-crunchingly painful and caused the hoodlum to gasp and fall to his knees. Neither assailant was still holding a knife. With those two down, Bear paused to look at her and catch his breath. She was glad he was on her team.

Then, before she could yell a warning, the formerly motionless, decked-out mugger who had been on the ground behind Bear, got up and bowled into him from a crouch. The slippery street proved Bear's undoing. He lost purchase, and the hood managed to knock Bear's legs out from under him. Bear went down on his shoulder with a hard thud. The successful mugger grabbed the backpack with the guns and took off down the alley at a dead sprint.

CHAPTER 53

3:15 p.m.:

Inside their suite of rooms at a hotel in Vilnius, Maddy had Will resting on the couch with an ice bag on the right side of his head. She and Bear had been watching her brother for several hours and she felt concerned.

Will opened one eye. "Where are we?"

"Vilnius. In the hotel room," Maddy replied.

"Maddy?"

"Yes, it's me, Will."

"Wow, my head hurts." Will gingerly moved the ice bag. "It's like there's a big bass drum in there."

"It probably does hurt. You got whacked upside your head."

"I did? What happened?"

Maddy exchanged a worried look with Bear. "We were in an alley, do you remember?"

"An alley...oh—right. *Merda!* We were buying guns. Guess that didn't work out, huh?"

"No, not so well."

"Cops are after me and we're on a doomed quest to find something...what are we looking for?"

"Something our ancestor Ramiro hid a long, long time ago. We think they're superconductive obelisks inside a *châsse* but aren't sure."

"Superconductors. Oh no. I remember now. Russians are trying to kill us."

"Yes, we're trying to stop them and figure out why they killed Dad and Maria."

"Maria. That's sad."

"It is sad, yes."

"But I can't cry about it. Boys don't cry."

"You're not a boy anymore, Will. You're a man and men do cry sometimes. It's okay to cry when your wife dies."

"Okay. I'm going back to sleep now."

Would he be himself next time he woke, or would they have to take him to a hospital and risk exposure?

CHAPTER 54

5:15 p.m.:

Two hours later, Will woke up again in the Vilnius hotel. The light streaming through the windows had the dim look of late afternoon and the rain had increased to a steady pitter-patter. He felt more like himself. His head was no longer killing him and his memory was back. Unfortunately.

Bear sat by Will's bed reading a book.

It was a decent hotel space. Tired of sleeping in hostels and trains, they'd gone for middle-of-the-road lodging in Vilnius. There were two beds that seemed about queen-sized and a comfortable couch that Will and Bear had taken turns using for a bed. The beds were clean and the shower hot. They had decided they'd be safer as a group in one set of rooms.

Will reached for the ice bag and reapplied it to his scalp with care. "Hey, Bear."

"Hey, Argones."

"You holding vigil over my not-so-dead body?"

"Ah, good. You are feelin' better. Your spunk is back."

"I was kind of out of it when I woke up before, wasn't I?"

"Yes. It would have been funny if we weren't so worried about you."

"Probably a concussion, huh?"

"That's our guess. We were thinking of taking you to a hospital if you didn't come around soon."

"I think I'll live."

"Happy to hear it."

"Where's Maddy?"

"She insisted on goin' to get some takeout. We got hungry and hoped you'd wake up soon and be hungry, too. Lunch didn't happen."

"We were going to do that after the botched gun deal."

"Yes. Sorry, you're hurt. The whole thing was my fault."

"How do you figure?"

"I was the one who found the guide and led us into that rat's nest."

"You don't get all the blame, buddy. We were willing participants and could have cried 'uncle' anytime."

Bear shook his head in disgust. "And what a stupid move to not load up a gun as soon as we walked out the door!"

"C'mon, Bear, don't be too hard on yourself. My skills are so lame. I'm embarrassed to have this lump on my head."

"What if one of you had gotten killed?"

Will suspected that Bear would have been more worried about Maddy's loss of life than his own, but he let it slide. "We didn't, Bear. Let's leave it at that."

"But now we're in a bad way. We lost not only the two diamonds but the entire sack of guns. We were able to recover your knife, though."

"Great. I'm starting to feel naked without it."

"Ha! We'll make a warrior out of you yet."

"Doubt that, but I do find some comfort in the blade. Thanks for finding it. I definitely need some practice."

"I think we all do," Bear said reflectively.

"Hey, how'd you get me home?"

"You were in and out of consciousness long enough for us to manhandle you down the alleyway and into a cab."

Will didn't want to focus on the memory. "Ah. I have a vague memory of puking."

"I wasn't going to mention that but, yes. When we stood you up you lost your cookies."

"Gotta love a concussion."

The hotel room door creaked open. Maddy walked in the door, wearing jeans and a black V-neck T-shirt. She carried a bag. "Will. You're awake!"

"Hi, Maddy. You can't kill me off that easily."

"And I see you're feeling better."

"Yes. For better or worse, the noggin seems to be firing on all cylinders again. Just a wee headache left."

Maddy smiled, her green eyes sparkling. "Good. You were pretty funny earlier."

"That's what Bear said. What's for din?"

"Sandwiches. Just went to the place down the street. Needed some air but didn't want to go far."

"Let's eat, then." He sat up and groaned. "Maybe I should take some pain meds. I think I can eat, and the head feels much better but why not take the rest of the edge off?"

"Good idea. I got you some aspirin while I was out, too. Here you go." She handed him the pills and passed around the sandwiches.

"Perhaps I can take advantage of your moment of weakness here. I think we need to claim this jaunt to Vilnius a bust and head to Bagan."

"You just love to be right, don't you?" Will took the pills and a tentative bite of his sandwich.

"Sure, who doesn't? But seriously. We've been here for days, haven't seen a thing, and the Rambo guns mission didn't pan out so well either."

The sandwich tasted better than Will suspected it would and he took a bigger bite. "I don't see that this morning's misadventure should weigh on whether or not we continue searching here."

Maddy pointed at the ice bag. "Well, what they have in common is that I've had bad feelings about both. The reason for this morning's evil feelings has revealed itself."

Bear spoke around a bite of sandwich. "Marshall, I feel bad about that. It's my fault."

"Nonsense. I don't see what you could have done differently."

Bear looked sheepish. "Could have loaded up a gun once we left."

She shrugged this suggestion off. "We should have been able to fight them off at close range without resorting to guns. And those guys were on us right away."

Bear grimaced. "Probably that guide. Got his pals and waited for us."

"I had a brief thought that it might be the Russians, but I think you're right."

"Yes, but, under the circumstances, I still should have—"

She interrupted, "Even if you want to call it a mistake, we all make them. And we learn from them. Which is why I think we should be making plans to head to Bagan."

She sure can be a single-minded creature. Will said, "You want to head all that way on just your gut?"

"Not just my gut, although I'm learning to listen to it. But also, we haven't found anything here! We've not found any evidence that this is the 'Center of the Pagan Empire.' All we've seen are howling iron wolves everywhere."

Bear put down his sandwich. "Those are pretty cool, though. I like the historical reference to when the grand duke chose this place as his capital. Plus, it was from a prophetic dream. You have to admit that part is cool."

Maddy looked at Bear. "I don't remember reading about the dream part. Can you fill me in?" She sat back and took another bite.

"Sure. It's a cool little story. One day, the Grand Duke of Lithuania, whose name was Gediminas, was on a hunting trip in the valley around the mouth of the river Vilnia. It was a successful hunt and Gediminas killed a bison. When night fell, the party decided to set up camp and spend the night there. While he was asleep, the Duke had an unusual dream in which he saw an iron wolf at the top of the mountain where he had killed the bison. The wolf was standing with its head raised toward the moon, howling as loud as a hundred wolves. When he woke up, the Duke remembered his strange dream and consulted one of his pagan priests about it."

Will took a bite of sandwich. "What did the priest say?"

"The priest told the Duke that the dream was a direction to establish a city there. The howling of the wolf represented the fame of the future city. That city's reputation would spread far and wide, as far as the howling of the mysterious wolf. So, the Grand Duke of Lithuania, obeying the will of the gods, immediately started to build his future capital and took its name—Vilnius—from the Vilnia river. Which is why we're here and why we see those iron wolves everywhere."

To Will, it looked as if Maddy had gotten lost in the story. She roused herself. "Very cool. What year was that again?"

"It was 1323."

"I rest my case."

Will shook his head at her pigheadedness. "I don't know, Maddy. It will take us days to get to Bagan. And we talked about the timeline. Isabella and Ferdinand could have placed this clue here."

"I don't think so. And we're spinning our wheels here, running around, looking at iron wolves, and not seeing any signs of Ramiro."

Will took the ice bag off his head and scratched his beard. "Have you had a dream about this place?"

She paused.

Will realized Bear didn't know about her premonitory dreams.

Maddy must have figured out the same thing because she turned to Bear to explain. "Sometimes—not often, but every now and again—I have a dream that comes true."

"Like Gediminas. Sounds neat."

"It is, except all of them that I can recall have been about bad things that have come true, not good things."

"Like what?" Bear asked.

She looked at the floor and her tone filled with sorrow. "Like a dream I had the night before Dad and Maria were murdered. Like a dream I had about my mom before she died."

"I'm sorry."

"And I had one the other night about AJ."

"Oh no. Really?"

"Yes. Of course, I'm hoping that last one isn't real. Don't know yet. But there's this unmistakable feeling when I wake up with a real dream. Hard to describe. Sort of a cold certainty."

"Let's hope AJ is okay. I think the question, though, was have you had one of these dreams about searchin' here instead of Bagan."

Maddy's voice rose. "No, I haven't."

Will could feel her temper start to simmer. Her face flushed.

Maddy gritted her teeth. "What if we split up? I could go without you guys."

"I don't think that's a good idea," Bear said before Will could.

"I agree. We stick together," Will said.

"Great. I'm buying tickets out of here tomorrow. Glad you're coming with me." Her tone was final.

CHAPTER 55

July 15, 10:45 a.m.:

The day after the embarrassing weapons incident in Vilnius, Maddy, Will, and Bear purchased airplane tickets to Mandalay, which was the closest airport they could get to Bagan on short notice. Then they found a store to acquire several extra throwing knives and a prepaid cell phone to use later.

Purchases completed, the three of them took a bus to a nearby village that the guidebook had recommended as a friendly spot to see Lithuanian farm life. Their flight was tomorrow, so they wanted to put the free day to good use by practicing with the weapons they did have and could check with luggage. Once in the quaint village, they spied a narrow lane, which led into the countryside. They'd only walked a mile before Will seemed to tire.

"What about this spot? Can we stop here?" Will asked.

The nagging worry Maddy had felt since Will had been hit in the head with the bully stick had started to fade, but he sounded exhausted, so she took a harder look at the glen to their right. It was a decent-sized meadow area behind a copse of trees, just off the narrow country road. She had dismissed it at first as being too exposed but they would hear a car, or people, coming from a distance.

After yesterday's debacle, it was clear she needed some aikido practice, Will needed throwing training, and Bear could use some preparation, too. If she had her way about it, Will would realize he also needed to begin to learn some self-defense beyond the knife. She was keen to become an aikido teacher, why not start today?

Maddy tossed the hair out of her eyes. "We can make it work. Bear, what do you think?"

"It's a little close to the road, but I think we'll hear folk comin'."

"I thought the same thing. Let's just make sure it's not soggy or anything."

They bushwhacked two yards into the clearing and then stomped around. It was a peaceful, bucolic setting, graced with short green grass, chirping birds, and several dark-winged butterflies that floated above colorful wildflowers.

Will pointed. "Looks fine to me. It dried quickly after yesterday's rain."

Will took a hotel blanket from his backpack and fanned it out on the ground. Today's skies were clear, and the temperature a little warm, so the spot he chose was in the shade on the far side of the meadow. "I need to rest for a minute."

"Me too," Maddy said.

She and Bear sat cross-legged near the blanket and drank some water out of their water bottles. After a minute of appreciating the shade and the quiet palette of nature, Maddy said, "Did you guys see anybody watching us today?"

"Are you trying to freak me out?" Will sounded peevish. "I'm still recovering from having the crap beat out of me yesterday."

"No, I just thought I saw somebody. A blond somebody. But, like you've been, I wasn't sure. It was a glance out of the corner of my eye." As she spoke, Maddy picked up a dark, jagged stone from the ground and fingered around its edges, as if it were a worry stone.

"Lovely," Will said, sarcastically.

"I'd rather know than not know. And I'm telling you because I think it would be good for you to learn aikido."

Will groaned, "Not this again."

"Will. Think about it. How'd that knife work for you yesterday?"

"Shut up." He sounded only half joking and rolled over to face away from Maddy and Bear. "Leave me alone."

Irritated, she snapped, "Sure, I'll just let you die next time because you can't take care of yourself."

"Hey!" He sat up. "Party foul. That wasn't nice!"

Maddy pitched the dark stone toward the other side of the meadow, angry. "It's the truth!"

Bear got up and walked out of earshot. Maddy watched him pull a few knives of his own from a sleeve and start to throw them at a large oak. Juvenile as the desire might be, Maddy wished he would take her side for once.

"Since when, in this day and age, is self-defense a requirement? I've certainly been able to put bread on my table. My boss loves me. And, after yesterday, I'm missing my job."

Maddy clenched her fists and brought her anger down a notch, back under control. "I have no doubt you're smart, Will, and have a great job, but yes, in this day and age, self-defense is still a useful thing to know. Didn't you ever get the heebie-jeebies walking down a side street in São

Paulo when toughs followed you? Maybe thinking they were going to roll you for your wallet?"

"Maybe."

"And, besides, we're in the middle of something huge here, something where knowing how to handle yourself could come in handy."

"I don't want to learn to be violent," Will retorted.

She paused and had an idea. "Let me show you something. Are you up for moving around just a little?"

He exaggerated a moan. "Sure."

"Okay. Come here. Stand like you're riding a skateboard. Front foot pointed forward, back foot perpendicular to it. Like this." She put her right foot forward and her left foot behind her, turned out. She straightened her back and bent her knees. "It's called *hanmi* stance."

Will stood and did as she instructed. "Okay, so what?"

"Bend your knees a little more. See if you can resist when I push on your shoulders. Keep your feet where they are. I'm going to try and push you off balance. Are you ready?"

"Yes."

Maddy pushed on his upper chest using the strength of her legs. Good. He was grounded and solid. She couldn't move him. "See that? I can't move you."

Will smiled. "I am taller than you and have you by a few pounds."

"Not the point. Now, I want you to think of something that ticks you off. Maybe the Russians who killed Maria. Maybe climate change. That Napa cop. Find something." She watched his face change. "Got it?" But she knew he did.

He nodded. She reached out and, with one hand, pushed his chest. He fell backward, arms flailing like a windmill.

"Hey!"

She laughed. The shocked look on his face was priceless.

Will scrambled back to a standing position. "Maybe I wasn't ready. Let's do that again."

Maddy raised an eyebrow. "With or without anger?"

"Both."

Maddy stood with her arms at her side. "All right. Think a kind thought. Or about what we had for breakfast."

He smiled his lopsided grin. "Ready."

She brought her arm up and pressed on his chest again, but she couldn't push him over, even though she tried. "Can't do it. Get mad again."

Will took a deep breath and his face changed. "Idiotic walrus Napa cop probably has me on the Most Wanted list by now. Ready."

"Ready or not, here I come!" As she said "come," she again pushed with one hand.

He lost his balance and stepped to the side.

"Huh," Will said, with a puzzled tone.

"Figure that one out, Mr. Science."

"If we ever get back to the real world, it might make an interesting case study." He took on a mocking tone, "How the body reacts in kind states versus states of hatred or anger." Smiling, he sat back down. "In the meantime, I concede the power of kindness."

"Good. That's the point of aikido. Gentle strength. You don't have to be a goon, be violent, or go around killing people."

"I don't have to be violent?"

She sat next to him, cross-legged. "No. Don't you remember this from high school? An angry or hateful opponent has already lost."

"Don't remember anything from high school except Jill MacIntyre's legs."

"Seriously? I don't even remember Jill."

"Hot. But okay, I'll think about it. Hey—what happened yesterday then?"

"Thanks for thinking about it—that's all a girl can ask. You mean why did my butt get kicked, too?"

"In a nutshell, yes. If aikido is so great, why'd we lose those weapons?"

"This is why I need some practice. I got ticked off watching your pretty little head hit the pavement. Their knife and the bully stick freaked me out, too. I was already off balance all morning and didn't focus well. I should have been able to neutralize all four of those attackers by myself—that's the kind of stuff we practice." Her face grew pink with shame, and she looked down. "The reality of a fight, I'm learning, is just different. The truth is: I choked." Shyly, she looked back up at him. "I'm sorry."

Will met her gaze. "No harm done."

She smiled. "Just your head. Maybe it knocked some sense into you."

"My head is fine. Good luck trying to knock some sense into it. We can try to find weapons again once we get to Bagan. Or maybe in Mandalay, where we land. It's a bigger town."

"I'm glad we got the disposable cell phone, though. We can use it in one of the airports along the way. Turn the lemons of all those stops into some sort of lemonade. I want to check on AJ."

"That first stop here in Europe would be better. In case the call is traced, we don't want an Asian connection. I need to make sure that walrus cop isn't after my hide, too."

"Good points." She stood. "I'm going to see if Bear will train with me. I need some practice."

"Wait. Maddy." There was an odd tone in his voice. Like a pleading uncertainty. Strange, maybe he was hurt worse than she thought.

She sat back down next to him and raised an eyebrow, questioning how she could help.

"I'm wondering—" His voice caught in his throat. "I'm wondering how you dealt with your fears. You know. Back in Jerusalem."

She softened her voice. "Feeling freaked out?"

"Yeah. A little. More than usual anyway. Had nightmares of my own last night. Falling dreams." He looked around nervously. His eyes lit on Bear. "And this whole thing. Knives. Guns. Bad guys. Russians. Superconductors. E-bombs. Slinking around in alleys. Getting my head whacked. Yes, my head is spinning."

"Wait, from the concussion?"

"No, from us on the run."

"I see."

"Part of me wants to ride like the wind out of here and go get lost in Alaska."

She put a hand on his arm for a moment to comfort him. "I understand that."

"But you're not freaked out. You faced down that guy in Jerusalem after dealing with the heights, the spiders. You even mastered the tunnel." He smiled and she ruffled his dark curls fondly. "What's your secret sauce? What did Samuel mean when he said I have to go in to get out?"

"'Going in is the only way out,'" she quoted.

"Yes, that's what he said. What did he mean? Did you have to go into something?"

She hugged her knees. *How to say this in a way his engineering mind can understand?* "It's a methodology. A procedure of sorts. It's a 'how-to' shortcut for dealing with emotions that aren't serving you." She looked him in the eyes and tried to put compassion and understanding in her gaze. "Like fear."

He swallowed. "Sounds useful right about now."

"I'm no expert yet, but what I'm learning is that if you feel the feeling you don't like, it will go away and stop tormenting you. That's what I did at the tunnel. It was the only way I could move beyond outright terror. But when I sat there and took the time to just be with it, it was scary for a minute, but I stuck with it, and it sort of dissolved."

"Really? Dissolved?"

"Like cotton candy in my mouth. Like going into the center of the tornado and finding it calm in there. Seriously, though, it brought back an icky memory with it. I don't know if that always happens, but I think that might have been what I was resisting. At any rate, it seems to have freed up some energy, and I've been able to start feeling my *ki*, or the Power, now, too."

"That sounds like more fun than feeling fear."

"It is." She smiled. "'Listen and feel the Power.'"

"What's that mean?"

"Another saying from Edith. It means that once you quiet your mind, you can start to feel the Power that is everywhere, even inside us."

Will tapped his fingers on his leg. "Is this some mystical martial arts woo-woo?"

"No. As a matter of fact, she told me our military is training soldiers in mindfulness."

"Interesting. They probably research the hell out of things like that."

"I'm sure they do. But why don't you see for yourself? Let me know when you've gone inside enough to deal with those fears and quiet your mind. Then we'll see. Deal?"

He smiled nervously. "Sure. Do I need to know anything else before I 'go in'? Some ancient secret Chinese breath technique?"

She swatted his arm. "You're hopeless. Just breathe into the feeling."

"Okay. Maybe I'll lie here and rest for a bit and try it."

"Just remember, it might get worse before it gets better, but your emotions won't kill you. You're safe. Bear and I will be right over there."

"Thanks, sis." He stretched out his lanky frame on the blanket. "Have fun practicing. Maybe you should deal with your resistance to handsome over there. I think he likes you."

"Oh stop." *So much for a good conversation.*

She walked over to where Bear hit near the same spot on a tree with each of his knives. *He does have nice shoulders. If only he were taller.*

CHAPTER 56

Baltic Airspace, July 16, 2:25 p.m.:

On the flight to Myanmar, Will was relieved that they'd left the airport without a hitch, even though the phone calls with the prepaid phone hadn't gone well. He was worried that Interpol already had him on their radar, or that the Russians had found some way to track them down. But they'd been able to move on.

He was feeling his oats today, or maybe it was the couple of tiny bottles of airplane alcohol he'd drunk on the first flight. With his fear of heights, his flying formula was always to finagle an aisle seat and then drink his way into oblivion so that he couldn't look out the window or think too much about being thousands of meters in the sky, hurtling through the air at several hundred kilometers an hour, in what amounted to a tin can.

Today, however, Providence had given him a window seat and he decided to sit there. Not only did he not feel like bargaining with Maddy over her middle seat, but he also, truth be told, felt a twinge of guilt about falling asleep yesterday in the meadow instead of trying to deal with any of his fears, which were still irritating the hell out of him. By sitting near the window, he knew he was setting himself up for a small test of his own. But on his own terms.

Maddy sat next to him, with Bear napping to her left.

Ten minutes after takeoff, she put down her paperback thriller—*isn't living this adventure enough*?—and turned to Will. "What can we do about AJ?"

"I don't know. You were right again, though. Your true dreams are downright creepy."

Maddy pulled her hair over her shoulder. "I just wish for once they'd tell me something useful, like how to help him."

"That would be nice. Let's recap what his foster mom told you. Maybe we can think of something."

"Okay. She told me that he went missing in the park. They were down at Golden Gate watching a comedy festival. Ellen DeGeneres was there. It was a big deal."

Will cupped his chin in his hand and stroked his beard. "Four days ago."

"Right. He played Hula-hoop with some girls—"

Will interrupted, "Already a ladies' man, a lad after my own heart."

"Good grief." Maddy rolled her eyes. "Anyway, the girls were the last ones to see him. The foster mom, Alice, got scared after the show ended, and AJ was nowhere to be found. She called the police. They canvassed the area."

"And forensics hasn't found anything?" Will asked.

"No. Foster mom thinks it's a pedophile. Led him off and grabbed him in the bushes."

"She's probably worried he'll end up dead."

"Yes. She didn't say that, but…" Maddy trailed off.

"It is a possibility," Will said.

Maddy shuddered. "True. But my dream had our blond-haired arch villain in it."

The wheels turned in Will's head. "Yes, that is disturbing."

"It is. What would he want with AJ?" Maddy asked.

The idea clicked into place. "Insurance." Will felt certain.

"What do you mean?"

"Assuming they exist, what if we find the obelisks inside the *châsse* first?"

"I hope we do."

"Then if the sniper tracks us down later and we don't give him what he wants, he has AJ as collateral."

"That bastard!" Maddy's hand hit the paperback with a *smack* and her voice was loud enough that several people in the seats across the aisle looked their way. Bear continued to sleep.

Will lowered his voice so that she would do the same. "What else could it be? If it is the Russian that has him."

Maddy scrunched her face in anger. "You're probably right. I just hate the idea."

"That might be part of their plan, too. Tick you off. Get you off balance."

A thoughtful look entered her eyes. "That's even more insidious. And it means our opponents may know something about working with energy themselves. Bad."

"Yes, bad. And based on the other phone call to Bella, we can't ask the authorities for help."

"You mean how our sister indicated the Napa walrus, I mean officer, wants you back in for additional questioning?"

"Yes, that," Will said.

"And has given you a week to return from your 'vacation' before he places you on that most wanted list?"

Will felt sick about it. "Yes, that again." He'd never been in trouble with the law before.

"He wouldn't be very helpful if he knew we were headed to Myanmar."

"No. We could use the CIA to get him off my back, but how do you call the agency exactly?"

Her tone was light, "Hello? Nine-one-one operator? Could you connect me to the CIA? Yes, we're trying to save the world here and could use your help. Yes, an artifact from a thousand years ago with unknown mystical powers. Yes, we think the Russians are after it, too, and want to kill us."

"I agree. We'd be the laughingstock of Langley. We need to find the *châsse*, see what's inside, and if it does appear to be dangerous, involve them at that point."

"Makes sense to me. It's our best chance to clear your name and save AJ. I'm going back to my book. It's pretty good."

"Okay. I'm going to try not to look out the window."

But as she turned away, he was drawn to looking out and down.

Small patches appeared so far below him that the landscape reminded him of the quilt that always used to lay folded at the foot of his Grandma Emma and Grandpa Max's bed. How high in the air were they? The world spun, as he feared it would. He shut his eyes and gripped his hands together.

Now I've done it! I'll end up losing my lunch. What did she say yesterday that I was supposed to do? The only way out is in.

After pushing the tiny gray button that only marginally reclined his seat, Will arranged an extra shirt under his head and tried to get comfortable.

In. Go into the feeling. How the hell does one do that?

Whenever he had these attacks of anxiety, he got dizzy and his stomach clenched. He decided to start with his stomach. It felt tight and hard.

Go into the feeling. What does it feel like inside there?

He was awkward and rusty, having spent most of his life trying not to feel these feelings. So, he tried breathing into the feeling.

Whoa! That made everything worse—tighter. I am going to puke! Wait, she said it got worse before it got better.

He controlled his breathing so he didn't hyperventilate. *Same breath in, same breath out. Breathe into that feeling.*

The tightness expanded, seemed to swallow him.

Now he felt as if he were falling, as in his falling dreams, the feeling of being out of control made his head spin.

Will was rooted to the airplane seat with terror.

And then he was back in time, in his mom's car, flying through the air and crashing, back when he was four. The memories were fresh and vivid.

For the first time in a long time, he remembered the details of the car crash when Mom died. She and Grandma Emma had taken him to a friend's birthday party down the road in Tahoe City. Maddy had been sick that day so she hadn't gone. On the way home, black ice had caught their car, sent it flying over an embankment for what had seemed like the longest eternity ever, and then crashed into a tree with a huge crunching sound, painfully twisting his left arm and cutting his chin as the car door buckled on him. *I'm not safe.*

From their silence, his mom's open, staring eyes, and the blood on his grandmother's face, he knew they were both dead. His screaming didn't bring them back. Touching their faces and their blood didn't wake them up. He was alone and not safe in that cold car.

Eventually, he had to leave them to get help. He walked half a mile in the snow by himself with a broken arm and bloody chin, crying, eventually finding a home filled with strangers.

Will allowed himself to feel all of it.

Not safe anywhere.

After a time, a switch, somewhere inside, turned.

I am safe. Right here, right now, I am safe.

It was a revelation.

New feelings flooded through him, replacing the terror he'd glimpsed a moment before. He felt lighter, his stomach settled and his head was no longer dizzy. *Wow—it worked.* Touch and go there for a minute, but like Maddy said, it didn't kill him.

Not safe, he mused. *All those feelings were based on that thought.*

From that psych class in college, he'd known the mind was a powerful thing. He recalled studies of athletes, using only visualization in their practice, who were able to outperform physically practicing teammates, but the implications here blew him away for a minute.

It was as if he'd been seeing the whole world through a set of glasses that had the words *NOT SAFE* written on them. Especially elevated parts of the world. And what a different place it was when he took off the glasses.

Will basked in the new feelings for a time, then he decided to test himself. With a sense of trepidation, he opened his eyes and looked out the window. He soon realized that it was a wonderful sight. He felt as if he were flying. He was a large bird, flying over the land. An oddly shaped blue jewel appeared in a field of green below, and he guessed it was a lake in the middle of a forest. It was beautiful. And didn't make him sick. Grinning, he realized he passed his own test.

After tapping her book to get her attention, he gave Maddy a huge smile and a thumbs-up. She looked at him, puzzled.

"I'll tell you later." He'd tell her about his experience at a better time. This place was too public.

He looked out the window again. In the distance, he could see mountains.

The sight of the mountains brought him back to earth. Even with his paralyzing fear gone, he knew that they still had an uphill battle to find the Aragon *châsse* and make it home alive.

And only a week until that walrus cop wanted him back in California. He was running out of time.

CHAPTER 57

Mandalay, Myanmar, July 17, 6:30 p.m.:

The encrypted phone in Ivan's pocket rang. He and AJ were in a dank hotel on the outskirts of Mandalay. His warder had gone to get food and supplies. Ivan didn't like the odd-eyed man. Pyotr was no better than the idiot who'd almost gotten Ivan killed in Napa by disobeying orders. Swearing, he touched the burn scar on his face, hoping it wouldn't scare his son back home.

His son, the rebel, was so different than AJ. The red-haired child, although discomforted, had proven clever but cooperative. The sniper liked to think it was because he was treating the boy decently.

Pyotr disagreed with his approach to the child, but Pyotr didn't know everything. Sometimes a carrot worked better than a stick.

Ivan answered the phone on the second ring with his left hand.

His right hand was infected from the bite wound. With his disease, he registered no pain, but it would need to be professionally treated soon or he could endure lasting damage. It could even kill him.

The encrypted, metallic-sounding voice on the phone held no pleasantries. "They have stopped in Bagan."

Ivan knew it was the baron and answered with the proper tone of respect. "Do our orders still stand?"

"Yes. Be careful. Be sure before you act."

"Yes, sir."

The phone went dead in Ivan's ear. As he put the phone back in his pocket, he reflected that his child's life was in the baron's dangerous hands. Like it or not, Ivan must do what needed to be done to keep his son safe.

CHAPTER 58

Bagan, Myanmar, July 17, 6:55 p.m.:

Although riding on the oxen-drawn cart in Bagan was a novel experience, Maddy was ready to be done traveling.

Yesterday, they were on the plane all day, spent the night in Mandalay, and, due to a lack of a working aircraft on the Mandalay-to-Bagan route, today had spent nine hours on the "seven-hour train." Several passengers had brought chickens in cages along for the ride, which seemed amusing at first, but didn't take long to lose its charm. Rather like the ox ride, the train had been fun for a minute, then bumpy and slow. It was an excruciating way to watch for those who might be following them.

In the interest of time, they had decided to skip finding weapons for now. The decision both relieved Maddy and made her feel more exposed at the same time. Will was already feeling anxious about needing to be back in California in six days, and Maddy was feeling the same press of time.

The climate in Myanmar, formerly known as Burma, was hot and humid, and July was the rainy season. Bear liked the sticky climate, saying it reminded him of his youth in North Carolina before he moved to Lake Tahoe, but she and Will complained it was too hot. For one, it made Maddy's hair look as if birds had set up camp there and fashioned a thousand nests. For another, the heat made her feel as if she were always walking in sand. She hated the humidity and pined for the dry air of California.

However, Maddy was intrigued by the culture. Their ox cart driver wore a cloth that looked like a skirt called a *longyi,* and both women and men chewed a red concoction made of betel leaves, slaked lime paste, and sometimes tobacco. Apparently, the mixture had a somewhat euphoric effect but caused a prevalence of oral cancer. She'd read it was also the cause of the population's ubiquitous missing teeth and red-stained mouths.

They wanted to scout the old town of Bagan before they ate dinner, so had caught the cart ride from New Bagan to Old Bagan. It wasn't far, but in the heat, she was grateful for every step she didn't have to walk, even though her thigh was feeling much better. She would focus on feeling grateful and worry about the bruises from the bumpy ride later.

The driver dropped them off at Tharabar Gate, a sturdy-looking stone structure from days long past. In front of the gate, on each side of it, were two shrines, one male and one female image, both in red hats with painted gold faces. They reminded Maddy of dolls she had played with as a child.

Bear read from his guidebook. "'Tharabar, the main gate of the eastern wall, is the only one left of the twelve gates of the walled city that King Pyinbya established in 849.'"

"So at least we know this town was around in Ramiro's day," Maddy said.

"Yep. Bagan became a central power base in the mid-ninth century under King Anawratha, who unified Burma under Theravada Buddhism. It's estimated that as many as thirteen thousand temples and stupas once stood here."

Will walked over to the stone gate and studied it. "That's a lot."

Maddy stood still and looked around. "I feel like we're on the right track but how many of those temples are still around?"

"There are twenty-two hundred, in various states of disrepair, but since they're all still considered sacred, we need to take off our shoes and socks before entering. And it's good we're wearin' long shorts as we're not supposed to show any knee."

"Okay, good to know. How long did people live here?"

It looked like a religious ghost town now, with only tourists milling about. Maddy hadn't expected it to be quite so wind-whipped and deserted. It reminded her of Bodie, a California town frozen in time that she visited once.

"Most historians think the Mongols invaded and sacked it in 1287," Bear replied.

Will joined Bear and Maddy. "So, for four hundred and thirty-eight years, it was alive and well. And the timing works from the Ramiro perspective. Shall we go in?" Will pointed through the gates and started moving through them.

Maddy was impressed by Will's calculator-like mind and surprised at how thick the gates were as they walked through. They'd been seeing temples dot the landscape for some time now, but the view inside the gate was amazing. "Wow."

Bear closed the guidebook down, using his finger to bookmark the page. "Look at that."

"Let's just be tourists for an hour," Maddy said.

"I could gaze at these abandoned temples and pagodas for days," Bear said.

Will swiveled his head from side to side. "We probably will, searching for a sign."

Maddy looked around, taking it all in. "I know, it would just be fun to be here without an agenda and appreciate the architecture."

"What's that tall temple over there to the left?" Will asked, "The one that looks like a white mausoleum with a golden tip at the top?"

Bear looked in the guidebook again. "That's Thatbyinnyu Temple—the tallest pagoda here. It measures just over two hundred feet tall. It was built in the twelfth century. The name translates to 'omniscience.'"

All of the temples needed to be searched. Awe and dismay filled Maddy. Her jaw dropped open and her right eye began to twitch.

They drifted toward the tall pagoda. It looked complex and there were so many similar temples and pagodas in the area. The tall one had seven terraces, all on one side. She counted over twenty spires, without even being able to see the back of the structure. As they walked around, they saw, on three sides of the ground floor, tall statues of Buddha made of brick and cement.

They took their shoes off and walked inside. On the ceiling and walls of the vaulted corridors, they found original mural paintings of people pursuing a variety of daily activities, painted in hues of tan, gray, and red. The lifelike action illustrated their lives with a delicacy, grace, and beauty that took Maddy's breath away.

While they put their shoes back on outside, they were accosted by an assortment of women and children selling wares. Several of the children and one of the women had golden colored leaves applied to their cheeks. Maddy figured they weren't stickers and wondered how they got them to stay on their faces in the heat. Even though some of the goods looked interesting, shopping was not top of mind at the moment, so they passed and walked on.

Everywhere she looked around the spire-fringed skyline, the gilded past contrasted sharply against the tumbledown present. Occasional groups of bald Buddhist monks moved in unison like schools of fish up and down the street. Stupas crowned with glitter-studded, miter-like spires and ascending tiers of roofs lined by lacy fascia woodcarvings, towered over copious amounts of overgrown weeds, stray dogs, relentless garbage, and clusters of overheated tourists.

She hoped this place still held the clue they were looking for among the ancient bricks and bushy bougainvillea. That missing *signum regis* was the key to keeping the Power of the obelisks from the hands of the Russians. She hoped it was here.

For a moment, one of the tourists looked like the burned Russian. Her breath caught. She stopped, touched Bear's arm, and said softly, "Hey."

Bear glanced her way. "What?"

Silently, she pointed toward the stupa where she had seen the slight, blond-haired man.

Will also stopped walking and glanced in the direction she pointed.

There was no one there.

Maddy shrugged one shoulder and took a deep breath. "False alarm."

"No worries," Bear said. "But would you like to walk in a different direction?"

"I would."

They turned right ninety degrees and continued walking down a new path.

Five minutes later, Maddy stopped to watch a pair of squirrels scamper from one temple to the walls and pediments of another. "Should we follow the same low, medium, high methodology we used before?"

Bear also halted and wiped the sweat out of his eyes with the back of his hand. "What if we look at the oldest structures first?"

Maddy liked Bear's solid, common sense approach. "Works for me. Does the guidebook have ages for the structures?"

"It does."

Will was playing with a medium-sized stray dog: young, mostly white, male. If it had a breed, Maddy didn't recognize it. Will had thrown a stick for it twice, making a new friend.

"Will, work for you?" Maddy asked.

"Sure, we can start there first and check the later structures if the earlier ones don't pan out. Anything built before Ramiro's time is fair game. What drew him here, do you think?"

"I know it looks ruined now, but in Ramiro's life, it was a thriving, well-known center of commerce and spirituality. It was out of the way, yes, but maybe he liked that," Bear replied.

"If I were trying to hide something and lived when he did, this would have seemed like a good spot," Maddy agreed.

Will threw the stick one last time. "Or maybe we're wasting our time here, too."

Sometimes Will's skepticism irritated Maddy and this was one of those times. "We'll never know until we look."

The dog followed Will as they moved. "Should I call him Buddy or Buddha?"

"Buddha might be insulting. But he'll forget you by tomorrow. Let's just go."

"C'mon, Buddy. Show me your town," Will said, and Buddy wagged his tail.

They searched for an hour before the beautiful, filtered light failed, and they could no longer see well enough to find any clue that might be hidden in the antique bricks. They headed back to New Bagan for dinner, tired and daunted.

The dog followed them for about half a mile. then it turned away, leaving them to walk the dark road back alone.

CHAPTER 59

July 20, 7:30 a.m.:

For two full days in Bagan, they looked at Buddhist temples, inside, outside, around each side, all to no avail. Not even the ghost of a clue presented itself and Bear could feel the twins' frustration. Will, in particular, was getting wound up, and Bear didn't blame him. The lone bright spot was that the dog, Buddy, and his wagging tail, had joined them each day.

They spied tourist balloons lazily circling the old city, and Bear secretly thought an aerial trip around the town might be romantic. Not so secretly, it might be a good way to search the taller spires of the city. As it had in Vilnius, the GoPro could help with their tourist disguise and the video would be amusing to look back on someday, if they made it through the rest of their adventure alive.

The town had two balloon tour companies. One had all red balloons, the other's fleet was entirely green. Over lunch one day, they overheard a tale that the green balloon company had experienced an accidental gas explosion several months ago. Despite the risks, Bear had talked the twins into a ride to increase their odds of finding a clue.

They arranged a tour with the red balloon tour vendor and were preparing for launch. In a staging area, next to their basket, several other balloons were spread out on a soccer field, which was about twenty minutes from town by bus.

The old English buses from WWII that they'd ridden to the launch site lined the outskirts of the field and tethered the balloons to the ground. Bear looked at the antique buses and imagined their long journey from England. He briefly recalled the bloody Burma Campaign. There was much history here, and he loved it.

"I'm not so sure about this." Will looked a little pale, not liking heights. Interesting that he hadn't voiced a concern at dinner last night when they'd planned the trip. "But the equipment looks cool, check it out." Will pointed to the noisy contraption that was burning gas above their heads and shooting flames up into the open belly of the balloon. "I wonder how that green balloon exploded."

"Maybe it's a not-so urban myth," Bear suggested.

Will turned to their tour guide. "Did one of the green balloons explode?"

"Not have much English. It not explode. It catch on fire and have to come down very fast. That is all."

Their guide was of Burmese descent, wore long shorts, no shoes, a light-colored T-shirt and had short, spiked, coal-black hair. His teeth were stained from chewing betel leaves. At least he still had all his teeth.

"Oh, thanks. That's reassuring," Will said with a smile.

The guide returned Will's smile. Based on the popularity of the tours, Bear guessed the locals could afford to make fun with the tourists and still do plenty of business.

Perhaps because it was the rainy season and fewer tourists than normal infested the area, they managed to get the balloon to themselves, along with the dog and the tour operator. Buddy had again tagged along and Will had done nothing to discourage his canine companion. The operator just smiled, nodded, and spat a red stream when Will asked if the dog could join them. They were all ensconced in a generous bathroom-sized bamboo basket with sides four feet high.

The spike-haired young man handed bags of sand from the bottom of the balloon over the basket's side to a cohort. "Hold on to the sides now," he said with one hand on a guy line.

Then he pulled a quick release and the balloon rose smoothly into the air. The ground fell away at what Bear considered a tad slower rate than most helicopters, but within seconds they were above the tree line. Will watched the ground and swayed from side to side like a tree in a windstorm.

Bear pointed toward the skyline. "Argones. Don't look down. Look at the trees, or out at the horizon."

Will pulled his eyes up, took hold of the railing, unobtrusively checked his knife scabbard under his sleeve, and stopped swaying. "Thanks, Bear."

Over the last few days, Bear had shown Will how to spin a piece of flat wood in the air to use as a knife target, and Will had become fascinated with the process, mumbling about trajectories, velocity, calculus equations, and such. Bear was just pleased that slowly, but surely, Will appeared to be getting more accurate and comfortable with his knives.

Maddy wore a baseball cap and twirled her ponytail in her fingers with a hypnotic rhythm. "This was a great idea, Bear, we'll be able to see a lot from up here."

Riding the air currents, they followed several other maroon balloons that had taken off before them. Crimson in its morning display, the sun had come up over the tree line only a few minutes earlier. In the spellbinding dawn glow, the golden Irrawaddy River sparkled and snaked in the distance and they began to travel downstream, toward Old Bagan and its famous pagodas. The still-almost-cool air smelled fresh and Bear's spirits lifted along with the balloon.

The guide moved to the other side of the basket, ignored them, and spat over the side. It was already a long way down. Bear wondered if the spit disintegrated in the air or if there was an unlucky sod below whose head would be the recipient of a large red droplet.

Will pointed. "Look at that temple. It looks like a golden ice-cream cone."

They were almost level with it. It was just a couple of hundred feet away.

"Golden spires everywhere." Maddy looked around as the operator's radio crackled. She pointed to another bell-shaped structure to the north, from where they'd come. "There's some even way back there."

It was true, although Old Bagan had a higher density of temples, the surrounding countryside had its fair share as well. Near where she had pointed, a batch of green balloons blossomed. One of the air ferries flared its gas and against the bright light, Bear saw what could be a blond-haired man. Hard to tell, it was several hundred yards behind them, at least.

The possible sighting made him wish again that they had been able to obtain weapons in Mandalay. He had been keeping his eyes open for sketchy types in New Bagan who might know how they could acquire some firepower. Unfortunately, the place was full of monks, not mischief.

Bear pointed to the specs around the guide's neck. "Can I borrow the binoculars?"

The guide handed them to Bear. They were beat up, not great quality to begin with, but they would have to do. He pointed them toward the cluster of green balloons and focused.

Maddy stepped closer to him. "What do you see, Bear?"

She smells good.

"I'm not sure yet." *Definitely not military-grade binocs.*

A blond man wore a blue polo shirt, and the other, a taller dark-haired man, sported a solid black T-shirt.

Bear handed the binoculars over to Maddy. "Take a look at that second green balloon. Tell me what you see."

She took the binoculars, focused them to her eyes. After a long ten seconds, she tore them off her face, turned her back to the green balloon, and swore vehemently under her breath.

CHAPTER 60

8:00 a.m.:

Maddy turned her back away from the green balloon and the Russian assassin. "I thought I saw him the other day, that first night we were here. It's the sniper." She swore and hit her thigh.

At the recognition of the threat, her stomach, which up to now had been doing fine with the heights, decided to do flip-flops.

"Seriously? Let me see." Will reached for the binoculars and Maddy handed them to him.

"He's with a taller, dark-haired guy. No AJ that I can see. Can you tell if they're looking this way?"

"I don't know. Hard to tell with these lame binoculars."

Maddy's voice cracked. "What do we do? We need a plan."

"How did they find us? That false clue should have sent them to the middle of nowhere." Will jerked the binoculars from his eyes and turned to face Maddy and Bear.

The guide continued to ignore them. The dog whined, sensing the fear.

Bear patted the dog's head absently. "They're looking for two men and a woman. They're a ways back there. At this distance, they're not going to be able to see much either, although they might have better equipment."

Maddy's hands were sweaty and she rubbed her palms together. "Could they hit us? If they shoot at us?"

Bear shook his head. "Too far back. But if the winds change and they get closer..." Trailing off, he looked at Will. "It would be best if they don't know it's us. Argones, you sit down here on the floor next to the dog. You'll be out of sight. Keep the binoculars. Continue scannin' the Russians for any information and Old Bagan for the clue."

Will sat down next to the dog, cross-legged. "Sure, I can do that. What will you two do?" He put the binoculars back to his eyes and began to scan through holes in the basket's weave.

Bear turned his back on the green balloon so that he was looking the same direction as Maddy. "We can't push the wind. We need a disguise. Are you up for being a couple?" He put his arm around her.

She almost rolled her eyes. "A couple? You mean you and me?" This was the oldest trick in the book. *Men...*

"Yes, they know we're not together, so they're not expectin' to see a couple. People see what they expect to see."

Heart pounding, thinking quickly, she turned to face him and looked into his arctic-blue eyes, now melting. They were in trouble. It would be a good hoax. "True. Okay."

He put his hand on her hip. "Can I kiss you?"

Slowly, she nodded.

It was awkward, lips touching, agreed to but unexpected. Suddenly, even more bewildering, a surge of energy flowed through her and lit her up. *His energy is...strong.* The kiss kindled a spark. She'd had her share of kissing. *But this is—*

Thought stopped, she gave in to the sudden fire and kissed him back.

The spark grew into a flame. Awareness of time fled.

After what could have been a minute, the dog whined again, and Will hit their legs with the strap of the binoculars. "Hey. Lovebirds."

Maddy pulled smoothly away and looked Bear in the eyes. *Had he felt that, too?*

His eyes beamed. He had felt something. She shivered and shook her head to clear it.

"What is it, Will?"

"You guys aren't going to believe this." From his spot on the floor of the basket, Will had the binoculars trained ahead, between basket sections, to Old Bagan. "I see a *signum regis* on top of one of those temples."

Maddy reached for the binoculars and Will handed them over without a word. "No way."

She focused them where Will was pointing and, sure enough, on the side of a medium-sized, bell-shaped cone was the telltale sign. At this distance, it looked rather small and, with the decay of years, some of the roof tiles that made up the sign had fallen off. Yet, the symbol was unmistakable: a thorned cross with a pointed bottom and flanged ends.

Maddy nodded. "That's it all right. I see the white mausoleum with the golden spire we looked at our first night here. The sign is second to the left of it. On the building that looks like an upside-down ice-cream cone. Happy birthday to us! Take a look, Bear."

She handed him the binoculars and watched him as he studied the temple. He was a smart, good-looking man with a kind soul. He also had a tall spirit and was sexier than she'd realized. Was that enough?

Bear interrupted her train of thought. "Yeah, there she is. Just to the right of the squat round one. I remember the temple it's on. It's the oldest one here and the only Hindu temple. Let me find it in the guidebook."

While he grabbed the book, Maddy looked back to the green balloon that held her father's killer. The balloon still looked small on the horizon. He was far enough back there that they could take a moment to study the clue.

Bear pulled the guidebook from his pocket and flipped through the pages. "Nathlaung Kyaung Temple. Square temple, with steep-rising upper terraces. Central pillar inside holds up the dome and it has Vishnu reliefs cut into the bricks." He looked at Will and Maddy. "How'd we miss it before?"

Maddy smiled broadly. "We were on the ground. I wonder if you can see the clue from the top of the tall temple? I'll bet you can since there were no balloons back in the day. We never went to the top. But I guess it doesn't matter at this point. We found ourselves the 'Center of the Pagan Empire.'"

Bear squeezed her arm. "I guess we have. But with our Russian tail, let me see if our guide can understand enough English to move this Hindenburg along any faster."

CHAPTER 61

9:15 a.m.:

To Will, the green balloon that contained the sniper seemed to get closer to them with every passing minute.

Proud of his accomplishment spotting Ramiro's sign, but concerned about the Russians behind them, he kept one eye on their pursuers and the other on the *signum regis*, which graced the temple ahead.

He was grateful that Bear and Maddy were now restraining themselves to standing next to each other, with Bear's arm over her shoulder. *Disguising themselves as a couple. Clever move, Bear, I'll have to remember that one.* He'd suspected that the energy between them would hit a flash point. It was only a matter of time.

Will continued to sit out of sight below the railing and wondered if the guide thought them odd. But the spiky-haired young man didn't utter a word, just guided the balloon and spat over the side. Will found the spitting somewhat disgusting, and seeing all the old men around town without teeth had made him glad he'd quit smoking.

Bear's urging of the red-mouthed guide to more speed proved futile. The sights were spectacular but there seemed no way to hurry the rest of their flight. The wind was the wind, after all.

Eventually, the landing field appeared. It was across the main road from a lonely pyramid-shaped stupa. Will was pleased that he'd made it this far without tossing his breakfast. Perhaps he had made progress on the plane about his fear of heights, but the imminent landing made him hold onto the binoculars with an iron grip. Before departure, they'd had to sign a waiver that discussed how the landing might be bumpy, and the basket might even lie on its side and drag for a while until it stopped. *Gee, doesn't that sound like a fun way to end our flight?*

As they lost altitude, their captain came alive. "Time to land. Need binoculars back."

Will hesitated before he handed them over. Looking through them had been a good way to distract himself from the anxiety of a crash landing.

"Face backward to the wind."

At the guide's direction, all three of them turned away from their landing zone and looked the other way, back toward their pursuer. Will hated to think of what would happen if the Russian, or Russians, caught up with them.

"Sit down on the seat and hold on to the rope."

Following instructions, they grabbed onto the handles woven into the basket sidewall.

"Lean back against basket padding."

The guide prodded Will, who had assumed a head-between-the-knees airplane crash-landing position. "Do not lean forward." He looked them over and also pointed at the dog, who he had made sit between Will's feet. "Now stay." He grinned, enjoying his own joke.

Will's active imagination was in overdrive, thinking about eating dirt in a crash landing.

The pilot yelled, "Landing positions!"

They all grabbed onto the rope a little harder.

Light as a feather, the basket touched down.

Other balloon employees grabbed the basket and attached guy wires. The balloon came to a gentle stop.

The entire landing was anticlimactic. Will shook his head at himself, chagrined.

Bear threw open the basket door. Maddy gave the guide a tip and they rushed onto terra firma.

A variety of transportation options presented themselves: buses, horse-drawn carts, motorcycles.

Bear pointed to a cluster of motorcyclists waiting at the edge of the field to convey people to their next destination. "How 'bout the motorbikes?"

"Sounds good!" Will replied.

They jogged over to the drivers. He would miss the dog but knew it would find another tourist from whom to beg leftovers. Their time here was now limited.

Bear pulled out some bills. "We need fast ride to Old Bagan. Near tallest temple."

"Okay," a young woman agreed.

Two other men pulled their motorcycles forward and donned helmets. Will, Maddy, and Bear each hopped onto the back of a bike.

"Hurry please," Will said into the helmet-covered ear of his driver.

The locals seemed happy to have an excuse to drive fast. They gunned their engines and took off.

Will looked over his shoulder and could see the green balloon just starting its descent. *Good, at least we have a head start.*

The side road that led to the landing field let onto the main road into New Bagan. The day had warmed and the rush of air dried the sweat on his face.

In a field to the right, a plaid-shirted farmer wore a straw hat while tending a flock of goats. When the motorcycle got up to speed, Will urged it to go more quickly. He imagined he could hear another set of motorcycles behind them and nudged the driver. "Can it go faster?"

"No, this is fast."

Their pack of three motorcycles passed a truck laden with long bamboo stakes that were tied together into bundles and overflowed the back of the truck by a good ten feet. In the oncoming traffic lane, a slow-moving herd of water buffalo loomed. Will's heart thudded as his driver careened around the bamboo truck and back into their lane, narrowly missing the lead buffalo.

He was used to this type of sharing the road from his time in South America, but it was still nerve wracking.

Then they were forced to slow down as they hit the main drag, which had red-and-white striped median dividers. They passed several shaded horse-drawn carts, holding tourists who were enjoying the relative cool under the awnings. A group of barefoot children rushed their motorcycles. They sang a chorus, "Change, throw us your change!"

Their rides crawled past the children. Impatient, Will bounced his leg up and down on the motorcycle peg.

The crowd got thicker as they approached the market area. Flooding the streets, women balanced platters on their heads that contained everything from slices of watermelon, to baskets of fresh cut flowers, to fish heads. They slowed to a crawl to avoid the women and the associated tourists.

Will could walk faster and almost jumped off the bike in his impatience.

A pack of homeless puppies wandered into the street, and his driver had to brake sharply. After Will recovered from getting thrown into his driver's back, he yelled into the dark helmet, "We have to get there soon!"

"Going now." The driver maneuvered around the puppy pack, found a clear route between a truck overloaded with men heading to a job and an oxen-drawn carriage, and then they were free of New Bagan.

Will looked over his shoulder again but he couldn't see any motorcycles following them. From walking between Old and New Bagan multiple times this week, he knew this stretch by heart, and it wasn't long until they left the paved highway and entered the dirt roads that marked the beginning of Old Bagan. They passed the Archaeological

Museum on their left and then leaned into a right turn at top speed, kicking up clouds of dust.

They drove by a small temple on the right, the round little stupa that they'd seen from the air, and then Bear was motioning for the driver to stop in front of their temple. The three of them dismounted, paid the drivers, and the bikes roared off.

Maddy looked up. "It looks bigger than it did from the air."

Bear stood on his heels and craned his neck back. "I don't see the sign from this angle."

"C'mon! Hurry! Let's go inside before they get here." Will started up the mud-brick steps.

Although there were no gaps in the stairs, like most temples in the area, this brick structure was showing its age. The pillars to either side of the once-proud, arched doorway had lost most of their stucco veneer, and only one of the four niches still had a statue inside.

From this perspective, it looked as if there were two open eyes masquerading as windows on the second floor. It gave the structure a haunted look.

Without pausing to take off their shoes, they ran through the doorway of the temple and into utter darkness.

CHAPTER 62

9:45 a.m.:

Inside the temple in the middle of Old Bagan, Bear's head was still spinning from the kiss he shared with Maddy while up in the balloon. *Oh my god. Oh my god,* kept marching through his head like a location-appropriate mantra. The sudden connection he'd felt, the fire, and her startling desire made him feel thrilled at the prospect of an intimate relationship with her.

And guilty, because he was still operating under "keep it quiet" instructions from VanOps and hadn't disclosed their interest. The kiss shifted the balance of his loyalty, though, and he vowed to rectify his sin of omission once he had a chance. She deserved to know, but he wondered how she'd take it. With the sound of motorcycles coming closer, he'd have to figure it out later.

It took a moment until his eyes adjusted to the gloom of the temple's interior. Both Maddy and Will had halted as well, just inside the door. Far enough in that they couldn't be seen by prying Russian eyes but not so far that they'd bump into anything.

Once he could see the stone floor, faded remains of wall murals, and the huge square brick pillar ahead, he moved forward. Common to other temples they'd seen, a circumambulatory passage surrounded the pillar.

Maddy walked in lockstep with him. "Now what?" They approached the pillar and she reached out to touch it.

Will touched one of the niches. "This must support the dome and tower above. What're the towers called?"

Bear ignored both questions since he didn't have a clear line of sight to their next move and knew Will didn't care what the tower was called in Sanskrit. "I read in the guidebook that these niches were originally adorned with different poses of Vishnu."

Maddy pulled her hand from the pillar. "Focus, guys. You're killing me. We're going to have to start praying to all known deities, including Vishnu, in a hot minute, if we don't figure out how to find the sign, or hide, or both. Hear those motorcycles?"

Bear did hear them. "You're right, they're getting closer. Let's look around. Maybe there's another sign inside here."

Maddy sprinted up a set of interior steps that Bear had overlooked in the gloom. "Since the sign was up on the tower, I say we look upstairs. And it will give us a little space from our stalkers. Let's go!"

Bear and Will followed. It was hard for Bear to keep his eyes off her long legs.

The second-story landing opened into a space that also had the square pillar from below thrust up through the floor. It was as if the building had been skewered, at least to the top of this room's ceiling.

Maddy looked around. "Will. Where's that flashlight? Hurry!" she whispered, as the rumble of the motorcycles sounded close. Too close.

Will pulled out his flashlight, put his hand over the top to minimize stray light, and flashed it around.

"I'm looking low, Will you look high, Bear, in the middle like before."

Bear did as she instructed and ran his eyes over the interior of the brick and mural wall as fast as he could.

Motorcycles were below them now. Bear risked a look out the window. Two men on cheap bikes were spinning up dust as they drove up and down the street looking for the three of them. A blue polo shirt and solid black T-shirt gave them away as the Russians.

"Over here," Will whispered.

Bear and Maddy walked to where Will was standing in front of a mural. Will pointed. In the upper right-hand corner, a *signum regis* hid inside a tree shape, and a tense piece of Bear's gut relaxed a notch.

Bear slapped Will on the shoulder. "Good work, Argones."

Maddy pressed the sign and a hidden pocket door to the left of where they stood slid open, revealing a dark, dusty staircase that led straight up.

Bear went first up the hot and dirty stairs. It was a short set and led to what was likely the inside of the bell they'd seen from the balloon. *That pillar below must hold up this floor.* He stepped off the stairs and had to bend over as he stood looking around in the gloom.

Maddy softly closed the pocket door, and Will tiptoed up the stairs.

The heat was intense in the small space. Filtered light from between cracks in the bricks provided dim illumination. Bear sat down to think. Will sat next to Bear, his long legs sticking out in both directions.

Maddy was the last to come up the stairs. "Good Lord, it's hot up here." Completing the small three-way circle, she peered out between the bricks. "Looks like our friends haven't left yet."

Will drummed his fingers on his thigh, his actions belying his confident words. "At least they won't find us here."

Maddy sat down. "Let's hope not."

Bear wiggled to get more comfortable on the rough floor. "I think we're pretty safe. They don't know where to look and couldn't recognize the sign."

"Sure, but how long are they going to linger down there?" Will asked.

Maddy looked around. "And why did the clue lead us up here?"

Bear took a deep breath to calm his nerves and looked around, too. There wasn't much to see. A handful of bricks had fallen onto the floor and above, in the narrow part of the bell shape, it looked as if missing bricks were part of the design.

In the distance, over the motorcycles, a group of dogs barked.

"I don't see anything and think I'm going to die of heatstroke," Will said quietly.

Maddy pulled a water bottle from her backpack and handed it to him. "If we could be so lucky."

Will took the water bottle from her and drank. "Feeling snarky, are we?"

He handed the bottle to Bear, who also drank. The water, at least, was cool and refreshing.

Maddy wiped sweat from her brow. "I'm hot, too. Does not help my typical lack of patience and, if you haven't noticed, there are men down there who want to kill us."

Bear wanted to cover all the bases and sometimes distraction was the best way to stop their bickering. "Argones, you're the tallest. Stand up and let me know what you see up there by those open bricks. But move quietly."

The motorcycles made him tense. He felt so naked without a gun.

Will stood until he was eye level with the open bricks. He turned around in all four directions, then reached out his arm and plucked something from one of the openings.

"What is it?" Maddy whispered.

Will sat back down and opened his hand. Maddy reached out and took the item. It was a polished, round metal object about two inches across. She moved it into the light to see it better. It caught a reflection, hurting Bear's eyes, and sent a beam toward the ceiling.

She frowned at it. "Maybe it's a mirror?"

Bear reached his hand out for it and she gave it to him. Although there was no glass, one side was highly polished. He examined it carefully. "I think you're right, Marshall." *Should I call her Maddy now?* "During the Middle Ages, glass mirrors went out of style for a while when folks thought the devil was lookin' at them from the unpolished, back side."

"Oh, please," Will cut in, still talking softly.

Bear could still hear those bloody motorcycles roaring up and down the street. "Those were different times, Argones. Anyway, the history of mirrors reflects the history of man in a way. I can fill y'all in later."

"Give us the abbreviated version," Will said.

Bear handed the mirror to Will. "The short history lesson is that mirrors have been around since before the Romans, so Ramiro was familiar with them and their uses."

Scooting to the edge where there was better light, Will examined the object further. "Hey, look at this!" He held it out to them. "Speak of the devil, it's got Ramiro's sign on the side opposite the mirror."

It sure did. "No devil there. So, it's a clue or somethin' we're supposed to use."

Will stood back up and looked out the brick hole where he'd found the mirror. For a minute, he looked around and then he said, excitedly, "What if it's a signal mirror?"

"Oh, could be." Bear's mind whirred. "That would be clever."

Maddy stood. Bear handed her the mirror and she handed it to Will. "Try it! But be careful. I still hear them down there."

Will took the mirror and peered through each of the open bricks. He turned to the south slot, the one that had held the mirror, and muttered, "I wonder..."

He put the mirror to the open slot and adjusted it. "Wow," he exclaimed and jumped back, hitting his head on the other side of the narrow space in the process. "Ouch." He slouched down, one hand on the back of his head.

Maddy reached her hand out to comfort Will. "Sit down and tell us what you saw."

Will put one knee on the floor and shook his head slightly. "That hurt."

"I'll bet. But what did you see?" Maddy asked.

"It surprised me. It *is* a signal mirror! When I used it, it caught light from another mirror at a temple down the way. It looked like it then beamed light to another."

"Wow! That is clever—low tech but extremely useful as long as you're up here during the day. It's likely they have relay mirrors at each of the other slots, too, to catch the sun as it moves through the sky," Bear remarked.

Will stood back up. "An old-time engineering marvel. I approve."

"But do you think you held it there long enough to signal whoever is looking for it?" Maddy asked.

"Probably not. I'll hold it there for a few minutes this time." He moved back to the narrow apex of the bell and adjusted the mirror. "This is so awesome."

"You're such a geek," Maddy said fondly.

Just then, the motorcycle engines shut off. Moments later, the sound of boots on a stone floor thundered throughout the building.

CHAPTER 63

9:57 a.m.:

Maddy's breath stopped with fresh fear when the boots began to thud two floors below.

She looked at Bear and he looked at her. He reached out and took her hand. It was hot and stuffy in the hidden top floor of the temple, and Bear's palms felt sweaty.

"Will," she whispered. "Grab that signal mirror and sit back down!"

Will did as he was told, completing the circle of their bodies again. Maddy appreciated that Will could move softly for a big man when he had to.

Had the Russians seen the signal light? A million thoughts raced through her mind. *Do they know we're up here, or are they looking into all the temples? Will they kill us if they find us?*

Looking from Bear's tense shoulders to Will's rapid breathing, she could tell they all were feeling the same fear. She reached out and held Will's hand, too. Maddy's muscles were tight as a bowstring and her heart slammed so hard in her chest, she swore the men downstairs could hear it.

This fear wouldn't do. She decided to close her eyes, breathe slowly, and try to calm herself.

The deep breaths helped. By God, she'd be prepared if they came.

Bear pantomimed his plan for a counterattack. "Let's be ready if they open the pocket door. Marshall, you move here, Argones here, and I'll attack from in front."

The twins nodded and silently moved into position. Holding bricks, Bear crept down the treads. Each sibling crouched on a side of the stairs. Maddy knew it would be a last, desperate stand with slim chance of survival.

Maddy, Will, and Bear listened. They hardly breathed. The dog pack that she heard earlier sounded as if it were drawing nearer. The sound of boots moved from the first floor to the second. They were all ready to spring into action.

Unintelligible Russian voices lofted up between the rafters like smoke from a fire.

Bear glanced at her reassuringly. She did feel comforted by his presence and tried to tell herself it was because he was good in a fight.

The Russians' movements echoed around the second floor. Maddy held her breath and willed the three of them to make no sound. Mentally, she rehearsed the counterattack should they open the pocket door.

The yipping and howling of the dog pack sounded close, perhaps outside in the street, and over the din of the dogs, the tone of the Russian voices sounded frustrated.

Boots clanged back down the stairs and the voices faded.

Maddy, Bear, and Will all heaved a muffled sigh of relief. Maddy's shoulders slumped a little and the three of them exchanged a thank-god glance.

Maddy moved to a crack in the wall and risked looking out. A block away, a group of monks headed toward them, ever-present oxen-drawn cart behind them.

In the street below, the pack of growling dogs surrounded the two Russian men. Buddy was in the front of the pack, looking vicious by showing his teeth and lunging forward and back. The Russians tried to shoo the dogs away as they looked around at the other temples. One of the men pointed to the other square-bottomed temple nearby, but the other shook his head and pointed to the dogs.

They got on their motorcycles and roared up and down the street to try to break up the dogs, but the dogs stood their ground. As the monks drew near, the motorcycles sped off into the distance and the dogs quieted.

Her shoulders relaxed. "I think they're leaving."

Bear walked back up the stairs and stood next to Maddy, placing a hand on her waist.

"Hope they don't come back," Will said.

"Looks like Buddy down there with his pals."

Will stood beside Maddy and hunched over to look out between the bricks. "I love that dog. Think the pack scared them off?"

"Either that or the large group of monks that is descending on the street had some effect."

"He gets some extra leftovers. Or maybe I can find him a home," Will said.

"Wow, there must be fifty monks down there. They're splitting up. Some are coming here, some going to the square temple next door, some circling that odd little stupa."

Soft sounds rustled below. Maddy could almost hear the distinct swishing of red robes.

A minute later the pocket door slid to the side and a voice came from below in accented English, "It is safe to come down now."

The three of them looked at each other, and Maddy spoke for the group, "Okay, coming down."

Maddy led the way down the steep staircase. Just outside the hidden door was a young Asian monk. He was bald, thin, and short, with ears that pointed up from his head in a way that was elfin-endearing rather than odd. His smile was warm and his eyes full of intelligence. "Which of you has the sign?"

"The sign?" Maddy repeated.

He looked from Will to Bear. "On your shoulder. One of you must have the sign, or else you do not come with us." His tone was matter-of-fact.

"Ah, that."

Maddy turned her back to him, wrapped her arms around herself, reached with her right hand and, bra or no, lifted the back corner of her shirt over her shoulder to expose the brand she'd won in Jerusalem. Rejecting embarrassment, she figured the young man would be more uncomfortable than she. Besides, she was irritated that he assumed one of the men had the sign and not her. When she turned back around, his face was a gratifying cherry color and he had turned away.

He pushed the sign of Ramiro on the mural and the pocket door slid closed.

"Sorry, had to ask. My name is Nanda. Welcome to the Order of the Invisible Flame. Follow me."

Gracefully, Nanda and his robes swished toward the staircase that led to the first floor.

Maddy made a mental note of the name of the order. She didn't recognize it.

Will put his hand on Nanda's shoulder. "Thank you. Are the men on motorbikes gone?"

Nanda nodded. "Yes, for now."

They walked down to the first floor and stood in the doorway for a moment with a handful of other bald monks. Maddy looked up and down the street. There was no sign of the motorcycles, nor did she hear them. The oxen and their cart stood still as a stone statue in the center of the hot dusty street. All was quiet.

Nanda removed a bag from beneath his robes and pulled out a battery-operated hair trimmer, scissors, and shaving cream. "We need to camouflage you as monks. Who is first to lose the hair?"

"No!" Maddy looked in horror at the trimmer.

In the same matter-of-fact voice, Nanda said, "Okay, you get caught, maybe die." Then he looked to Bear and Will. "What about you?"

Will sat down and gave her a pointed look. "You can cut mine. I don't want to die."

He could be such an ass sometimes.

The monk set to work with practiced ease, reducing Will's dark curly locks to dusty memories in no time. The beard went next and in less than three minutes, Will looked a new man.

Will rubbed his naked cheek experimentally. "This might feel good in the heat. That beard was getting pretty scratchy. Bear, your turn."

Without expression, Bear sat. His marine cut didn't have much hair to begin with, but his beard had gotten shaggy during their travels. It, too, fell to the floor. This monk was obviously the hair trimmer at the monastery, as he wielded the weapon efficiently.

Bear stood, and he, Will, and the monk all looked at Maddy expectantly. She realized she liked the couple disguise better than this monk disguise.

Bear rubbed his hand over his bald pate. "Ah, feels like boot camp."

Will had an evil, mischievous look in his eye. "It'll be a good look for you, Maddy."

Bear smiled at her as if to say he would still find her stunningly attractive. "It'll grow back in no time, Marshall. Better bald than dead."

Maddy groaned and relented, plopping on the floor in disgust. It had taken *years* to grow her hair to that length. She appreciated her hair and knew it wouldn't "grow back in no time." It would take at least three years. But he was right. If she were dead, it wouldn't grow at all. Perhaps she'd grow fond of hats for a while.

The raping and pillaging of her locks didn't take long, and she did feel cooler when it was done. Lighter somehow also, but she felt more exposed. Vulnerable.

"Here are your robes." Nanda handed them dyed robes from a bag and helped them put them on over their other clothes. "They will only help you not be noticed at a distance, so no need for the under-robe clothes we wear." Nanda scooped up the errant hair from the floor and put it in the sack.

Once disguised, they moved with the group of monks from the relative safety of the temple and to the oxen cart. The other monks who had broken away from the main group coalesced back into the whole.

They all continued walking up the street, Maddy, Bear, and Will in the center of the group. Buddy and his dog friends had dispersed around town.

Maddy looked around to make sure she looked like the other monks. Bear walked next to her. She touched her scalp. "I miss my hair."

His eyes shone. "You look fine."

She hoped he was telling the truth but doubted it. To change the subject she said, "Where do you think we're headed?"

"No clue, but they've either done this before or were expecting us."

"That mirror did the trick. Or maybe the Guardians called."

"Or sent a carrier pigeon."

She laughed. "They are rather low tech."

"Seems to work for them," Bear said.

"They've been at this a long time."

Their conversation faded in the heat.

Before long, they left the dusty roads of Old Bagan and walked to an alley behind one of the local monasteries. An old blue truck was being loaded with bags of rice and other supplies.

Nanda pointed to the truck. "We will take this truck to another monastery. You will meet the master."

True to his word, they finished loading supplies, ate some lunch, and the four of them got into the truck. Maddy folded herself into the small back seat next to Bear. The truck fired up with a cough and a rumble but managed to pull out of the alley in spite of its age.

As the blue truck headed out of town, twin motorcycles barreled toward them. One rider wore a blue polo shirt and the other a solid black T-shirt. Her heart caught in her throat for a moment. They all froze, but their disguise held, and the bikes continued deeper into New Bagan.

She couldn't help but wonder, *How long until they find us again?*

CHAPTER 64

2:10 p.m.:

For about an hour, the old blue truck rumbled along the dusty road that ran to the east of Bagan. Will was grateful to leave the town and the two Russian motorcyclists behind. Eventually, a single mountain peak became visible in the distance.

"That is Mount Popa, an old volcano," Nanda offered.

Will was curious. "What does Popa translate to?"

"*Popa* means 'flower' in English."

Conversation lagged for another ten minutes, and then a set of golden spires appeared atop a massive rock outcropping that jutted into low lying clouds. It looked like a Buddhist version of Camelot.

Maddy pointed. "What's that?"

"That is where we are going."

Out of the balloon and into the clouds. Just my luck. "Does it have a name? What kind of place is it?" Will was glad that he'd done some work on the whole fear of heights thing.

"It is called Popa Taungkalat Monastery."

Will was afraid to ask his next question but couldn't help himself. "How do we get to the top? I don't see a road."

Nanda laughed. "Good question. There are seven hundred and seventy-seven stairs. The supplies can go up by a rope but we climb the stairs."

All three of them groaned at the same time. Nanda laughed again. "I see you've been enjoying the stairs on all our temples in Bagan. Don't worry, most people make it. And the view is wonderful from above."

"It's the 'most people' part that I'm worried about." Maddy laughed and they all joined her.

Seeing the motorcycles with the Russians going the other way shortly after they had departed toward the monastery had done wonders for their moods. It felt good to laugh after so much tension.

A dog ran alongside the truck and barked briefly. Before they left the monastery in New Bagan, Will had given some money to the head monk and asked that he keep an eye out for Buddy. The man had promised that he would, so Will was happy about leaving his canine hero in good hands.

They dropped the truck off in the tiny but colorful town at the base of the rock outcropping, walked through the tourist zone—the entrance to which was flanked by statues of massive white and gold elephants—and headed up the stairs. Before long, their good humor faded in the warmth of the afternoon and the reality of the 777 steps.

Will moved slowly from getting up so early, from the excitement of the day, and from the heat. His legs ached and he had to pull himself up the stairs with the railing. His sister and Bear seemed cranky, too. It was also Will's turn to carry the backpack that contained their resources and, in the heat, it weighed on him.

He expected to hate the stairs. What he didn't expect were the diminutive monkeys that littered the broad, covered staircase. Also, he'd not anticipated his fear of heights to have lessened as much as it had. Oddly, he caught himself looking at the view without trepidation. It was a nice change. He wondered if it would last.

"This must be quite the tourist destination," Bear noted.

Proving Bear's point, Will observed the care that had been taken with the staircase construction. The stairs were broad and divided by a metal railing. They had been built wide enough for five people to walk abreast on each side of the divider. As they climbed, Maddy picked up trash until her arms were full then dumped it in a waste can. Blue-painted four-by-fours held up the metal awning, which did a good job of keeping the sun off their heads.

Awning or no, Will wondered if they'd all end up with a sunburned scalp anyway, just from having such pink newly-shaven heads. Bear looked decent as a bald man, but Will wasn't at all used to Maddy without hair. Her mane was such a part of her. She was forever playing with it, tugging on it. He sensed that she felt out of sorts without it, like he felt without Maria.

Nanda turned to Bear. "Yes," he replied. "The monastery sees many tourists every day, but especially during holy festivals like the full moon in December. Then many pilgrims make the effort. This site has much that is blessed. Many *nat* spirits live here and there are several relics, too."

Maddy nodded. "What's up with all the charming monkeys?"

Will had to agree they were cute, but they were everywhere. At least ten crawled on the railings. More were on the stairs, eating treats, and hanging overhead just under the awning.

Nanda replied, "Do not feed them. Do not hold any food in your hand. Don't let them come near you, and you'll be okay."

"I wasn't worried about them. Should I be? They're pretty adorable."

"No, they won't hurt you. Some tourists buy food for them is all. I wish they could go back to the jungle, where they could be at peace in their natural homes."

They walked up more stairs.

Halfway up, they stopped to catch their breath.

Then there were more stairs to ascend. The wind picked up and made the climb cooler, but also harder, as they had to fight against it.

Will hated anything even remotely stair-like by the time they reached the top. Still surprising himself, he didn't even care that they were in the clouds, thousands of meters in the air. He was just glad they had finished the climb.

At the top, Nanda left them to relax in a wind-blown section of the monastery that was tourist oriented. Covered benches looked out over the valley and the volcano. A snack shop offered beverages and light food. A decorative set of six golden spires, looking like complex giant Christmas ornaments, were set on pillars. Will marveled at how all the building material had been hauled up here. It seemed an unreal, daunting task. Yet, here it was, a fully functioning monastery on top of the world.

Will's breathing had almost returned to normal when Nanda appeared from a doorway and beckoned to them. "The master will see you now."

They followed Nanda single file through several doors, hallways, and small rooms. Eventually, they came to a ten-meter-square patio that held the pleasant, tinkling sound of a waterfall. A private sitting space was nestled in a corner, under a vine-covered pergola. The square patio was adjacent to a much larger space that held raised garden beds, benches, and potted trees. Will labeled that space as the Grand Garden and the secluded part of the patio as the Private Pergola.

The wind here, in the private section, was buffeted by the surrounding buildings, so fans moved the air to keep it cool. An old monk, bald and wrinkled, sat under the shade in a meditative pose.

The air smelled of jasmine, and Will could see the white-flowered plant growing up a trellis and across the pergola in several places. Other colorful plants that Will didn't recognize added to the ambiance. Overall, the impression was one of peaceful serenity.

Nanda motioned for them to move closer to the monk and sit down.

Will hesitated, as the man's eyes were closed, but Nanda was insistent and got them each settled on a cushion in a semicircle near the old man. Nanda sat down on the older monk's left and also donned a closed-eyed pose.

Will, Maddy, and Bear all looked at each other. Maddy shrugged. Will wondered if this were some other kind of test. Maddy closed her eyes, Bear followed suit, so Will did as well. He was tired after all.

As soon as he closed his eyes, Will sensed something unusual. His body relaxed and his mind became quiet. He was aware of a bird singing, the air from the fan rustling the plants, the water burbling in the waterfall. Will detected a ripple of strength from the old monk.

The beautiful moment stretched. And then the feeling passed.

"Master Mohan welcomes you!" Nanda said. "His Burmese and Hindi are excellent but his English is poor so he has requested I translate for you. Please, just call him master."

Will opened his eyes and found that everyone else had done the same. The master put his palms together in a prayer position, inclined his head, and pressed his fingers to the tip of his nose. Without having a clue if this was proper etiquette or not, Will, Maddy, and Bear followed suit.

"Please thank the master for seeing us. We appreciate his time and are grateful."

Maddy always knew what to say.

Nanda translated, and the old man smiled and nodded at her, pleased. Will noticed the master's brown eyes were alive with intellect and warmth.

Then the monk spoke again to Nanda, who repeated in English. "The master would like to know why you are here. Please take your time and speak your truth."

Maddy looked at Bear and Will and they both motioned for her to begin. She looked up at the pergola's ceiling vines for a long moment. "We have been told our ancestor Ramiro hid an object of great power. Men from Russia want this power, we think, to make war in the world. We wish to find the object before they do, so that we can stop a potential war and find the truth about our father's death."

"There are those who would use the Power you seek for evil deeds. I have turned away those with that intention." After Nanda translated, the old man nodded.

The master looked at Will expectantly. Feeling nervous at the talk of evil deeds, Will wasn't sure which part of the truth to share. "I, too, want peace in the world."

Even before the words were translated the old man was shaking his head. Nanda said, "He says you're not fully truthful. You must tell the entire truth for him to help you."

Will felt like he'd been hit with a stun gun. *How did he know that?* It was part of the truth, but he also knew that, deep down, his real driver was justice for his father and Maria. Not revenge, per se. It was justice he sought. As an engineer, he didn't believe in mystical powers. He closed his eyes. How best to communicate his thoughts?

Will opened his eyes. "These Russian men killed my father and my wife, both of whom I loved with my entire being. I don't know if there is power to be found but I want to know why my loved ones were killed and bring justice to those responsible."

The old monk nodded and smiled. Will felt heat in his cheeks and sipped some water. It was unnerving to have someone see your soul like that.

They all looked at Bear, who was uncharacteristically flushed. Will had never seen Bear fidget before, but he did now. He took a drink of water. His eyes darted around the patio. A band of perspiration broke out on his forehead.

Finally, he burst out, "I want to help Maddy succeed in this quest because I care for her. I want to keep her safe."

Will watched the reactions of everyone to this small outburst. Maddy colored and didn't look at Bear further. The old monk shook his head from side to side and spoke in Nanda's ear.

"What else?" Nanda translated.

Bear's mouth dropped open and his eyes went wide. He squirmed, held his breath, and his face turned bright red.

Will's curiosity was piqued. *What else could there be?* How did this master know their secrets? Bear clearly cared for Maddy, or was he faking that? Was there something Bear hadn't told them? Maddy started to narrow her gaze at Bear, probably also wondering what was going on.

The old monk just sat silently and watched.

Bear stood and paced up and down the patio.

What the hell was going on? Will could sense Maddy's blood pressure rising, likely with all the same questions he had. Only she had seemed to like that kiss and so was more invested than he was.

After several long minutes, Bear came back to the group. "Is there somewhere Maddy and I can talk? Alone?"

Uh-oh. Will thought. *This can't be good.*

CHAPTER 65

Popa Taungkalat Monastery, Myanmar, July 20, 5:35 p.m.:

Maddy could feel the anger coming on as she followed Nanda and Bear to a doorway on the other side of the monastery's large garden area. They sought privacy so that she and Bear could talk about whatever the master had flushed out of him.

Bear had looked more uncomfortable under the old master's scrutiny than she had ever seen a man look. Something was wrong here and she didn't think she was going to like it.

As they walked through the doorway, questions cascaded through her mind like a data dump on a computer screen.

What does he have to hide?

How is it that we've kissed once and now we have to 'talk' already?

Her old suspicion resurfaced. *Why did he come on this quest with us?*

Nanda dropped them at a table for two in a plain-looking dining hall. The sole distinguishing aspect of the place was that the floors gleamed with a brilliance she'd seen in expensive, high-end office buildings when she'd met clients to discuss software projects.

Bear sat across from her and, when they were alone, tried to hold her hands.

She pulled them away and got right to the point. "'Fess up. What's going on?"

Bear's face was a sickly green. "Marshall. Maddy. You have to believe me. I was going to tell you."

She leaned back and crossed her arms. "That is the wrong way to start a conversation."

"You're right. Okay. I'll tell you now."

"I'm listening."

"I don't know where to start."

She tried to keep her tone level, but it came out more sarcastic than she intended. "How about the beginning?" She was annoyed, after all, and it was starting to look as if she had a right to be.

"All right. When my last tour with the marines was up a month or so ago, I was approached by an agency to become an undercover agent." He paused and looked at her.

Her heart beat faster as her mind raced in two directions at once. She could already see where this was going as it related to their quest and didn't like what it implied on a personal note either.

What the hell? And he meant *to tell me?*

Her eyebrows shot up and a pit opened in her stomach. "An agency or 'The Agency'?" Her voice sounded wooden and far away.

"Yes, a department within the CIA, but more like a distant cousin with an open-minded, forward-looking focus. That's where their name comes from, like in vanguard. It's an ultra-deep black group within the Department of Extreme Threats called VanOps. Their charter is, um…" He paused, looking away. "Not conventional. They look for obscure or unusual threats. Ancient or futuristic. Things science can't explain."

"Things such as arcane powers that the Russians might want?" Her tone was cold. Ice-cold.

His eyes fell. "Uh, yeah."

"And you're on the agency payroll?"

"Um, not yet. Sort of. I mean, this whole mission, takin' care of you and Will. It was a test. Like your test at Jerusalem."

"I don't get it." With every new revelation, her anger rose a notch higher and her voice dropped a level lower.

"I've been a helicopter guy—gathered tactical intelligence, like enemy locations. But I've always wanted to do true undercover. Clandestine operations. This group, VanOps, it's the future. Cutting-edge physics. Modern warfare. They only recruit the crème de la crème. I had a pretty good rap sheet with the marines, and you may remember my dad was a general before he died. They're testin' even me."

"Bullshit. I don't know much about spying, but I think they're playing you."

The dam burst and Bear's voice broke. "They told me I couldn't tell you. I wanted to tell you from the start. I almost did on the ship, and then Will interrupted us. Remember? Maddy, please."

She did remember he had started to say something, but she just looked away, too angry to speak.

"And after we kissed. I hoped—anyway, I swore to myself that I would tell you. And I just haven't had a chance."

She tried to yank her ponytail and it was missing. That infuriated her even further.

"Maddy, I care about you. I always have and would have come along even if they hadn't asked me to keep you safe. I thought it would be a lark. I had no idea the Russians would catch up to us. We can call in backup from VanOps if you want. I'll likely not get the job, but maybe we need some extra firepower."

Now the words tumbled out of her mouth as she leaned toward him, hands balled into tight fists. "You're assuming this is still a group effort. How on earth am I to trust you, Theodore Thorenson, when you've deceived both Will and me since you sat next down to us at the Fire Sign Café? I feel betrayed."

It took all the willpower she possessed not to upend the table on top of him, or throw it across the room.

Bear looked down and grimaced.

She pounded her closed hand on the tabletop. It jumped. "What else does VanOps have up their sleeve? And what the *hell* do they want with us? Did you stop and think about that for a minute? What is their angle? How did they know what we were up to anyway? At that point, nobody should have known where we were. How did they know to hook you up with us? To keep us safe? Really. Sell me some Florida swampland while you're at it."

Bear didn't back down at her anger. Instead, something shifted for him, and he went on the offensive, looking her in the eye, leaning forward, and holding the table down with his palms. "Maddy. I can see how you are pissed off and that you feel betrayed. This is a big surprise and a lot of new information. But this group that's tryin' to help you is a bona fide government department. They've been funded in one way, shape, or form since the seventies when they studied psychic spies."

A part of Maddy liked that Bear could handle her anger, but she wasn't done. "So what? They're part of the CIA. Have you heard of water boarding? Snowden? You want to be one of those guys that torture people? That spy on Americans through their TV's and cell phones?"

"Of course not, but did you know what you call torture was legal, and there were only three men water boarded right after Nine/Eleven?"

Maddy leaned back in her chair. "No, I didn't know that. How do you know?"

"The former CIA Director wrote a book."

Maddy's tone was half sarcastic, half a question. "And you believe him?"

"I believe there are two sides to every story. Intelligence is the way to keep our country safe. More key than our armies, in my opinion. I believe I want to help keep America safe."

"By any means necessary?"

"No. I know right from wrong."

"Seems it might get a little murky working undercover. Seems it already has."

"Think about this, Maddy. I gave VanOps my word to keep you safe and stay silent. Was wantin' to keep you safe so wrong? And now that there might be some hope for us as a couple, my allegiance has shifted. I don't want to be the undercover guy that can't tell his significant other what is goin' on. I believe in trust."

"What's their position on that?"

"I honestly don't know. Haven't gotten that far yet."

"Something to consider with the job offer, I would think."

"Yes, I agree."

She took a deep breath and the tide of her anger receded. He had made some fair points.

He pressed. "What would you have done if you were me? If you had given your word and didn't see any harm in doing so? Thought you were doin' some old friends a favor even. A win-win."

"I need to think about that after I fully calm down. I learned a long time ago to not make decisions when I'm ticked off—I've always regretted them. So, let's set aside, for the time being, the question of did you owe me the truth before now. Let's go back to this department. What did you call them…VanOps? What do they want?"

"They didn't tell me."

"Okay. Got any guesses? You've had longer to mull this over than I have."

"My best guess is that they heard about these obelisks from somebody with loose lips in your rather large, extended family and want to make sure they don't end up in the wrong hands. Like I said, the Russians have been knee-deep in obscure spy territory for decades. VanOps couldn't have figured there was much of anythin' real behind it, or they wouldn't have sent a plebe like me."

"Could be." She hesitated. "Makes sense. And makes me feel a little better as well."

"We can call them in if you want."

"Funny, Will and I were joking about calling in the CIA on the plane. But I don't think so. No. My gut is not happy about how they've played this."

Bear's broad shoulders relaxed a notch. "I can understand that."

"Have you reported in or anything when we weren't looking?"

"No, my orders were simply to keep you safe, stay quiet, and call when we all got back to the States. I imagine they'll be fascinated by the obelisks, should they truly exist."

"Curious. Well, we've done well enough by ourselves so far, and if there's that much power at stake, I'm thinking I may not want them in the hands of the government. Do I have your word that you'll follow my lead on that? And that you'll fill Will in and let us know before you call?"

Bear nodded.

She relaxed and shrugged to release built-up tension. Bear got up, came around the table, and started to rub her shoulders.

"That feels good, but no. Hands off! You've given me too much to think about." Her tone was light, though.

"Rain check, Ms. Marshall?"

Maddy felt torn. "Maybe."

"I'll take it. Shall we rejoin the others? And how did the master know what I had up my sleeve?"

"Yes, let's go. Maybe we'll find out."

CHAPTER 66

6:15 p.m.:

In the middle of the mountaintop monastery, Will endured a long fifteen minutes before Maddy and Bear returned to the Private Pergola from a doorway on the other side of the Grand Garden.

The master had sat in a meditative pose with his eyes shut while Maddy and Bear were talking. Nanda was nowhere to be found, so Will also sat and tried to enjoy the early evening while wondering where the Russians were now and what secrets Maddy and Bear were discussing.

By the time he was anxious enough to consider getting up to go find them, they strode back to the patio. Will could tell that Maddy's anger had cooled. Bear looked wrung out, but a spring had returned to his step. Perhaps they'd kissed and made up.

Will recalled a fight a few weeks ago that he and Maria had over his bonus. He'd splurged, bought his Rolex, and she was ticked off he'd spent so much money. They worked it out, and he enjoyed the make-up session. He seriously missed her right about now.

As if on cue, when Bear and Maddy walked onto the patio, Nanda appeared from one of the other doorways. They all sat down on the cushions that faced the master.

"What did you learn?" the master asked Maddy, through Nanda.

Maddy looked at Bear. He nodded. She said, "Bear had made a commitment to others before we came on the quest. He has told me everything now."

The master shook his head and Nanda continued to translate. "What did you learn about yourself?"

"I'm confused. Wasn't this about the truth about why Bear came on the quest?"

"In part, yes, as your hearts must be pure to continue. However, I can see that his truth has been shared. But there is a lesson here for you, too, and that is more important in the long run. What did you learn about your anger?"

"My anger? He made me angry."

As Nanda translated, the master looked away. "Ah, so you did not learn."

Will was curious about where the old man was going with this line of thinking.

Maddy tried to pull at a ponytail that was no longer there. "I don't understand. Can you please explain? I would like to learn."

"Good. Think on this. Were you angry because of what he did, or because of your thoughts about what he did?"

"What he did. He withheld information from me." She nodded at Will. "From us."

He was dying to know what they had discussed. This was juicy. Instinctively, he knew that what she was about to tell them wasn't going to be good.

"No." The master corrected with a soft tone. "You interpreted his actions through the filter of your beliefs and judged his behavior as wrong. That is what made you angry. Try on a different perception of his actions and see if you feel differently. Can you respect him for keeping his commitment?"

Will didn't follow, but Maddy's face lit up. "So, my emotions are all my own doing?"

"Yes. Blaming others for your emotions robs you of your power."

Maddy looked stunned. "Oh, my. My thoughts generate my emotions."

That cleared things up for Maddy, but Will found it an odd concept. Not that he'd been overly emotional throughout his life, but they'd been raised to believe that other people's actions caused your emotions. It was the source of some friction in his own marriage—that money fight, for instance. He decided to mull over this concept later and test it out for himself. See if he could think himself happy, sad, or mad.

"Yes. Don't they teach you anything in school?" The master laughed. "This is important. Blocked feelings mean blocked energy. To maximize and control the Power that you will have access to, you must be able to control your thoughts and your emotions. You've passed a number of tests regarding fear and compassion, but it is my job to make sure you, the true you, are in control of the power. Not your anger or any other emotion."

Maddy nodded. "I see."

"So, before you leave, you must pass a test to show me that you can control your thoughts, emotions, and energy."

"What is the test?"

"You must be able to light paper on fire with your hands," the master said.

"What?" Will burst out. He couldn't help himself.

The master turned to him. "You did not pass the fear tests, but you may practice here as well. Since you have come this far, you may be able to retake the fear tests and someday join the Order."

"But no one can light paper on fire with their hands. It's impossible." As an engineer, Will felt the certainty about this in his bones.

"So sure? Nanda, please bring me some paper."

Nanda scampered off. The old man again closed his eyes. Will looked at Maddy, who raised one eyebrow and shrugged. Bear just looked curious and somewhat relieved to be out of the hot seat.

Nanda returned a few minutes later with a newspaper. He handed it to Will. It looked like a regular newspaper, a recent edition from Mandalay. Will sniffed it, studied it, and handed it back. There was nothing unusual about it that he could tell, without doing a chemical analysis. Nanda balled it up and put it in front of the old master.

Will's pulse quickened. *Can the master light this paper on fire?* He'd heard of yogis' supernatural feats, but he considered them nothing but quackery.

The master deepened his breathing. His eyes remained closed. Next, he cupped his palms in his lap. He moved his hands as if around an invisible ball the size of a grapefruit. This continued for about a minute.

At some point, the old man seemed satisfied with what he felt between his hands. He moved his hands toward the paper on the ground in front of him. The master didn't touch the paper but continued to cup it from about an inch away, all while moving his hands around it. Will was sure nothing would happen.

Whoosh! Flames erupted between the old man's hands, charring the newspaper in an instant. Will jerked backward and almost fell off his cushion.

The fire burned for a moment, then the master opened his eyes and looked at Will. "Please put the fire out with the water in your glass."

Will complied, shaken and confused.

The master smiled, looking delighted as a child that he had shocked Will.

Maddy and Bear also stared open-mouthed at the small pile of ashes in front of the master.

The master looked at Will and spoke through Nanda. "You're a thinker, yes?"

Will nodded.

"Think about this. You're familiar with the vacuum of empty space all around us?"

Will nodded again, unable to speak.

"Quantum theory predicts that it contains enormous residual background energy. Scientists call this 'zero-point energy' or ZPE. Am I right?"

Will moved his head in affirmation. He had a wealthy friend in Brazil who adored, over drinks, to share with Will his ideas about quantum experiments that verified those theories. Will had taken a few physics classes in college and liked to read about related advances, so had followed along. Will enjoyed the conversation and loved the fine wine.

"I am simply harnessing zero-point energy. You or anyone can do the same. We are all one."

Will still had a hard time accepting the master was using ZPE, but he had learned a long time ago, with the feelings he and Maddy shared, that sometimes science didn't know all. Maybe this was cutting-edge science and not a fake. Time would tell. The master turned his attention to Maddy.

"I will give you one exercise to practice. You'll have to figure out the rest. Do as I do. First, you listen. And feel the Power."

The master went on to show them how to sit on their heels, put their hands high above their heads in a prayer position, breathe into their guts and out through their hands while chanting and visualizing an energy pattern that moved up their spines.

Will squirmed, wanting to dismiss it as more yogic hocus-pocus, but the fire display was too fresh.

The three of them practiced for a minute under the master's gaze. Even Bear.

Sitting on his heels, Will's ankles started to ache. His arms trembled and he ground his teeth to keep his triceps tucked by his ears, hands held high.

Finally, the master had them inhale and relax. Will dropped his arms and balled up on the ground. After another breath, he sat up, extended his legs, and rubbed his quads. How could he be so beat from such a short exercise?

The master dismissed them. "I will see if you have any questions in the morning. Please enjoy a meal."

Nanda scooped them up and herded them toward dinner. As they left the patio, Will hoped Maddy was a quick study. *I'll never be able to do it and time is running out.*

CHAPTER 67

6:55 p.m.:

Bear felt awash in a tumble of emotions as they walked into the dining hall of the mountaintop monastery. Part of him was as shocked as Will had looked when the old master had lit that newspaper on fire. Another part of him, the larger part, was caught between the hope in Maddy's smile and the residual ashes of her anger.

And then he spied Juergen's tall frame and blond head in the dining hall, sitting next to stocky Dieter and hazel-eyed Elena at the end of a long bench. For some reason, they all sat on the same side of a table. *What are they doing here?*

Bear's emotional tangle coalesced into a dark, heavy ball and took up residence in the center of his chest. He swore under his breath.

Will and Maddy made noises of pleasant surprise and headed toward Juergen's table. Irritated, Bear followed along in their wake.

Will made it to the table first. "Hey, strangers! Can we join you?"

Juergen stood to shake hands with Will. "Hey, so good to see you! Yes, please, sit. Dinner is almost here."

Juergen looked the same as Bear remembered, still towering over even Will. *The guy must be six-six, maybe six-eight.* Abruptly, Bear felt like a hobbit.

Will sat across from Juergen, Maddy across from Dieter, and Bear took the end, away from Juergen and across from Elena, who engaged him in conversation.

Her golden red hair and round hazel eyes were still stunning. "So happy to see you all made it."

"We did and lost our hair along the way. Looks like you kept yours?"

Bear was distracted by the conversation that had sprung up between Maddy and Juergen. *Does she still care for him?*

Elena pushed her fingers through her locks to move the hair away from her face. "Yes. How'd yours disappear?"

"It's a long story. I'm surprised to see you all here. What is this place?"

"We've been here just a few days, but from what we can tell, on the outside, it's a Buddhist monastery and does function as such."

"Sure, but what's this Order of the Invisible Flame business?"

Bear became aware that the small talk between Will, Juergen, Dieter, and Maddy had ceased and they were all listening.

She flashed him a broad smile. "That is the interesting part."

Dieter took up the tale. "As you learned while at the Jerusalem Testing Society, everyone there is remotely royal, all descendants of Isabella and Ferdinand. You may or may not know that all the monarchs currently reigning in Europe, whether King Philippe of Belgium, Queen Elizabeth of the UK, or the kings of Denmark, Norway, Sweden, and the Netherlands, descend from Isabella I and Ferdinand II. Each particular family has its own traditions and I won't ask about yours, or share ours. However, what we all share is this common lineage."

Maddy tried to swing her hair, couldn't, and glared at Elena's mane. "What do Isabella and Ferdinand have to do with the Order?" Maddy had donned a baseball cap from their backpack as soon as they had entered the monastery and adjusted it instead.

"They set it up," Juergen replied. All eyes turned to him as he continued. "Set up the Order. What we've been told so far is that they established it after succeeding in a quest of their own. They wanted their children, and their children's children, to have a role in protecting the world from evil."

Bear's irritable mood bled into the conversation. "Evil such as the Jews and Moors that they ordered to convert or leave Spain?"

Juergen crossed his arms. "Popular culture has perhaps overstated the impact of the Spanish Inquisition."

Now Bear had another reason to hate Juergen. "Are you kidding me? But, hey, the Germans got the idea of killing the Jews from somewhere."

Elena disrupted the argument. "Cut it out, guys. That was all a long time ago. Anyway, the progeny of Isabella and Ferdinand were quite prolific. As Dieter said, almost all the royal houses of Europe trace back to them, except for the Russians."

"Any connection back to Alexander the Great?" Maddy asked.

"Not that I've heard of," Elena answered.

Dieter added, "All royal houses have a similar opportunity to join the Order. Although royalty doesn't today hold the power it once did, the secret brotherhood remains a powerful force for good. Each member helps in their own way. Some have been warriors, some diplomats, but most have been spies."

This caught Bear's attention. He wondered if the US Government was aware of this group and how much they had influenced history over the years.

Elena went on, "We're siblings, the three of us, and German if you couldn't tell." She chuckled and nodded toward Juergen and Dieter. "With guidance from the Order, one of our great-grandfathers joined the Nazi Party during World War Two to infiltrate the leadership and learn what he could to help the Allies. He provided intelligence that turned the tide of several battles on the eastern front. He survived the war, married our great-grandmother, and contributed in other ways before he died."

In spite of himself, Bear was intrigued by the concept of a secret sect of stately spies.

"So, anyone who passed the tests in Jerusalem can join the order?" Maddy asked.

Will jumped in, "And is the master the head of the order?"

"Yes, to both." Dieter answered.

"Why would a monk lead an order like this?" Will asked.

Bear could see the advantages.

"You have to admit it makes for a good disguise," Dieter said.

Will nodded, deep in thought.

"And how long do you expect to be here, training, before the next phase of your adventure?" Maddy asked.

Bear appreciated that she avoided asking for details.

"We understand that most people are here for a few weeks, to a few months. For some, it has been a college of sorts, lasting years."

Will's eyes widened at this comment.

"Are there others of us here now?" Maddy wanted to know.

"No, we're the sole group here right now," Elena replied.

The conversation wound down after that.

Monks served dinner and they all dove into the vegetarian fare with gusto.

Although Bear was intrigued by the dinner's revelations, he couldn't help but think that, with Juergen here, he'd never kiss Maddy again.

CHAPTER 68

At first light, Maddy woke in the monastery. Birds sang outside the window of her modest but rather comfortable room. A confusing dream about Juergen was fresh in her mind. He was massaging her shoulders while Bear looked on from across the room. She was enjoying the feel of Juergen's hands on her shoulders, but at the same time, she felt the weight of guilt and knew Bear was disappointed. Thank god it was just a dream.

Another, earlier dream played at the edges of her consciousness. It felt important. She tugged at the bed covers, rolled over, and allowed herself to drift.

After a little time following the feeling, the dream came back. She was Alexander III of Macedon, outside the town of Gaza on the edge of the desert, standing on one of the tall mounds his army had used to conquer the besieged city. It was a rare, private moment when his guards stood far enough away that it was as if he were blessedly alone. Twilight was falling and the air held an elusive note of coolness. In each hand, he held a heavy, dark red obelisk the color of blood.

Alexander ran his thumbs along the inscriptions cut into the sides of the strange thick spikes that had been found hidden in Batis' bedchamber. Alexander smiled. The tiny spears had been no help to the former gatekeeper of Egypt, whom he had ordered dragged by the heels from a chariot until the man expired an hour ago. Yet, Alexander knew the obelisks were considered vital or they wouldn't have been in the bedchamber.

The objects felt warm in his hands. Alexander allowed his mind to quiet, allowed his senses to expand. He could feel a subtle pulse inside the objects, dancing in time to his heartbeat.

Inspired, he pointed the objects at the setting sun. A small spark jumped from one obelisk to the other, causing Alexander to drop the rods into the sand. He swore and bent down to pick them up. Intriguing. Clearly, Batis hadn't known how to use the things. But then, he hadn't known how to defend his city.

Alexander held the obelisks again, sensing their strange pulse. Although he'd traveled the world, he had never encountered such devices. And they sparked! What he could do with a weapon that threw fire! Of course, he had stone-throwing machines and smaller bolt shooters. But those weapons had limitations, like the need for fuel. His army often fought in deserts, far from forests. Again, he raised the obelisks to the sky and attempted to repeat the spark. Nothing happened.

He had been hasty. He slowed down. What was the common beat he felt with them? It reminded him of making love, feeling his lover's pulse in time with his own as they moved as one. One of his lovemaking teachers from India had shown him how energy moved between bodies and how he could direct that energy by using his focused imagination. It worked well with his lovers.

He closed his eyes and found his energy. He directed it to swell in his heart before he raised his arms and sent it shooting out his hands. A rush of magnified feeling in his fingers startled him. He opened his eyes in time to see a small blue light flare from the red obelisk tips and arc toward the setting sun.

Magnificent!

Alexander's heart swelled with the victories to come.

Maddy's dream faded, but the feeling in her fingertips lingered. She flexed them, curious, but she had no time to dwell on it. Probably spurred from working the new yoga exercise from the master or that conversation last night about Alexander, Isabella, and Ferdinand.

The sky was just starting to show signs of blue when she rolled out of bed, freshened up, and decided to put dreams out of her mind to practice the exercise the master had given them last night. Before bed, she had practiced for half an hour and felt warm energy stir in her belly but nothing in her hands. Perhaps it would go better in the light of a fresh day.

There was a sheepskin rug on the floor, so she stretched for a few minutes and then assumed the posture he had shown them last evening. Balling up an extra piece of paper from her backpack, she placed it on the floor in front of her. She tucked her knees, sat on her feet, raised her hands above her head, and began to chant. The rhythmic sounds captured her mind.

Before long, she had moved into that listening state where her mind was quiet and she was fully aware of her surroundings and of her own energy. At first, her arms hurt from being over her head, but after a time, the pain faded and she became her breath and the chant. *Sat Nam, Sat Nam.*

Visualizing the energy in the way the master had shown them, she was aware that Alexander had done something similar in that dream. She focused. The next thing she knew, a hot flow of energy flared right up her spine from her lower back. It caught her off guard. She'd never experienced anything like that before. It burst into her head, like a wave cresting on a beach. Light, and a heady sensation of sweet velvet goldenness, filled her.

Eventually, the feeling faded and she brought her hands to her lap and tried to light a piece of paper on fire. It didn't work.

A curious mix of bliss and frustration filled her, and she decided to pursue breakfast.

After donning her monk robe again, Maddy grabbed her backpack and headed to the dining hall. She was almost there when the master appeared from a dimly lit corridor on her right, Nanda, his shadow, in tow.

Maddy repeated the hands to the nose greeting they were shown last night. "Good morning."

"A fast learner!" The master teased, through Nanda's translating ability.

"Perhaps," she countered. "I do have some questions for you about the exercise."

"It is early yet for the food. Would you like to step into my office?"

Why not? "Thank you. I would appreciate your guidance."

Nanda and the master turned and walked back the way they had come. Maddy followed at a close distance. The hallway was not straight, winding in a leisurely arc around to the right.

It wasn't long before they walked through a doorway and into a room with a large desk, an open space with cushions, and another rug on the floor in front of an altar. The best part of the room was a stunning picture window that looked out at Mount Popa, the nearby dormant volcano and the monastery's namesake.

Maddy stood for a moment and took in the panoramic, sweeping view of the sky with its wisps of orange and red clouds. She could work in an office like this. If she had to be in an office.

The master pointed to the cushions in front of the altar. "Please, let's sit here." Nanda lit a candle in front of a Buddha statue and sat down to join them. "Now, what is your question?"

"It has taken me years to be able to feel my energy at all," she began. "This morning, doing the exercise, I felt hot energy moving up my spine."

The old man nodded, eyes lit with understanding and delight.

"In aikido, we're always told that our power center is below and behind our navel. How do I focus that energy in my hands from that spot? Can you give me a clue?"

His face broke into a smile. He thumped his chest and said through Nanda, "The heart is the clue. It is like a lens that concentrates the sun's rays. Connect the heart to the power center with your mind's eye and try it again."

"Thank you." She bowed her head. "I will try later."

After Nanda translated, the master cocked his head, looked out the window for a moment, and turned to her. "I sense that you should try now."

She sat up straight with surprise at his interest but also knew time was short so she didn't argue.

As he had asked, she knelt and sat on her feet. Her arms went above her head and she began to chant. Although her eyes were closed, she could feel his attention on her.

As she chanted, she visualized her heart, big as the sun, getting energy from behind her navel.

"Good. Now imagine someone you love," the master said in a quiet voice.

Her thoughts bounced between Bear and Juergen, like and lust. She lost her sense of concentration.

He laughed. "A child. Imagine a child you love. That love is pure."

She obeyed. AJ filled her mind, and she imagined giving him a huge hug, her heart full and bright. That image steadied her and she could feel the energy grow in her heart.

"Now put your hands down, spread them apart as I did yesterday, and send some of that energy to them. See your hands getting white."

Maddy complied and could feel the warmth.

In the background of the room, someone moved. There were rustling sounds, like paper being crumpled. Something slid on the rug in front of her, a tray perhaps, but she stayed focused, sending heat to her hands.

"There is some paper on my tea tray in front of you. Cup your hands around it and continue seeing your hands white with heat from your heart."

She cupped her hands as he had done yesterday to let the energy and heat bounce between them. Doubts swirled in the distance, but she ignored her mind and focused on the chant, the heat, AJ. There was a white heat, a glow that she could sense, balled up between her hands. She concentrated on growing the ball of heat.

The sound was what she noticed first. A crackling, like when she used to light the kindling in the wood stove on a cold night in Lake Tahoe.

Fire!

Her eyes flew open, her concentration lost. But it didn't matter, the paper on the tray in front of her bore a tiny flame that was gathering momentum. A wide smile blossomed on her face, matched only by the twin grins that the master and Nanda wore as they looked between her and the paper.

She had done it!

Maddy glowed with pleasure. Relief that they could get moving again flooded her, too, and she knew Will would be pleased.

The master beamed at her for a long minute and then said something to Nanda in their language that she didn't understand. From around his neck, the master handed Nanda a small key on a long gold chain.

Nanda walked over to the master's desk and, using the tiny key, unlocked a drawer. He brought back a bright red-and-gold jewelry box and handed it to the master, who looked Maddy in the eyes. "What you seek are obelisks made of a special, ancient mineral."

He paused to let that sink in.

Maddy wasn't surprised, based on what they'd seen in the codex at the castle, and Will's scientific mumbo-jumbo. But it was nice to know they'd been right. She nodded at him to continue.

"These obelisks can be used as a weapon when you run your energy to them like you just did to the paper. Your energy amplifies the energy in the obelisks. Used together, they will burn with the energy of a thousand deadly suns. Be careful when you learn to use them and use them only for good. You must guard this secret with your life."

This news confirmed their assumptions. The obelisks were a weapon in their own right and perhaps could fuel an e-bomb. *No wonder the Russians want them!*

Maddy nodded again, more solemnly this time. A promise made.

The master turned the front of the box toward her and opened it. Her breath caught.

Inside the box was an ornate necklace, gorgeous in its jeweled splendor. The chain was finely worked gold, the ornament oval and about an inch long.

He handed it to her and she examined it. It had a gray-green precious stone in the center, upon which was carved a pyramid, surrounded by two smaller pyramids. The outer circle of gold around the stone was inlaid with tiny chunks of jade and garnet. There were two small pearls in the circle as well. She turned the amulet over. The back had a raised sixteen-pointed sun. Recalling the Egyptian symbols on the obelisks in the codex back at the castle, she wasn't surprised by the pyramids but didn't recognize the sun symbol.

"You will need this where you are going," the master said.

"It's...it's stunning."

"You might bring it back someday, but yes, for now, keep it safe, keep it with you, and use it to guide you to your last destination."

Maddy put the amulet over her head, moving her mother's necklace aside.

As soon as she tucked it under her robe, a helicopter whirred in the distance. The picture window revealed a dark spec on the horizon, growing larger by the second.

Where are Will and Bear? Juergen?

"You must go now. Nanda will help you leave. Remember to listen—"

On her feet and headed toward the door, backpack in hand, she completed the farewell, sure now what it meant. "And feel the Power."

She had found her power and knew where they needed to go, but with a helicopter bearing down on the monastery, would she live to find the obelisks?

CHAPTER 69

7:00 a.m.:

Will heard a helicopter in the distance.

He'd been awake for a good ten minutes, lying in bed, and reviewing the events of his evening after they'd all gone to bed in the Popa Monastery.

First, he cornered Maddy and had asked about the big secret that Bear was keeping about a prior commitment. In brief, she told him that Bear was training with a covert group of cutting-edge intelligence officers and would give him more details later.

Quite a surprise: Bear was a baby spy. Will had a healthy distrust of all thing's government, so although he trusted Bear, he was wary of this news and made a mental note to get the specifics from him.

Next, curious about everything the master had shown them, Will practiced the exercise in the tiny monk's cell that he was given as a bedroom. There was barely room for him to kneel on the rug next to the bed, but he knelt there anyway and worked the exercise for a while. He didn't feel a thing, and discouraged, had lain down on the comfortable bed to nod off.

Instead, memories of his time with his wife flooded his thoughts. The meeting at work when her smile lit the conference room on fire and he realized he found her attractive. Their first date at the Italian haunt in downtown São Paolo where they shared noodles and talked over espresso. The first time she spent the night on his live-aboard sailboat and they merged with the stars until the first light of day. Their large family wedding, lakeside, at the Parque Ibirapuera in São Paulo. It had rained, but they had a blast anyway. The night, a month ago, when she told him she was going to have their baby.

At the memory of the child, the grief had taken him over, and this time, he didn't fight it. It was an avalanche, a tidal wave, and drowned him in unfamiliar sorrow while the weight in his stomach and chest anchored him to the bed. Tears finally flowed, an unfettered ocean.

This morning, part of him felt so ashamed that he had cried that he wanted to hide under the covers. But he felt lighter and knew that it had been needed. Now he could get on with the business of healing his heart.

In the light of morning, he was considering how to accelerate their time here at the monastery when he became aware of the sound. At first, it was the distant, irritating drone of a fly.

Thirty seconds later, Bear knocked on the door. "Argones. Wake up! We've got to go!"

Will swung his feet onto the floor and started to dress in yesterday's clothes. "I'm up, I'm awake! How can you tell we've got to go?"

"I recognize the sound of that helo. It's military grade."

Expletives danced through Will's head. Within thirty seconds, he was dressed back in his monk's robe and had thrown open the door. Bear looked pale in the dim light of the hallway and had also chosen to keep with their disguise.

"I guess breakfast is out of the question?" Finding his own gallows humor amusing, Will laughed to himself.

"Shut up. Let's go find Maddy."

"Where do you think she is?"

"Let's start with the dining hall and that big garden area."

As the only pseudo public area that they'd seen here, it seemed a logical choice. "Let's go! But I do want to know more about the Bond business."

"Later!"

They ran.

Last night it had taken them just a handful of minutes to get from the dining hall to their rooms, but today it seemed to take an hour, even though they were running. Within seconds, Bear outstripped Will.

Soon they hit the dining hall. It was relatively empty, so they kept going, and when they came out into the Grand Garden Will could see why. Most of the monastery's young monks were milling about in the garden area, curiosity about the helicopter having drawn them away from their breakfasts. They were all looking to the south, and Will could hear the sound of the helicopter getting closer.

Frantically, he looked around for an exit. He had no idea how they were going to get off the mountaintop death trap. They'd be easy prey on those 777 stairs.

Will scanned the crowd. Although most monks wore look-alike robes, he was able to spy Maddy standing by Nanda near where the Grand Garden met the Private Pergola. She had also dressed in her monk's robe. Juergen, Dieter, and Elena were in the center of the open space, necks craning to look up at the helicopter, standing out like sore thumbs in their street clothes.

Bear saw Maddy, too. "There she is!"

She yelled for the monks to take cover, but in their curiosity, or helicopter-induced deafness, they ignored her.

As the noise became intense, Will and Bear pushed through the throng toward Maddy. They made it to the center of the Grand Garden. Juergen stood five meters away, hand shading his eyes so he could see better.

"Take cover!" Will shouted to him.

"What? Why?" Juergen demanded.

"It's military and might be after us!"

Comprehension lit Juergen's eyes and he began to push through the crowd toward Maddy. Bear and Will moved in the same direction. Dieter and Elena split and ran toward opposite walls.

Faster! They had to move faster!

Nanda motioned them to come toward him. He'd moved to one of the several doorways that lined the Grand Garden and held open the door. They were still eight meters away. The helicopter was closing fast from behind them.

Automatic gunfire ripped through the air. *Pop! Pop! Pop!* The stone patio behind Will's legs erupted and sharp bits of stone bit into both of his calves. He choked back a shout at the same time that Bear swore. Monks around them let loose primal screams full of surprise and dismay.

Juergen stumbled and fell. Will smelled blood and fear as the helicopter roared away overhead, its shadow blocking out the morning sun for a long black moment.

CHAPTER 70

7:27 a.m.:

Aafter the helo roared off, Bear felt a stabbing, shooting pain on the outside of his left arm and smaller points of agony on his calves. The back of Juergen's shirt was bloody. The noise of the rotors was still deafening and threatened to take him back in time to a mountaintop in Afghanistan that he'd rather forget.

Bear pulled himself into the present as he noted a telltale hole in the back of Juergen's left shoulder. Just to be thorough, he ran over and reached for Juergen's neck to see if there was a pulse at the carotid.

Juergen's neck felt hot and slippery with sweat. *No pulse!*

Will pointed in the direction the helicopter had gone. "We have to go!"

Knowing that it was hopeless but wanting to try everything, Bear pulled Juergen over his shoulders in a fireman's carry and headed toward Maddy and the open door that Nanda held. She stood just inside the darkness, still twenty feet away. Bear put his head down and sprinted toward her.

The helo raced back toward them and let down another trail of automatic gunfire fifteen feet to Bear's left. Will made the door. Lungs burning, Bear lunged toward the opening. And then the helo was past and Bear was inside.

They were in a broad hallway. Hands reached up to take Juergen off Bear's shoulders. They laid the body on the floor and Maddy repeated the exercise of trying to find Juergen's heartbeat. She choked. "I can't—"

Nanda leaned down next to her and also felt for a pulse. There was blood on Juergen's chest. The bullet must have gone clear through him. Bear could also see that Juergen's eyes stared up at nothing, so between that and the lack of a heartbeat, Bear knew the man was gone. Taking a deep breath to steady himself, Bear lowered his head in defeat. Remembering other fallen, his throat closed with emotion, and he shut his eyes.

In a moment, he realized that a small part of his heart felt lighter, relieved, for which he berated himself. Unless the man was a mole for the Russians who were following them somehow. The guy had seemed tense all the time.

Maddy looked at Nanda, beseeching him. "I don't feel anything. Nanda, do you?"

"No. He has departed." Nanda shut Juergen's eyes by running his left hand down over them. "I will say prayers later and we will arrange for burial. Now, I must get you to safety."

Tears welled in Maddy's eyes. She bowed her head for a moment, crouched next to the body. Will put his hand on her shoulder and Bear took the time to look at his left arm. He could still hear screams and commotion on the other side of the door. A bullet had grazed the flesh on the back of his arm, along the triceps muscle. It was a four-inch-long wound but gratefully not deep.

"Let me help," Maddy said. While he was looking at his wound, she had gotten control of her emotions and stood next to him.

She reached down, tore off a part of Juergen's shirt, and tied it around Bear's arm. Their eyes met for a moment, she touched his cheek, and he knew she understood his feelings and accepted them. In some way, perhaps she felt the same, as any conflict in her heart was over. A twisted knot, deep in his chest, loosened and he exhaled with relief.

"Come now!" Nanda said. "That may have to wait." He set off at a trot down the hallway.

Bear agreed with him and motioned for Maddy and Will to follow Nanda. Bear took up the rear guard, his calves complaining from shallow, bloody divots.

After heading deep into the compound for two minutes, Bear could still hear the helo, a distant fly buzzing around a corpse.

They jogged farther down the hallway, took a left, continued for another minute, and then pulled up in front of a narrow door. Nanda opened it and pulled out several brooms and mops. He reached up, pushed a small button, and the entire back panel of the closet shifted to the right, revealing a circular staircase cut into a dark narrow stairwell.

Nanda pulled a long black flashlight and a small pack from the wall and handed the flashlight to Maddy and the pack to Will. Maddy turned the flashlight on and pointed it down the tight spiral staircase. The tree-trunk-wide pole in the center supported stairs that jutted between the center shaft and the stone wall. The air smelled fresh, and Bear figured there were air shafts somewhere on the long way down. It was an impressive escape route.

"Secret stairs," Nanda said. "Not many know of them. They were built long ago and go all the way down, through the mountain, and come out about a mile from town, to the south. Be careful when you come out."

Maddy gave Nanda a quick hug, pulled back, and looked him in the eye. "Thank you for everything."

"You're most welcome. Now go."

They started moving down the stairs, following the small circle of light from the flashlight Maddy carried.

Nanda turned and closed the door. Quiet descended on the group and they halted.

Bear took a deep breath and regrouped. He sensed the twins did the same.

Will passed Maddy and moved down the stairs. "Sorry about Juergen. Shall we?"

"Yes, let's leave this place." Her voice broke a little. "I have what we need." She started to move down the stairs again, behind Will.

Will turned on his small keychain flashlight, aimed it down the middle of the spiral staircase to add additional light, and picked up speed. "You do?"

"Yes. I ran into the master on my way to breakfast. He showed me a few things. I was able to light some paper on fire, and he gave me an amulet."

Bear was amazed that she sounded so matter-of-fact about it. She was a fascinating woman. Or maybe she was in shock.

Will's tone was incredulous. "No way! You lit paper on fire, too?"

"I did, but don't know if I'll be able to do anything like it again. I've choked before, remember the alley in Vilnius? And the amulet is more important now."

"Can I see it?" Will asked.

"Of course, but we need to put some distance between ourselves and that idiotic helicopter pilot up there!" Now her tone was fast and high-pitched. Maddy's pissed off voice.

Will already sounded out of breath. "Maybe when we rest."

"You mean when we get to the bottom?"

"Oh god! You can't be serious. My legs are already burning."

"At least we don't have to run up them!" Bear said.

"Let's go as far as we can anyway," Maddy said. "I can*not* believe they found us again."

Will looked back. "Well, if the Russians were watching the temple area, they would have seen only monks leave. All the monks headed here, to Popa monastery."

"I suppose," Maddy snapped.

They moved as fast as they could down the steep stairwell. It seemed to go on forever, but Bear remembered how long it had taken them to climb the 777 stairs to the top originally.

After five minutes, Will slowed and then stopped. "I have to have a break. My legs are cramping." He sat down and used his flashlight to look at the back of his legs. They were dotted with red and streaked with blood in a few places.

Maddy sounded concerned. "Will, did you get shot?" She sat on the step above him.

He touched one of the red dots on his calf and his finger came away bloody. "I think it was from the stone chips flying through the air."

"That'll do it." Bear drawled as he sat down, too, and groaned a little. His legs were also sore and his arm throbbed.

"Let me see what's in your pack." Maddy took the pack off Will's back, rummaged around in it, and pulled out two bottles of water and several small raw potatoes. "No real first aid but you can rinse the wounds with water. Bear, are you thirsty?" She held out the bottles.

Bear and Will held out their hands and she passed out the water bottles. They drank and Will rinsed the worst of his calf wounds. Bear followed suit.

Bear realized his stomach was growling. "I'll eat the raw potato."

"*Eww.* Really?" Maddy asked.

"Sure, my mom used to give us slices with salt when she was cooking. Must be their form of emergency rations."

Maddy shrugged and handed him a small potato. Bear ate it with gusto. It tasted good and reminded him of happier times.

Will turned to look at Maddy on the step above him. "Can I see the amulet now?"

"Sure." She reached into her shirt and pulled up the end of a gold necklace, leaving the silver lion's head in place.

Will studied it in the light of his own flashlight.

Bear finished the potato.

"Cool. Looks like there are tiny pyramids on there. Want to see, Bear?"

Bear reached out his hand. "Yes, please."

Will handed him the flashlight and the amulet. Bear used the light to study the amulet.

It was a lavish piece of jewelry. Although the outside gold filigree held numerous precious gems, it was the center stone that held his attention. Inside were three pyramids, the third one a little taller than the other two and outlined. If Bear squinted, he could also see three much smaller pyramids in front of the first one.

"The Pyramids at Giza," he announced.

Maddy looked over her shoulder at him. "Are you sure? I thought so, but you're the historian."

"Yes, although there are a lot of other pyramids in Egypt, especially farther south of Cairo in the Luxor area and in the Valley of Kings, this series of three, with the three tiny ones in front of that first one, is unique in the world. They lie in the shadow of Giza."

Bear turned it over and ran his thumb over the raised pattern. "I wonder what the Vergina Sun is doing here?"

"Is that what it is? I didn't recognize it."

"Yeah, it's an ancient Greek symbol, possibly used by Alexander the Great's family. It has caused some recent controversy in Greece," Bear said.

Maddy held out her hand. "Hmm, the Alexander connection again. Well, hand it back and let's finish these stairs. Maybe we'll find out why we have it when we get there."

"At least we have a clear destination now. Looks like the Great Pyramid is the place to start." Bear handed it back to her and they all stood.

"Why are you thinking that, Bear?"

"It's outlined and the others aren't, and it's the most famous."

"Makes sense to me," Maddy said.

"Why not?" Will added, as they started moving down the stairs again. "First things first, though. Wherever this set of stairs leads, let's keep an eye out for a helicopter with machine guns."

CHAPTER 71

Bangkok Airport, July 21, 4:30 p.m.:

As the plane landed at the Bangkok airport, Maddy reflected that it had been an extremely long, sad, day.

Juergen's death left her with a hole in her heart and the last couple of hours were spent just going through the motions of getting away from the monastery. Part of the sorrow was stirred-up emotions from the loss of Maria and her father, but her heart also ached for the fresh loss of a friend, a colleague, and a handsome man to whom she'd been attracted.

Although she recognized that she could now pursue her feelings for Bear without conflicting emotions, the day was destined for mourning. It was not a day for new beginnings.

She also spent some time mulling over AJ's fate, wondering if her dream did herald danger for him, and questioning where he was, how he was, if he was safe. If he was even still alive.

And so the day had gone.

The secret staircase had led to the middle of nowhere. Once they had made the bottom of the circular staircase, they emerged into the darkness of an ancient cave. They surprised a few bats into flight, which got Maddy's heart racing for a moment, but otherwise the tall open space looked deserted.

To one side of the cave, a narrow shaft of sunlight cut the darkness. That brightness led to a short, slender tunnel that they squeezed through in turn.

Bear went first and reported the area quiet and clear. Maddy went through next, just mildly uncomfortable with the small, tight space. Will followed her through on his hands and knees. They came out on the side of the rock outcropping that held up the monastery, in the middle of a pile of rocks.

Once free of the tunnel, there was no sign of the feared helicopter, and they heaved a collective sigh of relief. Ten feet away from the entrance, she looked back and was shocked that the hole they crawled through was obscured by hefty rocks and dry vegetation. She had to admit that it was a shrewd escape route.

Away from the cave, the road lay a quarter mile away and the town farther to the north. They bushwhacked their way to the road and hiked the mile into town with local farmers for company. They were alert for the sound of the helicopter to return, but it did not, so they acted like monks on the way into town, talking all the way about how they'd been found.

Once there, they grabbed a quick breakfast, ditched their disguises in the bathroom waste cans, and caught a ride in a private car into Mandalay as backpackers. Maddy was glad to get out of the robe and get a hat on her head. She couldn't wait for her hair to grow back.

Later that afternoon, feeling quiet and subdued as a group, they purchased tickets to Cairo at the Mandalay airport. The only flights available had short layovers in Bangkok and Abu Dhabi. While in the Mandalay airport, they also purchased some clean clothes.

The first leg of their journey was on time, smooth, and uneventful, the type of flight that Maddy preferred. As they departed the plane and walked through the gate inside Bangkok's gleaming airport, she turned to Will and Bear. "What do you guys think about grabbing some computer time at an internet kiosk and doing some research on our destination?"

Will replied first. "Sounds good. The airport in Mandalay was a little light on technology."

She pointed past two gates on the left. "This airport looks like technology nirvana in comparison. I see a kiosk there—"

After being in the subdued light of the airplane for a few hours, the blue and white lights inside the gate area were so bright she had to squint. This airport reminded her of O'Hare in Chicago, all open space, girders, a clean white tile floor, and copious amounts of glass.

Bear motioned with his head. "There's another one beyond the departure sign, too."

"Yep, I see. That one does look less crowded, so let's head to it."

"Okay, I'll meet you guys there in a minute. I want to check on our departure gate and grab some sandwiches," Will said.

Maddy and Bear gave Will their sandwich order and then worked their way through the crowd to the internet kiosk.

Maddy paid for two fifteen-minute sessions and found a computer. Bear sat behind her. She signed in with the password coded on her receipt. "I hope the internet speeds here are decent."

"Especially since we all don't have a lot of time on this layover."

Maddy's fingers flew over the keyboard with practiced ease. "Yes. Exactly."

She was a little distracted as she familiarized herself with the computer. It was an older Windows 7 model, so she figured out where the Internet Explorer browser was located, downloaded and installed the TOR browser to maintain a level of anonymity, and opened up a search page.

Then she turned to Bear. He was looking a little scruffy from their travels and had put a blue bandanna over his bald head. *Didn't even have time to shave this morning.* His strong broad shoulders looked good under his new T-shirt. She had noticed a few women checking him out throughout their recent travels.

"So, you're pretty sure we start our search at the Great Pyramid?"

"Let me see the amulet again, if you don't mind," he drawled.

She handed him the amulet and searched for photos of the Great Pyramid. "Sure, take a look while I pull up some pictures."

Before the page with images had even loaded, Bear pointed. "See here?" He had the side of the amulet up that had the pyramids on it. "I just noticed. See how the largest pyramid, the one in the back, is the only one that has substance to it. The others are more like sketches."

She glanced down at it for a second until she got what he was talking about. "Okay, so let's go with that as an assumption. Check out these images." The page loaded. She went on. "Looks like the two upper chambers are called the King's Chamber and Queen's Chamber. There's a lower one, too, called the Subterranean Chamber. Oh wow, they recently found a buried secret chamber above the Grand Gallery, whatever that is."

"What about the exterior?"

"Well, there's no cap on this pyramid. It's got a flat top, but it has some sort of wooden surveying tripod in the middle where the cap would be. Since all the other clues mentioned the center of something, maybe it's under that tripod?"

Maddy noticed that Bear didn't seem to be paying much attention to the pictures. He'd probably memorized the layout from a *National Geographic* magazine when he was eight. She turned to him. He was looking, with glazed eyes, off into the distance. "Bear?"

"Hmm?"

"What are you thinking about?"

"The guards."

She realized what he was thinking. Of course, there would be guards. "Crap! You don't think we should wait until broad daylight, do you?"

"No," he agreed. "I don't. We've had too much company lately and I'm thinkin' a nighttime excursion would be better. We also have the need for speed."

"Yes, we do."

"What time do we land in Cairo?"

She rubbed her ear, considering. "Assuming all goes well in Abu Dhabi, around three a.m."

"The dead of night. It's perfect."

She sighed. "We won't get much sleep, but I think you're right."

They looked at each other and he nodded his head in time with hers.

He turned his attention back to the monitor. "Quickly then, there are a few details we need to know about. I'd like to make a plan that won't get us killed."

CHAPTER 72

Giza Plateau, Egypt, July 22, 4:10 a.m.

Will brought sandwiches back to Maddy and Bear at the airport, and discovered that they'd hatched an evil plan between them to rob him of any semblance of rest for the remainder of the night. While other passengers on the flight to Cairo slept, the three of them huddled together, whispering about how they were going to storm the pyramid in the predawn light.

At first, Will resisted the plan, but they reminded him of the annoying fact that he would soon be a wanted man by the Napa police force. He had no idea why the cops considered him a suspect for the murders that had started them on this adventure, but tomorrow, in fact, he needed to be in California, or else. They needed to end this quest and the sooner the better. He had to agree with them on that point.

Once they landed and obtained a ride, the car moved through Cairo with ease. The streets were deserted. The taxi driver dropped them off at the Sphinx View Bed and Breakfast, a stone's throw from the Great Sphinx, and walking distance to their destination.

The night was warm and a strong breeze stirred the palm fronds. The air seemed charged. Will could sense a storm approaching. *Rain in the desert? Just our luck.*

Maddy swung her backpack over her shoulders as the taxi's taillights disappeared around a corner. "Let's hope our driver just saw three tired tourists arriving late from the States."

Will looked at the B&B with longing, but excitement was starting to surge through him. "He's already forgotten us. Hope you don't mind getting wet, though. Feels like rain. Bear, which way?"

Bear took off at a brisk walk. "Follow me."

Will and Maddy followed.

"Our online research did say it rains here once in a while. We'll just have to deal with it," Maddy said.

Within a half block, they could see the desert on their left. Multiple pyramids loomed in the near distant darkness. The legendary Sphinx was right in front of them. Looking at its elongated paws and famous face, Will felt the thrill of standing at the crossroads of history.

"I've always wanted to come here," Bear said, reverence in his tone. "Did y'all know that the Great Pyramid was the world's tallest structure for over thirty-eight hundred years?"

"That's one hell of a long time," Will said.

Thunder boomed in the distance.

Bear went on, "Its ancient name was Khufu's Horizon. Even with skilled workmen regularly workin' around the clock, it took almost twenty years to build. The two other tall pyramids over there to the left were for his son and grandson."

"Aren't they still arguing about how they built all the pyramids?" Maddy pointed to the three smaller pyramids that lay between them and the Great Pyramid. "And what about these tiny pyramids in front of Khufu's?"

"Yes, the arguin' has gone on for centuries. Those little ones are for the wives."

Maddy's edged tone held a warning. "So, you're saying women have been the lesser sex for four thousand years?"

"There were matriarchal cultures in the time of Mesopotamia, but we digress." Bear did a good job dodging that bullet. "Let's work our way along the modern village until we can cut over to Queen Hetepheres's tomb through Eastern Cemetery."

He turned right on the small road that split the town from the desert.

Will pointed left, at several flat, low-lying structures. "You mean those?"

"Yes."

In the shadow of the ancient tombs, Will felt bare, a mast without a sail. Would he join Maria tonight? The town was asleep, and the blanket of clouds oppressive overhead. At least there was no moon.

They walked about thirty meters before Bear stopped and looked to their left. "Okay, now is when we stalk the shadows. We have to get over there behind the queen's tomb so that we can check out where the guards are stationed tonight."

All three of them looked around. Will didn't see a soul.

Bear gave a signal and they sprinted toward the Eastern Cemetery. Within a minute, they were inside the graveyard area, surrounded by rectangular squat-stone structures two or three times taller than Will. They zigzagged their way between the old buildings, alert for guards. Thunder continued to build, the gods bowling in desert lanes of sand.

Bear held up his hand. "Wait!"

Will looked around the corner. A guard paced in the distance, walking near the taller of the queen's pyramids, rifle on his shoulder. Will held his breath and the guard walked out of sight.

Bear motioned for them to trail him deeper into the series of old buildings. They followed, silently slipping between the darkest areas.

After ten harrowing minutes, they peered around a corner. The Great Pyramid loomed over them. Thunder boomed. The three wives' pyramids were right in front of them.

Bear motioned them closer. "Okay. We need to get the lay of the land and check out where the guards are. Let's each take a smaller pyramid. I've got the far one closest to the north side and the entrance. Maddy, you've got the middle one, and Will, you take this one to the left. Stay out of sight. Go see what the guards are doin' for ten minutes and rendezvous back here. Got it?"

Will nodded. His heart pumped wildly.

"Will, you need to scout that far corner of the pyramid. According to our research, the Japanese tourists who sneak to the top on a regular basis said it's the easiest to climb. Now go!"

Will sprinted for his small assigned pyramid. He had the tallest of the three, which was both a blessing and a curse. Although the heights on the plane hadn't bothered him, he didn't know how high he'd be able to climb but wanted to give it a go. It loomed before him and then he was at its base.

He looked around. Seeing no one, he began to climb, hugging the rocks and staying in the darkest shadows. Thunder clapped again, a little closer this time. Will shuddered. He still wouldn't call himself a fan of heights, but at least these were solid boulders and not a flimsy ladder beneath him. The rocks that made up the pyramid were half his height and many had begun to crumble. With each step, he checked his footing to make sure the rock would take his weight.

He scrambled almost to the top, looked down, was amazed that he didn't get dizzy, and decided that he was high enough to scoot around to the side and see if any of the guards were roaming nearby.

He peered around the corner. What Bear earlier had called the "Khufu Ship Museum" was a long white assembly, which contained an old Egyptian boat. The modern superstructure looked out of place here in the shadows of the last remaining wonder of the ancient world.

Will's breath caught in his throat and he cursed. *Merda!* In front of the maritime museum stood a single guard, blocking their path to the far corner of the pyramid.

CHAPTER 73

4:22 a.m.:

Bear was the first one back to the rendezvous point, after their attempt to get the lay of the land at the base of the Great Pyramid. *Hellfire! Where are the twins?*

He hoped nothing had happened to either of them, and he'd heard no commotion, so perhaps they were just tardy.

Time dragged. He checked his GoPro. Working. Tiny raindrops began to fall from the thick black cloud base above.

Before he could, in good conscience, go after Maddy to see if she was okay, she drifted around a corner into his line of sight. A second later, Will appeared too, from the opposite side. They converged on him.

Bear looked at Will first, as he'd had the most important assignment. "Will, what did you see?"

Will scratched at his stubbled cheek. "There *is* a guard. He's pacing in front of the boat museum. I don't know how we'll get past him."

"I was afraid of that. Maddy, what about you? You had the best view of the east side."

"Not much there. No guards but also no entrance and, from what our research showed, not a good run to the top. What did you see by the north entrance?"

Bear frowned. "Two guards. Both armed with rifles."

Will moved to crouch under a rock overhang. "We're screwed. Why don't we go find a hotel and come back in the morning? Besides, it's starting to rain."

Will's movement gave Bear an idea, which shifted his mood from frustrated to playful. "You pansy, scared of gettin' a little wet?"

Will began to puff up in annoyance, but Bear put a hand out. "I'm pulling your leg. This rain could help us out. Think that single guard is goin' to hang out in the rain, or go keep his friends company by the entrance where it's nice and dry?"

Maddy's eyes lit up. "Good idea. I'll go scout!"

Before Bear could protest, she slipped away.

Will and Bear shared a drink of water in silence under the overhanging ledge and Bear watched the silver bullets of rain fall from the sky. Thunder rolled and the first shards of lightning lit the sky in the distance.

Will pointed at the top of the pyramid. "Are you thinking we're going to climb that lightning rod?"

"Sure am. We could get inside tomorrow, but tonight's our best chance to check out the top. It's not exactly part of the tour package."

"You're insane."

"You don't have to come."

"Not climb one of the world's tallest structures in a thunderstorm? Why would I want to miss out on that?"

"The lightning is off in the distance. Maybe we can make it up and back before the storm moves this way," Bear said.

"Maybe pigs fly."

Maddy returned, a wraith moving between raindrops. She gave two thumbs-up. The guards were hiding from the rain.

Will mumbled expletives under his breath.

Bear grinned and his heart beat faster with excitement. He double-checked the video harness, wished again for a weapon. "Let's go."

Maddy led the way, veering left as she swiftly led them through the remainder of the tombs in the Eastern Cemetery.

They skirted the small pyramid Will had climbed and headed to the other small pyramids that were behind the boat museum. Maddy kept the tombs between them and the other side of the pyramid, in case one of the guards felt guilty and decided to leave the dry entrance. But the rain now was a steady drizzle.

Within heartbeats, they were at the last squat tomb near the southwest corner.

Maddy peeked around the stones looking for guards or other signs of life. Bear double-checked. The night was empty. Maddy gave the backpack to Will, who groaned. They all looked at each other and nodded.

Quiet as an animal hunting in the forest, Bear went first. He sprinted from the cover of the tomb to the corner of the Great Pyramid. He felt exhilarated, completely at home sneaking around the ancient monument in the night's darkest hour.

At the corner, Bear realized the online reports from the Japanese tourists who made this ascent regularly hadn't led them astray. Here the pyramid resembled a high-stepped staircase of steady, firm blocks, but on both sides, the ascent looked steep and crumbling.

After scrambling for a minute, he turned and was gratified to see Maddy behind him. Will was just a few steps behind her, taking the blocks easily with his long legs and arms. There were still no guards below. Bear breathed a sigh of relief, hoping against hope that he was right about this being the place to start.

Twenty minutes of hard, rapid, and slippery climbing finally brought the flat top into view between the slow but steady raindrops. Bear had been fantasizing about getting there for the last ten minutes. Lungs heaving, he cleared the top, made sure the twins were still hot on his heels, and paused to look around.

The view was magnificent, even in the rain. The lights of Cairo winked to the east. Khafre's pyramid in the near distance, which looked almost as tall as Khufu's, still proudly hung onto its limestone casing at the top, lending it the air of a stone mountain topped with snow. In a way, it reminded him of the peaks around Lake Tahoe.

Farther south, he could see the Pyramid of Menkaure, Khufu's grandson's tomb, and the smallest of the three. He was glad the GoPro was seeing it all. He'd treasure it later. If there was a later. Thunder rumbled.

Bear felt on top of the world, until the next crack of lightning, which lit up the nearby sky with an unnerving, searing jag that made the hair on the back of his neck stand straight up.

It was far too close for comfort.

CHAPTER 74

4:48 a.m.:

High above the dark, Egyptian desert, D'Angelo stared at the white-haired man who sat across from him in the spartan helicopter cabin. They both wore headsets to communicate. Ivan, the Russian sniper, sat next to the red-haired boy, and D'Angelo's agent, a pale-faced middle-aged man, sat in the back, manning the machine gun.

"Why did you have to kill that German?" D'Angelo asked.

The older man glared back. "This is our mission. You're getting paid well. What do you care?" His English held a thick Spanish accent.

D'Angelo wanted more money. "You've caused a number of international incidents. Including one in my Napa backyard."

"That driver wasn't following orders. But that's why you're on board. To help clean up our messes and give us the data on the early warning systems."

"I've done all that. But you've taken too many risks. The plan was to herd them along, not hurt them."

The old man pointed toward Cairo. "They're alive, are they not?"

"They are. But that Danish girl is dead, and so is the German."

"The German was a mole for us, and the girl, competition. As I said, none of your business."

The man had been reckless, and it had all been a pain in D'Angelo's ass. Way over what he'd agreed to with the baron. "Was the machine gun necessary at the monastery?"

"Would you rather they all slunk back to their homes?"

"Of course not," D'Angelo snapped. "But I've had to do far more than we agreed to keep the international community off your back."

Lightning flared across the dark sky, illuminating the pyramids in the distance.

"We had to keep them off balance, keep them running."

"It was a risky plan," D'Angelo said.

"Ivan is accurate. And it's paid off."

D'Angelo pointed to the gunner, who had followed the twins through Europe, and had kept a quiet eye on the Russians from a distance. "And now you want us to kill them?"

"Don't need them anymore. Remember, you get a bonus once we have the *châsse* in hand and they're dead."

D'Angelo remembered quite the bonus quite well. He wanted to use it to quit VanOps, and go live in Sicily with a certain, spectacular, young woman. The men stared at each other.

"What if I double it?"

D'Angelo stroked his chin. After a moment, he nodded his head.

The old man deftly tuned a listening device. "They've almost found it."

D'Angelo changed a channel and listened to Maddy Marshall's excited voice through the Russian bug that had been inserted into her mother's necklace. It did sound like the quest was coming to an end.

CHAPTER 75

4:50 a.m.:

When Maddy made it to the top of the pyramid, she was out of breath, her wounded thigh ached, and the rush from outwitting the guards was beginning to wane. But when the expansive view opened up before her, all thoughts of discomfort vanished.

"Wow, Bear, just wow! Can you believe this?"

"I know, isn't it amazing?"

"C'mon, Will! The view up here is beyond impressive."

Will scrambled up the last rock steps and joined them at the top. He took a few deep breaths and looked around. He smiled and she was surprised he'd made it to the top with his fear of heights. Evidently, he'd had some shifts on their journey, too. "Yes, it was worth the climb."

Mosquitoes buzzed around Maddy's head. "You'd think, with the rain, the mosquitoes would take the night off."

Bear walked over to the wooden, surveying tripod that took up a good portion of the rock-strewn, flat area at the top. "That would have been nice."

Maddy joined him and put a hand out to touch the slick wood. "What do you think that's for?"

"I think I read that they wanted to see where the capstone would've been."

"Was there ever a capstone?"

"Historians from the time of Christ say there wasn't one then, but the pyramid was already pretty old by their time, so hard to say."

Thunder sounded loud in Maddy's ears and then lightning cracked nearby. The way the sky lit up, it looked as if it might have even hit Khafre's pyramid next door.

Will jumped. "Hey, guys. I don't know if you've noticed, but I'm the tallest thing around and not interested in becoming barbecued William."

Maddy nodded and swatted another mosquito. She'd been thinking along the same lines. "I hear you. Let's search and see what we can find. Start under the tripod since most of the clues mentioned 'the center' as a key element."

She grabbed the monastery's long black flashlight from her backpack, Will pulled out his keychain flashlight, and they both began shining light around the wet stones. She moved the larger beam in an organized pattern. "Shouldn't take long. If there's anything up here to see, we'll see it soon."

Will began to say, "This is a wild-goose…" He trailed off, squatted down, and waved. "Hey, come over here."

"Here" was the pile of hay-bale-sized stones under the midpoint of the tripod. She and Bear moved toward Will and bent down next to him, swatting mosquitoes as they moved. "What do you see, Argones?" Bear asked.

Will pointed toward the bottom of one of the stones. "There's your symbol."

Maddy's eyes widened with shock and she reached out to touch it. "We've come a long way for this."

Will shook his head. "I don't believe it."

Maddy got down on her knees to study the symbol. Unmistakably, it was Ramiro's *signum regis*. Next to it was a small depression.

Bear touched her arm. "Wait! Listen."

Maddy did as he had requested. "I hear mosquitoes."

"Listen harder."

She strained and over the sound of the rain, sounding much like the mosquitoes, was the faint drone of a helicopter in the distance. She swore. "How did they find us *again*?"

The three of them locked eyes and looked at each other for a long moment. Maddy spoke first. "We've got to see if we can get the *châsse* and whatever's inside. It's the only weapon we might have."

"Okay, go!" Bear said.

Will started poking at Ramiro's sign. "Nothing is happening!" Panic laced his tone.

"Will. Shine your light against it. There." Maddy spoke in a rush. She was firing on all cylinders now. "See that little oval indentation next to it?"

Bear grabbed the flashlight from her hands and aimed the light. "Looks like there's a faint Vergina Sun etched into the oval."

It was a lock and she had the key. With agonizing slowness, she pulled the amulet over her head, turned the Vergina Sun side down to the rock, and pressed the raised pattern into the indentation.

For a count of two, nothing happened. She felt a click and that side of the stone swung inward revealing, in the light of the flashlight, a small blue-and-gold box. As she stared into the darkness, she wrenched the amulet back over her neck for safekeeping.

The helicopter sounded much closer now. The box was the *châsse*, but they were out of time!

Sweating, she reached in and pulled the *châsse* out of its miniature cave. It looked like a tiny house with a curved roof, about the size of a shoebox. Painted with a background of cobalt blue, there were gold images of winged angels on each side and on the sloping faux roof.

"Hurry, hurry," Will prayed.

Bear's head swiveled between her hands and the rain-soaked sky.

Pulse pounding in her temples, she opened the *châsse* with trembling fingers. Inside, wrapped in black silk, were two inscribed obelisks the color of rich rubies, or more darkly, she thought, the color of blood. She wondered if they were carved from a giant ruby, or garnet, or from some other rare mineral like the master had said, and wished for time to study the inscriptions.

She held them up to the light. "They're beautiful." They started to pulse as she rotated them. If she had to use them, she hoped like hell she wouldn't panic.

Will's tone held fear. "They better be useful. Here comes the chopper."

The helicopter was upon them. Its door opened and a man yelled. "I have the boy! Don't try anything."

Will was right about using AJ as insurance. Maddy shuddered. *Not AJ!*

She yelled, "No!" But the sound was lost in the whirr of the rotor blades.

The helicopter maneuvered to just above the pyramid and a rope snaked out of a side opening. Lightning flared in the distance and Maddy almost wished it would hit the metal bird.

A man slid down the rope and landed, feet first, on the stones. His gun was in his hand the second he landed. Her gut clenched with the recognition of the half-disfigured blond Russian who had murdered their father and Maria.

Inside the helicopter, another man grabbed the rope. Red-haired AJ was on his back, piggyback style. It was a swarthy-skinned, large-nosed man.

"You son of a bitch!" Bear yelled.

How did Bear recognize the man? Maybe he was part of VanOps. But there was no time to consider it. She only had eyes for AJ as he held on during the short descent to the pyramid's top. Instinctively, she moved toward him but stopped when the Russian's gun safety clicked off and he growled, "Don't move."

Instead, she reached out with her arms and pantomimed a hug. "Are you okay?"

AJ nodded and yelled, "Maddy, they want to take out early warning stations in America using some sort of bomb. Don't give them what they want!"

The man with the beak dumped AJ on the ground and backhanded him across the face. "Quiet!"

Maddy cringed at the blow, wanting to reach out and smack the man right back. *Take out warning stations with a bomb? Or an e-bomb?* She felt like her hands were already tied behind her back, helpless.

How could she stop them? She couldn't even keep the man from hitting AJ. Poor kid. She wanted to go to AJ, take him in her arms, and tell him it would be all right. Instead, she drank in the sight of him, relieved he was alive, comforted he could still smile after god-knew-what he'd been through. He looked older, thinner, but she was also reassured to see no blood or bandages. She also wanted to know what he knew about the e-bomb plot. But that would have to wait.

The next thing she knew, a tall, clean-shaven, white-haired man with olive skin landed on the pyramid from the helicopter somewhat less gracefully than the two younger men. She caught a whiff of cologne.

As the helicopter roared off, with help from a flash of lightning, she got a glimpse of the pilot through his window. His black hair was pulled into a stylish ponytail and he had dark skin, determined features. *Who is he?*

Then the white-haired man demanded her attention with a thick Spanish accent. "Give me those obelisks."

Expecting her to comply, he held out his left hand. It was missing the ring and pinkie fingers. His right hand held a pistol, pointed toward her midsection.

Maddy took a step toward him. Through their bond, she could sense both Will's emotional strength and his urging *not* to give up the obelisks.

Pausing, she studied the situation. On the other side of the tripod, AJ was standing between the scarred Russian and the guy Bear knew, or thought he knew. Both had guns and the Russian's weapon was pointed at AJ's temple. On her right, the old man was in the corner, closest to her. On her left, Bear stood next to her, angry and ruffled. And Will, face in a furious frown, stood next to Bear, almost directly across from the Russians. To say the odds were not in their favor was an understatement. She considered all her options and didn't like any of them.

Lightning arched across the sky, so close that she felt the hair on her arms rise, throwing the old man's face into ghostly relief. He seemed familiar somehow. He was tall, listed a bit. Had a receding hairline. How did she know this man?

The breeze shifted and brought the smell of Old Spice to her nose. In that instant, everything clicked and volcanic fury surged through her.

This white-haired man was the bastard that had locked her in the closet over and over again when she was young.

"You're our...*grandfather*." Her tone was menacing. Her anger, a blistering rage so hot her face seemed on fire.

He dropped his outstretched hand and laughed. "Yes, little Maddy. You're smart. The plane crash wasn't as bad as I made it look."

Will's eyes were wide, his tone incredulous. "You faked your own death?"

The lined face turned to look at Will. Comparing the two men, the family resemblance became clear—both tall, both olive-skinned, although Will's skin tone was lighter. They had matching green eyes. It unsettled her.

"Hello, Will. You're smart, too. Yes, I died to the world in the hopes your father would go on this quest, and I could follow him to the prize. I kept an eye on him through tapping his phone, and the receptionist of that attorney friend of his—she was a hot little number."

Will shook his head, sending droplets of water flying. "You had her killed."

"No choice once things were set in motion."

Maddy wanted to keep him talking. Buy time to think. "But why?"

"The throne. Ever since Carlos suggested we drown his twin, I knew it was my birthright. But then he was on guard and I could never find a way to remove him. I need the Power."

Maddy had known Prince Carlos for a scoundrel but to have truly murdered his own brother with the help of another took a special kind of evil. And if their grandfather had killed once—

Maddy's grip tightened on the obelisks as a significant piece of the puzzle clicked into place. "You! You killed our father! So, we would go on the quest and you could follow us."

"Your father was never on my side, he let me down. Never followed the clues. To make matters worse, he saw me on TV during the recent uprising in Jerusalem where I was trying to get to your precious Guardians. He was about to tell you I was alive. Why did you think he set up that little family reunion? I couldn't have that."

"Then why try to kill us?"

"I knew you'd go on the quest with a Russian sniper on your tail. Ivan was just herding you along. Until now."

Maddy shuddered. This obsessed man had killed his own son—and meant to kill them next.

"Why the Russians?" Bear growled.

"I made Slavic friends decades ago when on business for my father. They took me in after I 'proved my sincerity.'" He laughed and showed them his missing fingers. "One particular friend contacted me a few months ago, seeking a novel fuel source for his plans. So, you see, the timing was perfect."

"What about Maria?" Will cried. "Why did you kill her?"

The Russian looked down and shuffled his feet, but the black-haired man with the beak replied. "She was caught in the crossfire. It was unintentional. Now—please hand the obelisks over. This is also a matter of national security. We believe these obelisks will help our fight against ISIS and the Islamic terrorists."

"You're full of shit, D'Angelo," Bear spat the words. "And you're a traitor, too. These…these scum…killed Hana, Juergen, the twins' father, and Will's wife."

"You have a lot to learn about the covert world, boy, and motivation. Give us the obelisks and you've got a long happy career in front of you."

"To hell with you," Bear rumbled.

Maddy's chest grew warm with pride at Bear's words.

Lightning cracked again and the old man yelled, "Stop it! I'll have the obelisks or the boy dies now!" He looked at Maddy, stretched out his hand again. "Emma, give them to me."

Emma, her grandmother's name—his wife.

Emma, who had died with their mother in the car crash.

Emma, whom the king said she resembled.

More fragments of the mystery dropped into place, and she unexpectedly felt sorry for this old man who must have lost a piece of his mind over the death of his wife. And to have hungered for the Spanish throne to the point of ordering the death of his son. He'd have to live with that.

Knowing her anger would only play into his game, she put it on a shelf and breathed into her belly, into her power. She listened and became one with the rain, with the night, with Ramiro, with Alexander, with AJ and the love she felt for him. The obelisks thrummed in her hands. *I could use them.* But her grandfather was holding AJ and his release was more important. Maybe his life, at least, would be spared.

She stepped forward and handed the obelisks to her grandfather.

At that moment, everything happened at once.

As lightning crashed, her misguided grandfather tucked the gun into his belt, clutched the obelisks, and raised them overhead to the darkened sky. "The Power is mine!"

Several baseball-sized globes of blue-gold lightning poured from the obelisks. Maddy stared, transfixed, as the lightning balls, like drops of plasma from a blue sun, spun around in the sky for a long moment.

Then they boomeranged back toward the pyramid, toward their source. One of them brushed her grandfather's shoulder, another landed on his left foot. He stumbled forward, fell to the ground, his hands hit the pyramid, and he lost his grip on the obelisks, which rattled across the stones.

As she dived for the obelisks, Maddy nodded at AJ. Recognizing the signal the two of them had always used to start his aikido routine, AJ stomped down hard on the Russian's left foot. The child's attack seemed to amuse the sniper, but it caused him to look down, distracted, just long enough for Bear to pound into him with a football tackle. The Russian and Bear fell to the stones as a gun went off.

"Bear!" Maddy yelled.

Then thunder filled her ears and a serpent's tongue of regular lightning struck near the pyramid. It seared her skin, dizzied her, and knocked her down. After a count of three, she was able to stand up, obelisks in hand. She wobbled on her feet, alarmed about Bear, AJ, and Will.

However, before she could see how they were doing, her grandfather lunged for her at the same time that Will rushed forward, pushing their grandfather sideways, knocking the old man off balance and toward Maddy. As he fell in her direction, Maddy grabbed his arm and maneuvered him sideways with a fluid aikido move, adding further speed to his trajectory. She'd intended to simply move him aside, but on a piece of fallen stone, her grandfather tripped toward the pyramid's edge and tumbled part of the way down the slanted stone face. He landed with his head dangling from his neck, clearly dead.

Maddy stared at the body, still as a pillar of ice. A mixture of horror and relief stirred beneath her frosty outward appearance as she considered the ruthless justice, self-inflicted.

A rat-a-tat sound shattered the night. The helicopter, which had been out of sight, made a run toward them while laying down a trail of machine gunfire. It was clear to Maddy that to save AJ, Bear, and Will, her only choice was to use the obelisks against the incoming fire.

Hoping the pilot could eject, she prayed the obelisks wouldn't backfire on her like they had her grandfather and that she could direct her energy when it truly mattered. She found the deep well of her love, listened, and let her passion flare. She tapped into the Power to pour heat into her hands. An invisible flame filled her entire being, along with an intense sense of wonder so immense she felt she might burst. She flared blue fire at the helicopter, sensed it hit home, and the helicopter arced toward the desert floor.

Was that the sound of the rotors getting blown off? Did the pilot eject? She squinted, but through the rain and dark night couldn't be sure.

"Maddy!" AJ yelled.

Quick as a cat, she turned and barely registered the crash of the helicopter in the distance.

As she turned her gaze around, the Russian crouched over AJ. *Had the blond man been protecting AJ from the machine gunfire?* Next to the Russian, the man from the café wobbled on all fours, intent on a silver pistol that was lying on the stone a few yards away. Bear could be no help—he lay on the ground, clutching his leg.

AJ squirmed out from under the Russian and jumped on top of him. The sniper, eyes also focused on the lethal silver weapon, attempted to use his right hand to stand but his reddened hand gave way and he stumbled while trying to shake off AJ's weight.

In a vain attempt to end the threat, Will threw a knife at the off-balance sniper. He caught the Russian in the right cheek, and the Russian paused in his efforts to shake the boy.

Maddy also hesitated, not wanting to use lethal force against the Russian and concerned that balls of lightning might injure AJ. However, she knew aikido wouldn't help her if he got ahold of that gun. Apparently caught off guard, the sniper's posture gave her an opening that she might be able to use and still spare AJ.

Bear, Will, AJ: their lives were all in immediate danger. She had to risk it. With a deep breath, she raised the obelisks to the clouds. Her internal flame connected with her hands and blue balls of lightning sparked toward the Russian, her father's killer. The ball lightning seared a midnight-black hole through his lower abdomen.

He looked down toward his belly, eyes wide with shock, pale hands touching the charred edges of his shirt. AJ nimbly detached himself from the man's back while the assassin dropped to his knees and crumpled to the stones.

The sniper rolled to his side and died, a flash of relief passing over his features. Her gut clenched with the realization that she'd just killed a man. But maybe violence was a form of suicide as Edith had suggested.

There was one assailant left, no time for reflection. In slow motion, the man from the café sprawled to reach the weapon. He grabbed it with his right, outstretched hand, and pointed it at her as he rolled. His pistol flared white at the same time she sent blue lightning toward him. A split second later, a flare of jagged lightning roared out of the heavens and struck the tripod, which burst into flames.

The assailant's bullet slammed into her and ripped her chest backward. But her balls of fire returned the favor by burning a hole through his heart. As she dropped to the ground, the white-hot obelisks fell from her grip onto the pyramid's stone surface, and shattered with the sound of breaking dreams.

The remaining ball lightning spun over Bear's head as he looked down into her eyes. The balls looked like fireflies, lazily flitting through the summer sky.

And Bear. He was so tall. So handsomely tall.

CHAPTER 76

5:14 a.m.:

Staring at the carnage around the top of the pyramid, Will's fury faded with the deepening realization that his grandfather was dead and justice for his father and wife had been served.

A small reserve of energy fueled his movements. In the dim light of the burning tripod, he paused to be doubly sure that the blond Russian sniper, the intelligence officer who looked like a mobster, and his murderous grandfather were all dead.

He snatched up AJ and rushed over to join Bear at Maddy's side. Will knelt in the broken remnants of the obelisks, which fanned out around her shoulders and mixed in with the splashed blood from her wound.

"Is she okay?" Will asked.

Bear ignored the blood dripping from his own thigh while holding pressure on Maddy's chest wound. "Her pulse is steady. The bullet went through the right side of her chest below her collarbone. She's breathin' okay, but is losing a lot of blood."

"She's going to live?" AJ interrupted.

Will replied, "I hope so. The bullet missed her heart, but we still need to get her out of here or she'll die from shock! You too, Bear. How's that leg?"

Bear looked down at his leg. "I guess I should wrap it."

"Maybe one of these guys has a phone." Will stood, strode over to the Russian and the mobster and rustled through their clothes, finding nothing. Swearing, Will took the sniper's scorched shirt and the light jacket off the other body.

Will shook with frustration. He draped the large shirt over Maddy, cradling her head with one sleeve, then handed the jacket to Bear, who stood and tied the sleeves around his thigh.

How were they going to get out of here? Will took over applying pressure on Maddy's wound. *Can Bear and I carry her down the pyramid?* It wouldn't be easy.

Someone shouted in the distance.

Bear moved over to the side of the pyramid and looked down. "Looks like the cavalry is comin' to the rescue. Must've heard all the commotion."

"The guards?" Will asked with relief.

"What guards?" AJ asked.

"The men who guard the pyramid. They're on their way up here."

AJ moved off to stand next to Bear. "Good. They can help with Maddy."

Bear put his arm around AJ's shoulder.

While Bear and AJ watched the guards climb, Will looked out over the desert. He thought he'd seen the pilot of the helicopter blow the rotors and eject before the machine hit the ground, but he'd been distracted in the struggle and wasn't sure.

The rain was tapering off, as light gathered in the east. Will squinted to make out the flames of the ruined helicopter in the distant desert sands, but didn't see the pilot. Who was the pilot and where he, or she, now? Will didn't like loose ends.

AJ walked back over to Will and picked up one of the shards of obelisk. "This is cool."

Will looked at it. The rising sun shone around a cloud, caught the splinter, and flashed a scarlet prism on the stone surface of the pyramid. *Not a good idea to leave those pieces lying around.*

Will handed AJ the backpack. "Yes, very cool. Why don't you see if you can gather up the rest and put them in here?"

AJ obediently began to pick up the other pieces and put them in the pack.

Maddy's forehead felt cold under Will's hands. The bleeding had slowed with the pressure but he was worried. *What if the bullet grazed her lungs? What if it takes too long to get help?*

She was something, this sister of his. His heart grew warm with pride. While he'd failed miserably, she'd passed every test Ramiro had thrown at them, had learned to use the obelisks, and had saved their asses in the end. He shook his head with wonder. The guards clambered to the top of the pyramid.

They'd probably hand him over to the walrus cop. But he was glad they'd shown up. At least they could help carry Maddy down this ancient relic and get her to the hospital.

CHAPTER 77

Napa, California, August 7, 7:45 p.m.:

Two weeks after their victory in Giza, Maddy and AJ headed out to the private, western-facing patio as the golden rays of the setting sun lengthened over the vines of her father's vineyard. After surgery on her chest and shoulder, then a week in the hospital in Cairo recovering, they had all come back to the States.

It had taken them a few days to get things together for their father's funeral service, which had been held earlier in the day. Maria's would be held next week in Brazil. Even though she'd gone through a box of tissues, Maddy was grateful her sister had waited for the service until they made it back.

Looking out at the rows of vines and distant oak trees, she was glad to be home. She took a long, contented breath, settling into her patio chair. It had been a frightening but exhilarating adventure, and although Maddy was deeply troubled at having to kill to survive, she grinned to herself in surprise at how much she had enjoyed walking the knife's edge.

"C'mon, sensei, hurry up!"

"I'm coming, I'm coming."

Sensei. Her heart swelled with pleasure and gratitude. Although the bullet wound in her chest had not healed enough to allow her to take her next aikido test, with her newfound skills at directing energy, she knew she would pass with ease. She would be, at long last, on the fast path to becoming a martial arts teacher, so she didn't bother to correct AJ this time.

The patio table was set for dinner, and Will was already sitting at the table, sipping a glass of merlot. He'd found it in the cellar, a vintage their dad had bottled. She, Will, and her sister had inherited equal shares in the vineyard but they hadn't decided what to do with it.

"Can I go play with Damien?" AJ asked.

"You mean the dog? Squirrel?"

"I call him Damien."

"Sure. Have fun!"

AJ ran off and she sat down next to Will.

"How you holding up, sis?"

She let out a long deep breath. "I'm okay, a little tired is all. And my shoulder sure is sore. The service was beautiful but long. And there were a lot of people to catch up with."

"I'm glad Bella, Marty, and the kids decided to take an off-grid family vacation to stay safe."

"Me too. The photos of the kids in the river were priceless."

"Think Dad would have liked the service?" Will asked.

"As much as one could like such a thing."

"I hear ya," Will said.

They sat in silence for a minute.

Will sighed. "I think he and Maria would be glad we tracked down their killers."

"I'm sure they're glad we found the truth about why they were killed, and that justice was served in the end, although technically the killers tracked us down."

"True. We were hunted. Maybe Bear will have some insight on that when he joins us."

Maddy poured some wine for herself. "Hope so. And I'm glad we were able to stop the Russians from being able to fuel that e-bomb."

"No kidding. I'm just getting used to having internet again. Can you imagine if they had knocked out several military radar installations?"

"Scary. Bear said if they'd knocked out our eyes and ears, they could have deployed a high atmosphere nuke, which would have wiped out electronics over a wide part of the country. That would have allowed them to waltz right through our borders to wreak havoc. Grandfather's Russian friends would have been war heroes." Maddy shivered. "When I start to feel guilty about killing those two men with the obelisks, I remind myself of the lives we saved."

"Guilty? Those men were trying to kill us!"

"I know, which is why I did it, but it goes counter to all my aikido training."

"Sis, aikido seems great for hand-to-hand combat, even disarming an opponent at close range, but against guns from a distance?"

"I know. I want to discuss that philosophical conundrum with my sensei."

Will toasted the sky and drank. "Philosophy is a grand mental exercise. In the meantime, since it was kill or be killed, I'm glad to be alive!"

"Me, too," Maddy said. "I just wish there had been another way."

In slow motion, Will twirled his flashlight around his index finger. "While we're on the subject of killing, why do you think Grandpa did it?"

"You mean the whole thing? Killing Dad so we'd go on the quest?"

"Yes, what do you suspect was his motivation?"

"Well, I think he was obsessed."

"I'm thinking more about what drove him. What do you think drove that obsession?"

"Sounded as if he were a selfish, greedy bastard with no empathy whatsoever, who believed the Power and throne were his divine birthright, even though he failed the tests." Maddy sipped her wine. "Did I tell you the test he failed was the duel?"

"No."

"Yeah, Edith told me."

"Figures. No compassion there."

"Nope. And maybe helping Prince Carlos kill his twin when they were kids twisted his young mind into thinking he somehow deserved the throne. Or maybe he went off the deep end when Grandma died. Did you hear him call me Emma?"

"No, I missed that."

"Yes, and I've been meaning to tell you—when you and I were kids, whenever he and I were alone he used to lock me in the closet."

"What? When?"

"After Grandma died. In Spain, the king said I looked like Grandma Emma, so maybe Grandfather was punishing me somehow because he couldn't have her anymore. And I reminded him of that loss."

"That's weirdly insightful."

"It's just a theory." She paused. "He warned me he'd hurt you if I told anyone. But that's why I freaked out when you locked me in the bathroom before the Olympic games. Why I had a meltdown."

Will lowered his eyes. "Maddy, I am so, so sorry about that. I knew you didn't like to be confined and I did it anyway."

"Will. It was a prank. Then I broke my foot trying to break down the door, couldn't compete, and held a grudge for years. I blamed you. I'm sorry about that, too."

"But I knew it would mess with you. I guess I was mad since I always ended up playing second fiddle. You've always been a rock star. I'm sorry. You could have won gold."

"Maybe. I felt betrayed and held onto that resentment way too long. But, hey, we can laugh about it when we get old." She smiled.

He lifted his eyes to meet hers. "So, we're good?"

"Yes, we're good."

"So, you going to tell me about the secret you've been hiding since the castle?"

How'd he figure that out?

She swatted him with her napkin. "You're smarter than you let on."

"Sometimes."

"It was Catherine."

"I thought you guys had buddied up after that screaming incident in the Troubled Tower."

"We did. She turned out to be a bit of a wild old coot, but she gave me the missing page from the codex."

"What? *The* missing page? The one from the codex? No way!"

"Yes, way!"

"I want to see it!"

"I'll show you later. It's hidden in the house. I just wonder why it was created."

Will's eyebrows shot up. "Oh?"

"Well, it shows what I think is a group of stars, a constellation that I'm not familiar with. Perhaps it leads to the source of the obelisks. That's what Catherine thought and why she hid it."

"That's intriguing."

"Yeah, she was worried about Prince Carlos and trusted me to keep it safe and out of his hands."

They both drank a sip of wine. The warm, late afternoon and the wine made her feel mellow and happy. Maddy was glad she and Will had finally put their high school disagreement behind them.

A dog barked. She turned to watch AJ play with Squirrel. They were having so much fun.

Her heart melted, and she made a decision and turned to Will to fill him in. "Such a cute kid and he's been through so much. I've decided to adopt him, whether or not things work out with Bear."

"Sweet! That's awesome! So, I get to be an uncle?"

She smiled. "Yes, you do."

Maddy turned back to watch AJ and the dog, but while she watched, AJ tripped and then headed their way, crying a little.

"Maddy—sensei—I hurt my knee."

"Let me see it, little man."

She bent down and took a good look at the scrape, then dabbed a napkin in a glass of water and patted it on his knee. "There's only a little blood, you'll be okay."

AJ sniffled and wrinkled his freckled nose as if he were trying to get his emotions under control.

"It's okay to cry, you know," Will said.

Maddy looked at Will with suspicion. This was a new side of him. He'd seemed overly stoic as an adult, but she did remember he'd felt things deeply as a child, crying over a lost blanket, throwing a tantrum when their dad threw away his favorite shirt. He seemed serious now, though.

AJ looked up at him. "But I'm a boy."

"Boys cry too sometimes. And sometimes it's better to cry, feel it, and get over it, than to let it build up."

Maddy raised one eyebrow at Will over AJ's head, questioning. Will flashed her an "I've learned a thing or two, as well" smile.

"It hurts," AJ sniffled.

"Yep. And it will only hurt for a minute," Will said.

Maddy hugged AJ, who slumped in her arms, cried for just about ten seconds, then brightened.

"You're right. I feel better. Can I go play some more?"

Maddy waved her hand at the dog. "By all means." She turned to Will and teased. "Watch out or you'll make a good dad someday."

A shadow passed over Will's eyes. He scrunched his face, looked at the sky for a minute through his long lashes. "She was pregnant. Maria. I found out a week before she died. I was going to tell you—we were going to tell you when we met Dad here."

She reached out and held his hand. "Oh, Will."

"I'm okay. I finally let myself cry when we were at the monastery in the clouds."

"Good." She took a deep breath. "That's horrible. And I don't know what to say."

"Me neither. But at least I've learned a thing or two about emotions." His tone lightened. "Speaking of feelings, here comes Prince Charming."

She swatted him again.

Bear sauntered out of the French door, beer in hand, and looked at Maddy in a way that made her blush. "Hey, beautiful." He walked over to her and gave her a tender, lingering kiss, which lasted until Will cleared his throat.

Bear winked at her, tipped her hat off her head, and impishly rubbed his hand over the stubble that was her new hair growth. His beefy forearms had gained a new set of scars after their night on the pyramid. The tree-like marks looked like the forked lightning that had put them there.

She grabbed the hat from his hands with a smile. "Hey, stop that! Give me my hat back." She could not wait until her hair grew back.

He sat down across from Will.

"So, am I still a wanted man?" Will asked Bear.

"Stick with me, Argones, and I'll hook you up."

"Sounds dangerous. But what's the scoop? Were 'your people' that you told me about while Maddy was in the hospital, able to do anything about Pete, the crazy local walrus-mustache cop?"

"It's your lucky day or lucky year. In a nutshell, yes. Since you both cooperated with the, um, friends who visited us in the Cairo hospital, they've convinced the local Napa police that the true villains were subdued in a hush-hush operation overseas."

"There are many elements of truth to that," Will said. "And, regarding the 'cooperation,' there *was* a lot of natural lightning that night. Too bad it killed the sniper and your dirty director. We had to keep the obelisks secret to honor Ramiro's wishes."

"I understand. And no, they don't know about the Order either. But, by the way, the intelligence community doesn't always lie through their teeth."

"Sure," Will and Maddy said, sarcastically in unison.

"I hope you don't hate them too much. I have more news."

Maddy's heart sank. "They've offered you a job?"

"They have. Turns out the new director of VanOps was impressed by all our roles in the situation. He, the head of the Department of Extreme Threats, the Director of the CIA and the DNI—"

Maddy shot him a blank look so he added, "Director of National Intelligence. They all realized the old director was dirty as mud and had been in it up to his elbows as a mole for the Russians for some time. Too bad he died on the pyramid and his secrets with him. Much of the VanOps group is going to have to be rebuilt, as many of the players were compromised. The new director apologized that I'd been sent in that way and said it was a total farce. There is no such thing as that kind of testing."

"I'd wondered about that," Maddy said.

"Wondered? I remember you called bullshit on it at the monastery. I should have thought it through a little more, but I was excited, both to see you and to be workin' undercover. I'm ashamed to admit they tracked us through me and a chip in my new credit card. That's why he had me tag along."

Will took another sip of wine. "Bastard. We didn't think to sweep your stuff."

Bear reached into his pocket, pulled the silver chain out, and swung the lion around in circles. "It's good that you destroyed your phones. However, the Russians also bugged Maddy's necklace. I'm such a rookie, I didn't think to scan it either."

Maddy grabbed his arm and pulled the pendant from him. She looked at it. "Is it safe now?"

Bear clasped the jewelry around her neck. "It is. But the other news is he—the new director, that is—would like to interview you both, to see if you're interested in coming on board, too."

Maddy couldn't believe what she was hearing. "*What?*"

Will echoed her. "Are you serious?"

Bear smiled. "Yeah, it's somethin' to think about. D'Angelo had a dossier built on you both. Will, Sir Skeptalot, the new director thinks you might be a good fit for the 'red team,' which they use to challenge ideas. Your skeptical nature makes you a perfect fit for a job like that. And he likes your language skills. Maddy, he said your abilities to think on your feet, understand information technology, and defend yourself are a rare package. I tend to agree." He grinned.

Maddy felt thunderstruck. She would have to ponder the offer. She wasn't sure she trusted the lot of them but she was ready for a change.

She looked at AJ playing tag with the dog. There were considerations. If she got the job, she would miss spending time with AJ. Also, her dream of becoming an aikido teacher was within reach—she was ready to test for her next dan, nidan.

Bear must have noticed where she was looking as he also looked at AJ before he said, "Lots of time off between assignments." Bear paused. "Anyway, he also gave me some background on your grandfather."

Clandestine organizations might be untrustworthy, but they could be useful. "Go on."

"The CIA was keeping an eye on him because he turned up in Russia alive after his supposed death. Not a lot of American Spaniards over there running with nefarious crowds. Sounds as if he had some contacts from when he was younger, but when he showed up, they tortured him to see if they could trust him. That's how he lost those fingers."

"I remember he told us that," Maddy said.

"Well, he must have earned their trust. He married a Russian woman and worked his way up in a government organization designing weapons and making contacts high in the government, which he used in this final scheme. They suspect your grandfather's Russian son was the pilot of the helicopter. The only body recovered was a VanOps agent who matched the description of the guy Will thought he saw following us in Vilnius."

Maddy looked at Bear. "So VanOps was watching us, too."

"Yeah. That agent was as dirty as the old director."

Maddy frowned, unconvinced. "You sure you want to work for them?"

"I do. Most of them are the good guys. The new director also confirmed they were the group that had found out that the e-bomb weapon that went off in China was indeed made in Russia."

"What about the obelisks?" Maddy asked.

"Per your request, I sent the shards to Elena, and her friends in a German company ran some tests for me. Nice that she agreed to help out—I think VanOps would have been the better choice since they suspected the obelisks existed anyway, but I understand your concerns.

At any rate, the obelisks we found were made from an extremely rare superconductive material called lorandite."

Will scratched at his scruffy new beard. "Did I tell you or what?"

Bear turned to Will. "You sure did. The Germans have already found that it's a high-temperature superconductor, the highest found yet."

Bear looked at her. "Maddy, as your brother told us, the higher the temperature a superconductor works at, the more useful it is, since most of them work at temps well below zero."

Looking at them both, Bear continued, "The obelisks and this mineral are a great example of ancient technology that should not fall into enemy hands. That's what VanOps is all about, keepin' this kind of technology safe."

Will leaned forward in his seat with excitement. "Blah, blah, VanOps. You sound like a commercial. But superconductive and high temperature to boot! Ha!"

"You were spot on. Too bad they're now useless as a weapon. The director also strongly suspects that the Russian e-bomb does require superconductive material as fuel. My theory is that's how your grandfather talked them into killin' your father. Your grandpa figured the obelisks were superconductive and knew your father's death would set you on the path to find the obelisks. They must have intended to track you all along."

Maddy took a sip of wine. "Crazy. He sure was obsessed with the obelisks, to have realized they were superconductors."

"Well, the codex had many of the clues," Will said. "I suspected as much, too."

"You do have more modern, scientific training."

"He was a scientist, too." Will paused. "So, lorandite, huh? How rare is it?"

"It's extremely rare. And dangerous. Not naturally occurring. Probably came from a meteorite. Elena indicated that a cache of that material would be worth a fortune."

Will and Maddy exchanged a fleeting glance while Bear took a drink of his beer.

Maddy removed an errant leaf from the table top. "And it could have fueled one of those e-bombs?"

"All three e-bombs like they had planned. The director has taken AJ's story about their intentions very, very seriously. VanOps and other agencies are taking steps to safeguard our early warning system assets and to make sure they track down everyone involved in the plot."

Maddy laughed. "Glad we stopped it. I'm just getting used to my phone again."

Bear smiled. "The inscriptions carved into the obelisks that the GoPro camera captured are intriguing. I'm sure the director could offer some help translatin' the inscriptions if you change your mind about giving him access."

"Not likely," Maddy said. "How old were the things?"

"Well, the German carbon-dating indicated the obelisks were produced hundreds of years before Alexander the Great, so those images that we saw in the castle's codex could have been of him."

"You figured that part out, Bear. Alexander found the key to using them. With his military skill and having the obelisks as an advantage, he was unstoppable. And the obelisks somehow got from Alexander to Ramiro, who was clever enough to hide them," Maddy said.

"Yes, you saw what they did in the wrong hands."

"A weapon for the ages," Will mused. "If only they could have told us their stories."

Then, all three of their phones chirped simultaneously. They looked at each other.

"Sure, let's see who it is." Maddy looked at her screen.

"Looks like an encrypted email." She pushed a few buttons. "Let's see. Aha! A video."

Maddy opened the video and positioned the phone so all three could watch it. The master and Nanda came into view, along with the Guardians and their friends. Dieter, Elena, and a few others from their time at the school were there, too.

The master spoke, through Nanda. "Blessings, Maddy, William, and Bear Theodore. We've seen from the newspapers that the threat of the Russians getting the e-bomb fuel source is over and we know, from friends in Cairo, all about your role in this massive success."

He smiled, nodded, and paused to let Nanda catch up. Then he continued, with additional smiles. "I'd like to invite you to join our cause. Our Order, the Invisible Flame, has existed for over five hundred years to defend the world from those who pursue terror and bloodshed."

Maddy watched intently, delighted with the praise and the invitation.

The master went on, "Maddy, you've passed all tests so are already part of the Order. Come join us. Will, you'd need some additional training and testing, but it wouldn't take too long. Take as much time as you like to decide. We'll be here, under the Dome of the Rock, since the Popa Monastery location was exposed. We will hold a space for love and peace in the world at the intersection of three of the world's main religions. Come join us if you will."

Wild applause erupted from all those around the master. They were cheering! All of them were cheering. Her heart soared. Huge smiles played across the faces of Will and Bear.

The video over, she put the phone down and picked up her glass. "A toast! To Alexander, Ramiro, the ancestors who defined our past, and to the choices of our future."

As the sun nestled between the hills to the west, they raised their glasses, their eyes met and sparkled, the crystal clinked, and they smiled and drank, to both accomplishments and new beginnings.

EPILOGUE

Moscow, Russia, three days later:

Irritated, Baron Sokolov tapped his cane on the polished wood floor of his office. Usually, the hand-carved sea eagle head on the top of the cane gave him comfort in difficult times, but today he crushed it in an angry grip as he tap, tap, tapped it on the floor.

The source of his irritation, Pyotr, was running late. Pyotr had finally recovered from his helicopter crash injuries enough to get out of Cairo and schedule this debrief, but he didn't have the respect to be on time. The baron stared out the window at an overcast, late-morning sky above Pushkinskaya Square and tried to calm himself.

Tap. Tap, tap.

They had come tantalizingly close to recovering the superconductive obelisks. The blasted obelisks that he hadn't even believed existed at the start of the mission. But he had agreed to give Max Argones, the twins' grandfather, the requested sniper and other resources to pursue them because Max had argued that it was a low-risk proposition with a large reward.

Once the baron realized there was something to find, he had salivated over the possibility of knocking out the US early warning defense systems. Crippling the enemy would have boosted his career into the stratosphere. Hero, they would have called him. Would have held a feast in his honor. Now, even his morning tea tasted like ashes, and he glared at the antique samovar on the buffet table, tempted to batter it with his cane.

It had been tricky getting all the pieces in place to take out the radar systems without stirring up a hornet's nest of interest from others in the military. Too risky to take to the Kremlin until he'd had the superconductive material in hand. Yes, he would have needed approval to deploy the nukes to melt American electronics but he was certain his leadership would have jumped at the chance to wound their arch-enemy. The damage would have set the United States back years and would have given his country the chance to gain a technological edge.

That dream was now shattered, as if someone had taken a hammer to an icy Siberian pond. Fortunately, he knew how to be discreet, knew how to minimize the fallout of a failed operation. Most of the people who knew about the mission were already dead.

The intercom on his desk buzzed.

The baron pushed the flashing green button. "Da."

"There is a young man here to see you, sir," his administrative assistant said in Russian.

"Send him in now," he replied, also in Russian.

Swinging the door shut behind him, Pyotr Argones strode in, arrogant, unhurried. His tall, broad-shouldered, athletic frame angered the baron further. There had been a day when the baron's body was as lithe and strong as this spawn of the Spanish failure. The baron's hand tightened on the head of his cane until his knuckles were white as his hair. Yet now, the baron reminded himself, he wielded another kind of power.

Pyotr stood next to a chair on the other side of the antique desk. The baron stared at Pyotr. Pyotr stared back, his white iris disconcerting. Unnatural. Ignoring the discomfort, the baron pressed his position of authority.

Eventually, Pyotr broke the eye contact and dropped his dark head slightly in a gesture of submission or respect. Took him long enough. *If I let him live, I'll need to find a way to remind him that he's not as strong as he thinks he is.*

The baron gestured to the chair. "Sit."

As Pyotr sat, the baron regarded him. The moment stretched again as the baron gathered his thoughts on how to bring the man down a notch, yet still use him effectively.

When the baron spoke, there was disapproval in his tone. "Your father failed me, Pyotr. You failed me. My sources tell me the obelisks were destroyed. The twins have returned to America. Not only that, but they learned of our plan to take out their early warning radar systems and are taking steps to prevent us from using that tactic in the future."

Pyotr remained silent. No apologies, no excuses.

Interesting. "Why should I not kill you?" the baron asked.

"Perhaps I can still be of some use?"

"What do you have in mind?"

"Although the obelisks were powerful, my father believed there was some sort of map to the source of the obelisks."

"And?"

"And I'd like to find the map. Locate the twins, see if they know anything about the map, or the source. Then kill them."

"They are your niece and nephew."

"I have no feelings for them. And I'm the best asset you have to find them."

The baron turned his back on Pyotr by swiveling in his chair to look out the window on the gray morning. A single black raven perched motionless on a tree.

Pyotr's father had mentioned seeing a star chart once at the family castle. Other classified projects could utilize a cache of high-temperature superconductive material.

In particular, Russia and India were collaborating on an encryption-killing quantum computer that needed superconductive material to be successful. With a code-breaking computer like that, and his army of computer scientists, he could pull off a mega-hack of US banks, power stations, credit card readers, gasoline stations, food markets. With no power, food, or gas, there would be massive chaos. With so many gun owners in the country, they'd kill half their own population within weeks and then he and the military could invade, take over the government.

There was more to the plan of course, but those were the bones. It just needed that superconductive material to get started.

The baron turned his chair back around to face Pyotr. A single bead of sweat formed on the man's temple. *Good.*

"You may live for now. Here's what you're going to do."

AUTHOR'S NOTES

I hope you've enjoyed the story.

One of the things I always like is when an author shares fact from fantasy, so I wanted to return the favor for you.

Ramiro I was truly the first king of Spain and Isabella I and Ferdinand II, his descendants. Most of the current European monarchs are descended from their union, including the current king of Spain, King Felipe VI. It is also true that all the other monarchs currently reigning in Europe (King Albert II of Belgium, Grand-Duke Henri of Luxembourg, Queen Elizabeth II of the U.K., Queen Margrethe II of Denmark, King Harald V of Norway, King Carl XVI Gustaf of Sweden, and King Willem-Alexander of the Netherlands) descend from Isabella I and Ferdinand II. Also, the sovereign princes of Europe: Albert II, Prince of Monaco, and Hans-Adam II, Prince of Liechtenstein, are descendants as well.

The thorned cross was Ramiro's royal sign over a thousand years before it graced the cover of this book.

Female snipers were part of World War II for the Soviet Union. For example, Liudmyla Pavlychenko, or "Lady Death," was a Russian Red Army Soviet sniper. With 309 kills, she is regarded as one of the most effective military snipers in history.

It is a fact that scientists have recently identified superconductive bits in two meteorites: the Mundrabilla meteorite, found in the Australian Outback in 1911, and Graves Nunataks, a meteorite discovered in Antarctica in 1995.

Lorandite is a ruby red colored mineral that was mined in southern Macedonia from the Allchar deposit. Though rare, it is the most common thallium-bearing mineral. It also has superconductive powers. Superconductive minerals have been shown to illustrate the Meissner effect, which is the expulsion of a magnetic field from a superconductor. Quantum levitation is a process where scientists use the properties of quantum physics to levitate an object (specifically, a superconductor) over a magnetic source (more specifically, a quantum levitation track designed for this purpose). However, lorandite is not from a meteorite.

There are legends associated with lorandite and Alexander the Great, who purportedly had his phalanx cover their shields with the mineral and then would arrange battles to occur at noon. The movement of his troops occurred from west to east, which caused a strong reflection from the shields that blinded an opposing army. Many believe this is why the Macedonian symbol is the sun.

Regarding e-bombs and other EMP weapons, although much of the defense industry's work on these weapons remains highly classified, it is believed that high-temperature superconductors are used to create their destructive power. A good resource on the topic is "The E-bomb: How America's new directed energy weapons will change the way future wars will be fought," by Doug Beason, Ph.D.

The information on early warning systems is on the Internet. There is one in Northern California at Beale Air Force Base, one at Thule in Greenland, also Air Force, and one in England at Fylingdales, which is a British Air Force location.

Nat Hlaung Kyuang Temple in Bagan is a one-story temple. I added a second story to increase tension in the novel.

Several books have been written about the psychic spy program run by the CIA in the 1970s, and the military is training solders in mindfulness. The Department of Extreme Threats is my own invention.

There are several archeological images of Egyptians holding rods— they're typically cylindrical rather than in the shape of an obelisk.

Most researchers today agree that ball lightning is real, yet its nature remains controversial. It often appears as a glowing sphere which moves or drifts horizontally through the air. Typically, it's the size of a softball or grapefruit but sometimes appears as small as a dime, or as large as a bus. It can hover or bounce and lasts for only a few seconds, but can linger for longer. Sometimes it disappears quietly, and other times, explodes violently.

If you'd like to learn more about the Power that Maddy experiences, I suggest finding a local Kundalini Yoga class. There are many paths to that same destination. I hope you find your way, and remember to *Listen and feel the Power.*

CONNECT WITH AVANTI

Now that you've had the chance to read my story, I want to get to know yours. Find me on my webpage (http://www.avanticentrae.com) and drop me a line, or sign up for my newsletter to learn more about Fan-only specials and giveaways. Send me a mysterious idea to incorporate into a future tale, or an extraordinary threat.

You can also follow me on Facebook (avanticentrae), Instagram (avanti.centrae.author) or Twitter (@avanticentrae). Either way, let me know what you loved about *VanOps: The Lost Power* and what you want more of in the series to come.

CPSIA information can be obtained
at www.ICGtesting.com
Printed in the USA
LVHW030201010322
712197LV00007B/75/J

9 781644 371961